THE 34TH DEGREE

Also by Thomas Greanias

The Promised War
The Atlantis Revelation
The Atlantis Prophecy
Raising Atlantis

THE
34TH
DEGREE

A THRILLER

Thomas Greanias

ATRIA BOOKS

New York   London   Toronto   Sydney

ATRIA BOOKS

A Division of Simon & Schuster, Inc.
1230 Avenue of the Americas
New York, NY 10020

Copyright © 2011 by Thomas Greanias

First Atria Books hardcover edition June 2011

ATRIA B O O K S and colophon are trademarks of Simon & Schuster, Inc.

For information about special discounts for bulk purchases, please contact Simon & Schuster Special Sales at 1-866-506-1949 or business@simonandschuster.com.

The Simon & Schuster Speakers Bureau can bring authors to your live event. For more information or to book an event, contact the Simon & Schuster Speakers Bureau at 1-866-248-3049 or visit our website at www.simonspeakers.com.

Manufactured in the United States of America

10   9   8   7   6   5   4   3   2   1

Library of Congress Cataloging-in-Publication Data

Greanias, Thomas.
 The 34th degree : a thriller / Thomas Greanias.—1st Atria Books hardcover ed.
  p. cm.
 1. Intelligence officers—Israel—Fiction. 2. Arab-Israeli conflict—Fiction.
3. Middle East—Fiction. I. Title. II. Title: Thirty-fourth degree.
  PS3607.R4286A55 2011
  813'.6—dc22   2011003088

ISBN 978-1-4516-1239-4
ISBN 978-1-4516-1240-0 (ebook)

For my mother, father, and sister

METEORA, GREECE, 1943

1

It was on the Feast of the Ascension, forty days after Easter 1943, when an agent of the British Secret Service turned up at the doorstep of the Monastery of the Taborian Light and Philip knew his life as a monk was over.

Wrapped in his black cassock and hood, Philip had been on his knees with his brothers in the sanctuary, celebrating the resurrection and ascension of the Lord Jesus Christ, praying in eager expectation at the blessed hope of His return. This was as he had done for over twenty years, ever since he renounced his former ways and retired to the Monastery of the Taborian Light.

The monastery was perched atop one of the many otherworldly peaks of Meteora, the most remote and mysterious region of Greece. A thousand feet below lay the village of Kastraki, nestled in the foothills. Clinging to its gray granite summit, undisturbed by war or petty human conflicts, the Taborian Light was an impregnable retreat where the Eastern Orthodox monks could witness the unfolding of earthly affairs below and reflect on the eternal.

Here Philip made it his ambition to lead a quiet and peaceful life, just as the apostle Paul had instructed the original church at Thessaloniki. Toward that end, he had allowed his gray hair and beard to grow long, making him seem older than his fifty years, and cloaked in the humility of a monk, he tried to make himself as small and wiry a figure as possible.

But his shapeless cassock could not hide his hard physique or the alert, confident movements of his limbs. Nor could his hood completely veil his eaglelike nose and sharp features. Locals who glimpsed his face during a rare trip to the village never missed his shining black ramlike eyes, set wide apart, gazing placidly from beneath his bushy eyebrows. Their faces would darken with fear, and they would scurry away. Whether they recognized him or not, they instinctively knew he was not one of them.

The sound of hurried footsteps broke Philip's trance, and his quick black eyes darted up to see Brother Vangelis whisper into the Archimandrite's ear. The old monk's face, barely visible behind his great beard and the misty veil of burning incense, fell as he looked at Philip, and the peace that Philip had known for twenty years left him.

So the day has come, Philip thought, and with it the dread.

Philip crossed himself three times before he rose from the floor. With a silent nod, he acknowledged the Archimandrite, took a deep breath, and left the sanctuary.

The visitor was in the narthex, admiring a wall painting of *The Four Horsemen of the Apocalypse.* He was dressed like a Greek peasant, and with his high forehead, long aesthetic features, and beard, he bore an absurd resemblance to a saint out of some Byzantine icon. But his blue eyes and fair skin betrayed him. When he spoke, it was in perfect Oxford English.

"Commander Lloyd, British Intelligence," said the Englishman, looking him over. "You must be Philip. You're smaller than I thought."

That was what most men thought. Philip lowered his hood and watched Lloyd drop back a couple of steps in fear.

"They were right after all," said Lloyd, marveling. "The face of a hawk and the eyes of a ram."

Philip narrowed his eyes. "What do you want, Commander Lloyd of British Intelligence?"

"Why, the same thing the Nazis want," Lloyd replied. "The Templar Globe. More precisely, what's inside the globe."

An uneasiness Philip hadn't felt since his early days now gripped his heart, and he blinked as though he failed to understand. "I'm sorry, I don't know what—"

"The Maranatha text," pressed Lloyd. "The one the apostle Paul wrote to the Thessalonian church in the first century. The one that dates the end of history and the return of Christ."

2

Philip looked at Lloyd, well bred and impatient. He is as I once was, he thought, and decided to be gentle but firm. "Even if there ever were such a text, Commander, what makes British Intelligence believe it has survived the ages?"

Lloyd had a ready answer. "When Arab Muslims besieged Constantinople in the eighth century, the Byzantine Greeks defending the city were able to save themselves with a miraculous and secret weapon. A compound that burned when it came into contact with water. A substance that became known as Greek Fire. Now, the exact formula used by the Greeks remains a mystery, but we know it included the compound naphthalene palmitate. Better known as napalm."

"Which is hardly a secret anymore," Philip observed, "as napalm is commonplace in your bombs and flamethrowers."

"But the Byzantine Greeks deployed it in a different and, in some ways, more potent form twelve hundred years ago."

Philip shrugged. "I hardly see what Greek Fire has to do with the Maranatha text."

"The defenders of Constantinople used Greek Fire aboard their war vessels as a missile to be hurled from a catapult. By destroying the wooden fleets of the Muslim Arabs, Greek Fire blocked the spread of Islam into Europe. Rumors swirled among the ranks of the retreating Muslims that the Byzantine Greeks discovered the formula for their infernal fire encoded in the contents of the legendary Maranatha text. That is why, seven centuries later, when Constantinople finally fell to the Turks in the fifteenth century, bands of Muslim invaders turned over every stone in the city to find it."

"But the text, I take it, was not to be found," Philip said guardedly.

"No. During the siege, the Greeks had no choice but to turn to the Knights Templar to smuggle it out of the city to Rome, where it would be safely beyond the reach of the Ottoman Empire. But it never reached Rome. Instead, it ended up with the Freemasons at their Three Globes Lodge in Germany, founded to protect three golden globes from King Solomon's temple. Two of those globes ended up with the American Freemasons, who buried them beneath Washington, D.C., at the founding of the United States of America. The third remained in Germany until Greece finally won its war of independence from Turkey in 1830 after four hundred years. The third globe, with the Maranatha text inside, was returned to its original home, a secret monastic order descended from the original Thessalonian church, whose members can trace their ancestry through the laying on of hands to the apostle Paul himself."

"An interesting tale, Commander."

"Yes, and I have another one for you," Lloyd said. "This one took place a century later, during the Greco-Turkish war in Asia Minor in 1922. An aide-de-camp to Kemal—the great warrior Hadji Azrael, the Angel of Death—shocked the empire by laying down his sword, renouncing Islam, and embracing the Christian faith of his enemies."

Philip's heart skipped a beat. Unconsciously, he placed his left hand over the large, ornate cross that hung from his neck.

Lloyd continued, "There was a secret ceremony with the patriarch of the Eastern Church himself, the laying on of hands, and a new name for this once sworn enemy of Greeks, this killer of Christians. Ultimately, his orders sent him to the monastic order that guarded the legendary Maranatha text he once sought to destroy. He became its protector and wore a gold cross with a sapphire omega set in the center. The very one you seem to be wearing, Philip. Or should I say, Hadji Azrael?"

3

In his former days, Hadji Azrael would have known exactly how to deal with a man like Commander Lloyd of British Intelligence. The Englishman never would have been heard from again. But the Way of Christ demanded mercy. And so Philip reluctantly showed his visitor to the Archimandrite's chambers, a sparse room with a hard bed and a rough-hewn table around which the three men sat on straw chairs.

The Archimandrite eyed Lloyd and fingered his black worry beads. "How did you find us, Commander Lloyd?"

"The Koutras family in Kastraki," Lloyd explained in passable Greek. "They were hiding me from the Germans. Young Gregory knew the secret bridle path to the Taborian Light."

The Archimandrite turned to Philip, who nodded that this was probably the case.

"I see, Commander," said the Archimandrite. "And since when is British Intelligence so interested in spiritual things?"

"It's Hitler's interest that concerns us, Archimandrite. Fact is, Greek Fire changed the course of history. Hitler believes it can do so again. Only this time it's the modern fleets of the invading Allies he wants to burn before they land on the beaches of Nazi-occupied Europe." Lloyd produced a document from inside his tunic. "This communiqué was intercepted between Ankara and Berlin. It's a telegram from the German ambassador to Turkey, Franz von Papen, to the Nazi foreign minister, Ribbentrop."

He handed the document to Philip, who looked it over carefully. It was an English copy of the German original and said that an SS general, a certain Ludwig von Berg, had discovered the location of the Monastery of the Taborian Light.

This was terrible news, Philip realized, even worse than he had feared. It meant they must flee Meteora at once or risk having the

Maranatha text fall into German hands. That must not be allowed to happen.

The Archimandrite must have sensed his distress, for he asked, "What is it, Philip?" When Philip told him that the Germans had located the Taborian Light, the old monk's face turned white, and he crossed himself. "Lord, have mercy on us all!"

Philip turned to Lloyd. "Who is this General von Berg, Commander?"

"You mean the Baron of the Black Order?" Lloyd said. "Only the most dangerous man in the Third Reich, after Hitler and Himmler—and more cunning than both of them put together."

Philip passed the communiqué back to Lloyd, who pocketed it.

"As you can see, Hadji Azrael, our interests are purely political," Lloyd told him, patting the bulge in his tunic. "Churchill simply wants the Maranatha text out of Hitler's reach for the rest of the war."

Philip wasn't so sure. The communiqué contained several puzzling references to a microfilm of a first-century copy of the Maranatha text, a copy allegedly unearthed by British archaeologists in Palestine. As far as Philip knew, there was no such copy, only the original text now buried beneath the monastery's crypt inside the Templar Globe. Obviously, there was more to this intrigue than Commander Lloyd of British Intelligence was telling them. "And what does Mr. Churchill propose, Commander?"

"That I smuggle the text out of here on horseback to Kalambaka, hitch a ride on the Thessaly Railway to Volos, and then board a certain ship to neutral Istanbul. There I entrust the text to the Patriarch of the Eastern Orthodox Church himself for safekeeping until the end of the war."

Lloyd's offer was too generous for Philip to believe. But he could see it made an impression on the Archimandrite, who began to nod as he worked his worry beads.

"Surely, Archimandrite, you're not seriously entertaining this stranger's insane proposition?" Philip asked.

The Archimandrite sighed. "Better the text be with the Patriarch than in the hands of the Antichrist."

That was presuming the text ever reached the Patriarch. Philip did not trust British Intelligence. Nor could he trust the judgment of his superior, who, never having killed a man, clearly was at a serious disadvantage. At times the Archimandrite seemed to forget that the heart of man was, above all else, cruelly deceptive and exceedingly wicked. But Philip, responsible for thousands of deaths, knew the human heart all too well.

"I am bound by a sacred oath to protect the Maranatha text," he said. "I must insist that I be the one to deliver it to the Patriarch."

The Archimandrite shook his head. "You know that is not possible. There is a death sentence on you the moment your feet touch Muslim ground. No, Philip. Brother Yiorgios will accompany Commander Lloyd to Constantinople."

Lloyd frowned. "Brother Yiorgios?"

"Our silent brother," said Philip, trying to conceal his bitterness. "We found him some months ago, roaming the hills not far from here, the last survivor of a monastery the Italians plundered. He has never said a word of that unspeakable evil. We put it all together when we saw his cassock and heard the reports."

"He keeps everything to himself," said the Archimandrite, who raised an eyebrow at Philip. "An example to us all."

Philip added, "Vangelis insists he goes out at night into the woods to speak to the devil."

The Archimandrite dismissed the notion with a wave of his gnarled hand. "That one sees a devil behind every fig tree."

Seeing that his superior was not going to allow him to accompany Lloyd, Philip switched tactics. If reason failed to move the Archimandrite, then perhaps the unreasonable would smoke out the Englishman. "I say we burn the infernal text and be done with it."

"You would destroy God's revelation?" The Archimandrite looked at Philip in horror. "Come to your senses, Philip!"

"I've told you my suspicions, Archimandrite. Paul warned our forefathers to beware of any unsettling letter supposedly coming from him that talks about the Lord's return."

"Just a bloody minute," said Lloyd, his eyes shifting back and forth between Philip and the Archimandrite. "You don't think the text is genuine?"

"A genuine forgery," Philip told him. "The Bible itself speaks of such a letter, one allegedly written by Paul that claims the last days have already come." He looked the Archimandrite straight in the eye. "Perhaps the Maranatha text is the false report Paul mentions in his second letter to the Thessalonians, the very letter from hell he warns us to consider at our own peril."

"Perhaps, Philip," said the Archimandrite, suddenly sounding tired beyond his considerable years. "But how can you be sure?"

"The very nature of this text contradicts Paul's repeated warnings to us not to entangle ourselves with endless timetables and futile speculations. Can't you see, Archimandrite? There is something very diabolical about this text. Death surrounds it! Look what it does to men."

Philip was pointing to Lloyd, who at first was startled by the gesture but soon found his tongue and turned everything Philip had said to his advantage.

"Archimandrite, if what Hadji Azrael says is true, then you must help us," he argued with rising passion. "If you don't, if the Maranatha text should fall into Hitler's hands, you will fan into flame the all-consuming fires of Armageddon. And if Jesus Christ should come back today or in a thousand years, it will be you who must stand alone before His throne of judgment with the innocent blood of millions of women and children on your hands. And these words of mine will judge you when they are replayed for all to hear. How will you account for yourself?"

It was a dirty trick that had its desired effect on the Archimandrite. The mere thought of what Lloyd said seemed too great a burden for the old monk to bear. His shoulders drooped, and a faraway look filled his eyes. "Yes," the Archimandrite repeated with resignation, "better the text be in the hands of the Patriarch than the Antichrist."

Philip could not believe this was happening. "But, Archimandrite—"

"The matter is settled, Philip." The Archimandrite grasped his rough wooden cane and rose slowly to his feet. "Brother Yiorgios will accompany Commander Lloyd to Constantinople. The Patriarch will decide what should be done with the Maranatha text."

"The prime minister's sentiments exactly," chimed Lloyd, grinning in triumph as he looked at Philip.

Philip stared at the floor, unable to suppress the restlessness in his heart. "To let the text leave this monastery is to open up a Pandora's box of evil," he warned. "Who knows where it could end?"

It was a question that neither the Archimandrite nor Lloyd was able to answer, for at that moment Brother Vangelis burst through the door.

"Germans!" he cried, out of breath. "Coming up the hill!"

4

It was a sight Philip had to see with his own eyes from the monastery's watchtower: The Death's Head battalion must have started for the Taborian Light that morning, having shaken the dust of the nearest town, Kastraki, off their jackboots. What was once a sleepy village nestled a thousand feet below the towering rock formations of Meteora was now a pillar of black smoke rising up behind the twenty-four SS paratroopers as they converged on the granite summit.

They were far closer than Philip had imagined just a moment ago.

He knew they had come off their conquest of Crete, these *Fallschirmjäger* in field-gray uniforms and rimless steel helmets. Hand-picked by Reichsführer Heinrich Himmler himself, they were the pride of the Waffen SS. These days found them loose on the Greek mainland, clearing the mountains of partisans and performing special missions for Himmler's second in command, the mysterious SS general Ludwig von Berg.

Leading the way up was the Baron of the Black Order himself, handsome and wholly evil. One hand held a Schmeisser machine pistol, the other a leash with a terrified Gregory Koutras straining at the end. The boy tried to shout a warning. Von Berg yanked hard on the leash, choking off his cries.

Philip was no stranger to the art of war and the effects of military regalia. But even he felt a chill at the sight of Ludwig von Berg marching toward the monastery in his smartly tailored black dress uniform, black boots, and black leather accessories. Above his sleeve's cuff title was the diamond-shaped SD patch of the *Sicherheitsdienst,* or SS intelligence service, which meant he was the worst of the lot. Flanking him were two *Fallschirmjäger,* with their machine pistols.

The Baron of the Black Order looked younger than his reputed age of forty and radiated venal power. Glints of gold hair were visible beneath his black cap, and his clean-shaven cheeks tapered down to a twisted smile. His beaklike nose and upper lip, in particular, gave him the air of a predator. But it was his eyes that dominated his appearance, those clear blue eyes with a gaze that could pierce armor plating.

Even from afar, Philip felt the stare of the Death's Head badge on von Berg's cap. The silver skull-and-crossbones insignia signaled the general's willingness to give and take death in the holy cause of national socialism. But it was also a grim reminder of the invincibility of the Baron of the Black Order, of the silver plate in von Berg's skull and his seemingly supernatural ability to survive an assassin's bullet on more than one occasion. Even Philip had heard of the joke within the ranks of the SS: The baron had nine lives, and for each life, the world was a worse place.

Philip turned from his perch and rushed down to the cave beneath the monastery. Commander Lloyd stood at the secret exit tunnel with Brother Yiorgios, who clutched the ornate golden Templar Globe containing the legendary Maranatha text. The globe was the size of a round watermelon but looked visibly heavier in Yiorgios's arms. Six monks stood by, ready to roll back into place the large mosaic slab that hid the tunnel.

"You'll come out in the Pindos chain of mountains," Philip told them. "From there you are in God's hands. Now go."

5

Inside the marble crypt beneath the monastery, Philip joined the Archimandrite and the rest of the monks of the Taborian Light huddled together in the dark. It was musty from the bones of the saints buried in the alcoves around them, the temptation to cough and betray their presence all too real.

Philip could hear the scrape of jackboots on the floor above as the storm troopers stripped priceless mosaics from the walls. He was sure the incense and smoke from snuffed-out candles had already informed Baron von Berg that the monastery had not been abandoned. But even if the Nazis should torch their monastery and burn it to the ground, yes, even then they would rise from the ashes like the phoenix and rebuild it all, just as they had done after the Italians, the Turks, and every invader before them.

"Outstanding, really," the voice of Baron von Berg boomed above. "These Greek Orthodox monks have transformed their faith into an art form. Unfortunately, I suspect their art will outlast their faith. Yes, several icons here would make excellent additions to the Führer's collection. The best ones I keep for myself, of course. Along with the Maranatha text."

Suddenly, something like thunder rumbled overhead, followed by a flash of light as the marble slab to the crypt was lifted away. Fear seized them all as they looked up to see the face of evil staring down like an austere icon painted inside the dome of a church. The face of SS general Ludwig von Berg smiled at them, but his voice addressed somebody else.

"Unfortunately, Standartenführer Ulrich, you will have to join the martyrs in making a rather abrupt departure from this world. You and Himmler didn't really think you could run off with the text and keep it a secret from me?"

From somewhere out of view came the cry, "I know who you are, von Berg! Himmler told me. You can't get away with this. We know who you are!"

"To whom are you appealing, Ulrich? Reason? Justice? God? According to the SS rules that you have chosen to live and die by, you stand outside the jurisdiction of German state courts and even those courts of the Nazi Party. I am your judge now, and I know no justice except my own."

Philip and the monks could see Ulrich's back pressed against the low wall of the crypt. Something about him seemed oddly familiar to Philip.

"You are mad, von Berg, insane."

"The Reichsführer chases fantasies, and you call me mad? Hardly, Ulrich. Oh, I'll keep this so-called Maranatha text, but not to indulge the Führer's mysticism. There's a war going on, and the last thing we need is this apocalyptic nonsense further clouding the Führer's judgment. Now, if you will please hand over your SS dagger, Standartenführer. Quickly, we haven't all day."

Philip heard the shuffle of boots and then saw Ulrich's own men take hold of him. Then a black sleeve reached forward and removed the dagger from its sheath.

"See the words engraved on its hilt? Yes, say them out loud."

Ulrich's hoarse voice replied, "Blood and honor."

"That's right, Ulrich. Your blood, my honor."

There was a flash as the blade caught the light. Ulrich screamed.

"You see, there is an art to dying," von Berg's voice mused above Ulrich's cries. "In one stroke, a traitor is killed and decrepit monks become martyrs. Of course, it may help you to consider yourself a martyr. Every faith needs them, even our own. I can only wonder when you wake up whether it will be in the same place as those you are about to join."

The monks saw Ulrich fall backward into the crypt, pushed by the stiff hand that still lingered in the air overhead. They shrank back in fear to avoid the falling body and felt the ground shake when Ulrich hit the floor.

Philip bent over the crumpled, robe-clad body and turned the head to see the German's face.

Brother Yiorgios!

In that instant Philip realized that Yiorgios was a Nazi spy, Commander Lloyd of the British Secret Service was dead, and the Baron of the Black Order now possessed the Maranatha text.

Lord Jesus Christ, have mercy on me, a sinner!

Then he felt something like raindrops and smelled petrol in the air. When he looked up, the Baron held a lit cigarette over the open crypt.

"See you in Valhalla, Ulrich. You, too, Hadji Azrael."

Finding himself at his enemy's mercy, Philip rose to his full if short height and looked up. "It is true that I answered the call of the muezzin to prayer as a child; that I have made the holy pilgrimage to Mecca; that I once lived by the sword of Allah. But now I serve the Lord Jesus Christ in the order of the Taborian Light."

"The last of a dying order, I might add," von Berg said. "And you'll fare no better than your brothers. Where is your precious Jesus to save you now?"

Philip stared at the burning cigarette above. Realizing that he was about to die, he resolved to depart this earth in a manner worthy of his calling. He must not allow a moment of personal weakness to blemish the cause of Christ. Nor must his hatred of this evil man keep him from extending the Lord's forgiveness. "Oh, He is coming soon, Baron von Berg. You need not worry about that. His reward is with Him, and He will give to everyone according to what he has done. He will repay you for your wickedness. But if you repent now, He will forgive you."

"Is that so?" Von Berg smiled as his fingers dangled the cigarette. "You should have kept the vengeful faith of your former life, Hadji Azrael. If you had, the Maranatha text might be yours. Now it is ours."

Philip watched in horror as the Baron dropped the cigarette into the crypt. The flicker of light grew larger and larger until it bounced off the wall and scattered its tiny, glowing ashes across the floor. For a moment they seemed to melt into the darkness with no effect. Then a sudden flicker of light exploded into a burst of fire, illuminating the horrified faces of the Archimandrite and the brethren. A second later, the inferno engulfed them all like the flames of hell.

LOS ANGELES, PRESENT DAY

6

Sam Deker awoke from his nightmare, gasping for air in the dark. He felt his bare chest for burns but found only electrodes. The polysomnogram monitor on the nightstand beeped loudly. He lunged wildly for a switch with a free hand until it finally shut up. Then he sat up in bed and blinked.

Slowly, his eyes began to adjust to reveal what appeared to be a small hotel room. Besides his bed and nightstand, there was a dresser with a TV on top, and a chair with his clothes and leather gym bag. He noted the single door to his left and the heavy drapes to his right. Only the surveillance camera in the corner gave away his location, bringing him back to the present.

He grabbed his Krav Maga watch from the nightstand. The glowing dial told him it was 5:24 A.M. He hadn't even made it to six this time. He picked up his military dog tag with the engraved Star of David and slipped it around his neck. Then he stood up and pulled back the window curtains. The glass towers of Century City still reflected only stars in the predawn light.

Deker stepped outside his room into the deserted suite of doctors' offices at Advanced Sleep Labs. He blinked under the bright fluorescent lights as the sole nurse on duty stood up from her computer station and walked over to the checkout counter. Her name tag read GISELLE. Deker remembered she was still a student at UCLA Medical School.

"Good morning, Sam," she said. "Did you get any sleep this time?"

Blinking in the harsh office light, he wasn't in the mood to report on the jumbled images of ancient texts, Greek monks, and a Nazi monster slowly fading from his head. "You tell me, Giselle," he said as he signed out.

She hesitated. "Dr. Prestwick will interpret the data and call you in a couple of days," she said, referring to the sleep specialist he had never met but to whom his own ENT physician had referred him. "But your spikes are off the charts." She leaned closer with a conspiratorial smile. "Either your nightmares are so real that your body thinks it's being skinned alive, or you're still dreaming about me."

It wasn't what he wanted to hear, but he smiled and said, "That must be it."

7

Deker's black Audi squealed out of the medical building onto Avenue of the Stars and turned west onto Santa Monica Boulevard. He passed the Century City shopping center and went through the McDonald's drive-through for coffee; he didn't feel like bantering with the baristas at Starbucks. Then he took a right onto Veteran.

The Federal Building loomed ahead.

The nineteen-story white monolith overlooked the Los Angeles National Cemetery, America's largest veterans' cemetery after Arlington, and was ground zero for protests in L.A. It also housed the region's FBI headquarters.

As chief mason with M Building Systems, the L.A. contractor hired for the building's $400 million renovation, Deker was supposed to ensure that "no extraordinary environmental circumstances" would result from the modernization. Meaning: As long as the building was still standing when all the work was done, Uncle Sam was happy.

He passed the stone pillars of the nearly half-mile-long fence surrounding the complex. He had installed a few of them himself. The pillars protected the FBI headquarters from truck bombs and other terrorist threats, and the white walls of the building were designed to be blast-resistant. But new federal guidelines following the terrorist attacks of September 11, 2001, required a complete renovation, including two hundred thousand fully grouted and extensively reinforced concrete units for backup and partition walls.

He entered the rear lot and parked at the construction site next to the 405 freeway. Crews were already at work removing asbestos and continuing seismic upgrades. These renovations were exempt from local requirements for a full environmental review, which had riled the residents of nearby Westwood, along with the already un-bearable traffic congestion.

He walked behind his car and opened the trunk to remove his bag. Inside were his Masonic apron and trowel. Anytime a federal public works project involved cornerstones, there was usually a low-key ceremony of some kind. It had been that way since the founding of the republic.

He slipped his bag over his shoulder and shut his trunk door to see several armed FBI agents swarming him. The lead agent, a twenty-something punk kid like himself, gave him the death stare.

"Sam Deker," he said. "You're wanted for questioning in connection with an imminent terrorist threat. Come with us."

8

Deker sat in the glass conference room on the fifteenth floor, overlooking Wilshire and the cemetery, while two feds argued outside the door. The agent who had detained him in the parking lot was going at it with a tall, thin African-American woman whom Deker recognized as Wanda Randolph, the unflappable former chief of the U.S. Capitol Police's subterranean RATS division in Washington, D.C. The man stormed off in defeat, and Wanda walked in through the door, a thick file folder in her hand.

"Still can't sleep, Sam?" she asked softly as she sat down at the table opposite him.

"What am I doing here?" he demanded.

"The FBI here gets a little nervous when they learn that a man of your particular background and talents is skulking around the foundations of their headquarters."

Deker noted her use of "they" to refer to the FBI, which suggested she still might be working for General Marshall Packard at the Pentagon's research agency, DARPA. A bad sign for him.

"Why are you here in L.A.?" he asked her. "Did you finally wise up and ditch Packard and his lunatics?"

She said nothing, only smiled.

Dammit.

"What do you people want?" he demanded.

"To help you, Sam."

"Help me?" he repeated. "You're the ones who sicced the FBI on me."

"The FBI was already onto you, Sam," she said, and opened his file. "And frankly, I'm curious to see how much they've got on you before we make it all go away. Aren't you?"

So that was the bait. Packard was going to ask him to do "one more for the Gipper" and get a clean slate, or else.

"Fine," he said. "What have I done?"

"What haven't you done?" she said. "They've got you joining the U.S. Army after your father was killed in the north tower of the World Trade Center during the 9/11 attacks, then graduating at the top of your class at West Point. As a Ranger, you disobeyed orders in Tora Bora and went after Osama bin Laden yourself instead of letting the local Afghans do it."

"They let him go," Deker said. "We had him. *I* had him. You were there. You know it."

She shrugged innocently and continued. "They've got the Israel Defense Forces requesting your services from DOD to help them defend the Temple Mount in Jerusalem from both Arab and Jewish extremists." She paused. "And they've properly flagged Rachel Alter's death as a turning point in your psych profile."

Deker swallowed hard and said nothing, seething at this blatant ploy to throw the worst experience of his life in his face. He and Rachel, barely nineteen, were engaged when she died from an explosive he had created to take out a Hamas leader. The accident with Rachel was a tragedy.

"Interesting," Wanda Randolph concluded. "They note your discharge from the IDF but give no reason. But they do say you were deported from Israel a year later for being a 33rd Degree Freemason."

"I thought it was time I actually did something constructive with my life," he told her. "You know, build things instead of destroy them. That's a crime?"

"Dang, no, Deker. Not in America. I've seen Masons get medals for their service to their country. But it's a problem in Israel if you're cutting a white Melekeh cornerstone from Solomon's Quarries for a Third Jewish Temple, seeing as it would have to be built where the Dome of the Rock mosque currently sits. The FBI concluded that the Israelis decided you were thinking about blowing up the Dome of the Rock."

Deker blinked. "And I am being held here by the FBI on what charge?"

"On being psycho," she said. "They think you're a walking time bomb waiting to go off, and that you sure as hell don't belong in federal buildings, especially theirs."

"Bullshit. You know that's not true."

"But they don't, Sam," she said, closing the file and tapping it with her finger. "And they also don't know about the terrible torture you endured at the hands of those Palestinian extremists."

"They were Jordanian GID," Deker corrected her.

"Jordan's intelligence agency is a U.S. and Israeli ally," Wanda said. "That's nonsense. It was those bastards in the Alignment who pumped you full of photosynthetic algae and light waves in order to take control of your brain. They seemingly sent you back in time to 1400 B.C. and the ancient Israelite siege of Jericho, but it was only to break you down and extract what you knew about Israel's secret fail-safe in case of attack."

"It wasn't a psychosis, it was real," Deker said flatly, and realized he was fingering his IDF dog tag hanging from his neck.

"Of course it was real," Wanda said, sounding like she was playing along with a lunatic. "You were an ancient Hebrew spy sent by General Joshua bin Nun to scout the walls of Jericho before the Israelite invasion. You made love to a beautiful enemy named Rahab who was a dead ringer for your beloved Rachel. In the end, you not only saved Israel—past and future—but established the bloodline that gave the Jews their king David and the world Jesus Christ. For these heroics, the modern state of Israel thanked you by dishonorably discharging you from its armed forces."

Deker knew how ridiculous it all sounded. Wanda Randolph had proved her point.

What really happened to him was that he had been broken into a million pieces. So many pieces that he could never put himself back together again. Once he was a warrior who broke things. Now he was broken beyond repair, a ghost wandering sleep labs by night and construction sites by day in an apron and waving a trowel like he could make his world of hurt disappear and become whole again.

But he could never know real peace in his heart, never rest until he found out for certain whether his visions, nightmares, whatever they were, had actually happened. The uncertainty since Jericho had stolen his sleep, his peace, maybe even his soul.

Deker took a deep breath and looked at her. "You said you could help me. Help me how?"

"Help you know what's real and what isn't," she told him, and stood up. "But we've got to move. We don't have much time."

"*We* don't or *you* don't?" Deker said. "What if I decide you can't help me?"

"Then these boys here at the FBI will give you all the time in the world you need to decide," she warned him. "But by the time you do, this offer will have expired. You've got to make up your mind, Deker, if you want to make up your mind. Get it? It's now or never."

He couldn't argue with her logic, however crazy it sounded. And he had run out of options for answers.

"Fine," he told her. "Let's go."

They took an elevator down to the subbasement of the Federal Building and emerged inside a garage with a fleet of black Escalades and several presidential limousines. The fleet was based here for the president's trips to Los Angeles. A presidential golf cart emerged from a dark tunnel with a faceless driver and none other than Marshall Packard, former U.S. secretary of defense and now head of the DOD's research and development agency, DARPA.

"Climb aboard, Deker," Marshall said as the cart pulled up.

Deker turned to let Wanda Randolph get in first, but she had vanished, and he was standing alone. He climbed in back next to Packard. "So where are you taking me?"

Packard said, "Back in time."

9

As the cart scooted off into the dark tunnel, Packard turned to Deker and said, "You look like hell. When's the last time you got a decent night's sleep?"

Packard knew damn well that Deker couldn't remember his last decent night's sleep. It had been at least a few years. They passed a guarded gate at a tunnel cross section, were waved through, then sped up, the golf cart's electric engine humming in the dark.

Deker sat back in his seat and sighed. "Not since I met you, Packard. So what exactly is this mission you have for me?"

"The *Flammenschwert*, Deker. The so-called Sword of Fire warhead that the Nazis built that could turn water to fire. The original Greek Fire. The Nazis, in their misguided mythology, believed it derived from Atlantean technology. You self-righteously destroyed the last of it under the Temple Mount, so that we couldn't get our hands on it, and nor could anybody else. Well, now we need to get it back, or at least the formula that created it."

Deker pondered the odd juxtaposition of his nightmare about the Baron of the Black Order and this conversation. His sixth sense was on high alert.

"How is giving you the power to scorch three quarters of the planet going to help me sleep at night?" he asked sardonically.

"Because you'll have peace of mind knowing that you kept it out of the hands of those Alignment terrorists who tortured you," Packard said. "Our intel says they're scouring Greece looking for any clues to rebuild the device."

"They're going to come up empty-handed," Deker said. "That secret was locked inside the head of SS general Ludwig von Berg. IDF files say he went down with his sub in the summer of 1943. Then the sub slid down the Calypso Deep, lost forever."

"It's something else the Alignment is after," Packard went on. "They want the formulas that General von Berg used to create the weapon. They believe those formulas came from a first-century biblical text that has since been destroyed. But we don't know for sure. We want you to tell us, and hopefully tell us what it says."

"The Maranatha text?" Deker asked.

"Now, how the hell did you know about that?" Packard demanded.

"I dreamed about it last night," he said. "Von Berg stole it from some Greek monks in Meteora who had been hiding it."

"This is amazing," Packard said. "Your brain did that all on its own, connecting bits and pieces of information you had come across and putting them together."

Packard's surprise sounded fake to Deker. He began to wonder if his recent nights at the sleep lab were really about him extracting information from the dark recesses of his own mind, or if in fact they were about DARPA somehow implanting information. Perhaps to make him more amenable to accepting an otherwise intolerable mission. The timing was simply too suspicious.

Deker said, "But the only reason the Alignment tortured me in the first place was because it knew I had a state secret inside my brain. The information you're after now was in the baron's brain. He's been dead for almost seventy years."

"Not quite," Packard said as they pulled up to the underground entrance of some vast structure that Deker guessed was the nearby Veterans Administration Hospital. "He's inside those walls. Get ready to meet the Baron of the Black Order."

10

SS general Ludwig von Berg turned out to be a slice of brain tissue trapped inside a glass slide and illuminated by a powerful beam of light. Walking to the lab beneath the VA Hospital, along a musty basement corridor in dire need of renovation, Deker felt like he was walking down some cosmic time tunnel to 1943.

Even the tall, trim man in the white lab coat with the brain slice seemed out of date, the way academics sometimes do. General Packard introduced him as Dr. Gordon Prestwick.

"This slice was removed from von Berg's brain by Nazi doctors in 1942," Prestwick said. "Von Berg had survived a bullet to the head in 1941 on Crete, where a metal plate replaced part of his shattered skull. For some reason, he had the plate replaced a year later. We found this sample, along with some other things, frozen at a secret Nazi base in Antarctica years later. Perfect for the 34th Degree Project."

"The 34th Degree?" Deker repeated.

"Yes, right," Prestwick said. "My grandfather Jason worked for the OSS, which was the predecessor to the CIA. He was also, like you, a 33rd Degree Freemason, the highest level in the Scottish Rite. He was my inspiration for the Pentagon's 34th Degree Neuro-simulation Program."

Deker said, "So what is it?"

Before Prestwick could answer, the lab door burst open, and Wanda Randolph entered with several medical technicians carrying a metallic organ transplant container.

"The medevac just landed," she announced.

Deker watched technicians unpack a complete human brain and place it like a slab of meat in a machine. To his shock and disgust, the machine began to cut the brain into paper-thin slices, which were then quickly frozen and encased in glass slides.

"What is that?" Deker asked. "*Who* is that?"

"That's Chris Andros, the Greek shipping billionaire who died minutes ago at UCLA Medical Center at the ripe old age of ninety-two," Packard said. "We and his family have been preparing for this process for some time, as he was the last living eyewitness to the events of 1943 that we've been discussing. We've already sliced and downloaded the brain of his wife, along with other participants of the era. Time is of the essence, or we lose our ability to extract information."

Deker understood now that the morning had been a setup. Packard must have been monitoring him for months. He couldn't disguise his anger. "You're not slicing my brain up," he said flatly. "That's not the kind of inner peace I'm looking for."

Prestwick actually found that funny and laughed. "No, of course not," he said as he helped the technicians slide the glass-encased brain slices into an optical drive. "At least not until you're dead. The brain slices enable us to download data into optical computer drives. So once the transference is made, storage isn't the issue. The problem is interpreting the data. That's where you come in. You're aware of Second Life and IMVU on the Web?"

Deker nodded. "Virtual communities where people connect and interact through avatars or digital representations of themselves that they create."

"The 34th Degree program is just such a virtual community, only its avatars are real people, or were," Prestwick said. "The idea was originally to allow U.S. authorities to interrogate terrorists they had already killed."

Deker glanced at Packard. "A virtual Gitmo," he observed, referring to the U.S. detention center for terrorists in Cuba's Guantánamo Bay.

"Precisely, and with no human rights issues, as the subjects are already dead," Packard threw in helpfully. "Better still, the 34th Degree allows us to view a terrorist attack or some other historical event from many points of view."

Deker asked, "What if you're missing a key participant because he blew himself up?"

Dr. Prestwick smiled and held up his finger. "The 34th Degree hypothesizes and creates that point of view based on the other information it has—the same way computers can do a 360-degree around a subject or object when surveillance cameras have captured only one side of the picture. The problem is that the 34th Degree is not quite at your level of advancement."

Deker saw what looked like an electric chair in the corner. "You're not strapping me into that thing. Get some other guinea pig."

"We've tried that already," Packard said. "Nobody else is as singularly talented as you are, Deker. When those Alignment interrogators pumped you with that photosynthetic algae, it changed something in your blood and neurology. You respond to light waves differently than we do. Your brain can make synaptic connections nobody else's can, even if we send the same light waves to their brains. We are simply repeating your torture without the torture. Just a little hole in the head for the fiber-optic cable and light waves. The straps are so you don't hurt yourself while you're under. Trust me, you won't feel a thing."

There was more than one way to interpret that. "And what do I get in return?" Deker asked as he slipped into the chair, which was comfortable enough. "I forgot."

"A clean slate with the FBI," Wanda Randolph said, as if to remind Packard. "Maybe even a good night's sleep."

"Oh, yeah," Deker said. A clean slate. A good night's sleep. They sounded like euphemisms for a lobotomy. "What if I never wake up?"

"Well, then we can slice your brain up to see what you discovered," Prestwick said without irony.

Seconds later, Deker was strapped in the strange metal chair, an IV pumping photosynthetic algae into his right arm. Now that the benzocaine anesthetic had taken hold, Prestwick fastened a shunt with a glowing purple fiber-optic cable to Deker's skull. It looked like a syringe gun. Once Prestwick pushed the button, the hair-thin fiber-optic line would inject itself through his skull. That would enable the team to send flashes of light from the brain slices directly into his brain.

"Now, let me frame your 34th Degree mission for you in 1943 terms," Prestwick said as the anesthesiologist put a mask over Deker's mouth. "Think of these glass slides of brain slices as a slide show. We are going to load them up one at a time. First the slide from my own grandfather, then Baron Ludwig von Berg, then Chris Andros. You must ultimately identify with him."

"Why?" Deker asked.

"Because he's looking for the text, too," Prestwick said. "If you become dominated by a strong presence like the Baron and identify too much with him, you will do everything you can to keep the contents and location of the Maranatha text from us. But you need him, because he can take you places nobody else has been."

"Okay," Deker said. "So I'll experience all these episodes in your slide show until they're loaded and running together."

"Then the 34th Degree program, together with your brain, will fill in any empty spaces," Prestwick said. "You asked me what the 34th Degree was, Deker. It's total omniscience. You will know more than we do. You will know everything. You know what that means, don't you?"

Deker nodded soberly. It meant that if this crazy experiment actually worked, then his trip through time to the ancient battle of Jericho in 1400 B.C. had been just a torture-induced psychosis. This lab, this chair, these people, were real. Everything else was illusion. He could finally sleep easy. If it failed, then perhaps reality was back in 1400 B.C. or 1943 A.D. or whenever, and this life was the illusion.

Except the intel.

The intel, as he had learned the hard way long ago, was always real.

Packard nodded enthusiastically. "I can't think of a Mason who wouldn't die for this kind of opportunity," he said. "Consider this your 34th Degree."

"Sure," Deker said slowly.

"No worries," Prestwick said as he quickly made some adjustments. "The next burst will send you back. You will see, feel, and experience everything that these people did at this significant moment for them in 1943, starting with my grandfather. Are you ready?"

Deker nodded. In spite of himself, the terror from his previous torture seized him, and he gripped the arms of the chair tightly.

"Okay, then," Prestwick said, and pushed the button. "Here we go."

Deker felt a surge of energy coming into his head, then a blinding light, and finally, a black tunnel engulfed him.

1943

11

Jason Prestwick hurried along Fifth Avenue with a teddy bear from FAO Schwarz tucked under his arm. A phone call in the middle of the night had instructed him to pick up the cub at the famous toy shop and "carry it to a certain floor of a building in Manhattan," the New York headquarters of the Office of Strategic Services.

Now, as he neared Rockefeller Center on this sunny afternoon of May 11, 1943, Prestwick slowed down and ran a quick check on a possible tale. At sixty-two, the Yale University professor knew he was hardly the sort one would associate with the spy trade, what with his tall, awkward frame, ill-fitting Harris tweed sport coat, shaggy gray hair, and round spectacles. Still, one had to be careful. No doubt some top-secret information about Operation Maranatha was stuffed inside this absurd teddy bear, and he was the courier.

The professor of classical Greek had been recruited in 1939 by the British Secret Intelligence Service as a cryptanalyst. After helping William Albright and the ULTRA team crack the Nazis' secret Enigma codes, Prestwick had brought his formidable cipher and code-breaking skills to the Research and Analysis branch of the OSS, America's fledgling spy agency. He later transferred to the agency's Secret Intelligence section in order to serve as an OSS liaison with Britain's Special Operations Executive, or SOE, created by Churchill "to coordinate all action by way of subversion and sabotage against the enemy." That meant helping resistance movements in Nazi-occupied Europe and engaging in all sorts of splendid intrigues designed to "set Europe ablaze." For a frustrated academic like Prestwick, itching for cloak-and-dagger action, it was the perfect sort of work, even if he was a deskbound case officer and not a field agent behind enemy lines.

Prestwick passed under the statue of Atlas in front of the 630 Fifth Avenue entrance, crossed the lobby, and stepped into the nearest elevator. Already he fantasized about the good news on Maranatha. It was his greatest "caper," as he liked to call his operations, and he looked forward to celebrating that evening at the Stork Club. Maybe he'd win back some money at gin rummy from a certain air force colonel and then share highballs in the Cub Room with a certain lovely starlet. The band would strike up "That Old Black Magic," and they'd dance the night away. . . .

The offices of British Passport Control were on the thirty-sixth floor at the end of a deserted hallway. A New York police officer sat outside on a wooden chair, dozing off under the *Times* as Prestwick walked by. The front-page headlines reported that Axis forces in North Africa were on the eve of official surrender.

Inside the reception area, a young blonde in a short skirt smiled at the teddy bear and pushed a button beneath her desk. The buzzer unlocked the door to the office of Bill Stephenson, code name INTREPID, the agent who coordinated joint American OSS–British SOE operations from New York.

As soon as Prestwick stepped into Stephenson's office, he could sense something was off. Somebody else was seated behind the spymaster's desk with his back toward the door. A cloud of cigar smoke hovered over his bald head. When the chair turned, Prestwick found himself face-to-face with Winston Churchill. Prestwick's jaw dropped.

"Don't just stand there gaping, man," said the British prime minister. "Come in and close the door."

12

Prestwick sat on the edge of his stiff chair. Across the desk, the great round face seemed to hover over the dark bow tie with white polka dots, disembodied from the prime minister's navy blazer. Holding that blazer together over the expansive stomach was a single brass button. With each puff the great man took of his cigar, the button came alarmingly close to popping off. Prestwick wondered if it would be poor etiquette for him to duck should it fly toward his face.

"In less than eight weeks, the largest invasion force ever assembled in human history will land on the shores of Sicily," Churchill began. "We are talking about more than five hundred thousand American and British troops."

Churchill unrolled a large map of the Mediterranean across the top of the desk, placing the teddy bear as a weight on one corner. Over Nazi-occupied Europe, the prime minister had drawn the outline of a huge crocodile stretching from Spain in the west to Greece in the east.

"This is our first assault on Fortress Europe and the first big seaborne landing on a coast held by the enemy."

Churchill thrust his Havana up the soft underbelly of the crocodile to make his point. His fingers were long and thin, almost delicate. This always surprised Prestwick, perhaps because his memories of their previous chats were invariably dominated by the prime minister's gruffness.

"As this is precisely what the Germans are expecting, the Combined Chiefs of Staff asked the British SOE and the American OSS to come up with several deception operations designed to convince the Germans that Sicily is only a cover, that the bulk of the Allied invasion force will land in Greece. The idea is to force Hitler to spread his coastal defenses thinly rather than concentrate them on Sicily, our intended point of entry."

None of this was news to Prestwick, and he wondered where the prime minister was going. "I believe I understand the fundamental concept, sir."

"My men at SOE got the ball rolling with Operation MINCE-MEAT," Churchill continued, apparently irritated at the interruption. "They arranged for a corpse, wearing a British officer's uniform and carrying documents referring to an invasion of mainland Greece, to be floated off the Spanish coast. Two weeks ago this 'Major Martin of the Royal Marines' washed up on a beach near Alicante and was found by local fishermen. His papers fell into Nazi hands, as planned, and, I understand, are making quite an impression on the German High Command."

This Prestwick hadn't heard. "Why, that's wonderful news, sir!"

"Mmm," Churchill grunted, neither confirming nor denying what Prestwick had said. "Not to be outdone by London, you proposed your own OSS operation."

"That's right, sir," Prestwick replied, trying not to smile. "Operation Maranatha."

"Tell me, then: How did this inspiration come to you?"

"Gladly, sir." Prestwick straightened in his chair. "While Major Martin was intended to dupe the German military and intelligence authorities, we also appreciated Hitler's contempt for these traditional sources of information. He often consults his astrologers and numerologists before making any major decisions. Ultimately, he relies on what he perceives to be his infallible intuition. In the past we've encouraged this superstitious streak by propping up our own bogus astrologers, publicizing their prophecies in the world press and then using American OSS and British SOE agents to make them come true. Our Hungarian friend de Wohl's prediction of SS general Heydrich's death and our use of Czech assassins to carry it out is a case in point. So when we caught wind of Hitler's interest in Greek Fire, I naturally considered ways we could turn it to our advantage. That's when I recalled a fantastic tale I heard from a young Muslim warrior during one of my travels some years ago."

"The infamous Hadji Azrael," stated Churchill.

Prestwick nodded. "Hence Operation Maranatha," he said. "The word 'Maranatha' is Aramaic and means 'Lord, come.' It was a greeting used by the early Christians to express their hope in Christ's return. That's how the legendary lost epistle of Paul to the Thessalonians became known as the Maranatha text—because it predicts the end of the world and the return of Christ. I simply arranged for a microfilm of a bogus Maranatha text to surface at our OSS outpost in Istanbul, which you correctly suspected of being infiltrated by Axis agents. In addition to its references to the Second Coming, Armageddon, and all the fire-and-brimstone rhetoric we find in Bible prophecy, the bogus text by implication singles out Greece as the first point of entry by any invasion forces from the Middle East, Allied or Divine."

Here Prestwick couldn't help himself and had to add, somewhat shamefacedly at his own brilliance, "I even encrypted it with an ancient Greek military cipher just to make Hitler's numerologists think they had tapped into the Greek Fire formula."

"So I'm told," said Churchill, puffing his Havana. "That was quite . . . clever."

"All in all," Prestwick concluded proudly, "I'd call it an apocalyptic piece of theater designed to exploit Hitler's fascination with the supernatural."

There was heavy silence, and Prestwick waited expectantly for Churchill's congratulations. When they didn't come, he began to feel uneasy.

Finally, Churchill said, "And knowing Hitler's obsessions, you never considered the possibility that he would attempt to obtain the original Maranatha text?"

"We suspected the microfilm would whet Hitler's appetite, sir, but we never dreamed the Nazis would find a real text, because . . ." Prestwick trailed off.

"Because a real text couldn't possibly exist?" Churchill asked. "Quite presumptuous of you. Indeed, this revelation of yours has turned into a divine comedy, and it's that devil Hitler who will be laughing."

Prestwick felt a hollowness in his stomach. "Excuse me, sir?"

"We just got these photos from C in London this morning." Churchill pushed a file across the desk to Prestwick. "The Nazis beat us to the text. Operation Maranatha is blown."

Prestwick's heart sank. With trepidation, he opened the file and shuffled through the grisly photos. The charred remains of Orthodox monks lay strewn among the smoldering ruins. "Dear Lord. I take it this was once the Monastery of the Taborian Light?"

"Not one stone left unturned."

"And Commander Lloyd?"

"Dead," said Churchill. "This is the Baron's handiwork."

"General von Berg?" This was even worse than Prestwick had thought. He pushed the file of photos back across the desk.

"The implications, of course, are catastrophic," said Churchill. "If the Nazis suspect your bogus Maranatha text is a plant, they'll *know* Greece is only a cover and that we'll be landing in Sicily. And they'll be waiting for us on those beaches, all their forces concentrated. Hundreds of thousands of British and American lives are on the line, Prestwick."

Prestwick stared at the map of Europe, everything Churchill said sinking like lead in his stomach.

"What I want to know," demanded Churchill, "is how long before von Berg appreciates the differences between his text and your microfilm? How long before this time bomb of yours goes off?"

Prestwick's mind, numbed for a moment by the realization that it was his head that would roll on Churchill's altar of bungled Allied operations, now started to race. "The beauty of passing my forgery in the form of a microfilm, of course, is that the film is only a photographic reproduction of the text and not the text itself. That eliminates the danger of the Nazis dating my 'ancient' papyrus and discovering it to be discolored 1940 Canadian bond paper. Furthermore, my papyrus appears to be only a fragment of a larger document. My guess is that's precisely the case with the text from the Taborian Light. Therefore, rather than compare the two versions side by side, the Germans could in fact see them as complementary."

"It's those alphanumeric codes of yours I'm worried about," said Churchill sharply. "I sincerely doubt that the document von Berg has found, if genuine, is similarly encoded."

That was true, Prestwick realized. Churchill had him there. "Perhaps," he suggested weakly, "there's still time to change the invasion plans?"

Churchill stopped him with a cold glance. He then waved his hand over the map and spoke as if by rote. "The toppling of Mussolini. The domination of the central Mediterranean. The ability to level threats at the soft underbelly of the Axis in southern France and the Balkans. Not to mention the possibility of drawing Turkey into the war on our side." Some cigar ashes fell onto Greece, and the prime minister brushed them off. "These are highly desirable goals."

There was little Prestwick could say, so he thought it best not to say anything.

"No," Churchill concluded. "According to what you've told me, we must obviously steal that text, or destroy it, before von Berg cracks the codes and discovers the secret of Operation Maranatha: namely, that our text is a fraud."

"Steal the text from the Baron?" Prestwick was incredulous. "Impossible!"

"Good God, nothing's impossible," Churchill replied. "It can't be impossible, not with more than half a million troops on the line. But you're correct in assuming that if von Berg has the text, it will be difficult to find. A traditional commando unit is no good, not until we know exactly where von Berg has hidden it. Fortunately, I know of someone close to von Berg, an insider who may be privy to the text's whereabouts and could be induced to help us."

Churchill passed Prestwick a photo of a striking young woman. Large, sad eyes gazed out of one of the most beautiful faces Prestwick had ever seen, crowned with a shimmering mane of black hair that fell behind her shoulders. Prestwick was seduced by her wide and well-formed mouth. "Who is she?"

"Von Berg's mistress," Churchill explained. "Aphrodite Vasilis, an Athens socialite."

"She can't be over twenty-one."

"Exactly," said Churchill. "And if anybody else besides von Berg knows about the text, it's Miss Vasilis. She's the chink in his armor, his Achilles' heel. If we can get through to her, we can get to the text."

"But how, sir?" asked Prestwick. "Knowing the Baron, she's probably just as well defended as the Maranatha text. And I'm sure he's trained her never to talk to strangers."

"That's why we're going to send her an old friend."

"An old friend?" Prestwick was curious.

"A special man I have in mind," Churchill went on. "A man I believe is capable of persuading Miss Vasilis to help us."

Prestwick adjusted his tie and leaned forward expectantly. "And who would that be, sir?"

"His name is Chris Andros."

Prestwick frowned and sat back in his chair. "Of the Andros shipping family?"

"The same," said Churchill. "I knew his father well. General Nicholas Andros of the Greek army, one of Greece's greatest war heroes. He was killed on Crete two years ago during the Nazi invasion. His brother-in-law now runs Andros Shipping in Athens, under Nazi supervision. He also runs guns for us to the Greek Resistance."

"And this son of General Andros. Where is he now?"

"Here in the States." Churchill drew out a file. "You'll discover that Chris Andros is a fiercely independent, proud young man who seems hell-bent on emerging from his father's shadow on his own terms. That's why he left politically scarred Greece and came to America." He pushed the file across the desk.

Prestwick opened the file, and a photo fell to the floor. He picked it up by the corner and saw a rather dashing young man no older than twenty-five standing in what he recognized as Harvard Yard. For a Harvard man, Prestwick thought, this Andros cut a fine figure: medium height, good shoulders, and a trim, athletic build. He had black wavy hair, clear dark eyes, an aquiline nose, and a firm jaw. But it was his broad grin that made Prestwick hate Andros, for it was the kind of winning smile no decent man could hate and no warm-blooded woman could resist.

"A handsome man," he observed, unable to hide the envy in his voice. "Too handsome, really, for a spy."

"Good looks aside, Prestwick, Andros has proved himself in action, which is more than I can say for you."

Stung by this tasteless exposure of his faults, Prestwick replaced the photo of Andros in the folder. He thumbed through the rest of the documents, hoping to glean some vice or character flaw that he could put to good use. "What makes you think Miss Vasilis will assist young Andros?"

"She was his fiancée before the Nazis invaded Greece and cut off their engagement."

"Ah."

Churchill added, "Those letters in his file are love letters the two wrote to each other between the time of their engagement and the middle of 1941, when all communication ceased. Our girls in Bermuda intercepted them. From what they tell us, Andros knows nothing about the new man in his former fiancée's life. As for Miss Vasilis, she still thinks he's at Harvard, as do the Germans."

"But he's not there anymore?"

"Dropped out as soon as the Germans invaded," Churchill told him. "Tried to get back to Greece for personal reasons, but couldn't."

"So where is he now?"

"The United States Military Academy."

"West Point?" Prestwick could see there was more to young Andros than he at first imagined. "He's a soldier, just like his father?"

"I wouldn't put it to him that way, Prestwick, but it's all there in your file. You'll recruit him, train him at the Farm, and then slip him into Greece. There he'll make contact with the girl and, ideally, steal the text."

Prestwick glanced at the file in his hands, keenly resenting that his career now rested with a young, untested man he hadn't even had a hand in selecting. "But what chance does a rank amateur—even if he is a West Pointer—have against the likes of the Baron?"

"Young Andros is our only chance," Churchill said. "He knows the language and the land of Greece better than any of our own. He also has, as you people in New Haven put it, the proper 'connections' in Athens. Let's see how he fares with Miss Vasilis. If her feelings for him are anywhere near what she's expressed in those letters, she'll help."

"And if not?"

"We have another little Greek tragedy in the making. And you'll be part of it."

"Excuse me?"

Churchill drew out a second file. "According to your OSS records, Yale cut off all your funding just before you joined SOE." He grew reflective. "This war is the best thing that ever happened to you, isn't it? If it came to an end, you'd have nowhere to go, would you?"

"Would you, sir?" Prestwick shot back, and then, seeing the frown on the prime minister's face and realizing the enormous offense of his insult, hastily added, "Would any of us, really?"

Churchill reached over and tapped his cigar on an ashtray. "You don't have any friends, do you, Prestwick?"

"Plenty, sir, in every department."

"Those are colleagues, Prestwick, acquaintances." Churchill sat back in his chair and looked at him. "I'm talking about those individuals with whom you spend your leisure. You don't have any of those in your life, do you?"

Prestwick felt cornered and didn't like it. He always felt uncomfortable whenever he considered his personal relationships, or lack thereof, and wondered what the prime minister was driving at. "No, sir."

"You were married once, too. What happened?"

"She left me."

"I'm sorry."

"It was because of my work," Prestwick put in hastily, feeling he had to provide some sort of excuse. "She couldn't come to grips with my devotion to scholarship."

"The same scholarship the academic community could do without?"

Prestwick thought Churchill's cruelty deserved a response. But it eluded him, and he was forced to face the cold truth that he had squandered the better part of his life on dubious research and lost the only woman he ever loved.

Churchill said, "We can't afford to have any of our lonely masterminds wandering about in vulnerable conditions."

"Vulnerable? I'm afraid I don't understand, sir."

"I think you do." Churchill produced a thick envelope and pushed it across the desk.

Prestwick picked up the envelope and opened it. It was stuffed with American hundred-dollar bills. "There must be several thousand dollars in here, sir."

"Just enough to cover your gambling losses," said Churchill, giving him a knowing look.

Utterly humiliated, Prestwick pocketed the cash. Desperately, he tried to recover his dignity in the face of all this unpleasantness. "I can explain, sir."

Churchill held up his hand to inform him that no explanation was necessary. "That young actress, by the way, is one of Hoover's," he added. "She has more than enough secrets to pry loose from the hearts of private citizens without your wasting her time. Or compromising our secrets to the FBI."

Prestwick swallowed hard. "I won't, sir."

"Good," replied Churchill, and he repeated the point of their little conversation lest it be lost on either of them. "It is paramount that the Nazis believe we're about to invade Greece, Prestwick. You'll do whatever it takes to convince them. Understand? Or else, for you, this war is over."

13

Or else, for you, this war is over. As far as Prestwick was concerned, harsher words were never spoken. Churchill's warning was unmistakable, and it made an indelible impression. Suddenly, Prestwick felt old and used up, crumbling inside like the yellowed pages of some old, dusty, and forgotten book. "This war is my life, sir."

"Then you'll do everything in your power to make sure Andros succeeds in his mission."

As Churchill spoke, the bookcase behind him opened to reveal a secret exit. Two American Secret Service agents were waiting to escort the prime minister.

"I must be going," Churchill said, putting out his cigar. The great man rose to his feet, brushed off the cigar ashes from his blazer, and rolled up his map of Europe representing millions of lives. "I'm expected at the White House this afternoon to meet with the president and the Combined Chiefs of Staff. Hopkins is waiting for me outside in the car."

Prestwick nodded and picked up the folder, realizing there would be no gin rummy tonight, no starlet, no dancing. Instead, he'd spend the night like he did nearly every night: translating some obscure document or reading a report. Then he saw the stuffed bear still sitting on the desk.

The prime minister was squeezing through the bookcase when Prestwick caught up with him. "Sir, what about the teddy bear?"

"Almost forgot, Prestwick, thank you." Churchill clutched the cub by the throat. "A gift for one of the president's grandchildren. Good of you to pick it up for me. Now, no more mess-ups. Knowing the Baron, he's already two steps ahead of us."

14

Baron von Berg raced through the Bavarian Alps in a staff Mercedes, late for a conference with Hitler and his generals at the Führer's holiday house at Obersalzberg.

Von Berg was driving with the top down, having placed the dead body of the chauffeur who tried to kill him in the backseat. No doubt Himmler had sent the fool to greet his plane after failing to hear from Ulrich in Greece, von Berg thought. Unfortunately for the driver, the Baron had performed too many similar assassinations for the Reichsführer to fail to recognize that something was up. He took care of the swine shortly after they passed through the village of Berchtesgaden, when he forced the driver to stop so he could answer nature's call.

Himmler had tried to kill two birds with one stone in Greece, von Berg realized: eliminate the Baron and obtain the Maranatha text. Now he would get neither, for the text was safe in Greece, and von Berg had no intention of missing this meeting, not with the truly significant document inside his leather briefcase on the seat beside him.

As the autobahn curved east, von Berg could see more majestic mountains in the moonlight. Yes, it was good to come home to his beloved Bavaria, good to be alive. So good that the thought of the Reichsführer working up some remorse and breaking the bad news to the Führer of the Baron's unfortunate end at the hands of religious fanatics made him smile. He pushed the pedal to the floor, and the Mercedes took off.

15

Hitler's holiday house at Obersalzberg was reached by a precipitous road that wound its way up Mount Kehlstein and ended at a bronze portal blasted into the rock. Here an SS guard snapped to attention as Baron von Berg proceeded to drive through a long marble tunnel lined with chandeliers. When he emerged in the vast underground garage at the other end, he stopped the Mercedes, and an SS valet opened the rear door only to discover that the passenger was dead.

"His shirts weren't pressed, and he was always on time, never early," von Berg explained to the terrified attendant, jumping out of the driver's seat. "Now, I won't be long, so inform the airfield in Berchtesgaden that my private plane will arrive and take off in three hours. Unload the globe from the trunk and have it brought up to the house. In the meantime, have my car washed and get that blood off the backseat. You might also inspect the wiring under the hood before we leave, to ensure we don't have any unfortunate accidents, because you'll be my driver."

The parking attendant gave him a stiff-armed but shaky Nazi salute. "*Zu Befehl*, Herr Oberstgruppenführer!"

"Excellent. Carry on. And don't scratch the fender this time."

Von Berg stepped into the waiting elevator and sat down on a gray leather seat. As the polished brass cage began its slow three-hundred-foot ascent up the shaft in the heart of Mount Kehlstein, he glanced at his watch and turned to the sleepy SS guard operating the elevator. "Rather unusual for the Führer to hold a situation conference this early, wouldn't you say? He's not exactly what I would describe as a morning person."

"Ach," replied the operator with a nod. "He is having trouble sleeping these days and keeps us all up every hour to accommodate him."

"And accommodate him we must. Is my delivery here?"

"Yes, Herr Oberstgruppenführer." The operator pulled a hook on the floor to reveal a lower compartment. Below were two SS orderlies with a large object draped in canvas: the Templar Globe. They would exit on the lower level of Hitler's house.

"Very good. Have it ready when I call."

When the elevator reached the top, von Berg proceeded to the anteroom of the Berghof, Hitler's holiday house. Oberführer Rattenhuber, the Nordic-looking chief of the SS bodyguard, seemed very surprised to see him, as though he had just seen a ghost. He was so surprised, in fact, that he failed to ask General von Berg to hand over his pistol when he brushed past without waiting to hear the magic words "The Führer will see you now."

16

Hitler was standing in front of the large picture window, looking out at the hills of Salzburg while he addressed his generals, his hands clasped behind his back. He was wearing the field-gray military uniform. At the sound of von Berg's footsteps, he turned sharply with a frown that quickly became a smile.

"Von Berg, at last!" he said, walking over and warmly clasping von Berg's hand with both of his own.

"*Guten Tag,* Chief," replied von Berg, dispensing with the ingratiating "Heil Hitler" of outsiders.

"I see the rumors of your death are greatly exaggerated. Please sit down."

Von Berg nodded and looked at the disappointed faces of the four men seated around the long map table. They were General Alfred Jodl, chief of staff of the Armed Forces High Command; Admiral Karl Doenitz, commander in chief of the naval staff; Admiral Wilhelm Canaris, chief of military intelligence; and, finally, von Berg's boss, Reichsführer Heinrich Himmler, chief of both the state and the secret police, looking paler than usual, von Berg thought, as he took his seat next to the devil and smiled.

"As I was saying," Hitler continued, "now that Rommel's overrated Afrika Korps have disgraced us with their defeat in Tunisia, the Allies hold the whole North African coast, with General Eisenhower's army at the western end of the Mediterranean and General Montgomery's army at the eastern end. That the Allies will use their new position to launch an invasion into our Fortress Europe there can be no doubt. Our entire southern front is exposed from France in the west to Greece in the east. The only thing between us and them is the moat that is the Mediterranean."

At this everybody nodded, Admiral Doenitz in particular,

acknowledging that the Mediterranean was his fleet's responsibility to defend.

"But where will they land?" asked Hitler. "That is the question, and we must know the answer if we are to crush their armies on the beaches. I shall hear reports from our two intelligence chiefs. Canaris, you first."

Admiral Canaris nodded to an SS orderly, and the curtains were drawn and the lights dimmed. Two tapestries at opposite ends of the room lifted to reveal a projector on one wall and a movie screen on the other. Below the screen sat a large chest with built-in speakers and a large bronze bust of Richard Wagner on top. The film began by showing a funeral procession that von Berg recognized as Catholic.

"This footage was taken by one of our agents in Spain," said Canaris, narrating. "Two weeks ago the body of a British courier, a certain Major Martin of the Royal Marines, washed up on the shores near Huelva. Apparently, his plane was shot down over the Mediterranean. He was carrying two letters from the Imperial General Staff in London to General Alexander and Admiral Cunningham in Tunisia. Abwehr agents managed to photograph the contents of the letters before the British authorities claimed the corpse from the coroner."

These men will believe anything, thought von Berg, as his former master proceeded.

"A careful analysis of those letters reveals the Allies are going to attack Sardinia and Greece," Canaris explained. "The British Eighth Army, under General Montgomery, and the American Seventh Army, under General Patton, will strike Sardinia from their positions in Tunisia. But that will be a diversionary blow. We believe that the main target of the operation will be an invasion of Greece."

A map of Greece appeared on the screen, complete with animated arrows that pinpointed where the enemy would strike.

"From their positions in the Middle East, two divisions of General Wilson's Ninth Army are detailed for landings on the west coast of Greece. The Fifty-sixth Infantry Division will land near

Kalamata, and the Fifth Infantry Division will land on the stretch of coast south of Cape Araxos. We expect them to be joined by Montgomery's Eighth Army and Patton's Seventh Army for the advance up the Greek mainland."

Von Berg watched Hitler's eyes glaze over as Canaris continued his narration.

"At the same time, we must reckon with the probability that Wilson's other divisions—how many he has, we don't really know—will invade the east coast of Greece, taking the Dodecanese islands in the process. The code name for this operation, according to the documents found with Major Martin, is Husky. Lights."

Curtains were pulled back, and Hitler asked for comments.

Himmler cleared his throat. "As the Führer is aware," he began, "SS agents in Istanbul recently intercepted their own Allied communiqué, one that contained a secret microfilm."

"Yes, yes," said Hitler, eyes widening with interest. "Go on, Reichsführer."

"That microfilm confirms the Abwehr's analysis that the Allied forces now gathering in Palestine, Egypt, and Libya are intended for Greece. Increased partisan activity in Greece provides further proof, including a rising number of supply drops to the Greek Resistance by American and British aircraft."

Hitler said, "Von Berg, you've just come from Greece. Is what the Reichsführer says true?"

"It is true, but . . ."

"But what?" Hitler asked expectantly.

"I am troubled that documents as vital as these should so conveniently fall into the hands of the German High Command."

Canaris responded quickly. "If you are suggesting, General von Berg, that Major Martin is a plant to dupe us, I can assure you that the general staff has considered this possibility and concluded that he is genuine and his documents above suspicion."

Hitler looked to Himmler, who said nothing, then back to von Berg. "You are not convinced?"

"The Allies simply want us to spread our coastal defenses thinly rather than concentrate them on their intended point of entry—Sicily."

Canaris shook his head. "Any attack on Sicily or one of the Italian islands will be diversionary."

"That's what they want us to believe, Admiral," said von Berg. "It is Greece that is the cover. Allow me to introduce my own intercepted communiqué. Nothing less than the Anglo-American invasion plans, complete with changes made by General Montgomery himself."

Himmler frowned as von Berg opened his briefcase and produced a copy of a U.S. military report. There were glances across the table and immediate interest as von Berg passed the report to Hitler. Von Berg then stood up and looked down at the map.

"Gentlemen, may I present to you the real Operation Husky—the Allied invasion of Sicily." Von Berg found a pointer and traced the routes of the invasion forces. "The assault begins with a landing by night by the American Eighty-second and British First Airborne Divisions, followed by a landing of eight seaborne divisions simultaneously—four American, four British."

There were murmurs across the table.

"Ten divisions!" exclaimed Doenitz.

Canaris said, "That's twice as many as we've got in all of Sicily."

"All the same," von Berg insisted, "the American Seventh Army, under General Patton, will race up the west coast of the island. The British Eighth Army, under General Montgomery, will race up the east coast. Together they will converge at Messina. From there they will cross the channel and invade Italy." He sat down.

"Italy!" cried Canaris. "I think you're gravely mistaken, von Berg."

The room grew very quiet as an angry Hitler slapped his hands on the table, rose to his feet, and began to pace the floor. "There are two possibilities," he said. "Either this Major Martin is a plant, or this report from General Montgomery is a plant. Both can't be correct. Either the Allies are invading Greece, or they are invading Italy by way of Sicily. Now, if my intelligence chiefs can't agree on anything, perhaps my military chiefs can." Hitler turned to Doenitz. "You have just seen the Duce, Admiral. What are his views on Anglo-American intentions?"

"Mussolini, Kesselring, and the Italian High Command all feel the Allies' next move from North Africa will be a jump into Sicily and then an advance up the boot of Italy."

Hitler turned to General Jodl. "And you, Jodl?"

The former Bavarian artillery officer stood over the map table. With the pointer, he tapped Sicily, Sardinia, and Corsica. "Even if the Allies captured all three Italian islands, it is unlikely they would invade Italy herself, as von Berg suggests, because in Italy our reactions would be swift and strong. In Greece, however, our reinforcements and supplies would be slow."

Jodl drew an imaginary line from the Middle East to the southern tip of Greece. "An invasion of Greece by General Wilson's army in the Middle East poses the greater danger, because it threatens to interrupt not only our supplies of bauxite, copper, and chrome from the Balkans but also oil from Romania's fields at Ploesti."

"Yes, yes." Hitler nodded enthusiastically. "I tell you, this is what I dread. This is what we cannot allow to happen."

"Furthermore, if the Allies invade Greece, it is probable they would use it as a springboard to advance up the Balkans through the historic Vardar Valley route used by the British and French in the Great War." Jodl drew an imaginary line from Salonika in northern Greece up through Belgrade, Budapest, Vienna, Prague, and finally, with a loud tap, Berlin.

The impact was not lost on Hitler, who seemed visibly shaken at the thought of history repeating itself. "Yes," he finally concluded, "Sicily is too heavily defended to be taken easily."

After composing himself, Hitler began to speak in the third person, something he often did when issuing formal orders. "The Führer does not agree with the Baron nor the Duce that the most likely invasion point is Sicily. Furthermore, he believes that the Anglo-Saxon order discovered by Abwehr agents is genuine and confirms the assumption that the planned attack will be directed mainly against Greece." He paced back and forth. "The Führer prepares the following order: 'The First German Panzer Division will be sent to Greece, to support the three German infantry divisions and the Italian Eleventh Army there.'"

"But the First Panzer Division is in France!" von Berg protested. "You're going to pull a complete panzer division out of the war and transport it all the way across Europe to Greece?"

"The First German Panzer Division will establish its headquarters at the Greek town of Tripolis," Hitler went on sharply, ignoring von Berg. "It is ideally situated in the Peloponnese to command resistance against any Allied landings at Kalamata and Araxos. Now, all of you, leave me. I need a few minutes with General von Berg and the Reichsführer."

They all left the room—Jodl, Doenitz, and, finally, Canaris. When they were gone, Hitler glared at von Berg.

"It is enough that my political and military intelligence services are at odds; that much I expected. But dissension within the SS? Von Berg, I asked you for a simple text, and you bring me this—this obvious forgery." He looked at the report and gave it to Himmler. "Montgomery's handwriting, indeed. How much of a fool do they think I am?"

"Clearly, the Baron was premature in introducing this analysis without my approval," said Himmler. "My staff shall look into the report more thoroughly before making any formal recommendations."

Von Berg knew that would be the last he would ever see of the report. He also knew that Hitler's hunch about Greece had less to do with General Jodl's cool logic than with his own heated passion about the Maranatha text.

"Tell me what happened in Greece," said Hitler. "The Reichsführer, for some reason, thought you may not appear here at all."

Von Berg glanced at Himmler, still lacking color, as well he should. The bastard probably had a communiqué in his pocket ready to produce at the right moment, informing Hitler that his favorite underling had been killed in Greece by mad monks. Nevertheless, von Berg would not reveal that he had actually obtained the Maranatha text. Who knew where that would send Hitler?

"A tragedy. That's what it was," von Berg said. "Those religious fanatics burned themselves and gutted the entire monastery in the process."

Hitler asked, "And the Maranatha text?"

"Not to be found." Von Berg looked at Himmler. "Unfortunately, Reichsführer, we also lost Colonel Ulrich. Were it not for him, I wouldn't be standing here before you."

"Nonsense, you have good luck," insisted Hitler. "Even when surrounded by fools, fate spared you now, as it has before. You were failed by your protectors, just as I am."

He was referring to rumors and recent attempts on his life. Von Berg, however, not wishing to provoke Himmler just yet, spoke in Ulrich's defense. "To the contrary, my Führer, I recommend a Knight's Cross for the Standartenführer, awarded posthumously. His actions were most noble. Tragic he should die at the hands of religious fanatics, but it was not in vain."

He snapped his fingers, and two SS orderlies walked in with a heavy object draped with a white cloth. "A gift for the Führer. From the Monastery of the Taborian Light in Meteora."

The orderlies snapped the canvas away to reveal the great golden Templar Globe.

Hitler stood back, surprised and awed. He walked over and closely examined it, a bit fearful. "Striking," said the Führer. "This was taken from the *Zu den drei Weltkugeln*?"

"From the Lodge of the Three Globes, yes," the Baron replied. "But it is far older than old Prussian Freemasonry. The monks in Greece believe it is one of three globes that once graced King Solomon's Temple. Would you like it kept here or stored with the other icons?"

Hitler didn't answer; he simply stared at the globe. "This is what I saw in my dreams. I am sure of it. Another sign, Reichsführer."

Von Berg was wary of whatever bizarre new tangent the Führer was embarking on. Hitler's physician, Dr. Karl Brandt, attributed his constant fatigue to stress. Von Berg would not have been so generous with his diagnosis. It was at Brandt's urgings that Hitler set up his headquarters at Obersalzberg in March in the first place, allegedly for a three-month vacation. Now overwork and isolation had made him more exhausted and irritable than ever. This, more than anything, thought von Berg, would explain the fascination with miracle texts and a search for some divine deliverance.

"A sign?" von Berg repeated. "I'm not sure I understand."

"Come, I'll tell you as we stroll to the Eagle's Nest," Hitler told him. "I have a surprise waiting for you there—Professor Xaptz."

"Professor Xaptz?"

"A specialist in ancient Greek literature that the Reichsführer has found. He has solved the riddle of the Maranatha text."

17

Professor Xaptz was a small man with round spectacles and dubious credentials. He had been recommended to Himmler by one of Hitler's most despicable and corrupt supporters from the old days, a fanatical Jew-hater named Julius Streicher. The professor's high-pitched, nervous laugh rose above the clatter of teacups, coffee, and assorted cakes now being served in Hitler's teahouse, a twenty-minute walk from the Berghof and perched on one of Hitler's favorite lookout points over the Berchtesgaden Valley.

A few minutes later, after Hitler, Himmler, and Baron von Berg had settled into their easy chairs around the coffee table, Professor Xaptz began:

"As you know, I have been charged by the Reichsführer with unearthing and protecting the ancient history of our Aryan civilization. This mission has taken me to the ends of the earth, even Antarctica, where General von Berg established a submarine ice base for the Reich."

Von Berg flinched at the mention of Antarctica, seething once again at the memory of the ridiculous expedition that had cost him two crew members and several months of his life.

Professor Xaptz was part of a team of archaeologists and "scholars" that Himmler had sent to Antarctica to prove Hitler's master race theory, specifically the fantastical idea that the Nazis descended from the First Race—the mythological Atlanteans. They and their doomed city were first described in the fourth century B.C. by the ancient Greek philosopher Plato, who himself allegedly relied on source material dating well before the ancient Egyptians.

It was all pure fiction, of course, but the money, manpower, and military support that were being diverted from the war were not.

Yet, despite the Nazi occupation of Greece and access to all the pre-Greek Minoan ruins he could ask for, Professor Xaptz had not been able to show any hard evidence to support his wild speculations. So it didn't surprise von Berg that Xaptz would resort to turning the Führer's attention to Antarctica, where any ruins would be impossible to find, much less unearthed two miles beneath the ice, but which was as fertile ground as any for wild speculation and pseudoscience.

Von Berg had been forced to lay claim to the entire ice continent for the Reich by establishing a secret submarine base in East Antarctica, from which Xaptz and his ilk "worked" for three weeks. The only good that came of it for von Berg was an ideal locale to stash some of the army's unstable biotoxins so that they could not infect and destroy Germany before the Allies even landed.

Meanwhile, Xaptz had creatively established the idea of a "chain of knowledge" from the Atlanteans to the Nazi SS. This chain started with the Atlanteans and moved on to the Minoans, Egyptians, Greeks, Knights Templar, and Freemasons—all of them clay vessels to hold the enlightened knowledge of Atlantis. At the end of this line—beyond the 33rd Degree of the Masons—lay the knowledge of "First Time," which in turn contained secrets of the "end times" upon which rested Hitler's vision of a Thousand-Year Reich.

Again, a huge distraction from the war and impending Allied invasion with real ships, guns, and tanks. And now once again they were entertaining this charlatan with their attention.

"For the past few weeks I have had the honor of serving under the Reichsführer to examine the Maranatha text as represented by a captured enemy microfilm. The text claims the apostolic authority of Paul and predicts the end of the world. As there is no papyrus for me to date, I have had to rely on content alone to determine the text's authenticity. Nevertheless, I have completed a preliminary analysis and made some remarkable discoveries."

He produced a marked-up enlargement of the microfilm. "The Book of Revelation tells us that the celestial armies of Christ will gather in the Valley of Megiddo. That's in present-day Palestine, now occupied by the Allies. The Maranatha text says as much and implies that the most likely point of entry into Fortress Europe from these invasion forces will be Greece, repeating the spread of Christianity two thousand years ago."

"I told you, Reichsführer!" Hitler said to Himmler. "I was sure of it!"

Von Berg looked at Himmler and then eyed Xaptz incredulously. "How on earth did you arrive at such a convenient deduction?"

"I'll show you." Xaptz pointed to letters he had circled in the text. "By skipping certain letters, we see certain words appear—"

"Excuse me," interrupted von Berg, turning to Hitler. "Why should the good professor be searching for encoded words in an ancient document? What sort of scholarship is this?"

"Explain it to him, Herr Professor," Hitler said, waving his hand.

Xaptz frowned at von Berg. "Down through the centuries, there has been considerable debate in the Judeo-Christian tradition as to whether the Bible is literally inspired by God, word for word, letter for letter. Some Orthodox Jewish researchers, most notably Dr. David Stein, have gone so far as to search for encoded messages throughout Scripture that defy human explanation. By skipping letters in the Book of Genesis, for example, the Hebrew name for God, Elohim, appears 147 times. Because the probability of that happening by chance is about one in two million, the premise is that the Book of Genesis is divinely inspired."

"Do you personally believe this?" von Berg asked Xaptz.

"The consensus among many biblical scholars is that an editor pieced together the Book of Genesis from several ancient sources, known as the D, P, E, and J documents," Xaptz told von Berg, then turned to Hitler. "Of course, my Führer, this documentary hypothesis collapses if the present findings hold up."

"This is all very interesting, Herr Professor," said von Berg, "but what bearing could it possibly have upon the course of the war?"

Professor Xaptz's response was defiant. "The ninth chapter of the Book of Esther refers to the hanging of the ten sons of Haman. They were enemies of the Jews. Hidden among their names is the Hebrew date for 1946: Judgment Day, if you will. I would think any reference to the twentieth century is quite relevant."

"Why 1946?" asked Hitler, clearly troubled by what he had just heard.

"I suppose it means the war will be won by one side or the other by then."

"But which side, Herr Professor? I must know!"

What was left of the thin veneer of infallibility of the Führer, the military genius who had conquered continental Europe, disintegrated, as it often would during these tea-time conversations when he would openly share the opinions he tried to hide from military types such as Jodl and Doenitz, rightly fearing their ridicule.

"For that answer, I refer you to the thirty-first chapter of the Book of Deuteronomy, where the Lord told Moses his descendants would forsake God and break His law. Verse seventeen says, 'Then my anger will be kindled against them . . . and I will devour them.' When that section is scanned for every fiftieth letter, the Hebrew word for 'holocaust' emerges. That means a burnt offering or fiery destruction of life."

"Clearly a divine affirmation of your Final Solution, the extermination of the Jews," added Himmler to Hitler. "Of your messianic mission and the certainty of the Thousand-Year Reich."

"Why, of course, I see now," said Hitler. "I thought of it, and now I am sure. Even the miserable Scriptures of subhumans cannot hide the reality of my destiny and their destruction." He turned to von Berg, who nodded dumbly. The notion that an ancient document could predict a genocidal madman like Hitler was almost as absurd as the reality of watching him actually believe it.

Hitler produced a German Bible and opened it to the bookmark at the thirty-first chapter of Deuteronomy. "Show me here, Professor, circle the letters."

"It won't work in just any translation, my Führer. I need the original Hebrew Torah. I suppose the Masoretic text that dates to

the tenth century is precise enough. But even then I'd have to translate the alphanumeric codes."

"I see. But of course."

Von Berg could only gaze with wonder at the disappointed
Hitler. The man should be removed from leadership immediately,
he thought.

"In the case of the Maranatha text we see in the microfilm, I'm
dealing with first-century Greek and not the Hebrew Dr. Stein ana-
lyzed. But here, too, if we use only every fiftieth letter, we discover
words such as 'Armageddon' and 'judgment' hidden among the letters of this lost epistle to the Thessalonians."

"Fascinating," Hitler muttered.

"Why fifty, Herr Professor?" von Berg asked. "Why not thirty-
seven or forty-four or any other number?"

"The number fifty is seven times seven plus one," Xaptz answered simply. "Seven is a special number in the Bible, especially in
the Book of Revelation, and we cannot forget there are seven days
in the week of the creation myth. There are also fifty days between
Passover and Shavuot, as the Jews celebrate those holidays, and
Easter and Pentecost, as they are recognized by Christians."

"But of course," von Berg replied. "That explains everything."

Hitler nodded in agreement, failing to appreciate the Baron's
intended sarcasm.

"Some letters can be translated into their numerical equiva-
lents," Xaptz continued. "Alpha, for example, is equal to one, beta is
two, zeta is six, and so on, so that hidden among the letters of this
microfilm is what appears to be a rather complex code of some sort.
One that, if we could unravel it, would tell us the exact date of the
end of human history as we know it."

"And provide us with the formulas for Greek Fire," said Hitler.
"Go on, go on."

"Unfortunately, it is all inconclusive, you see, because we have
here only a fragment of the Maranatha text and not the text itself.
And I am not so much of an expert as Dr. Stein."

Hitler turned to Himmler. "Then get me Dr. Stein."

Himmler cleared his throat and, in a low voice, reminded the Führer, "Sent to Dachau in thirty-eight. Died two years ago."

"I see," Hitler murmured. "Is there nobody else?"

Xaptz said, "There is an American I am aware of who has done some work in this field, though it is not his specialty. Professor Jason Prestwick of Yale University."

Hitler nodded. "The one referred to in the Allied communiqué we intercepted along with the microfilm."

"The same, Führer. Naturally, he is beyond our reach at this moment, though probably just as puzzled if they have shown him this microfilm."

Von Berg had heard enough of this fantastic conversation spoken in such calm, reassuring tones between the quack professor and the chancellor of Germany. He could restrain himself no longer. "Has it occurred to Herr Professor," he said, "that Prestwick is perhaps in the employment of the American intelligence services and that this microfilm is an elaborate hoax?"

For a moment they were all silent. Xaptz began to twitch nervously.

Himmler laughed. "You give the Allies too much credit, Baron von Berg. What purpose would such a forgery serve?"

"To exploit our fears about the Allied armies gathering in the Middle East." Von Berg addressed Hitler, eye to eye. "They know we have a fairly accurate assessment of Patton's Seventh Army and Montgomery's Eighth Army in North Africa. But Wilson's Ninth Army in the Middle East is another story. We don't know how many divisions are down there, much less if any of them are even close to being ready to mount a large-scale invasion. The Allies understand our strategic dilemma, so they devise mystical nonsense such as this Maranatha text to deceive us."

"To what end, von Berg?" asked Himmler from his chair, sounding as if he'd had enough of the Baron's tiresome doubts.

Von Berg kept his eyes locked with Hitler's. "As I said earlier, to make us fear an invasion of Greece and move the focus of our attention away from their intended point of entry."

Hitler sighed. "Which you still insist is Sicily?"

"Yes," said von Berg, "and again I must remind the Führer of my opinion that we don't need additional German divisions in Greece. Once they are there, they cannot be easily moved, certainly not in time to counter an Allied invasion of Italy."

A faraway look filled Hitler's eyes as he considered the implications of the logic, and for a second von Berg dared to believe that reason would prevail. But the Reichsführer dashed any such hope to pieces.

"What is it you're hiding in Greece that the presence of more German troops makes you so uneasy?" Himmler removed his silver pince-nez and polished the lenses as he squinted his small eyes at the Baron. "You're not still pursuing research on atomistics, Jewish physics, are you? The Führer ordered the *Flammenschwert* Project abandoned. We don't want a Sword of Fire. We want a Sea of Fire. We want Greek Fire to protect our shores from invasion."

Hitler snapped out of his trance. "Yes, von Berg," he said with newfound authority. "We've already been through all this with the armaments ministers. Last year, before he died, Todt told us that an atomic bomb is not worth our time. And Speer says that even if we were to pursue such a weapon, the earliest we could deploy it would be 1946. By then, as Professor Xaptz has shown us, the war will be over. Besides, von Braun's rocket research at Peenemünde looks much more promising."

At this point, thought von Berg, no weapon could save Germany if Hitler remained in power. Already Hitler's failure to appreciate the stealth of the U-boat had cost Doenitz's underproduced fleet the Atlantic. His blindness to the speed of the Messerschmitt Me 262 jet fighter had cost Goering's battered Luftwaffe the skies of Europe. Now his ignorance of the power of the atomic bomb could cost Germany the war.

"The ultimate weapon is Greek Fire," Hitler went on, his eyes sparkling at the mention of the subject. "Greek Fire will provide us with the ultimate defense against any Allied invasion—a ring of fire around the continent. In the twinkling of an eye, we could set our coastlines ablaze, burning the Allies before they even set foot on our shores. Just like that." He snapped his fingers. "What are you doing about it, von Berg?"

"My team of scientists is working around the clock on a synthetic formula for Greek Fire," he answered, although that was a lie. "They are using the latest advances in science to test various combinations of naphtha, sulfur, petroleum, bitumen, potassium nitrate, and other compounds in search of the formula."

Hitler glared at him. "I don't want a synthetic formula, von Berg," he demanded, his voice growing louder. "I want the real thing. I want the Maranatha text. That's all I ask. Just bring me that infernal text! I want it before the next weapons conference!"

Von Berg realized that the next weapons conference was on his fortieth birthday, less than a month away. "But that's on the second of June."

"Which gives you three weeks, von Berg. Don't disappoint me."

"Oh, I won't."

Von Berg knew that Germany's only hope at this point was the restoration of his monarchy and a peace settlement with the Allies. The *Flammenschwert* bomb would make it all possible once Hitler was out of the way. All he needed was a few weeks—precisely what the Führer was granting him. Until then he would keep the Maranatha text out of Hitler's hands or find a way to use it for his own ends. He rose to his feet. "But if I should find that this Maranatha text contradicts the contents of the microfilm, you will reconsider my hypothesis concerning Sicily?"

"Yes," Hitler sighed. "I will reconsider."

18

Chris Andros stood fifty yards away from Adolf Hitler when he turned to face the Führer, lowered his right arm, and fired three bullets from his Colt .45 automatic into the madman's face. The cigarette dangling from Hitler's mouth exploded in a small cloud, the smoke lifting to reveal two holes for eyes. An awed silence was broken by cheers and pats on the back from the fellow cadets who surrounded Andros at the outdoor firing range of the United States Military Academy at West Point.

"What did I tell y'all, the best in the West," proclaimed First Class Cadet Billy Hayfield. He lit a cigarette for Andros and turned to the fourth-class cadets. "Now pay up, plebes."

There were groans as the young men began to part with their money, much to the delight of the big, grinning Texan.

Andros, meanwhile, popped his Colt back into its open holster and stared at the makeshift target as he smoked his cigarette. This was as close to a real Nazi as he had gotten in the war, a war that seemed so far away from these green meadows and rolling hills on the banks of the Hudson. To Andros, the river symbolized the uncrossable gulf that separated him from Nazi-occupied Europe and the woman he loved.

"Three hundred dollars!" Hayfield exclaimed, as he finished counting the money. "There's gonna be a good time in the city this weekend!"

No sooner were the words out of Hayfield's mouth than Andros heard the rumble of an approaching vehicle. The small crowd of cadets dispersed rapidly. Hayfield was still stuffing his pockets with cash when the jeep braked to a halt, engine still running.

"Superintendent wants to see Cadet Andros," said the driver, an MP whom Andros vaguely recalled from a particular card game. "Pronto."

"General Wilby?" Andros asked, snuffing out his cigarette.

The MP was stone-faced under his white helmet.

Andros exchanged a long glance with Hayfield before climbing into the jeep.

"Hey, I'm part of this, too," Hayfield confessed as the MP shifted gears. "I didn't mean to take O'Brian's last cent, but he insisted on playing. . . ."

But the jeep carrying Andros was gone.

19

The jeep pulled up in front of the cadet chapel, a Gothic edifice on a hillside that soared above the surrounding woods. Andros turned to the driver and asked, "I'm supposed to find the superintendent in here?"

The MP didn't give an answer, and by this time Andros wasn't expecting any, so he went up the steps and under King Arthur's sword, Excalibur, which hung above the entrance.

Inside, it was cool and dark. Carvings of the Quest for the Holy Grail glowed dimly from the light filtering through the stained-glass windows. Andros let his eyes adjust and looked down the cavernous chapel toward the altar. A lonely figure sat in the first pew with his head bowed. Andros took off his cap and proceeded down the aisle beneath the procession of flags that arched overhead.

When he reached the front pew, however, he was surprised to find not his superintendent but an elderly gentleman in an ugly tweed suit and crumpled shirt. The man was hunched over an open briefcase, sorting papers.

"Excuse me," said Andros, "I was looking for General Wilby."

The man raised his angular face. Two small green eyes regarded Andros from behind thick, round spectacles. "I'm afraid the superintendent won't be able to attend this little meeting, Cadet Andros," he stated in a slow, mannered, and annoying voice. "Allow me to introduce myself. I'm Colonel Prestwick."

Andros frowned as he looked at the long nose and thin lips. This Prestwick didn't look like any sort of military officer he'd ever seen, much less one with the rank of colonel.

Prestwick said, "Come, sit down. Nobody will bother us, I assure you. The MP will see to that."

Andros sat down in the pew next to Prestwick. "What's this all about . . . Colonel?"

"You are the son of General Nicholas Andros of the Hellenic Royal Army?"

The reference to his father made Andros shift uncomfortably. "My name is Chris Andros. I'm a second lieutenant in the United States Army. That's who I am, Colonel Prestwick."

Prestwick cleared his throat. "Yes, well, it seems you haven't been as straightforward about your commission in the U.S. Army with your family or fiancée as you are with me. Indeed, they think you're at Harvard. These letters are all addressed to your old Cambridge address, and your letters are posted in Boston."

Prestwick handed over what Andros immediately recognized as photostats of the love letters he and Aphrodite had exchanged before Athens fell to the Nazis in the spring of '41.

"Our offices in Bermuda intercept all transatlantic correspondence," Prestwick explained, adding, "I must tell you, your romantic prose had our girls swooning."

"What's the meaning of this?" Andros demanded, angry and embarrassed that his words should be exposed to strangers. "Who do you think you are?"

"I told you. I'm Colonel Prestwick. I'm with the OSS."

Andros had heard of the OSS, the American spy agency, but if this man was one of its so-called intelligence officers, he feared for the future of the country. "I'm sorry, did you say OSS or SS? I didn't know the American government spied on its citizens."

"We don't." Prestwick sniffed as he smoothed out his tie. "That's the FBI's job. Our interests are more global. That's why we opened your letters; we could tell they had been opened and resealed by our German friends first." Prestwick removed the photostats from Andros's hands and replaced them in his briefcase. His manner suggested that their contents were classified and that Andros was privileged to have even glimpsed his own correspondence.

Andros never liked mysteries, and he was sure he didn't like

Prestwick. "So are you accusing me of being a spy, Colonel? Is that it? Are you going to kick me out of the academy?"

"Quite the contrary," Prestwick said. "Your little white lies have established the perfect sort of cover for you. The Germans have no knowledge of your military background. That's why I want you to work for us at the OSS. We have a rather special assignment for you in Greece."

A hollow pang of anxiety filled Andros's stomach, and he stiffened in the pew. Had Prestwick said Greece? The subject of Greece always brought to the surface painful reminders of his inadequacies as an Andros. But the possibility of learning what had happened to Aphrodite was simply too overpowering to resist. He looked at Prestwick with deep suspicion. "What's in Greece?"

"A document of fantastic military significance."

Andros narrowed his eyes. "What sort of document?"

"The enemy's encrypted plan for the defense of Greece, disguised as an ancient text."

Andros leaned forward with interest. If the OSS was interested in the defense plans for Greece, that meant Greece was no doubt the likely target for the impending invasion of Europe. Liberation would be close at hand for Aphrodite and his cousins. "And where in Greece is this text, exactly?"

"That's what we want you to find out for us," Prestwick explained. "All we know is that it's in the possession of this man here." He handed Andros a blowup of what had been a group shot. "It's the most recent one we have on file."

Andros found himself looking at a handsome German wearing the uniform of the Kriegsmarine. He had deep-set eyes and light, slicked-back hair under a cap with a white top. "A U-boat commander?"

"At one time," Prestwick said. "Bills himself as an international businessman. Baron Ludwig von Berg. In reality, he's a top-ranking general in the SS."

Andros passed the photo back to Prestwick. "Never heard of him."

"You're not supposed to; he's too important," explained Prestwick. "Among other things, he heads the foreign intelligence section of the SD. That's the secret intelligence department of the SS. Next to Hitler and Himmler, we consider him the most powerful man in the Third Reich. Of the three, he's certainly the most dangerous. And that's saying a lot."

"And he lives in Greece?"

"On a vast estate outside Athens when he's not in Berlin, although sometimes he disappears from both locales for weeks at a time. Where, we don't know. But based on private intelligence sources in Switzerland, we suspect it's his special research laboratory."

"Where you think he's hiding this cipher containing the defense plans."

"Yes," said Prestwick. "Furthermore, we believe somebody close to him, an insider, may be persuaded to divulge the location of this facility."

"And who would that be?"

"His mistress."

"I see." Andros smiled wryly at the audacity of these OSS people. "You want a spy to seduce her into spilling the location of this document and compromise her lover?"

"That's the general idea, yes."

"Somebody to go to bed with her, encourage her to talk?"

Prestwick nodded. "I suppose if need be, yes."

Andros leaned back and crossed his arms. "Then you don't need me, Colonel. I'm not the man you're looking for. What you need is a gigolo, some lowlife scum accustomed to taking advantage of women."

"What we need is a well-connected civilian in Athens," Prestwick replied. "Again, I cannot emphasize enough how your little white lies to your friends and family have established the perfect sort of cover for you. The Nazis have no knowledge of your military background."

Andros could see that Prestwick failed to understand that the military was not simply part of his "background," as typed on some government report, but his very life. To give it up would mean giving up the essence of who he was or, rather, who he hoped to be.

"You're in perfect physical condition for this mission," Prestwick continued, reading from a file. "You've completed parachute training. You're a crack shot with pistol and rifle. You won't need to worry about the operation of radio equipment or demolition work for this mission. According to these records, your only failure here at West Point is your abnormal fear of water, which seems to have prevented you from becoming an Olympic-caliber pentathlon champion. But I suppose such a handicap is understandable, considering the circumstances of your mother's death."

Andros tried to picture his mother's face as he remembered it from family photographs. But all he could see was the face of Baron von Berg smiling at him from under the U-boat commander's cap. He tried to push the image out of his mind, but the pain wouldn't go away. Neither would this OSS colonel, he realized, not without some help.

"The British must have scores of secret agents in Athens," Andros told Prestwick. "Are none of them up to this task?"

"Several British agents have approached von Berg's mistress," Prestwick explained. "She hasn't turned any of them in, but she's rebuffed all efforts to help us, no doubt fearing for her family."

Andros asked, "She's Greek, then?"

"Yes."

"A collaborator?"

Prestwick nodded.

Andros stood up to leave and said, "Then she should be shot."

"She very well may be, by German or Greek, I couldn't predict," Prestwick remarked. "But we were hoping it wouldn't come to that." He pulled a photo from the file and handed it to Andros. "After all, she is such a beautiful girl, wouldn't you agree?"

To Andros's astonishment, he was looking at Aphrodite's face. "This is a joke."

Prestwick's face was serious as he shook his head.

Andros shoved the photograph back. "Then it is a lie."

"No lie, Chris." Prestwick took the picture but didn't put it away. "It seems she's been no more forthright with you than you've been with her."

Andros felt sick. The Germans might as well have blown up the Parthenon or desecrated the Sistine Chapel. His knees gave way, and he sank back into the pew next to Prestwick, his mind swirling in confusion.

"Apparently, the Baron and his men moved into her family estate in Kifissia after the invasion," Prestwick explained matter-of-factly. "She had to cooperate unless she wanted to wake up one morning and find her family had disappeared—*Nacht und Nebel*, Night and Fog, as the Nazis call it—at the hands of the Gestapo. Frankly, I don't think she had much choice."

Andros managed a weak laugh. "You obviously don't know Aphrodite," he said. "With her, it's always a choice. She would rather die than be forced to do something against her will."

"All I know," said Prestwick in a patronizing tone, "is that the Baron protects her and her family not only from the Gestapo but from those Greeks who would just as soon hang them out to dry for collaborating. That is why she has shunned all approaches from British SOE agents in Athens, even though she secretly helps the families of the Greek Resistance through the Red Cross. That is why you must go back to Greece. You were born for this mission."

Andros recoiled at the suggestion. He had fought too hard to escape the complicated political situation in Greece and his father's legacy to go back now. He had invested too much of himself into his new life in America and into carving out his own future and sense of identity to throw it all away. That was what this man was asking him to do, however lofty the vernacular. And for what? To be a spy. Spies, Andros knew, were a lower form of life, held in contempt by men such as his father and his West Point comrades.

"Think about it, Chris," said Prestwick. "In a few weeks or months you could be one of hundreds of thousands embarking on the largest invasion in human history, a human guinea pig to test the enemy's defenses. Or you could be the one who paves the way for the invasion's success, saving tens of thousands of lives, perhaps millions. You might even win us the war."

Andros wasn't thinking about the war or his sense of duty or even his desire for revenge against the Germans; if anything, his father's folly in chasing the Great Idea had taught him to distrust any overt appeal to boyish pride. He was thinking about Aphrodite as he looked again at the photo Prestwick was holding. Those clever eyes, seductive lips, and long, dark, shiny hair were all he had left in this life. No mother. No father. Not even his precious honor. All the medals and glory in the world would be worthless if Aphrodite wasn't there for him to embrace when this war was finally over.

He was also thinking about von Berg. It did not surprise Andros that this monster had risen from the primordial ooze of the Kriegsmarine that had murdered his mother. Nor that he belonged to the same fraternity of murderers who had invaded his homeland and slaughtered his father. But the thought that this beast could be lying in the same bed with Aphrodite filled him with a rage he never would have believed possible. It was a rage he would have to control, he realized, if he hoped to kill the rabid animal.

Andros knew what he had to do. He looked Prestwick in the eye and, in a firm voice, said, "When do I go in?"

"Four days," said Prestwick, who expressed no surprise at the decision. "In the meantime, we're sending you to the Farm for some special advanced training."

"'The Farm?'"

"Our most elite school for spies," Prestwick explained. "We're bringing in an instructor especially for you, to prepare you for your mission. We won't have much time, but hopefully, we can break some of the traditional military habits you've picked up here at West Point and teach you a few new tricks as well. Now the MP outside will escort you to your quarters to pack your belongings. You will speak to nobody."

Andros rose to his feet. "You don't waste any time."

"At this point in the war, we can't afford to," said Prestwick, replacing his papers in his briefcase.

Andros nodded. "Then I'll be going."

Prestwick watched Andros walk up the aisle to the back of the chapel and disappear. He then closed his briefcase and went into the chaplain's office, where Major General Francis B. Wilby was sitting with Andros's official West Point file.

"He's no spy," said Wilby. "He's a soldier, the best I've seen in years. That crazy outfit of yours is no place for a man like him."

"Nonsense, Superintendent," Prestwick replied, taking the file from Wilby. "He's an accomplished liar and will serve us well."

Prestwick struck a match, touched it to the corner of the file, and dropped it into the metal wastebasket. "The name of Chris Andros shall be struck from every record, Superintendent. West Point's top cadet never existed."

20

His decision to drop out of Harvard and enroll in the United States Military Academy even before America entered the war would have shocked his American friends and relatives—had he told them. But Chris Andros felt it was his duty to uphold the honor of his family's name, a name that to Greeks was synonymous with war and greatness.

Chris Andros was named after his great-great-grandfather, a legendary merchant skipper of the Greek islands during the war of independence. A master in the saltwater sport of fireboating, the old sea dog would approach Turkish warships at night in dispensable vessels packed with gunpowder, pitch, and sulfur. Once they were close enough, he and his crew would light the powder train, cast off in their longboat, and enjoy the fireworks from a distance. His end came at Missolonghi. Surrounded by Turks, he and the remaining defenders set fire to the ammunition stores and blew themselves up, taking their enemies with them. This act propelled an inspired Anglo-French fleet to sink the Turkish navy in the Battle of Navarino in 1827 and thus secure the birth of modern Greece.

Chris's great-grandfather Byron and, later, his grandfather Basil built the Andros Shipping dynasty, chiefly through hard work and fortuitous marriages that consolidated some of Greece's most prosperous shipping lines. On rare occasions they engaged in smuggling, not for money but on principle, sending arms to those who fought for freedom in various parts of the world. Eventually, his uncle Dimitri brought the family's business to America, anchoring Andros Shipping West in Boston Harbor.

His father, Nicholas, however, chose a different path. He shunned the family trade altogether and, against the wishes of Basil, chose to train at the Kriegsakademie in Berlin as a military officer.

Inspired by the idea of a greater Greece, he returned to Athens to take his commission in the Hellenic Royal Army. But to make peace with Basil, he announced that he would take Anastasia Rassious of the Rassious shipping family as his wife.

Chris Andros never knew his mother. At the time she was carrying him, the Great War had broken out across Europe. King Constantine, defying the Greek people and the Allies, decided to support his German brother-in-law, the kaiser. With the Greek government on the brink of collapse and civil war looming, Nicholas sent Anastasia to America to stay with Dimitri and his cousins. By the time Chris was born in 1917 in a Boston hospital, Greece had sided with America and the Allies against the Germans and was suffering the ravages of war. One month later, the ocean liner on which Chris and his mother were sailing was sunk by a German submarine. Anastasia died in the icy waters of the Atlantic, but Chris was plucked alive from the hungry waves.

God, how he hated the Germans.

After the Allied victory, he was returned to Greece—a grim reminder of his mother to his father, Colonel Nicholas Andros, and an answered prayer to Basil, who already had decided that Chris would one day take the helm of Andros Shipping in Greece.

Grandfather Basil made sure Chris's education started early, bringing a British governess to the family's estate in Kifissia. From Miss Robinson, he learned to read Shakespeare, Milton, and, in her weaker moments, American authors such as Mark Twain. Especially inspiring were the speeches of President Woodrow Wilson, whose call for a League of Nations captivated Chris's young mind with its vision of a new world order governed not by violence but by an open understanding of the rights of all nations, the small as well as the mighty, to determine their own destinies. Above all, from Miss Robinson, he learned of the glory that was ancient Greece and of the country's contributions to European civilization.

Even as a boy, he could sense that the modern Greek nation paled before its ancient glories. A simple drive from his northern suburb of Kifissia to the docks of Piraeus to see the family ships proved that much. Passing through the hot, winding, tortuous streets of Athens, he couldn't help but notice the ramshackle storefronts, refugees, and street children, even though Nasos the driver took pains to stay on the main boulevards. As for Greece's place in the world, Nicholas said the country was prized only for its strategic position in the Mediterranean and would forever remain the pawn of world powers unless it seized the initiative to become a great state.

Nicholas tried to do just that with what became known as the Great Idea—Greece's ill-fated quest to invade Turkey and reestablish a new Byzantium, with Constantinople as its capital. The Hellenic Royal Army came within sixty miles of Ankara before the tide of battle turned and they were routed. It was only by the grace of God, Nicholas later said, that he and his troops eluded the bloodthirsty Hadji Azrael, whose legions of holy warriors decapitated thousands of Greek stragglers. The Great Idea thus became Greece's greatest military defeat in centuries. Nicholas returned to Athens only to see the Greek prime minister, commander in chief, and other senior government officials tried and shot for their failure. His father barely escaped trial himself, and the country fell into political turmoil.

From then on, his father, now General Andros, was a nervous man, caught between coup and countercoup. Because Nicholas favored a Greek republic based on American-style democracy, he was accused by royalists of being a republican. Republicans in turn accused him of being a royalist because of his belief that the Greek people should first prove themselves capable of establishing a stable government, strong military, and modern economy before they spent endless hours debating the role of the king. "Better to make the monarchy irrelevant before we depose it," Chris's father used to tell him.

Chris didn't much like King George II. The man wasn't even Greek but a Dane, an unemployed European monarch whose royal family had been assigned to Greece by the Great Powers sixty years earlier. The Greeks had rejected their first monarch, young King Otto of the Bavarian House of Wittelsbach. Chris thought they should do the same with the House of Oldenburg. Greece was for the Greeks.

Chris had mixed feelings about his father. He admired the man, even though he was something of a fascist, dealing ruthlessly with those who represented "security threats" in Greece. But Chris resented his father's legacy. Being the son of General Andros was the worst of all worlds. Family friends would compare him to his father and invariably find him lacking. Meanwhile, political enemies would confuse him with his father's fascism. They would threaten him in order to even old scores with Nicholas or attempt to convert him to their self-aggrandizing politics in order to embarrass his father.

By the time he was twelve, Chris Andros despised the intrigues of Greek politics, having visited his cousins in America for the first time and come back with the realization that the outside world offered a saner, more pleasant existence—in particular, baseball, jazz, and blondes, all of which were rare commodities in Athens. So the next year, after the death of Basil, who had spoiled him rotten and whom he adored, Chris persuaded his father to allow him to attend a preparatory school in America. That way, he reasoned, he could escape his father's legacy and become his own man.

He had met her at a dance one summer night in Athens when he was home from school on vacation: Aphrodite Vasilis. She was the daughter of a wealthy tobacco merchant—an Andros Shipping client, in fact—and the most beautiful girl he had ever seen. Eyes of amber, hair shining black, and a soft mouth that simply begged to be kissed outside under the moon and mango trees. That she was Greek only added to her value in his eyes.

She had so completely turned his head that even life in America couldn't compare with her company, and he made every excuse to come home to visit his father during school breaks. It was a magical time in his life, despite the arrival of the Depression in America and the regime known as the Fourth of August in Greece. Even he had to admit that under the dictator Metaxas, some stability had returned to Greece. Andros Shipping flourished under the leadership of his uncle Mitchell Rassious; his father found some fulfillment in modernizing the Greek army with German weapons; and his own love for Aphrodite cast a spell of enchantment over his adolescent years.

Finally, in the summer of 1939, after his first year at Harvard, it was her turn to visit him, and together they went to New York for the World's Fair. They wandered through the effervescent architecture of the futuristic exhibition buildings, astounded at demonstrations of a new medium called television, 3-D movies, and other visions of the World of Tomorrow. The Futurama exhibit in the General Motors Building particularly fascinated Andros as their comfortable electrically driven chairs took them on a simulated airplane flight across the future America of 1960, crisscrossed by an intricate highway network carrying thousands of automobiles. "This highway thing will never work in Greece," he told her afterward. "Too many mountains. I can assure my uncle Mitchell our shipping business is safe for now."

With America coming out of the Depression and the arrival of such modern high technology, life seemed to open up before Andros. For here was American optimism, a bright future and the woman of his dreams to share it with. The ominous thunder of war rumbling across Europe seemed so far away. Standing there before the fair's trademark spike-and-ball centerpiece—the soaring six-hundred-foot Trylon and great geospheric Perisphere—with the glittering Manhattan skyline as a backdrop, he asked Aphrodite to marry him. She replied with an enthusiastic yes, and they pledged their unwavering loyalty to each other.

Andros said, "I promise I'll come back to Greece with a ring."

But he never came back.

War broke out again in Europe, and a glory-hungry Mussolini, unwilling to remain in Hitler's shadow, issued Metaxas an ultimatum to surrender without a fight. Metaxas hardly had time to utter his famous retort of "No!" before Italian forces in Albania advanced into Greece in overwhelming numbers. The Greek army, led by Field Marshal Papagos and General Andros, then stunned the world by driving Il Duce's illustrious eight million bayonets back into Albania. Only Hitler's intervention the next spring could rescue Mussolini. No match for the overwhelming force of the modern German war machine, the Greeks, even with the help of the British Expeditionary Forces, were crushed in a matter of six weeks. General Andros, who resolved to fight to the finish, died with his men on the island of Crete, but not before destroying five thousand German paratroopers in the bloodiest fighting of the war. That was of little comfort to Chris, however, who had lost his father and found himself alone in America, powerless to help and tortured with regret. Haunting him was the sense that he wasn't there when his father, fiancée, and country had needed him most, and in missing that one crucial moment of his life, he had missed it all.

God, how he hated the Germans.

Cut off from Greece and Aphrodite by the war, cut off from his father forever, he did the only thing he could to restore any sense of honor to himself. Though America was officially neutral at the time, he asked a certain U.S. senator—who was indebted to Andros Shipping—to nominate him to West Point. One month later, he swore an oath to defend the Constitution of the United States with his life. Three months later, the Japanese attacked Pearl Harbor, and America declared war on the Axis.

As in previous wars, the U.S. Military Academy reduced the length of its course to three years. Together with his academic credit from Harvard and his outstanding demonstration of skills in military and physical training, Andros rose to the top of his class by May 1943. At last, Andros felt, he had made something of himself. No longer was he simply a privileged heir to a Greek shipping dynasty. Now he was a second lieutenant in the United States Army. He had earned the respect of his peers, his superiors, and, most important, himself. Come June, he would graduate for assignment to combat duty, most likely to join the force long rumored to be gathering for an invasion of Europe.

Andros dreamed of landing with the Allies in Greece. He would lead his U.S. Army troops off their transports in Piraeus, vanquish the fleeing Nazis, and liberate Athens. Yes, what his father had begun in the valiant defense of Crete, he would finish by returning to Greece a conquering hero.

Now that dream was dead.

21

B ack in his quarters at the central cadet barracks, Andros started packing.

All that was left when he was finished was the picture of Aphrodite he kept on his desk. It was a better photograph than the one Prestwick had shown him, taken in happier times. For several minutes he gazed at her angelic face, embittered by the seeds of doubt that Prestwick had managed to sow in his heart.

"I'm coming, my love," he said, packing the picture and frame into his sack and pulling the strings. "Just like I promised."

Andros drew out his Colt .45 automatic and moved to the window overlooking the parade grounds. The grass was golden with the last rays of the setting sun, and the trees cast long, thin shadows. After taking one last look out over the Hudson, he checked the bullets in his clip and rammed the clip home into the Colt's chamber.

"I'm coming for you, too, Baron von Berg."

22

Aphrodite Vasilis was swimming in the mouth of the Chali-kiopoulos Lagoon on the Greek island of Corfu while two of Baron von Berg's SS bodyguards watched nervously from shore. High above them, overlooking the lagoon from its lofty hill, was the Villa Achillion, the Baron's estate. No doubt more SS were watching her from the terrace. She knew that if she should so much as take in a mouthful of water and choke for but a moment, the Baron would have their heads when he returned to the island.

"You look so hot and uncomfortable, boys," she called out in Greek, splashing some water, teasing them as she often did. "Don't you want to come in?"

Hans looked like he very much wanted to join her, but Peter spoke sharply to him in German and offered him a cigarette instead. How anybody could smoke outside in the heat of the day Aphrodite could never understand, but it was an addiction her father the tobacco merchant had always encouraged.

She sighed and let her eyes drift across the sparkling water toward Pondikonissi, or Mouse Island, the farther of two islets that floated offshore. Legend said that the islet was Odysseus's ship, the one Poseidon turned to stone. Seen from a distance, the dark mound did indeed resemble a vessel enshrouded in somber cypress trees. It was crowned at the top by a tiny whitewashed monastery from the eleventh century, the Church of the Pantokrator, an inviting refuge.

"Suit yourselves," she called, and broke away toward the islet. They started calling out after her in angry, fearful tones, but she ignored them and made her way to the islet.

Upon reaching it, she rose from the water, wrung her long black hair, and let the beads of water roll off her bronzed body. At the foot of the whitewashed steps, she found her robe hanging on a peg along with some slippers. One look back toward shore showed Hans watching her through his Zeiss field glasses, to make sure she was all right, and Peter radioing the others on the villa's terrace. She slipped on the robe, tied the belt, and ascended the steps that spiraled up to the treetops.

At the top of the hill, she emerged onto a cobbled terrace and entered the tiny monastery. It was to this hiding place that she often came, to shed her pretentious ways with the Baron, to light a candle for Chris, and to confess her life of sin to the Orthodox priest, whose wizened old face now nodded gravely as she began to cry once more in the dark.

"The Baron returns today, Father John," she said. "Please grant me God's forgiveness."

Father John raised an eyebrow. "For what you have done, child, or what you are going to do?"

Aphrodite felt embarrassed to discuss such things with a priest who had sworn off the temptations of the flesh. Still, the old man smiled in a way that hinted that before making his vows, he had not passed through life without knowing its pleasures.

"What's done is done," she confessed, and told him once again— for her own justification rather than for his understanding—how she had met Baron Ludwig von Berg that summer day in '42 when he was wheeled into her Red Cross hospital in Athens with a gun-shot wound to the head.

23

A phrodite had been acquainted with the brutal realities of death and dismemberment ever since she joined the Greek Red Cross as a nurse, with her friend Princess Katherine, in the early days of the war. She had become a nurse because she was tired of serving no higher purpose in life other than being beautiful, a role her parents and others were content to let her play but which she despised. At that point in the war, the Greeks were whipping the Italians and morale was high, and the work helped crowd out her worries about her brother fighting at the front and her fiancé far away in America. That was before the Germans invaded and she began to attend to the smashed bodies of British Royal Air Force men, Greece's new defenders. Then came that fateful Sunday morning when the Herrenvolk finally entered Athens and hoisted the swastika over the Acropolis. The Germans ruthlessly began to clear the beds of major hospitals, throwing the wounded out on the streets to make room for their own.

She also had been familiar with the German troops, who soon filled the streets of Athens. Their gray-green uniforms were soiled, their faces harassed and hungry. They traveled in large groups and carried so-called occupation marks, *Reichskreditkassenscheine*, which shopkeepers were forced to accept. They grabbed everything in sight, emptying shelves and decimating what was left of the Greek economy. What they didn't buy, they simply took, such as Aphrodite's car parked at the tennis club; when she walked outside, her driver stood alone at the curb, arms raised in exasperation.

She experienced famine in the winter of 1941–42, when children with swollen bellies and the skeletons of old men and women haunted the streets of the city. More than three hundred thousand Athenians starved to death in two months, and whenever a lifeless body dropped, only the ration card of the forgotten soul was remembered by survivors, a means to prolong their own suffering. The city had become an extermination camp, and there was little she could do at the hospital except watch the poor and weak die.

What she had not been prepared for was a German like Baron Ludwig von Berg. For three days he lay there in his hospital bed, hovering between life and death, his face invisible behind the bandages wrapped around his shattered skull. The miracle was not only that he survived but that, through it all, he carried himself like the perfect German officer and gentleman. When the wrappings were lifted, he turned out to be younger than she had imagined, and better-looking, considering the silver plate in his skull. He also was obviously quite taken with her. Only his icy blue eyes betrayed a hint of ruthlessness and the sense that whatever charming things the Baron might say were not necessarily what was in his heart.

It was a Greek sniper who'd shot him. The Gestapo had rounded up some three hundred hostages in reprisal, according to one of the SS guards posted outside the private room. She later learned from the doctor, however, that the bullet dislodged from the Baron's skull came from a Czech Česká of the type favored by SS intelligence—he had most likely been shot by one of his own men. She could never confirm this, as the doctor disappeared shortly thereafter, along with the Baron himself.

When she told her family about the Baron, her father recognized the name as that of a wealthy German industrialist who came to Greece every so often to check on the supply of chrome and other raw materials. Her brother, Kostas, however, spat in contempt. "A 'gentleman,' you call him? Stupid girl. He's as bad as that playboy fiancé of yours in America. I don't know why you still pretend that coward Andros loves you. He's an embarrassment to his father and to Greece. Tell me, where was he when we were risking our necks against the invaders? Where is he now?"

Ever since he returned from the front, Kostas had been a bitter man, especially after the Italian Brenero Division under General Paolo Berardi "triumphantly" entered Nazi-occupied Athens. "We whipped these boys in Albania, this very division, sent them running through the snow and mountains to their mothers," Kostas had said. "Now they dare return and call themselves victors!"

Then Vasilis Tobacco was obliged to accept the "Mediterranean drachmas" the Italians brought with them as payment for what little tobacco the company was still able to produce beyond what the Germans confiscated. An overconfident Rome had printed the currency before its failed invasion of Greece in October 1940.

This was the last straw for Kostas, who, with the first tobacco consignment, hid a bomb in one of the cases on the docks in Piraeus. The Greek stevedores who loaded the cargo aboard the Italian transport said nothing about the extra weight. The ship blew up at quayside, sinking to the bottom to the cheers of the Greek dockers. At the same time, when the first tobacco crop arrived in Germany, it was immediately confiscated by Nazi officials, who opened it to find neither tobacco nor explosives but sand and sawdust. Since that time Kostas had become even more deeply involved with the Resistance, to depths their parents did not care to probe.

"Mark my words," Kostas told her. "That Baron is no gentleman, and your playboy is no son of General Andros."

That night the sound of screeching tires woke the family. Aphrodite's usually reserved mother burst into her daughter's bedroom in her nightgown, making the sign of the cross, screaming, "The Gestapo!" Behind her mother, Aphrodite could see her pudgy father throwing on his robe as he hurried downstairs to answer the pounding on the door. When Aphrodite pulled the curtain back from her bedroom window, she saw three black Mercedeses in the drive and several men in black leather greatcoats and carrying machine guns.

With the commanding Gestapo officer was a Greek interpreter, wearing the yellow armband of collaborators. He said Kostas Vasilis was wanted in connection with acts of sabotage on the docks in the Piraeus district.

The Gestapo officer then presented two clippings from the Nazi-controlled Greek newspapers *Vradini* and *Proinos Typos*. The first reported a fire in a box factory in Piraeus. The second carried a story on a cotton mill in the same district that had gone up in flames. The damage was estimated at thirty million drachmas.

"These two fires destroyed supplies for German troops in Africa and on the Russian front," the German said through the interpreter. "And then there are the robberies from the Piraeus electric company. We believe Kostas Vasilis was involved in all three acts of terrorism."

Aphrodite's mother was hysterical, her father speechless. Aphrodite came halfway down the stairs, listening while her father said he didn't know where Kostas was. He had slipped out the back, in fact, through the gardens and over the wall. So when the Germans searched the house, they found only her and brought her downstairs.

"Ah, what have we here?" asked the Gestapo officer, fondling her long black hair. "Pretty Fräulein, do you know where your brother is?"

Aphrodite was blinded for a moment by the headlights of the cars in the drive, their white beams shining through the open front door like spotlights. She shaded her eyes and shook her head.

"In that case, we'll take you."

Her mother had begged for mercy, and her father had offered the Gestapo officer his secret stash of gold sovereigns, when the silhouette of a tall, dark figure suddenly appeared in the doorway.

"The girl goes nowhere, Standartenführer."

The Gestapo officer turned with a start and clicked his heels. "Herr Oberstgruppenführer!"

Aphrodite blinked and saw Baron von Berg emerge from the light. The man whom she had tended in the hospital was now wearing the black uniform of an SS general. The wrappings around his head were still visible beneath his black cap.

"What seems to be the problem, Standartenführer?"

"This family has been harboring the terrorist Kostas Vasilis. As we cannot find him, we shall take them to Averoff prison and lock them up as hostages."

"That won't be necessary," said von Berg. "As of this moment, I am requisitioning this home as my own in Athens. The Vasilis family shall stay on to manage the estate."

"But, Herr Oberstgruppenführer—"

"That is all, Standartenführer. This Kostas Vasilis, should you find him, is yours. Even so, he is not to be executed immediately but held as a prisoner. This will discourage his friends in the Resistance from future acts of sabotage. His family, however, will assume their place in the New Order by serving me."

And so the Baron had requisitioned the house. He did so for her "protection," at first from the Gestapo and later from the Greeks themselves, who labeled the Vasilis family collaborators even after her brother finally was captured and imprisoned. As for Aphrodite herself, the Baron anointed her his personal attending nurse and flew her to the Villa Achillion on Corfu to supervise his recuperation. The only health risk she discovered on the island was to her brother and parents. The Baron assured her that if she ever revealed the location of his secret retreat to anyone, they were all dead.

The only things that kept her alive were her visits to Athens to see her parents, her secret work of feeding and clothing the families of Resistance fighters through the Red Cross, and her hope that someday her brother would be freed and her fiancé would return.

24

"I hate him, Father John," Aphrodite told the priest with tears in her eyes. "I hate what he's done to me and what I've become. But I love my family. If I stop pleasing him, who knows what will become of them?"

Father John shrugged. "That, only the Lord knows. All I can tell you is that making peace with the devil is no way to seek God's favor."

"What choice do I have, Father?" There was anger in her voice.

He raised his hand, and she caught the glint of a fisherman's knife. "You could always kill the swine."

She sighed. "If only that would release my brother or provide an escape for me and my parents. But Ludwig is the only protection we have from the Gestapo." She hesitated. "Besides, you're forgetting that I tried that once before, remember?"

He put the knife away, crossed himself, and sighed in despair. "And what happened?"

"He told me he liked that in a woman."

Father John shook his head in utter disbelief. "Truly, this man is possessed!"

"No, Father, I'm the one who's possessed. That's the problem. I'm the personal property of Baron Ludwig von Berg." She felt rage and despair and humiliation at her helplessness. "If only the Allies would hurry up and start the liberation. Greece would be free. My brother would be free. *I* would be free."

Father John nodded sympathetically. "I wish the Lord would come today and fix Hitler, but he hasn't," he said. "The Lord is not a genie, granting our every wish. His thoughts are not our thoughts, nor our ways His ways." Father John raised his other hand, which was missing two fingers. He, like other Orthodox priests, had fought against the Italians and Bulgarians along the northern frontiers on the mainland, just across the channel. During the winter in the mountains, he'd lost his fingers to the cold. Most other men lost more: hands, legs, their lives, but worst of all, their souls.

"So what are you saying, Father?"

"Sometimes the only thing we can do is wait. You must endure. The Lord is not wringing His hands, wondering what to do about Hitler. He knows exactly what He's going to do with that Antichrist."

"Well, I wish He'd hurry up," she replied. "I don't know how much longer I can last. One of the guards has acted inappropriately toward me, and I fear for his life should the Baron find out. And my own."

He paused. "What about this Greek you are betrothed to?"

"Christos? He's half a world away." There was bitterness in her voice. "In the beginning I used to pray that he would come and rescue me from all this. I was just being a silly girl, of course; Greek women know better than to trust the men in our lives. They're either oppressive, like the Baron, or impotent to help me, like my father, my brother, and Christos. I'm afraid you and the archbishop in Athens are the only two men in my life who haven't let me down yet. Now please bless me, Father, for I'm about to sin."

She knelt before him.

"You are a remarkable woman, Aphrodite Vasilis," Father John said with admiration and resignation. "Let us pray to the Lord." He placed the end of his stole on her head and prayed.

"O Lord God, show Thy mercy upon Thy servant Aphrodite, and grant unto her an image of repentance, forgiveness of sins, and deliverance, pardoning her every transgression, whether voluntary or involuntary."

He placed his right hand on the stole over her head and pronounced Absolution. "May our Lord and God Jesus Christ, through the grace and bounties of His love toward mankind, forgive thee, my child, Aphrodite, all thy transgressions. And I, His unworthy priest, through the power given unto me by Him, do forgive and absolve thee from all thy sins. In the Name of the Father, and of the Son, and of the Holy Spirit. Amen."

She watched his hand as he made the sign of the cross over her. He was waiting for her to give thanks to God for His goodness, as was the Orthodox way, when they heard the ominous roar of an engine.

"He's back," she said grimly, and rose from her knees.

They stepped outside onto the terrace and looked to the sky. Bursting out of a cloud was the Baron's plane. It came in low over the lagoon and passed over the tiny church like a giant vulture.

"Any parting words of wisdom, Father?"

"Resist this man."

"God knows I've tried, Father. I can't promise you I won't sleep with him when I know what means he'll use to force me. I won't deny it. I won't lie to God."

"Then at least thank God for His forgiveness and promise Him you'll do your best to resist this man."

She sighed and lowered her eyes. "O almighty and merciful God, I truly thank Thee for the forgiveness of my sins," she recited impatiently. "Bless me, O Lord, and help me always, that I may ever do that which is pleasing to thee, and sin no more. Amen."

She lifted her eyes and watched the plane clear the trees at the end of the lagoon and drop out of view. Hans was furiously waving her back to shore, and Peter was halfway toward the monastery in a rowboat. The Baron was back in time for afternoon siesta, and he would want her comfort.

25

As the Stork began its descent, von Berg looked out the window. The island of Corfu lay like a jewel in the northernmost part of the Ionian Sea. The most lush and tropical of the Greek islands, its southern tip was a few miles west of the mainland, its northern under a mile from Albania. For him it was the perfect island retreat, far away from the Byzantine politics of the Third Reich.

The pilot tipped his wing and made a slow turn over the Chalikiopoulos Lagoon for the final approach. The plane barely cleared the steeple of the monastery on Mouse Island, skimming the blue water until it finally dropped down onto the airstrip.

Before Corfu became part of Greece, it was a British protectorate; now it was occupied by the Italians, who'd replaced the local Nazi forces when the Germans moved on to the invasion of Russia.

Commandant Georgio Buzzini, the nervous Italian officer temporarily in command of the island, was in full dress uniform when von Berg stepped out of the plane. As far as von Berg was concerned, Buzzini was a bumbling idiot. His round face, hooded eyes, and baritone voice bestowed upon him all the military graces of a stage extra from a third-rate Italian opera.

"General von Berg!" He saluted. "You have several cables and reports from Berlin waiting for you."

Von Berg looked over the squat man's shoulder toward his awaiting Mercedes. The top was down, and Franz, his driver, stood outside and opened the back door.

"Thank you, Commandant, but I'm anxious to get home for siesta," said von Berg as he proceeded toward the Mercedes, Buzzini close behind.

"All is well, I take it, General?"

"If the commandant is referring to the mental health of the

Führer, I'm afraid not. In fact, soon you'll have even more German company. The Führer has personally ordered the First Panzer Division over from France. It should arrive in a few weeks, along with further reinforcements for Greece."

Buzzini frowned as von Berg settled into the backseat of the Mercedes. Franz shut his door, climbed behind the wheel, and started the engine.

"That would make four German divisions in Greece," Buzzini said. "So they fear an Allied landing?"

"No, just you Italians."

The commandant laughed nervously.

All this idiot can do is laugh at my jokes, von Berg thought. "I'll come to Corfu Town to look at my cables in a day or two."

"Any time the general wishes—"

But the Mercedes shot off before the Italian could finish his sentence.

"Thank you, Franz," said von Berg as they left the airstrip behind and began to make their way through the countryside.

Franz looked up into the rearview mirror and smiled. "Anytime, Herr Oberstgruppenführer."

Franz was a fine young soldier who would rather be on the front fighting than be anyone's driver, von Berg thought, but his ability and loyalty as a protector made him indispensable. He was not only a crack marksman but an excellent skier, the only bodyguard who could keep up with him on the slopes in northern Italy during the winter months. That the two bore some resemblance—same height, similar smooth features, and blond hair—when targeted in a rifle scope also came in handy on occasion. Franz had two bullet scars in his left shoulder to prove it.

"I could have used your services while I was gone, Franz. These other drivers, they have no manners, I tell you. I'm glad to be back. Anything happen while I was gone?"

Franz hesitated and then looked up. "Karl . . . touched the girl."

Von Berg could see Franz's eyes in the mirror, searching for his reaction. Karl was one of his best men, too familiar with the consequences of any advances toward Aphrodite to pursue such folly. Unless, of course, von Berg realized, Karl wasn't expecting him to return from the monasteries of Meteora or his meeting with Hitler in Obersalzberg. That would mean the fool had thrown in his lot with Himmler and Ulrich.

"How very daring of him."

They passed the village of Gastouri, and the road climbed through geraniums, cypresses, and olive trees toward von Berg's estate.

26

The Achillion was a pretentious palace in the neoclassical style and was completely at odds with its tropical surroundings. But von Berg considered it home for a number of reasons, not least of which was that it was built in 1890 for Empress Elizabeth of Austria. Later, Kaiser Wilhelm II of Germany made it his summer home until the Greek government confiscated it in 1914 and let the French turn it into a hospital. Now it belonged to Baron von Berg, courtesy of Adolf Hitler, who had intervened on his behalf with Mussolini.

Von Berg had made a few of his own modifications when he moved in. The vast, beautiful gardens that surrounded the estate were booby-trapped with mines triggered by pull igniters and pressure switches. Also, any low-flying intruders who approached from the sea and managed to elude Italian radar would be greeted by a camouflaged FlaK 38 antiaircraft gun. Its quadruple barrels could fire at a rate of 900 rpm and had a ceiling of 6,500 feet. Quite formidable, especially as it was fitted with the latest generation of sights. Finally, despite objections from the Italians, the entire estate staff was German, handpicked by von Berg himself, from the chefs to the Waffen SS guards and Dobermans that patrolled the grounds. Surrounding the premises were an electric fence and signs that said the estate was a clinic for convalescing soldiers.

The SS guards snapped to attention as Franz brought the Mercedes through the electric gate and pulled up to the entrance. Von Berg got out and walked up the steps past the sentries.

Inside the front door, to the right, was a chapel with frescoes on the walls. Von Berg poked his head inside to see if Aphrodite was there, as she often was, wasting her prayers on a God who didn't exist, but the chapel was deserted. He moved on, briefcase in hand, passing a series of rooms adorned in Pompeian splendor.

Von Berg's office was on the first floor at the end of the hallway. Here, in what used to be Kaiser Wilhelm's study, rested the Maranatha text. The troublesome papyrus lay enclosed in a glass case in the corner of the ornate room. Standing next to it was Karl, von Berg's once trusty, lantern-jawed aide, buffing the glass with his sleeve. When von Berg walked in, he snapped up straight and smiled. "Does this please the general?"

"It's just fine, Karl." Von Berg didn't even look at the text as he walked up to the portrait of King Ludwig II behind his desk. It pictured the Bavarian monarch wearing the regalia of St. George. The Baron pulled the portrait open on its hinge to reveal a secret wall safe, dialed the combination, and placed his briefcase inside. Upon closing the door and replacing the portrait, he turned to Karl and asked, "Where's Aphrodite?"

Karl didn't flinch. "She should be back from her swim any minute now."

"Fine." Von Berg could only admire the ice-cold self-assurance of his protégé, and inwardly, he complimented himself for being such an excellent role model. "And where have you been?"

"Downstairs in the labs."

"Of course you have." Von Berg decided that Karl knew too much about what went on beneath the Achillion and had to die. "I'd like to see you upstairs in the master suite in a few minutes."

A puzzled look crossed Karl's face. "As you wish."

Von Berg went out into the front hall and climbed the majestic marble staircase to the second floor and the master suite. On his bed lay a change of clothes, and he could hear water running in the bathroom.

"The perfect temperature, Herr Oberstgruppenführer," said his maid as she came out with his robe. "Just as you like."

She was a heavyset, middle-aged, and plain mule of a woman who knew her place. That was exactly what he liked about her. "Thank you, Helga."

Helga nodded and left, closing the door behind her.

Von Berg unfastened his tie and moved to the open window

overlooking the sweeping gardens. Here stood an outstanding statue of the dying Achilles, by the German sculptor Herter, as well as lesser statues of Lord Byron and the melancholy empress Elizabeth herself. Best of all, the gardens offered von Berg a panoramic view of the Chalikiopoulos Lagoon, Mouse Island, and, beyond that, the mainland. And there on the sand, walking along the shore like a Greek goddess, was nature's most exquisite treasure of all—Aphrodite Vasilis.

If he had a flaw, von Berg realized, it was his love for this Greek girl. Not that he believed in love as such. Love implied an equal footing for both partners. But life in this meaningless universe had made it clear to him that the stronger must always subdue the weaker. So it couldn't be love, he rationalized. No, perhaps it was his instinctual recognition that he was attracted to her for reasons beyond her physical beauty.

For one thing, she wasn't weak, like other women. He detected a strength in her that he found truly admirable. She wasn't one to be bullied, though bullied she had to be if he wanted to control her. But threats of physical harm to her proved fruitless. She would rather have both breasts cut off and her face mutilated before she bowed down to the Gestapo. That was happening in many Greek villages these days. The only way to motivate Aphrodite, therefore, was to threaten another innocent victim. This compassion for others was her only vice, and he used it as a last resort because it was a tacit admission of his own failure to control her.

There was also her love of poetry, which they shared, although she preferred Lord Byron to his beloved Goethe. Lately, however, he had seen her toting a slim volume by the aviator poet Michalis Akylas, a major in the Hellenic Royal Air Force who had been shot dead in Athens the year before. Poets who died of natural causes, von Berg decided, were preferable to those who died from German bullets; they didn't stir the same resentment in Aphrodite toward him.

Then there was the way she carried on behind his back, secretly working with Archbishop Damaskinos whenever they were in Athens, using her Red Cross mercy missions to funnel money and relief supplies to the families of killed and imprisoned Resistance fighters. She didn't know he knew this, but he did and approved of it. He had tested her with his own agents, posing as British spies, and knew that she was loyal to him. In short, she could play the game.

The worst thing about her—the best thing, really—was her independent spirit. For a man like himself, one who had to conquer and defeat to validate his existence in this insane world, she proved to be the ultimate challenge. Hitler, after all, could be stopped with a single well-placed bullet. The Allies, too, could be blackmailed into favorable peace negotiations with the nuclear threat of *Flammenschwert*. But the human heart was a different game altogether. After all, he couldn't make Aphrodite love him. She was beyond his control. This fact frustrated and infuriated him, because it reminded him of the other things in life beyond his control: his impending madness and, ultimately, death.

He looked down at Aphrodite drying off on the beach. She then climbed into the back of the *Kübelwagen* with Hans and Peter. They started down the coast road to the Achillion.

Perhaps if I can make her love me, he reasoned, I can defeat the demons of madness and frustrate death.

Or, if I fail, she will be the cause of it.

27

When Aphrodite returned to the mournful palace, she was told the Baron was waiting for her on the second-floor veranda. There she found that a table for two had been prepared, the white china and silverware that bore Ludwig von Berg's monogram gleaming in the sun. A few feet away, next to a bust of one of the nine Muses, stood Ludwig, looking out over the hills and ocean.

He was out of uniform and thus seemed less lethal and more relaxed, dressed as he was in a white linen suit. When he turned, his blue eyes brightened.

"The best view in all of Corfu," he said as he crossed the terrace and embraced her. "My little Nausicaa."

Nausicaa was his pet name for her; it was the name of the princess who'd found Odysseus shipwrecked on her island. Ludwig fondly drew the parallel to her finding him in a hospital bed and nursing him back to health. That they ended up here on Corfu—the very same island, possibly, from Homer's myth—only made their relationship that much more romantic. Or so Ludwig maintained, conveniently forgetting that she hadn't come to Corfu of her own free will.

"Did you miss me?" he asked. "I've missed you. You know, I almost didn't make it back here alive."

"I don't know what I'd do without you."

He gave her a rueful smile. "That's what I like about you, Aphrodite. No flattery. Complete honesty. An independent opinion. That's rare in the New Order."

"Then maybe we should go back to the old order, Ludwig. You and your countrymen can pack your bags and leave my land. Then my family and I can get on with our lives."

"And leave you to a future without me?" he said, taking her

arm and escorting her to the table. "The thought is too much for me to bear."

An SS waiter she did not recognize held her chair for her as they sat down. He proceeded to pour some Mavrodaphne wine into two glasses. It was the first sign that something was wrong: Karl usually poured Ludwig's wine after tasting it. When she looked at Ludwig, he raised his glass to toast her. "To my little Nausicaa."

"Where's Karl?"

Ludwig paused, swallowed some of the sweet red wine, and set the glass down. "Karl is ill," he replied. "A bad bottle of wine. Fortunately for us, we do not have to drink from the same cup, do we? Come, now, you aren't even touching your food."

She looked down at her plate, where some lamb was already cut up for her. There was no knife in her place setting because Ludwig had ordered the staff to keep sharp objects out of her reach when they were close to each other. "I'm not hungry," she informed him. "I'm too worried to eat."

"Worried?" His penetrating eyes looked intently at her above his cruel smile, a look that always made her fear for her life. "Whatever about?"

"About Kostas," she said. "Did you inquire about Kostas?"

He frowned. "Yes, he's doing as well as can be expected at a place like Larissa. I made sure he received your letter. As for any release, right now that's impossible. But I'm working on it."

It was always *I'm working on it*. Aphrodite bit her tongue. She knew she couldn't press him too hard about Kostas's case; she was fortunate to get the news she did about him, and fortunate that Ludwig's SS bodyguard detail "protected" her family in Athens. Fortunate to be alive, even, and so well cared for. Still, somehow, she didn't feel alive.

"It's just as well," Ludwig went on. "If your brother were released, he'd probably turn right around and do something foolish again, maybe even come after a German like me. All he'd manage to do is get himself killed. No, my sweet, I think your brother is safer at Larissa."

Knowing her stubborn brother, Aphrodite realized that Ludwig was probably right. But Ludwig failed to understand that a Greek would rather enjoy one day of freedom and die than live a thousand years in slavery. Indeed, if Kostas ever found out the means by which he was being kept alive, he would hang himself in his cell. Or, if he ever got free, he would probably show his appreciation for her efforts by calling her a traitor and a slut before killing her with his own hands.

"There's a furrow in that lovely brow of yours," Ludwig observed. "What are you thinking about?"

She decided to take advantage of her private audience with the Baron to advance her agenda. "I'd like to get back to Athens to see my family," she told him.

What she really wanted to do was secretly help Archbishop Damaskinos distribute food and clothing to the families of the Resistance. Then she could feel useful again.

"Yes," Ludwig said knowingly, "I'm sure you would. But I'd like to relax here for a few days and regain my strength."

That meant sleeping with her. The thought revolted her.

"Which reminds me," he said as he finished eating and tapped the corners of his mouth with his napkin, "tonight I thought we'd enjoy a walk along the beach. But for now let's get out of the heat of the day and enjoy our siesta. I have something to show you in my bedroom."

"Can't we stay outside just a little while longer?"

"You've been out long enough, my little Nausicaa. Indeed, I understand you eluded Hans and Peter during your swim."

She said nothing. Whenever she resisted him, Ludwig would punish not her but somebody else. He knew that while she was more than willing to make herself a martyr, she couldn't bear to see the pain of innocents. Finally, she said, "Please, Ludwig, it was my fault. Don't blame them."

"You went to visit your friend the priest on Mouse Island, didn't you?"

Not Father John, she thought. Dear God, no. She had to be

careful about what she said, because it might cost somebody his life. "You have your retreat, Ludwig," she answered simply. "I have mine."

"I hope you're not betraying any confidences to the old man."

"What confidences do I have to betray? You never tell me anything. Besides, he's under a vow before God. The confession is inviolate. He'd never repeat anything I've told him, even under torture."

"I can always find out."

"Please, Ludwig," she begged him. "He's an old man who lives there all alone. He hasn't hurt anybody. Let him be."

"Perhaps you have a point." He slid back his chair and rose to his feet. "Let's sleep on it."

Defeated, she slowly stood up and let him take her hand. As he did, she caught him checking her nails to make sure Helga had filed them down. That was so she couldn't scratch his eyes out. Ludwig took no chances with his personal safety, especially during lovemaking, when he was most vulnerable. He could never let his guard down. He was always on top of her and never closed his eyes. As a result, she saw, he couldn't enjoy it fully. But then, he didn't make love to her for his own pleasure. It was to dominate her completely. To tell her that, her little rebellions aside, he was in control and she was his slave. What he enjoyed was dominating her, and it began long before they entered the bedroom.

They passed between the columns of the Ionic peristyle into the palace. She could hear the faint strains of Wagner's "Death March" coming from the hidden speakers of Ludwig's phonograph. He always had it playing when they made love. So conditioned was she to that morbid music that already the terror of what was to come overwhelmed her. Every time she slept with him, it felt like dying, and when it was all over, it was like waking up from a nightmare only to find life worse.

She trembled as they approached the open doorway to the master suite, Hans and Peter posted as guards on either side. She frantically searched their eyes for acknowledgment, some sort of contact, to let her feel she was not alone, but their gaze was fixed on some distant point, their faces stone cold as she and Ludwig walked by. The doors closed behind them, and the music swelled. They were alone.

"Now close your eyes," Ludwig told her.

She reluctantly obeyed and let him lead her to the foot of the bed.

"Open them."

She opened her eyes and saw the great portrait of Empress Elizabeth of Austria that hung over the bed. It had always been there. Then she looked down and saw the black nightgown on the bed.

"Paris," Ludwig explained. "I don't know why I bought it, because I knew once you wore it, I'd want to tear it off in seconds! But it is a great find, and I thought it should fit you well. Try it on."

She looked at the fine prewar detail and ran the smooth fabric between her fingers. It reminded her of another nightgown she had seen in New York, one she never got to wear.

"You seem so sad, my love. You don't find it attractive?"

"It's lovely, Ludwig. It's just . . ."

"You don't find me attractive?" He said it in a playful tone, but she didn't laugh.

"Christos bought me something like this in advance of our wedding night."

Ludwig's eyes darkened. "You know, I'm beginning to wonder if your Chris Andros is even a real person, or some imaginary figure you've dreamed up to distance yourself from me."

Aphrodite was beginning to wonder, too. She said nothing. She didn't have to say anything. The mention of Chris always aroused Ludwig's jealousy. Her fiancé's unseen yet always-felt presence had proved a useful weapon against Ludwig. Unless Ludwig was ready to fly to Boston, he'd never get within a thousand miles of Chris. These were the moments when she appreciated that Chris was an ocean away, outside the reach of the Third Reich. For now. Ludwig often joked about where she'd like to live in New York when the Nazis won the war.

"My little Nausicaa, at least see how it looks in the mirror."

She walked over to the wardrobe with the full-length mirror

inside the door. When she opened it, she held the gown before her in front of the glass. She could see him behind her, sitting on the foot of the bed, admiring her, his eyes shining.

Out of the corner of her eye, however, she saw something in the shadow of the wardrobe. The sleeve of Ludwig's uniform, she thought, until she saw the hand and looked up to see Karl hanging by his neck with one of Ludwig's black ties, his bulging white eyes staring at her.

It took several seconds for her to find her voice and scream, scream above the blare of the Death March, scream so loud that Hans and Peter and the whole world could hear her.

But nobody came through the door. Nobody ever came. And after her voice became nothing more than wisps of air pushed out by her tired lungs, she felt an arm wrap around her waist and draw her to the bed.

"There, there, my love," said Ludwig. "Don't worry. Nobody else will ever touch you."

His soothing voice was as tender as his embrace, and when he began to undress her, she didn't protest. She simply cried in his arms, cried because of him and yet to him, because there was nobody else to comfort her. Not her brother, who was locked up in some dank prison cell, nor her fiancé, who was somewhere in America, half a world away.

28

Andros guessed they couldn't be over twenty miles outside Washington, but Prestwick was mum as the black Chevrolet with District of Columbia plates hummed through the Maryland countryside in the middle of the night. The driver, some sort of government agent, stared woodenly ahead.

Andros could see that Prestwick was enjoying himself. "You like keeping people in suspense, don't you?" Andros asked.

A perverse smile crossed Prestwick's face. Only when the Chevy rolled up to a locked gate an hour later did he finally announce their arrival. "The Farm. Or, as it is officially known, RTU-11."

The official sign said something about an army gadget testing center, but Andros could make out the dim outline of a large country manor at the end of the long drive. So this was the OSS school for spies.

"The whole estate is about a hundred acres or so," Prestwick explained as they started up the drive. "Belongs to a prominent industrialist from Pittsburgh. OSS is leasing it for the time being."

At the entrance, a rotund woman whom Prestwick introduced as Gertrude greeted them and escorted them upstairs to spacious, comfortable bedrooms.

"A regular Waldorf you have here," Andros observed, pressing down on the soft bed. "Is this how you toughen up your secret agents, Jason?"

Gertrude had warned them that they should use only their first names. Security precautions. Still, Andros detected an unnaturally chummy atmosphere here that confirmed his perception of spies as dilettantes, men of leisure who had little to offer their countrymen like this Prestwick.

"Don't you worry," said Prestwick, who was standing by the window looking out. "We'll get started in the morning with some of the more practical aspects of your survival behind enemy lines."

Andros nodded and began to unpack his sack. He drew out a cigarette from his pack of Vargas and lit it with the gold lighter Aphrodite had given him.

Prestwick coughed from the smoke and turned away from the window. "A nasty habit for a West Pointer," he observed. "My reports said nothing about you being a chain-smoker."

Andros shrugged and propped up his picture of Aphrodite on the nightstand. He placed the gold lighter in front of it. "Maybe you shouldn't put too much faith in those reports of yours."

"And maybe you should keep your mind clear of distractions." Prestwick was frowning at Aphrodite's picture. "From now on you must focus only on your mission."

"She is my mission."

Prestwick ignored the remark. "There's a bible in the top drawer of your nightstand. I suggest you begin with that tonight."

Andros opened the drawer and found the OSS training syllabus. He scanned the table of contents: silent killing, firearms, ciphers, undercover operations, escape, explosives.

Prestwick said, "Those areas pertinent to your individual mission are highlighted. Study those sections thoroughly."

Andros thumbed through the syllabus. "I'll commit these passages to memory tonight."

He tossed the syllabus on the bed and moved to the window where Prestwick had been standing. A peek behind the curtain revealed well-manicured lawns rolling on under the night and the shimmer of a swimming pool. Andros paused a moment and looked again. Swimming laps in the pool was a shapely woman. What kind of crazy outfit was this? At the sound of Prestwick's rapping, Andros let the curtain fall and turned around.

"Your closet." Prestwick opened the door to reveal clothing.

"Your prewar Savile Row suits, custom-made Italian shoes, all the trappings of a playboy. Standard uniform for your cover."

"Cover?" Andros asked suspiciously. "What cover?"

"That, you'll find out tomorrow morning in the study, seven sharp. In the meantime, try to get some rest." Prestwick stopped in the doorway and looked back with a self-satisfied smile. "Pleasant dreams."

29

The next morning Andros found Prestwick in the study with a stocky, gray-haired man of about sixty. They were looking over some papers and sipping coffee when he walked in.

"Chris Andros, this is General Bill Donovan, head of OSS," Prestwick began, dispensing with the first-name rule. "He was kind enough to break away from his office to join us this morning."

"Anything to meet the son of General Andros." Donovan quickly extended a hand and looked at Andros with unusually bright blue eyes. "Met your father while touring the Balkans in 'forty-one, just before the Germans invaded Greece."

"Really?" Andros was genuinely interested as they sat down around the coffee table, Donovan and Prestwick on the couch, he on a chair. Andros knew "Wild Bill" primarily as a millionaire Wall Street lawyer and former attorney general. But he was also aware that the Hoover Republican was a hero of the Great War and the only American to have won the Congressional Medal of Honor, the Distinguished Service Cross, and the Distinguished Service Medal—the nation's three highest military decorations. As a result, he immediately commanded more respect from Andros than Prestwick had.

"A great leader, your father was," Donovan continued. "Spoke fondly, if sadly, of you. But he'd be proud to see you now."

"Would he?" asked Andros, self-conscious about his suit and the mention of his father.

"Hell, yes," said Donovan, studying Andros's physique. "If anything, you've become *too* fit since you've last worn those clothes. That won't do. Prestwick, have a tailor alter them for young Andros here."

Prestwick mumbled something as he scribbled a note to himself.

"We don't want you looking too firm when the Germans consider your request," Donovan explained, offering him some coffee and a Danish.

Andros declined. "What request is that, General?"

"Why, the request you're about to present to the Germans, telling them you want to go back to Greece."

"What? You want me to let the Germans know I'm coming?"

"Didn't Prestwick tell you?"

Prestwick cleared his throat. "I'm afraid I haven't gotten to that part yet, General."

Andros stared at the two men incredulously. "I'm supposed to simply hand myself over to the Nazis? This is insane. I thought—"

"That we'd somehow sneak you into Greece by boat or parachute drop?" Donovan shook his head. "Normally, if we were simply dropping you off in the mountains to link up with the Greek partisans, that's what we'd do. But you're too well-known in Athens and could be spotted if we tried to slip you in covertly. Have you heard of a Major Tsigantes?"

Andros nodded. "A well-known republican in the Greek army."

"Too well-known," Donovan said. "Last September the Allied GHQ–Middle East slipped him into Athens on a secret mission. He was to contact political and military leaders in order to organize a non-Communist resistance movement. But he was betrayed by an informer and killed in a gunfight with Italian *carabinieri* in his hideout."

"I see."

"Besides," Prestwick added, "such covert infiltration would defeat the purpose of the cover you've gone to such great lengths to establish with the girl. According to your letters and every other piece of information the Germans have on you, you've been attending Harvard all this time."

Donovan nodded. "Perfect for when you approach the German Legation in Bern."

"Switzerland now?" Andros leaned back in his chair, waiting to hear what was next.

"You'll be going there on a humanitarian mission to secure the safe passage of Red Cross food and medical supplies to the suffering people of Greece," Donovan explained. "The International Committee of the Red Cross, after all, is based in neutral Switzerland. And it remains an association of private citizens entrusted by governments with official missions."

"What exactly is my official mission?"

"You simply want to approach the German Legation in Bern and request that the Germans lift their counterblockade so Andros ships can bring relief supplies into the port of Athens. Of course, in order to personally oversee their distribution, you'll insist on being in Athens yourself as a neutral Red Cross observer."

It sounded too simple to Andros. "What makes you think the Germans could possibly go for this?"

"They've done it before," said Donovan. "The famine in Athens during the first winter of occupation was so desperate that the Greek government in exile in Cairo was able to persuade both the British and German authorities to lift their respective blockades and allow relief supplies to be shipped in via Turkey. Under the agreement, an International Red Cross administration was set up in Greece, staffed by Swiss and Swedes, which distributed Canadian and American wheat shipped into Greece with safe passage guaranteed by all belligerents."

"But that was over a year ago."

"Famine is still a reality in Greece," Donovan insisted. "The metropolitan of Athens, Archbishop Damaskinos, has been on the backs of the Germans for quite a while to allow more supplies in. The military authorities support him because they still fear disease spreading from the civilian population."

Andros frowned. "More important to you, I suspect, is that this gesture of mine is sure to attract the attention of Baron von Berg."

"He can hardly refuse such a gift, considering how good he'll look in the eyes of the Greeks in general and Aphrodite in particular. As a baron, he fancies himself a statesman, a member of the elite, anything but one of Himmler's SS swine." Donovan stood up and paced the floor. "We couldn't dream up anything better. As Chris Andros, you have a natural entrée into the same circles of Athens society that surround Baron von Berg. Furthermore, Aphrodite Vasilis is a high-profile member of the Greek Red Cross. Nobody would question your perfectly understandable motivation to meet with your fiancée."

Andros brooded over the proposal. "I'm not comfortable using the Red Cross as a cover," he said. "Aphrodite has devoted herself entirely to its humanitarian aims. I don't want to jeopardize her work or that of others."

"Merely a public excuse to get you into Athens and provide a context within which you can meet Baron von Berg," Donovan said. "Operation Trojan Horse, that's what we've dubbed your mission."

"Clever," said Andros. "But let's say I get all the way to Switzerland. Let's say the Germans approve the shipment of relief supplies. What good is it if von Berg doesn't allow me into Athens to oversee their distribution? What then?"

Donovan exchanged glances with Prestwick. "There are worse places to wait out the war than Bern," Donovan pointed out. "But as you said yourself, we think the good baron will intervene on your behalf. He obviously knows about you and the letters that Aphrodite has written to you. Unless hers are totally fraudulent—and there seems no reason to believe so—then he knows her heart is with you. We think he'd be eager to meet you."

"I think he'd be eager to put a bullet in my head and get me out of the way," Andros said.

"Von Berg isn't like that, Andros. He is a keen competitor. He would want to meet you out of curiosity—and beat you as a man before Aphrodite. He can't win her affection by killing. He has to beat you some other way. Furthermore, he has the unique authority to permit this venture," Donovan said. "Aren't you eager to meet him?"

"I'm eager to put a bullet in his head."

"Well, the Greeks already did that in 'forty-two, Andros. He miraculously survived, with the help of a metal plate in his skull."

Prestwick said, "Besides, you won't have a gun. That would tip them off that you're up to mischief. There must be nothing military about your manner."

"Then I'm defenseless!"

"Not true," said Donovan. "The least we can do is give you a sporting chance. That's why we've flown in Captain Whyte from the Scottish Highlands. Teaches the silent killing course at SOE's special training school at Lochailort."

30

Captain Erin Whyte turned out to be none other than the shapely woman Andros had seen in the swimming pool the night before. The daughter of Scots Presbyterian missionaries in China, the fresh-faced captain was the protégée of Major William Fairbairn, the British supercop known as "the Shanghai Buster" whose skills were honed after thirty years in the streets of the most violent, drug-infested city of the Far East. Now SOE's femme fatale of the martial arts, silent killing, and other dirty tricks looked Andros over as they stood outside the manor.

Erin was twenty-nine, a knockout five-seven in her gray fatigues. She wasn't a glamorous, exotic beauty like Aphrodite, thought Andros. But her athletic build, shoulder-length blond hair, and natural good looks beguiled him. Especially the freckles on her small, up-turned nose, which crinkled as she squinted at him in the sunlight. He couldn't imagine this girl hurting a flea, much less teaching him the finer points of killing.

"Last thing we need is some American gunslinger in Athens spraying bullets," she warned him, "blowing away Nazis at every corner."

Her tough talk seemed completely at odds with her tender voice. Yet her words possessed unusual power. Perhaps it was her very proper British accent, courtesy of the empire and its outstanding schools in the Far East. That might explain how she could draw him in with her down-to-earth Scottish warmth and still keep him and other men at a safe distance with a formal air that seemed to say, "I'm not that kind of girl, so don't get any ideas."

"Since you won't be packing your iron, you have to be trained in unarmed combat, learn to kill with stealth and speed. Understood?"

Andros nodded curiously as she walked over to a straw-filled dummy and placed a German helmet on its head.

"Remember," she told him, "you've always got a weapon in your pockets: a nail file, a pin, a fountain pen. Any one of them can produce instant death if you know how to use them. So can your hands, knees, head, elbows, and fingertips. Now, watch me."

She proceeded to attack the dummy with a flurry of hard punches. The relentless body blows began to build to an excruciating crescendo, and it was with some relief that Andros witnessed the final, brutal kick to the miserable dummy's head. When it was all over, the straw brains of the decapitated German lay strewn across the ground, and Erin Whyte smiled with satisfaction.

Andros could only marvel in wonder at this force of nature. He began to pity the fools in the field who underestimated her. Fools whose heads were filled not with straw but with dreams. Fools like him.

"Always go for the side or back of the head, never the top," she said as an afterthought, picking up the helmet and hanging it on the dummy's stump of a neck. "Now you try."

For the next few hours Andros did his best to follow her instructions. They were rather long and complicated, although they invariably ended with the same final instruction: "And then kick him in the groin." This last bit of advice she demonstrated with unusual relish. But when she ordered him to dismember the straw guts of the dummy—or rather, what was left of the German—he couldn't hide his reluctance.

"What is it?" she demanded.

"I'd just as soon use my Colt .45," he explained somewhat sheepishly. "It's . . . cleaner."

"Death is death," she replied. "Just because you make it clean doesn't make it less cruel."

Andros realized she had a point.

"War is a dirty business," she went on contemptuously. "You must put aside all pretense when it comes to fighting. There is no decency. No soldier's honor or etiquette. Only victory or defeat. Survival or death."

Andros asked, "What if I simply want to search a prisoner?"

"Kill her first."

Kill her first. Kill *her.* A chill shot up Andros's spine, and he snapped his head up at Erin, whose pretty face revealed nothing. Did she mean he had to be prepared to strike at women as well as men? Or was that a slip about Aphrodite? A sudden dread stirred inside his stomach. Maybe that explained the real reason for Captain Erin Whyte's presence—to get him used to the unthinkable notion of silencing a beautiful woman like Aphrodite. . . .

"What if that's inconvenient?" Andros asked, surprised to hear his voice falter.

She must have seen something in his eyes, because her voice softened somewhat. "Make him lie face to the ground, hands out in front of him," she said. "Knock him out with the butt of your pistol—should you have one—or with the heel of your shoe. Then search him."

Andros nodded but didn't take his eyes off hers. They were an earthy brown, he finally noticed, and they seemed to regard him with true affection, almost pity, before they looked away.

"But never, never stop just because you've crippled the enemy," she reminded him, toughening up as she went along. "If you've broken his arm or leg, it's valuable only because it makes it easier to kill him and—"

But she had already confirmed his fear.

31

"Of course you might have to kill her. Before she kills you."
Prestwick took another bite of the apple pie Gertrude had baked as they sat in the library after dinner. Andros wasn't hungry.

"She's a wild card, Chris," Prestwick continued. "She's lived with this man a year now and has a brother in a German camp. She may have turned, for all we know. Who knows how she'll react to your arrival? One whisper to the Baron, and your fate will be sealed. She could be the key to unlocking the whereabouts of the text—or a knife in your back."

"You're wrong, Jason. She won't betray me."

Prestwick put his fork down and looked at Andros. "How can you be so sure? When was the last time you were in Greece? The entire country has changed quite a bit under the occupation, and not just Aphrodite. Old alliances have disintegrated, and new political winds have swept Greece. The debate these days is no longer between the royalists and republicans; everybody wants to abolish the monarchy. The brewings of civil war are under way between the two most important resistance groups, the right-wing republican army of General Napoleon Zervas and the left-wing army of the National Liberation Front. If they're not killing Germans, they're killing each other. Personally, I find this fratricide revolting. You, however, might find it life-threatening, if you're not careful."

"So what are you telling me?"

"I'm telling you that you can trust no one, including your beloved Aphrodite." Prestwick helped himself to some coffee.

"So you're saying I'm all alone."

"Not entirely," Prestwick replied, stirring his cup. "Ah, Miss Whyte."

Erin walked into the library wearing a neat blue suit and white blouse. "Captain Whyte to you, Colonel," she reminded Prestwick as she took a seat next to him opposite Andros and smiled. "Hello, Chris."

Her hair was wet and her legs longer than Andros had remembered. He could only conclude that neither military nor civilian clothing could safely contain her figure.

"You?" he said. "You're coming to Athens with me?"

"No, but I'll be close by," Erin answered. "The SOE chief of Athens himself will be your contact. Brigadier Andrew Eliot. His code name is Touchstone."

"How will I find him?"

"Don't worry about that," said Erin. "He'll find you. He's a master of disguise. He'll coordinate clandestine support for your mission and serve as your commanding officer in the field. You just try to get close to Aphrodite."

"I intend to," he assured her.

"This might help." Erin held out a ring box from Tiffany & Co. of New York. "It's the engagement ring you're going to give to your betrothed."

Andros opened the box to see a glittering two-carat solitaire set on a gold band. The irony was that the dirty bastards at OSS had gotten it exactly right—it was the same ring he had chosen for Aphrodite. "You don't miss a beat, do you?"

"We don't intend to miss anything," Erin said. "That's why we've hidden a bug inside the box, courtesy of our wizards in the lab. You'll carry it at all times. This way Touchstone and his agents might pick up on some clues in your conversations that would otherwise elude you. They'll also know your whereabouts and perhaps be able to help in case of an emergency."

"The only emergency I fear is von Berg or the Gestapo finding this bug on me," Andros replied.

"I wouldn't worry too much about that," said Erin. "That engagement ring is of great sentimental value to you, so having it on your person is hardly unusual. Besides, the size of the diamond will most certainly detract attention from the discardable box."

"I'm sure you're right," said Andros, snapping the box shut and slipping it into his suit pocket. "The greedy Gestapo will keep the ring and throw the box into the trash with my corpse."

"In any case," said Prestwick, ignoring Andros's cynicism, "that ring is your excuse to be alone with Aphrodite, to ask her where von Berg keeps his important papers."

"Which reminds me," Andros said. "How will I describe this encrypted text to her? You haven't even shown me what it looks like."

"If she knows anything about the text, she'll know what you're talking about." Prestwick sipped his coffee. "What she'll do about it is another question entirely."

Prestwick's guilty-until-proven-innocent attitude toward Aphrodite annoyed Andros. "What if she knows nothing?"

"Oh, she'll provide you with something," Prestwick warned. "If not the text itself, or at least its location, then—"

"Then a knife in the back. I heard you before," said Andros. "Let's assume true love prevails. What then?"

"Once you obtain the information or the text from Aphrodite, Touchstone will arrange for your escape from Athens the night before that Red Cross ship of yours leaves."

"Me, Aphrodite, and our families," Andros insisted. "I'm not leaving without them."

"Yes." Prestwick sighed, setting down his cup of coffee. "You, Aphrodite, and your families will escape from Athens and arrive at a secret guerrilla base we've established in the Parnon Mountains of the Peloponnese, some miles north of Monemvasía in the province of Laconia. There you'll hand over whatever you have concerning the text to Miss Whyte. She'll be the new senior British liaison officer to the EOE."

"The EOE?" repeated Andros, looking to Erin.

"The National Bands of Greece," she explained. "It's a new resistance force of some two hundred Greek partisans, or *andartes*, drawn from both the left-wing National Popular Liberation Army and the right-wing republican National Democratic Army. We consider the National Bands to be the most elite unit within the Greek

Resistance. These *andartes* are the commandos who will go after the text once you've provided us with its location. That's if you haven't already stolen the text itself. They also, we hope, will go on to coordinate the competing resistance groups in the Peloponnese. Their cooperation is vital to the success of any Allied invasion."

Andros nodded. "But what happens to us?"

"Your mission will be accomplished," said Prestwick. "A submarine will pick you up the night after you arrive at the secret base. I'll be on that submarine. Together we'll arrive in Alexandria and then join the Greek royal family and government in exile in Cairo until Greece is liberated."

"Which, from what you've told me," said Andros, "could be within weeks."

32

The headquarters of the OSS was hidden inside an anonymous complex of drab brick-and-limestone buildings in the old gasworks part of Washington, D.C. As the black Chevy carrying Andros and Prestwick turned the corner of Twenty-fifth and E streets that Sunday afternoon, Andros could glimpse the Lincoln Memorial a few blocks to the east before they turned again into an unmarked driveway.

General Donovan's office was in the Q building of the complex. The OSS chief was on the phone when Andros and Prestwick were ushered in. He motioned them to two chairs in front of his desk.

"They just came in," said Donovan, and hung up. "That was Captain Whyte at the airstrip. She says the plane is ready. She also says that after four days at the Farm, so are you, Chris."

"Ready as I'll ever be, I suppose," Andros replied. "You're sure the Swiss will allow this?"

"The Swiss have replied in typically Swiss fashion." Donovan drew out a telegram from his desk drawer and read from it. "They say they consider your 'diplomatic mission' a matter of interest to both Bern and Washington and will be glad to provide you with a visa. But they regretfully add that they cannot guarantee your safe passage into or out of the country."

"Meaning they aren't expecting me anytime soon."

"Not when Switzerland is surrounded entirely by Axis troops in France, Germany, Austria, and Italy." Donovan put away the Swiss telegram.

"So how do I get in?"

Donovan held up a Pan Am ticket labeled PRIORITY ONE. "We've got you on a Clipper flying out of New York tonight for Lisbon."

Andros reached for the ticket, but Donovan pulled it away. "But it won't be you on that flight."

Andros sighed in frustration and sat back in his seat. "Of course not."

Donovan said, "Under normal circumstances, after arriving in Lisbon, you'd hop a Lufthansa to Madrid and Stuttgart, and from Stuttgart board a Swissair to Zurich. But since flights on Lufthansa are no longer possible for American citizens, we're going to send you three out on a Flying Fortress to Blida, Algiers."

"Colonel Prestwick and Captain Whyte are coming with me?"

"Only as far as Algiers," Donovan said. "From there we'll put you on a Skytrain transport and drop you into Switzerland by parachute during the blackout."

"A parachute drop," Andros muttered. "I wish you would have told me. I could have prepared myself mentally."

"Nonsense," Prestwick cut in. "According to General Wilby at West Point, you did quite well in paratrooper exercises with the Rangers. As for the drop outside Bern, there's not another European capital so close to the countryside. You'll be in the city within a half hour."

"That's right," said Donovan. "An agent code-named Watchmaker will be waiting for you at the designated drop zone. He'll drive you to a safe house in the city where you'll spend the night. The next morning you'll check into the Bellevue Palace Hotel."

"Just like that, I pop up in Bern? Won't the Swiss question the circumstances of my arrival?"

"They'll question, but your visa should keep you out of trouble with the Bupo," Donovan said. "My guess is they'll assume that after your arrival in Lisbon, you made it by Spanish plane to Madrid and then crossed France by train or whatnot, with the help of some friends in the French Resistance."

"Ah, yes, I forgot about my friends in France." Andros shook his head in amused wonder at the considerable depth of Donovan's deception. It seemed second nature to the OSS chief.

Donovan glanced down at the papers on his desk. "Now, a few

more things and we're done." He handed Andros a file. "Read this. It's your operation order."

The order outlined the operation code-named Trojan Horse and gave Andros the field name of Sinon. It concluded with the phrase NOW DESTROY NOW DESTROY.

"Understood?" asked Donovan, striking a match.

"Wait a minute. Sinon is the name of the defecting Greek captain in Virgil's version of the Trojan-horse story."

"Yes, he misleads the Trojans by telling them that the Greeks have sailed away and left the horse behind as an offering to please the gods. Now, please, the match is burning."

Andros held on to the order. "Why not Menelaus, king of Sparta and Helen's husband, who won her back from the Trojans?"

"Depends on your point of view," said Prestwick. "After all, Helen may not have been all that eager to leave Troy or her lover Paris."

Andros glared at him. "If that's a thinly veiled allusion to Aphrodite and von Berg in Athens—"

"Really," said Donovan as the flame descended down the matchstick, "now is not the time to question our nomenclature. Dammit, Andros, just burn the order."

Andros sighed. He touched the paper to the flame and dropped it in the ashtray on Donovan's desk.

Donovan let go of the matchstick and blew on his fingertips. "There," he said, then slid a sheet of paper across his desk to Andros. "One more thing."

It was an OSS employment contract:

> The employer shall pay the employee the sum of $150 in the currency of the United States of America each month while said contract is in force. . . . This contract is a voluntary act of the employee undertaken without duress.

Included in the contract was a five-thousand-dollar life insurance policy, to be awarded to anyone Andros designated.

Andros looked up at Donovan. "What is this?"

"A mere technicality." The OSS chief smiled and handed him a pen. "You know, red tape."

Andros wrote the name of his beneficiary, signed the contract, and slid the document back to Donovan.

Donovan read it and smiled. "Aphrodite Vasilis. You're a confident man, Andros."

Andros looked at Donovan and then at Prestwick. "One of us has to be."

33

President Franklin D. Roosevelt sat at his desk in the Oval Office of the White House, reaching for a fresh cigarette while he listened to Donovan on the phone. When he hung up, he placed the cigarette at the end of a long holder and looked across at Churchill. "They've just taken off, Mr. Prime Minister."

"Andros should be in Bern by tomorrow night," said Churchill, puffing away on his Havana. He offered the president a light.

Roosevelt inhaled and then released a stream of smoke. "Dulles is in for quite a shock when he gets the news that Andros is coming. So what happens now?"

"A lot depends on how things go in Bern, Mr. President. But I expect Andros to be in Athens by the time I arrive in Algiers next week to meet with General Eisenhower. At that point, things are wide open."

Roosevelt nodded his understanding. "Our first American in Greece," he noted. "I should have liked very much to have met him."

Churchill grunted. "He has his own reasons for going. If we wrapped it up in the Stars and Stripes, he'd be more suspicious than ever."

"Yes, I suppose." Roosevelt swiveled his wheelchair around and wheeled himself to the window. "He suspects nothing, then?"

"About the Sicily invasion and why we really want the Maranatha text? No," said Churchill. "If anything, he believes we're about to invade Greece."

"Which is what you want him to believe," said Roosevelt at the window, staring out as he smoked.

"The important thing is to ensure the Germans still believe the target of the Allied invasion is Greece," Churchill insisted. "If

Andros can steal the Maranatha text before von Berg compares it to our fake, I will be delighted."

"But if he can't?" Roosevelt swiveled around in the chair. "If Andros is caught?"

"Then his attempt to steal the Maranatha text, together with Captain Whyte's efforts to increase Greek partisan activity, can only reinforce Hitler's fears that Greece is about to be invaded."

"I see, Mr. Prime Minister," said Roosevelt thoughtfully. "So you expect Andros to fail."

"Counting on it, I'm sorry to say," Churchill confessed. "That calculating know-it-all Prestwick even worked out the chances of Andros fulfilling his mission statistically. There are three chances in ten that Andros will be incapacitated before even arriving in Athens: His plane could be shot down in the Mediterranean, something screwy could happen in Switzerland, that sort of thing. If he does make it to Athens, there's one chance in three that he'll be found out and captured. If he's captured, there's one chance in two that he'll be interrogated by the Gestapo."

"But in his case, the rules don't apply," Roosevelt said. "The Nazis know he's coming. So he really has no chance, does he?"

"Not really," concluded Churchill as he put out his Havana. "But it's better for one man to die than millions."

34

The landing lights of the Flying Fortress blinded Jack Mac-Donald for a moment before it touched down at Blida, the Allied air base outside Algiers. MacDonald watched the B-17 taxi to a corner of the field under the stars. The thirty-year-old red-haired Scot then stamped out his cigarette with his flying boot and zipped up his leather bomber jacket. The scarf at his throat blew in the desert wind as he crossed the runway toward the Pegasus. His black-painted B-24 bomber was awaiting takeoff behind a line of other Liberators ready to strike Wehrmacht supply lines in southern France.

Wing Commander Rainey, his copilot, was running down the checklist with the navigator when MacDonald clambered into the cockpit and clamped his earphones over his cap.

"Our package is here," MacDonald said, angrily flicking the switches on his instrument panel. "Just once in this bloody war, I'd like to drop a real bomb on a real German target, preferably the Reich Chancellery in Berlin."

As it was, Captain Jack MacDonald of RAF Squadron 624, one of Britain's Special Operations squadrons, was too good a pilot for typical bombing runs and felt condemned to a career of flying secret supply missions to resistance forces in the Balkans and southern France. Tonight's fantastic orders involved the delivery of an American OSS agent.

"So they're serious?" Rainey asked. He was twenty-two, with a baby face. He looked at MacDonald in disbelief.

"Mission orders confirmed—it's Switzerland," MacDonald told his amazed copilot. "We're going to risk our necks crossing France to drop some American Joe in a neutral country, no less. We'll probably slam into the Matterhorn and burn before we get there."

MacDonald wasn't afraid of dying. He just wanted to take down with him as many Nazis as hell could hold.

He had never flown before he joined the RAF in 1940 and, as a child, had been afraid of heights. But after his wife and daughter were killed in the London Blitz by German bombers, he couldn't get up in the air fast enough to pay back those Nazi bastards. And pay them back he did. Flying twin-engine Bristol Beaufighters in the night skies over the Channel, he engaged and destroyed eleven incoming German bombers during the Battle of Britain. Bombers were such easy, slow-moving targets in the air. He could soar past their operating altitude, fire from overhead, and blow them out of the sky in one pass. He could also outfly their Messerschmitt escorts.

He pursued his prey with such reckless abandon that he became a legend in the RAF. His suicidal tendencies, however, made it difficult for him to hold on to copilots. Rainey had stuck with him the longest. MacDonald had been shot down four times and earned a Distinguished Service Order and Distinguished Flying Cross in the process. But his medals couldn't bring back Carol or little Sarah.

Because of his skills in night interception, the geniuses at the Bomber Command had the brilliant idea of transferring him to Squadron 624. Who better to stick in the cockpit of a B-24 bomber than a former ace who could outthink and outmaneuver any night fighters the Luftwaffe sent his way? Unfortunately, they wanted him to drop not bombs but secret agents and supplies behind enemy lines. It was a more constructive use of his abilities, he realized, but less therapeutic. His two tours of duty had inflicted little damage that he could see to the Third Reich. One *real* air strike was what he needed—the mother lode—and then maybe he could let go of his bitterness.

But it wouldn't be tonight.

"I think I see our Joe now," Rainey said.

MacDonald looked out his cockpit window. Their mysterious passenger, clad in expensive civilian clothing beneath his half-zipped flight suit, stepped out of the darkness at the edge of the flight line. He was talking to a woman in a Royal Marine uniform and some wiry old man in a tweed sport coat. The lovely lass then gave the Joe a kiss and disappeared into the night.

"Well, now, would you look at that," MacDonald said. "How come we never get that kind of send-off?"

The American Joe was nodding as he and the old man ran across the tarmac toward the Pegasus. The old man, having trouble keeping his hat on against the rushing wind of the plane engines, waved good-bye.

Rainey said, "Isn't that the professor from OSS who—"

MacDonald cut him short. "The same. Now I *know* we're in trouble."

It was over a year before that MacDonald had been in the operations room when Professor Prestwick proposed an insane operation "guaranteed to destroy the Third Reich" by demoralizing the Führer. According to OSS psychoanalysts, this could be best accomplished by exposing Hitler to obscene quantities of pornography. For this, Prestwick wanted MacDonald's squadron to drop the magazines and photographs. It was only after MacDonald raised bloody hell that he learned the new U.S. Army Air Force had already refused to have anything to do with the professor. The mission was scrubbed.

"Why are we the ones who have to drop this American?" Rainey asked. "Why don't the Americans handle their own?"

"Because they're too smart to risk the life of a single airman for those maniacs at SOE and OSS."

"Cargo on board," said the tailgunner over the intercom.

Rainey socked the starter button, and the four Pratt & Whitney Twin Wasp radial engines whirred, coughed, and kicked over. The navigator opened his logbook and penned a terse entry for the flight record. Date: 17 May 1943. Type of aircraft: B-24 Liberator. Length of flight: Nine and a half hours. Number of landings: Zero.

The B-24 taxied onto the runway behind the other Liberators, which one by one lifted off into the darkness. A moment later, MacDonald shoved the throttles forward, and the Liberator picked up speed down the airstrip.

"Tail's up," said Rainey as the tachometer moved to takeoff speed.

MacDonald took a deep breath, pulled back on the yoke, and felt the Pegasus leap off the desert floor and into the night sky. "Here we go again."

After a quick glance at his compass, he turned on a heading that led toward France and Switzerland. The logbook recorded the destination simply as "Combat mission—SECRET."

35

It was cold in the fuselage where Andros sat beside a pile of stores and the trunk that would be dropped with him. For most of the flight, they were in a cloud, although every now and then Andros could glimpse the bright Mediterranean moon lurking behind the black shadows. His jumpmaster, Cecil Cates, a young rogue who claimed to be the illegitimate son of a British lord, was too busy jiving to popular tunes from Radio Algiers on his earphones to hear the intercom when it crackled.

"Feel like a smoke, Joe?" It was the captain. "Come up to the flight deck."

A minute later, Andros stood behind MacDonald and Rainey. To Andros, the pilot looked like a red-haired devil and his copilot a cherubic hostage hanging on for dear life. Andros smoked a Varga while MacDonald went over the details of the drop.

"The plan is that we follow the formation up the Rhone," Mac-Donald began, referring to the river below them. "When the other bombers near their target, we'll peel away toward Switzerland while enemy radar and antiaircraft artillery are focused on them."

"This ruse works?" asked Andros.

"Sometimes. Other times the Luftwaffe sics night fighters on the formation, and we get caught in a flak barrage and have to scrub the mission. Last week we lost one of our best pilots when the Jerries shot him down over Greece. Good man, too."

"Greece? What was he doing there?"

"Reconnaissance," MacDonald replied. "He was photographing enemy coastal defenses and artillery positions on the Ionian islands when antiaircraft fire brought him down. That's why the Pegasus here is hitting the ceiling at twenty-eight thousand feet. The Swiss have set some of their antiaircraft batteries on the mountains to boost their range. They don't have radar and almost never score a hit. But I'm not taking any chances, seeing as we're about to violate their airspace."

They were flying high over France now, the Rhone River below them to their left, the Alps to their right. Andros thought he could make out Mont Blanc in the distance and, beyond that, the Matterhorn.

"We'll be approaching the target soon," MacDonald said. "You better get back and make final preparations."

Andros put out his Varga and turned to leave.

"Hey, Joe," said MacDonald. "The woman back in Blida. She your girl?"

"No. Mine is in Greece."

"So they send you to Switzerland. Figures."

Andros left the flight deck as the bomber peeled off from the rest of the formation. The sharp banking must have alerted Cates, because the jumpmaster had removed his headphones by the time Andros made his way to the back.

A few minutes later, Andros was hooked to the static line while Cates checked his parachute pack. They sat around the rectangular escape hatch in the floor through which Andros would jump.

"Obey the system of lights," Cates told him. "Red to get ready and green to go."

Cates lifted the cover of the hatch, and Andros felt a violent rush of freezing air and the deafening roar of the four engines. "Now, when the green light flashes," Cates shouted, "wait for my 'Go.' I'll signal by dropping my hand on your right shoulder."

Andros nodded and looked down through the chute. He could see mountain peaks and deep gorges shrouded in snow and realized this was a far cry from his practice jumps over West Point.

The aircraft started banking steeply. Andros realized that MacDonald was looking for the signal fire. As the plane circled, Andros could see the T formation of bonfires flicker in the darkness below, looming larger as the Pegasus cut its speed and lost altitude.

The "action stations" red light flashed. Andros swung his legs over the hole and into the void. He was numb with cold.

The green light flashed, and Andros felt Cates's hand drop onto his shoulder. "Go!" shouted the jumpmaster.

Andros pushed his trunk over the chute and watched it disappear into the night. Then he stiffened over the hole and dropped into the wind-slip of the four engines.

A second later, he was free-falling in space.

36

The blast of the slipstream sent him somersaulting through the night skies, gasping for breath. He pulled for his parachute to unfold and felt the welcome tug of the black canopy snapping open. He swung like a pendulum toward the earth.

Looking down, he could see only the dim plains, no lights from the blacked-out Bern—and no lights from the signal fire.

There still seemed to be a long way to go when he hit the ground and had the wind knocked out of him as the canopy collapsed over him. When he pulled it from over his head, the Pegasus was gone. There was no sign of any signal fire or reception committee.

After making sure he was free of injury, Andros gathered up the parachute and searched for the trunk. He found it about fifty yards away.

Andros had shed his flight suit and jump boots and was tying the laces of his wing-tip dress shoes when he heard what sounded like the heel of a heavy jackboot on rock. He instinctively reached for his Colt .45 automatic, which he did not have, only to discover that he was surrounded by several goats wearing wooden bells.

Apparently, he had jumped onto a large farm outside Bern; now he could make out the dim outline of a farmhouse cut against the distant horizon. He could also smell something foul in the air and looked down to find his wing tips ankle-deep in goat dung. He groaned.

His ears picked up the faint hum of an engine. He turned to see the shadow of a vehicle coming quickly up the road, which, along with the fence that ran beside it, became visible when the car flashed its two blue running lights as it rolled to a stop.

Andros left the trunk, hopped the fence, and ran over to what turned out to be a British Triumph.

"You made it after all, Sinon," said the surprised driver, a compact, middle-aged man sporting a neat leather driver's cap, jacket, and gloves. He then apparently remembered his signal. "I'm the Watchmaker."

Andros leaned into the open window. "My trunk."

The Watchmaker eyed the trunk by the side of the road and grimaced. "Too big for my Triumph, I'm afraid. Hide it in the bushes. I'll come back for it later."

A dog barked in the distance, and a light went on in the farmhouse.

"Hurry, let's go," said the Watchmaker. "The clock's ticking."

Andros did as he was told, climbed in, and they were off.

A half hour later, they entered the medieval city of Bern, passing through darkened arcades and streets invisible in the blackout. After crossing what the Watchmaker told Andros was the Kirchenfeld Bridge, they rolled to a stop along the bank of the river Aare.

"You're going to 23 Herrengasse," the Watchmaker said, handing Andros a map. "Just follow the directions and enter through the garden."

Andros found himself in a picturesque part of town, knocking on a door with a sign outside that read: ALLEN W. DULLES, SPECIAL ASSISTANT TO THE AMERICAN MINISTER.

37

Dulles regarded him warily as they sat in front of the fireplace in the spacious club room of the Herrengasse flat. The Swiss station chief, known simply as Number 110 in the OSS message codebook, was younger than Andros had expected, a dapper fellow in his forties with slicked-back dark hair and a round, intelligent face. He was wearing an elegant silk bathrobe and leather slippers and was smoking a pipe.

"You're certain you weren't followed?"

Dulles's sour expression made it plain that he did not appreciate receiving unexpected guests in the middle of the night, especially those with manure on their shoes. He seemed to regard Washington's brutish intrusions into his delicate operations here in neutral Switzerland with visible disdain. Andros had felt unwelcome from the moment he walked through the door, and he resented it.

"You never know," said Andros, loosening his tie and lighting a Varga.

Dulles shook his head. "This is another one of Wild Bill's crazy ideas run amok," he said. "Donovan's attitude is to try anything that has even the slightest chance of working. His disregard for standard operating procedures is reckless. Reckless."

The words did little to reassure Andros. "So you don't think Prestwick's plan will work?"

At the mention of Prestwick's name, Dulles removed the pipe from his gaping mouth and stared. "Did you say Prestwick? Good Lord, don't tell me *he's* behind this!"

Andros wasn't sure what to say, so he tapped his Varga over an ashtray and shrugged. "You know him?"

"The man used to report to me when I headed our OSS offices in New York," Dulles explained. "Our psychological chief, Dr. Henry

Murray of Harvard, spoke of him when he shared with me his fear that the whole nature of the functions of OSS is particularly inviting to narcissistic characters."

"Narcissists?"

"You know, those types attracted to sensation, intrigue, the idea of being a mysterious man with secret knowledge."

That certainly described Prestwick, Andros thought. Indeed, he was beginning to get the impression that outside of the sensible Dulles, the entire organization must be filled with Prestwicks—those paranoid misanthropes who read too many spy thrillers and whose tendencies toward the unconventional bordered on the psychotic.

"Now you must tell me what they told you," Dulles went on, looking very grave. "What did Donovan and Prestwick say was your reason for coming to Switzerland?"

"You mean my cover?" asked Andros. "I'm here on a humanitarian mission to secure the safe passage of Red Cross food and medical supplies to the suffering people of Greece."

"That's not any sort of cover at all. The Germans would see through that in a second." Dulles frowned. "You mean they didn't tell you?"

Andros had a sick feeling in his stomach. "Tell me what?"

Dulles sighed. "Publicly, your ambitions may be humanitarian, Chris, but privately, you're here in Bern for more selfish reasons. Specifically, you're here to unblock Andros Shipping funds. Andros Shipping is a Swiss corporation, is it not? And quite a few Andros ships sail under Swiss registry?"

Andros, bristling with anger, could see once again that the OSS knew a lot more about him and his family than he knew about them. "My grandfather didn't feel his funds were secure in Greece," he explained, "considering the constant political turmoil."

"Even Switzerland wasn't safe enough for the Swiss when it looked like the Nazis were going to invade a few years back," Dulles replied. "The banks transferred their assets and national gold reserves to New York. At the time, America was officially neutral. But

Washington was concerned that many so-called Swiss corporations were nothing more than fronts for Nazis like Baron von Berg. Hence Executive Order 8389."

"Executive Order what?" repeated Andros.

"Signed by the president on April 10, 1940, it empowered the Treasury Department to draw up a blacklist of world firms doing business with Germany and to secretly prepare to block any of their funds that had been sent to New York. That in fact happened on June 14, 1941, when Washington froze all Swiss assets in the United States. It's been almost two years that we've enforced the blacklist."

"Which, I'm beginning to suspect, includes Andros Shipping."

"Along with about thirteen hundred other Swiss firms that ever sold any goods or provided any sort of service to Germany."

Andros could barely contain his rage. How dare Donovan and Prestwick entangle his family's business with their intrigues!

Dulles simply puffed his pipe and looked into the fire. "It's the perfect cover," he said. "To unblock Andros Shipping funds, you naturally attempted to prove to Treasury that Andros Shipping is non-German. As this is impossible without a full register of shareholders, you contacted Swiss bank affiliates in New York. But when you tried to trace the actual ownership of Andros Shipping, you hit a brick wall."

"That's because Swiss shares are *bearer* shares," Andros said automatically. "They're registered in the name of the shareholder's bank, not the shareholder himself. And Swiss law forbids banks from revealing the names of depositors or shareowners."

Dulles nodded. "Which is why you've come to Bern yourself— to see your family's private banker."

"Pierre Gilbert?" Andros felt truly unnerved at the vast amount of intelligence the OSS had gathered on him. "What on earth does he have to do with this?"

"As a director on the board of the Swiss Bankers Association, Pierre Gilbert works closely with the Swiss National Bank in the negotiation for international treaties and agreements affecting the banking trade and its customers. You want him to work on your behalf. Specifically, you'll ask him to get the Swiss Clearing Office to certify that your blocked account in New York is not German-owned. The agency has been supervising all Swiss-German trade."

"He'll never do it," Andros insisted. "Pierre would bleed to death before he broke the Swiss banking code or enlisted others to do so."

"We know that," said Dulles. "But our intelligence sources here tell us that Gilbert & Co.'s biggest depositor is none other than Baron Ludwig von Berg himself, whom we suspect has spies at the bank. Remember, von Berg has a vested interest in tracking Swiss industry and finance. We're confident that whatever you say to your family banker will make its way back to him."

"So von Berg learns that Pierre turns me down flat. So what?"

"So you approach the German Legation. You offer to smuggle precision technology on Andros ships carrying Red Cross relief supplies to Greece. For a price, of course."

"*What?*" Andros sat up in horror. "I'm a smuggler now?"

"You're a desperate man, Andros, a playboy with no money to play with. The fact is, with all its funds blocked, Andros Shipping is in dire straits. It cannot continue to cover expenses and pay employees out of capital much longer. Nor can it support your lavish lifestyle, now that you've squandered what is left of your personal financial resources."

"The only thing I've squandered is my sanity," Andros said. "What makes you think the German Legation will believe this revolting cover?"

"Because it makes sense," Dulles insisted. "You've come to Switzerland under the noble guise of securing Red Cross aid for the Greek people, but really to unblock Andros Shipping funds. When you can't unblock your funds, you devise this smuggling scheme."

"All right, then," said Andros. "Perhaps I am desperate enough to make such an offer. Why should Baron von Berg take me up on it?"

"According to private Swiss intelligence services, as well as the Swiss Army's N1 special branch and the Buro Ha, Baron von Berg has an entire network of agents here engaged in industrial and financial espionage. We also know that he's constructed some sort of secret research facility in Greece. Your offer to smuggle precision components via neutral ports of call is just what the Baron is looking for."

"And he'd believe I'd turn my back on my own country?"

"Which country? The American government has turned a deaf ear to your argument that by keeping Andros Shipping on the blacklist, it's dissipating many of the assets it wants to recover. All that's left for you is the draft. At least in Greece you have family, a girl, and a chance to rebuild what's left of Andros Shipping. That's if you play your cards right with the occupation authorities and use the Red Cross gesture to ensure a favorable reputation in postwar Greece, whichever side wins."

Andros shook his head. "Quite a coward you people have made me."

Dulles seemed unconcerned. "Tomorrow morning you'll check into the Bellevue Palace Hotel," he said, speaking to the fire. "We'll slip you out of here before dawn. A cab will drop off your trunk later. And then you must promise to never come knocking at my door again."

"You don't have to worry about that," said Andros. "I don't plan on coming back."

38

It was early morning on the island of Corfu when Baron von Berg came down the steps of the Achillion and got into the back of his Mercedes. He was in the full black dress uniform of an SS general. He avoided wearing the black around Aphrodite but preferred it whenever he went into Corfu Town, if only to put the fear of God into the Italians and see Commandant Buzzini jump.

"A beautiful morning, Franz," he said as they drove along the seafront boulevard toward town. "Beats Berlin these days, wouldn't you say?"

"Yes, Herr Oberstgruppenführer."

To their right, the sun was rising over Garitsa Bay. To their left was the old town, its colonnaded houses dating back to the island's days under British rule. Straight ahead was the old fortress with the Italian flag flying overhead and, beyond that, their destination, the Palace of St. Michael and St. George.

The former residence of the British governor and the Greek royal family was now the headquarters of the Italian commandant. Franz turned in through the triumphal arch known as St. George's Gate and braked to a halt at the Doric colonnade along the front of the palace. Von Berg got out and went up the steps past the Italian sentry.

Inside, a corporal was sitting behind a table at the bottom of the stairs, pretending to busy himself with paperwork, when the sound of von Berg's boots made him look up, fix his eyes on the black uniform, and leap to his feet.

"The commandant is expecting me," von Berg announced, proceeding up the stairs without bothering to check in, leaving the corporal to pick up the phone and, in a frantic voice, warn Buzzini's office.

Sergeant Racini, the commandant's lanky young aide, was just replacing his receiver when von Berg appeared. Racini looked up helplessly. His big, pointed nose and small eyes reminded von Berg of a nervous rat sniffing the air for a whiff of cheese. Without wasting his breath on the fool, von Berg brushed by Racini's desk and burst into Buzzini's office.

Buzzini was still in the middle of his Italian breakfast, chewing a tiny sandwich and sipping ersatz espresso. At von Berg's appearance, he coughed up his espresso. "General von Berg," he said, standing up and wiping his small, petulant mouth. "This is most unexpected."

"But so much more fun, Commandant," von Berg replied, noting the rolls of fat quaking beneath the commandant's tunic. The man was a disgrace to all men in uniform. "You have my mail?"

Buzzini shot a fiery glance at the helpless Racini, who had followed von Berg into the office. "The general's cables from Berlin, Sergeant," Buzzini ordered in his baritone voice. "Bring them to me."

The ratlike Racini disappeared and returned with several dispatches. Buzzini took them from his aide and handed them to von Berg. "Anything else?" he asked politely, although von Berg could detect the rage bubbling beneath the surface of his dark, fleshy face.

Von Berg ignored him and moved to the window and quickly sorted through the various dispatches to learn what the Italians had seen. Mostly routine, except for a special order from the naval high command and an encoded signal from German minister Otto Carl Kocher in Switzerland.

"I'd like to be alone for a few minutes," von Berg replied finally. "Could you wait outside?"

At that moment Franz entered the office with what looked like a small typewriter. He proceeded to clear the top of Buzzini's desk and put down the Sonlar coding machine.

Buzzini turned red, his eyes flashing in anger and his loose jowls quivering. "This is an outrage, General. This is *my* office! I am the commandant of Corfu!"

"A commandant who can receive nothing except what is given

him by the Reich, including this island," von Berg responded. "And what is freely given to you can just as easily be taken away."

Buzzini stared at him, livid. "General Vecchiarelli will hear of this, von Berg. Come, Sergeant."

With that, Buzzini and his aide left the office, closing the door behind them.

Von Berg shook his head. The commandant had little reason to hope that his new boss, Vecchiarelli, would fare any better than his old boss, Geloso, the former commander of all Italian troops in Greece. Already plans had been drawn for the Germans to disarm and replace the Italian Eleventh Army in Greece and, if necessary, to occupy Italy. Operation Alarich, Hitler called it, after the fifth-century Teutonic conqueror of Rome.

Von Berg handed Franz the encoded signal from Switzerland. "Decode this," he said, and turned his attention to the naval dispatch. He could always gauge Hitler's reaction to his intelligence reports by the orders handed down through the various services. This one from the naval war staff confirmed that Hitler had rejected his stolen plans for the Sicily invasion and instead was sold on the idea that the Allies would be invading Greece. It was dated May 20 and labeled MOST SECRET.

"Listen to this, Franz," von Berg said, beginning to read the order aloud. "'In the opinion of the naval war staff, the possibility of enemy landings in the eastern as well as the western Mediterranean must be reckoned with.'" He paused. "Now, that's a novel thought."

He skimmed several more paragraphs offering the revelation that the enemy would probably make an initial landing where there would be the least resistance and where the greatest results could be expected in the shortest time.

"'Landing attempts are most likely to be made in the Greek west coast area, where the Corfu-Arta-Pyrgos region offers the greatest prospects of success,'" he continued. "'The German admiral commanding the Aegean is ordered to take over control of the minefields the Italians are laying off the western coast of Greece. German coastal defense batteries also are to be set up in a territory under Italian control. German R-boats are to be sent from Sicily to the Aegean.'"

"Motor torpedo boats to Greece?" asked Franz, busy with the Sonlar. "For what purpose, Herr Oberstgruppenführer?"

"To establish R-boat bases, command stations, naval sea patrol services, and other safeguards, now that almost the whole coast of Greece, as well as the Greek islands, are threatened." Von Berg crumpled up the report. "No wonder Buzzini is so edgy. He doesn't want German company, and neither do I at this point. With the *Flammenschwert* reaching the crucial assembly phase, the last thing we need is the attention that more divisions in Greece will attract from the Allies and Berlin."

"I have it, Herr Oberstgruppenführer." Franz held out the decoded signal, and when von Berg read it, he felt a sensation of surprise he hadn't experienced in a long time.

> TO SS OBERSTGRUPPENFÜHRER VON BERG, PERSONAL. MOST SECRET.
>   UNUSUAL ARRIVAL IN BERN MAY INTEREST YOU. CHRIS ANDROS OF GREEK SHIPPING FAMILY SEEN LEAVING FLAT OF AMERICAN OSS SPY DULLES AND CHECKING INTO BELLEVUE PALACE HOTEL. NATURE OF VISIT UNCLEAR BUT INVOLVES MEETINGS WITH RED CROSS REPRESENTATIVES FROM GENEVA. SWISS FOREIGN MINISTER MARCEL PILET-GOLAZ CONFIRMS VISA HAS BEEN ISSUED. KOCHER.

Von Berg stared at the message, filled with a strange mixture of fear and excitement. Chris Andros, he thought. My God, you do exist after all.

For too long he had been haunted by the ghost of Andros, not because the man was any threat in himself—that remained to be seen—but because of Aphrodite. While he could remove a dagger from her lovely hand, he could not remove the poison from her blood: her love for this infidel. And just when he was on the brink of deposing Hitler, rescuing continental Europe, and establishing global peace, this devil Andros has chosen to surface in Bern after four years. Why now, of all times?

Franz cleared his throat. "Trouble, Herr Oberstgruppenführer?"

"Perhaps, Franz." Von Berg put the signal down on Buzzini's desk and picked up the commandant's coffee cup. He took a sip and frowned. Terrible stuff. No wonder the Italian was always in a bad mood. He put it down. "I need you to draft a signal for Bern."

Franz stiffened to attention in his chair. "*Zu Befehl,* Herr Oberstgruppenführer."

Von Berg perceived Andros as a psychological threat to his control of Aphrodite and his plans, which he now began to see were intertwined. What was the use of being a sovereign without her? His mission suddenly lost its meaning. But how could that be if he didn't believe in meaning? He pushed the thought out of his mind and began his dictation.

"'To German minister Kocher, personal, most secret, et cetera,'" von Berg began with a wave of his hand. "'Interested in Andros arrival. Would like to greet personally, see what business he has in Bern. Arrange proper reception in person of Agent Barracuda. Expect detailed report as soon as possible. Von Berg.'"

"No more, Herr Oberstgruppenführer?"

"Not yet, Franz." Von Berg stood at the window and looked out at the lush green spiniada of Corfu Town. "So, Herr Andros, you return. Let's see what kind of a man you really are."

39

Andros paid the cabdriver and walked up the steps of the venerable private banking firm of Gilbert & Co. It was in a small, austere building in Bern's Old Town, its presence marked only by a discreet brass plaque set in the wall. A porter greeted Andros as he entered, asked him to state his business, and directed him to the second floor.

Andros ascended the stairs to a reception area leading to the private executive offices. Here a smiling mademoiselle, a blonde in a red cashmere sweater, took his Burberry raincoat. Her pale blue eyes seemed to linger in admiration of his athletic build beneath the three-piece suit. In the most exquisite French, she informed him that Monsieur Gilbert would see him in but a moment.

Andros took a seat and surveyed the shabby but elegant reception area. The faces of several generations of Gilberts looked down from the oil paintings on the walls. For well over a century, the bank had remained in family hands, an outgrowth of their merchandising business. It was one of only a few private banks in Bern, as most were in Geneva, and the only one with a French surname and not German. Like the other private banks, Gilbert & Co. was unincorporated and, as a rule, never published its balance sheets.

Andros remembered that his father had preferred the modern big banks of Zurich, but his grandfather had insisted on conducting family business affairs in this manner, with a personal touch. In addition to the close attention Gilbert & Co. paid to client requirements, the unlimited liability of the bank's partners had led his grandfather to believe they might be more cautious with their management of the Andros portfolio than the gnomes of Zurich.

What Andros was curious to know was which one of the bank's employees was von Berg's spy. Whoever it was would say a lot about von Berg and his selection of associates. If what Dulles said was true, then the spy would have to be somebody high enough in the bank's management to be privy to the private affairs of such depositors as the Andros family. Higher still would be that *other* bank employee, the one Dulles failed to mention to him but who Andros guessed existed, the employee who had tipped off the OSS to the presence of a German plant in the first place. Dulles no doubt knew the identities of both men. Andros knew neither, but the maddening reality was that he was known to both.

The mademoiselle returned and ushered him into Gilbert's office. Andros hadn't seen Pierre in years, but when the tall, gray-haired man, elegant in boutonniere and black suit, rose from his desk, the family resemblance to the paintings in the reception hall was unmistakable.

"A pleasure to see you again, Monsieur Andros."

Gilbert's eyes regarded him keenly, and his smile was civilized. The Swiss banker asked no questions about what Andros was doing in Bern or how he had gotten there. Nor did he show any inclination to find out. His was a face that had seen everything.

"Please, sit down and make yourself comfortable."

An officer of the bank, a big, bald man whom Gilbert introduced as Monsieur Guillaume, stood silently by his side, as was the practice. He regarded Andros warily from under his heavy eyelids. Does nothing ever change in this country? Andros thought as he sat down.

"And how can I help you, Monsieur Andros?"

"My inheritance. I'm here to check on its status."

"Yes, I am sorry to hear about your father. A great man."

"A dead man, Monsieur Gilbert. Life goes on."

"But of course, we must eventually attend to business," Gilbert said, taking a file from his desk. "You must excuse me, Monsieur Andros, but it has been some years since I last saw you. May I see both your American and Greek passports for proper identification?"

"Certainly," said Andros, handing the passports to Gilbert.

Gilbert called in his receptionist, the blonde, who answered to the name of Elise, and gave her the passports. She promptly disappeared, presumably to check the passports and any photos and signatures on file.

"Your family account is numbered," Gilbert said. "Do you have the code?"

Andros repeated the four-digit number. Gilbert nodded to acknowledge the number's validity, and Elise returned with the passports.

"Thank you, Elise. You are free for the evening." Gilbert admired her form as she walked out before he returned the passports to Andros. "Your assets, Monsieur Andros, following your grandfather's instructions, are in the form of bearer shares of Andros Shipping. They are secure."

"My so-called assets are frozen, and I can't touch them."

"This is true," Gilbert responded. "The American blacklist is an unfortunate turn of events for all of us."

"As things stand, my ships can arrive only at ports of call in neutral countries or the designated 'Swiss ports' of Genoa, Trieste, and Marseille. At this pace, my inheritance will be worthless at the end of the war, because Andros Shipping is dissipating many of these assets you inform me are so secure."

Gilbert shrugged. "What more can we do, Monsieur?"

"You can help me get a full register of shareholders to prove that Andros Shipping is not German-controlled. Only then can I get my funds released in the States."

Gilbert smiled. "Besides breaking federal and cantonal law, how else can I help you?"

"You see some problems?"

"Two of them. The first is Article 47 of the Swiss criminal code. Monsieur Guillaume?"

The mute bank officer now recited Article 47 from memory: "'Whosoever as agent, official, employee of a bank, or as accountant or accountant's assistant, or as a member of the banking commission, or as a clerk or employee of its secretariat, violates the duty of absolute silence in respect of a professional secret, or whosoever induces or attempts to induce others to do so, will be punished with a fine of up to twenty thousand francs, or with imprisonment of up to six months, or both.'"

"And the second problem?" asked Andros.

"Article 273 of the code," Gilbert replied. "Monsieur Guillaume?"

"'Whosoever exploits trade secrets in order to make them accessible to foreign governments or foreign enterprises or foreign organizations or their agents, and whosoever makes such trade secrets accessible to foreign governments or organizations or private enterprises or to agents thereof, will be punished by imprisonment.'"

Gilbert turned to Andros and smiled. "Surely you don't want to see your family banker in jail. I could hardly be of any service to you there."

"But there must be a way to identify the shareholders of my own company," Andros persisted. "You are a director on the board of the Swiss Bankers Association, Monsieur Gilbert. You have friends at the Swiss National Bank. Surely, with their help, you could persuade the Swiss Clearing Office to certify that Andros Shipping is not German-controlled."

Gilbert's response was firm. "If cantonal law says Andros Shipping is Swiss, then it is Swiss. This is what I have argued with the American government and what I will continue to argue. I will not, however, break federal laws by revealing information about my depositors, and I certainly will not beseech other bankers to do likewise. The Swiss banking system owes its position in world finance to its tradition of absolute confidence between banker and customer. Any deviation from this tradition of secrecy would shake confidence in Swiss banking."

"But this is in your personal and collective interest," said Andros. "The shareholders' interest."

Gilbert shook his head. "To bow to American pressure would place our Swiss honor and neutrality at stake, Monsieur Andros. If we bow to American pressure today, who says we won't give in to German pressures tomorrow? You Americans seem to forget that any assets a German national channels into Switzerland are completely beyond the reach of the Nazis, too. The world is filled with governments eager and demanding to see what is in Swiss safe-deposit boxes. Even now we fear a Nazi invasion."

Andros remembered Woodrow Wilson's admonition that "in the next war there will be no neutrals." Men such as Pierre Gilbert would never accept such a view.

"We have spent billions on civil defense," Gilbert continued. "Should it come to invasion, we are ready to give up Bern, Geneva, and Zurich to the invaders and burrow into our Alps. But even if war should scorch the entire face of the planet, we will emerge from our mountain fortress in the end, still intact and still neutral, ready with our hard currency to rebuild the world."

Andros looked at Pierre Gilbert and smiled blandly. "Your confidence is reassuring. I can see our family fortune is safe with you."

Pierre Gilbert half-closed his eyes and placed his hand over his heart. "Always, Monsieur."

40

As the cab turned down the Kornhausplatz and passed the Ogre Fountain, Andros leaned back against his seat and closed his eyes, going over in his mind his conversation with Pierre Gilbert.

If the Swiss banker was puzzled by his cover, he didn't show it. Nor did the quiet Monsieur Guillaume, who Andros guessed was the bank's link to von Berg. He had to be—always silent, always listening in on Gilbert's conversations. Who else could there be? Well, now Monsieur Guillaume had something to talk about.

When Andros opened his eyes, they had arrived in front of the colonnaded Beaux Arts facade of the Bellevue Palace Hotel. He got out of the cab and went inside, passing between the Ionic columns that supported the lobby's stained-glass ceiling. On his way to the elevator, he saw several patrons of the Bellevue bar in deep leather chairs, diplomats from the Federal Palace next door, eyeing him over the rims of their drinks.

Perhaps they knew what he was up to, perhaps not. At this moment, as Andros stepped off the elevator and approached his Louis IV suite at the end of the floor, he didn't care. He was tired of his cover, and tonight, for the first night in several, he would get some good sleep.

He slipped his key into the lock and was about to turn it when he heard water running inside. He looked up to make sure he was at the right suite and listened again. This time he heard nothing. He turned the key and pushed the door open.

She was sitting on the bed, the blond head-turner from the bank, wrapped in a towel. Across her lap lay his May issue of *Esquire,* which she had fetched from his wide-open and most likely thoroughly searched trunk. So he had guessed wrong. He owed Monsieur Guillaume an apology.

"Did Monsieur Gilbert send you?" he asked her in French, closing the door. "Or are you really a little French tart with a well-heeled clientele, Elise? It *is* Elise, isn't it?"

Her pale blue eyes glanced down at the *Esquire*. "'Hollywood's Best Bet,'" she said in broken English, reading from the racy American magazine. She smiled and turned a page, revealing a striking pinup girl: one in an evening dress who literally was pinned to a target by arrows. "'Warner Brothers' newest starlet, Dolores Moran, eighteen, blonde. Five foot seven of proportions. Waist twenty-five inches, hips and bust thirty-five inches, weight one-twenty.'"

Whether she was one of Baron von Berg's lethal spies or Swiss Bupo, Andros couldn't be sure. Knowing Prestwick, Andros wouldn't be surprised if she was one of Dulles's OSS agents and they were testing him to make sure he could keep his cover as a playboy. Of course, he couldn't be sure and had to play the game. The game was what disgusted him.

She tossed the magazine on the nightstand and picked up the pack of playing cards Prestwick had packed, the backs of which depicted the Varga Girl striking various poses as Elise riffled the deck. "Naughty, naughty, Chris," she said, then switched to her sensuous French. "A man like you doesn't have to look."

Andros shrugged and walked over to the dresser. He began to take off his suit coat, then his cuff links, all the while watching her in the mirror. "A man like me is too busy to do much else."

"Too busy to make love to me?" She loosened her towel to proudly display her full, round breasts.

Andros looked at her in the mirror and cringed inwardly at this déjà vu. His first time with a woman had been in a hotel room in Geneva, a present for his sixteenth birthday from his grandfather Basil. She was a sensuous brunette who took special pleasure in initiating him into manhood and later begged him not to leave. At Harvard, there had been a couple of cold, stiff New England girls from Vassar. They were much less exciting than the French woman and incomparable to what Aphrodite would offer him on their wedding night. No sooner. He could never press Aphrodite for that; he had demanded angelic purity from her.

"What are you waiting for?" Elise asked, sounding impatient.

So this was the way it would be, Andros thought: He must break either his cover or his faithfulness to Aphrodite. The irony was that the success of his mission, which he equated with saving Aphrodite, hinged on the Germans buying his cover. He wondered what Aphrodite felt when she faced this decision with von Berg. He was losing only the purity of his devotion to her. She had lost her virginity.

"I haven't even had dinner yet," he told Elise, "and already we indulge ourselves with dessert?"

He loosened his tie and turned off the light so he couldn't look at his face in the mirror before he turned around. He hated games. He hated Prestwick and this whole spy business. Most of all, as he thought of Aphrodite, he hated himself for what he was about to do.

As he approached the bed, he could see her shape in the darkness and her arms reaching out to embrace him and pull him into her.

"Love me," she groaned. "Love me."

He thought of Aphrodite and the first time they had kissed under the mango tree that night in Kifissia. He thought of their subsequent secret rendezvous at the top of Likavitos Hill and her guilt-ridden expression when the priest from the nearby chapel caught them kissing. He thought of that night in New York when they could have made love but hadn't, deciding they would wait for their wedding night. That wedding night now seemed further beyond their reach than ever.

Aphrodite, he thought, please forgive me.

41

One thing Andros had to admit that night as they lay awake in bed was that Elise—if that was her real name—threw herself into her work. She also proved with her relentless, breathless questions that she knew Swiss banking inside and out.

"Pierre has a theory about the Andros fortune, darling," she told him as she drew hearts on his chest with her finger.

"Really?" By now Andros could see that Monsieur Gilbert was not the discreet Swiss banker he had portrayed himself to be. Unless this woman had worked her bedside charms on him, too. "And what theory is that?"

"He thinks your father transported more than Greek wine, grains, and tobacco."

"Opium? Ridiculous."

"No, darling. Arms, guns, explosives. Most recently, to Franco during the Spanish civil war. He got to feed his favorite fascist causes and send his son to the best boarding schools at the same time."

"Interesting," Andros replied. "What do *you* think?"

She sighed. "I think how terrible it must feel to be sitting on a fortune and not be able to touch a single franc." Her forlorn voice sounded as if it were her money they were talking about.

"So what do you suggest, Elise?"

"You could wait out the war here in Bern with me. We could make love with the Alps behind us and a lifetime ahead, whichever side wins."

She didn't mean it. He even doubted she expected him to believe her. He smiled to himself as he resisted the impulse to say "Yes, darling, yes. That's what I want to do. To spend my life in these sheets with you," then watch her charm herself out of that. But it would do nothing to advance his agenda—getting into Greece—or, for that matter, hers, which was finding out his agenda.

"A pleasant thought," he said absently. "But what if my company should go under in the meantime? I don't think you count paupers among your acquaintances, and that's what I'll be. And then I foresee a rather abrupt end to our relationship, don't you?"

She laughed. "Chris, darling, you really are too funny."

Andros looked toward the window, where the darkness outside was brighter than in the room. "No, I think the answer is in Greece."

"Why would you risk your life to go back to Greece, darling?" She rubbed her hand across his chest. "What does Athens offer you that Bern doesn't?"

"Family, for starters. My uncle Mitchell and grandmother are in Athens. I'm naturally curious to see how they're getting along."

"What else?"

"Money. If I can get enough cash to keep Andros Shipping afloat, then the trip will be worth it."

"But what good is your money if you are dead, darling?"

"Let's just say I have business to attend to."

She laughed and kissed his neck. "Monkey business."

"You mean the black market?" he said, innocently putting the idea in her head. "I'm sure with my ships, I could make out pretty well by the end of the war. What do you think?"

"I think that if you are intent on abandoning me for Greece, I do have a friend who could possibly help you. . . ."

Andros grew still as she continued to draw hearts on his chest with her finger, sighing with affection. He wondered if she could feel his heart beat just a little faster. "You think this friend of yours could help?"

"More so than the Americans or the Swiss, I should think."

"And where could I find this friend of yours?"

"Oh, at the German Legation. He's a military attaché, so lonely, being apart from his family and all, quite pathetic. Not at all like you."

And what *am* I like? Andros asked himself. Elise was giving him what he had been after, but it had cost him his moral integrity. He had broken his vows to Aphrodite and slept with the enemy. How much more like the enemy would he have to become in order to win this war? It was a moot question, he realized grimly. Now that he was in the game, there was no room for wavering. "The German Legation, you say?"

"Yes, but he won't be in until Monday, which gives us the entire weekend together—"

"Darling," said Andros, completing the thought.

42

Major Ernst Dietrich, the assistant military attaché to the German Legation in Bern, was a stiff, wooden man with black hair cut short and a bored, dull face. After a lonely, uneventful weekend during which his mistress never returned his calls, he was in his office Monday morning, working through some papers, when his secretary came in and said that a certain Herr Andros was outside asking to see him.

Dietrich had never heard of any Andros, unless he was somehow connected with the shipping concern, and immediately was suspicious. All the same, he could use a diversion from his never-ending office chores.

"Show him in," he told his secretary, "but come back in a few minutes to remind me that my other appointment is waiting."

The secretary disappeared, and Dietrich pulled open his drawer and pushed a button to begin recording. As an officer in the Abwehr, he was always interested in a possible tip, although one rarely came knocking at his door—not one that was genuine, anyway.

When Herr Andros entered, Dietrich was surprised to see a young, handsome Greek-American in a Savile Row suit. Dietrich had been expecting someone older and more distinguished-looking.

"Herr Dietrich," said Andros as they shook hands. "Elise DeMoulin recommended I see you."

That explains the lonely weekend, thought Dietrich. "Please, sit down, Herr Andros."

Andros took a seat, and Dietrich sized him up as yet another of Agent Barracuda's small fish, thrown his way because she and the SD did not deem the Greek important enough to bother with. He would keep the conversation as brief as possible.

"How can the German Legation help you?"

"It is I who wish to help you, Herr Dietrich," said Andros. "I propose a business arrangement that would be of mutual benefit."

"What sort of business arrangement?" Dietrich asked, unable to think of anything of value that this man could offer him.

"Smuggling," Andros said. "I offer you regular, reliable passage through the Allied blockade."

Dietrich leaned back in his chair and eyed his visitor. The Allied blockade had been in effect since 1939, the result of which was that no shipments destined for Switzerland, whether on Allied or neutral ships, were allowed into the ports earmarked for handling Swiss imports unless accompanied by the corresponding permit or so-called navicert. "How would you manage that, Herr Andros?"

"I am here on a humanitarian mission to secure Red Cross supplies for the people of Greece," Andros explained. "In the process, I have also managed to secure safe passage for my other commercial vessels that fly the Swiss flag and are bound for neutral ports." He produced the certificates with British letterheads, notifications that would allow passage of such ships through the blockade.

To Dietrich's amazement, the documents actually appeared genuine. "Herr Andros, where did you get these?"

"Courtesy of the blockade authority," Andros said. "Normally, navicerts are issued on an individual basis and only after the exporting firm has filed a special application. Under the new inverted system, the blockade authority issues the Swiss government a block permission to distribute navicerts for agreed-upon quantities of imports. Thanks to my contacts in the Swiss government, Andros Shipping has been authorized to carry the bulk of the latest consignments, about forty thousand tons, under the Swiss flag."

It made sense to Dietrich now. Perhaps Herr Andros was telling the truth. Perhaps not. Perhaps this was a trap.

"All you have to do," Andros went on, "is arrange for your consignments to be loaded in falsely marked crates at neutral ports of departure such as Rio, Stockholm, Lisbon, or Istanbul. Thanks to my navicerts, the Allies will then allow my ships safe passage through the blockade to the designated Swiss ports of Genoa, Trieste, and Marseille, all of which are occupied by the Axis. There we unload the consignments, and you can carry them by rail to Germany or any destination you like."

Dietrich considered what this man was saying but could only wonder why he should come to the legation in broad daylight, when his visit could be spotted so easily by Allied spies and Swiss Bupo. He handed the navicerts back. "Tell me, Herr Andros, why would you jeopardize your neutrality to help the Axis?"

Andros looked a bit sheepish. "I must confess that I first approached the American Legation here with the idea. But they accused me of already doing for Germany what I am proposing to you. That is why Andros Shipping is on the blacklist." He threw up his hands in a gesture of futility. "If such is my position with the Allies, I might as well be compensated."

"What form of compensation do you seek?"

"A hundred thousand American dollars."

"One hundred thousand dollars!"

At that moment Dietrich's secretary returned to remind him that his nonexistent appointment was waiting.

"That is not within my authority," Dietrich concluded, although the prospect of establishing a secret, secure supply route through the blockade under the noses of the Allies was too attractive to pass up. "Excuse me for a moment, please."

He left Andros waiting in his office and darted to Herr Kocher's suite. Inside the large, tastefully appointed room, he found the German minister seated behind a huge desk below an equally imposing oil painting of Hitler. Seated opposite him, to Dietrich's surprise, was the SD's top agent in Bern, the Barracuda herself. Once again Dietrich realized he was the last man in the know, for as he approached Herr Kocher's desk, Elise gave him a defiant smile and demanded, "Well?"

Dietrich, resigned to the probability that the minister knew more about the situation than he did, explained, "Andros wants to strike a deal with us, Herr Kocher, to smuggle supplies through the

Allied blockade. The navicerts have already been issued. He wants one hundred thousand American dollars."

The minister exchanged glances with the Barracuda before he leaned back in his chair and looked at Dietrich pensively. "This must be a trap, a trick to compromise us," Kocher responded. "Suppose this Andros is an agent provocateur, here to make a deal with us and then expose us. His rendezvous with us is proof enough to the Swiss to have us kicked out of the country."

"I have investigated Andros thoroughly," the Barracuda assured the German ambassador with what Dietrich considered unnerving confidence. "I can confirm that he is a blacklisted businessman in danger of losing Andros Shipping altogether without some immediate hard currency. He also strikes me as a man who would go to any extreme to obtain what he wants."

"But one hundred thousand dollars—so large a sum," Kocher said.

"I didn't say that's what he wanted, Herr Kocher," said the Barracuda. "He could very well be a spy. But whatever he's after is worth our attention."

"Whatever he's after, I'm in no position to grant him, certainly not one hundred thousand dollars," said Kocher. "Dietrich, you inform Herr Andros that we'll be in touch. When you return, we'll draft a cable to Berlin to see how we are to proceed."

43

The cable from Berlin was on Commandant Buzzini's desk by noon. Unfortunately, it was in a sealed envelope, so the Italian couldn't read what Berlin had forwarded to General von Berg.

Buzzini looked at the "most urgent, most secret" envelope in his hand. What sort of mysterious correspondences did the good Baron have with Berlin? And what sort of nefarious Nazi work proceeded within the Achillion that he—the commander of an island occupied by Italian forces, no less—was not allowed to know?

Before Buzzini knew what he was doing, he had torn open the envelope and found himself staring at gibberish. They've coded it, he realized with horror. He would need von Berg's personal key to decipher it. He got on the phone. "Sergeant Racini, come here immediately."

The sergeant from Palermo appeared instantly and could see the panic in his superior's eyes. "What is it, Commandant?"

"This cable for the Baron. I've opened it by mistake."

Sergeant Racini's eyes widened. "You have opened the Baron's mail?"

"Yes. From Berlin."

"Mother of God!" cried Racini.

"Fortunately, it is encoded, so I have not comprehended its contents."

Sergeant Racini sighed in relief.

Buzzini asked, "Can we reseal it somehow?"

Racini looked at it and shook his head. "The risk is too great that he would know it had been opened and resealed."

Buzzini paced the floor nervously. "Then I want you to deliver it to him personally. With my apologies."

"Surely you cannot ask me—"

"Go, Racini. He is at the Achillion." Sensing the sergeant's hesitation, Buzzini barked, "Now, Sergeant."

Sergeant Racini picked up the cable with trembling fingers and left the office. Buzzini looked out the window and watched Racini's staff car drive off toward the Achillion. Then he sat down at his desk and wiped his brow.

44

In his underground laboratory hundreds of feet beneath the Achillion, von Berg was talking with his chief physicist when Franz came in with word that a Sergeant Racini was outside with a signal from Berlin.

Von Berg frowned. "Why didn't you take it?"

"He insists he deliver it to you personally."

"I see." Von Berg looked around the cavernous facility. A thousand centrifuges whirled while scientists and engineers in white jackets monitored their controls. With Hitler's weapons conference only one week away, time was running out. "I wonder what Berlin wants now." He turned to his physicist. "Dr. Reinholt, you may proceed," he instructed, and left with Franz.

They entered a maze of underground corridors. As they passed, Waffen SS guards posted at key intersections smacked their leather boots together and gave von Berg stiff-armed salutes. They were yet another precaution of von Berg's to protect this vast research and development complex he had constructed beneath what to the British, the Greeks, and even the Germans appeared to be an ordinary residential estate on an island naval installation manned by an Italian garrison.

It was here in these secret laboratories that Germany's best scientists, plucked from their respective industries by von Berg, worked around the clock. Not to develop new and better chemical weapons for use on the Russian front, nor to produce the rocket fuel for von Braun's A-4 rockets that Hitler had been demanding. Nor to chase Hitler's Greek Fire. No, a project as important as the *Flammenschwert*—Germany's first atomic bomb—required single-minded devotion and zero interference from Berlin. Here his scientists could proceed unencumbered by the uncertain whims of the Führer that so often impeded any real progress in weapons development.

Raw materials and supplies for his atomic program were easy to come by. Von Berg simply performed the same maneuvers for himself that he did for the German navy and, later, for Himmler in breaking the Versailles Treaty: They came into Piraeus on Andros ships in crates marked as grain and food. From there he slipped them onto Corfu via submarine and assembled them here in this underground facility.

They emerged into the cavernous loading bay where von Berg's submarine, the *Nausicaa*, was being serviced by her crew. Rounding the horseshoe quay, they passed a pile of crates and stepped into an elevator. The doors closed, and they ascended through hundreds of feet of rock to his study in the Achillion.

A few minutes later, von Berg walked down the front steps of the Achillion and saw the rat Racini. "Yes, Sergeant," he said in a manner that made his irritation plain to the Italian. "What is it that is so urgent?"

"This cable came for you from Berlin, General von Berg." The sergeant held out the envelope with an unsteady hand.

Franz took the envelope, examined it, and passed it to von Berg. "It's been opened."

"So it has." Von Berg looked at the cable inside. "Franz, please take this inside and translate it while I dismiss the sergeant here." Franz left, and von Berg looked at Racini. "The commandant's negligence I've long suspected, but treason? What do you have to say about that, Sergeant?"

"It was an accident, General. An accident. I swear to God." Racini's voice was shaking. "The commandant, he thought it was for him."

Von Berg held up the envelope. "But of course, Sergeant. Seeing as how the outside clearly has my name in German, I understand how the good commandant could make such a silly mistake."

"He is terribly sorry, General. Terribly sorry. I am terribly sorry, too."

"Yes, I am sure you are. Now go back and tell Buzzini he is lucky this time that the dispatch is ciphered."

"And why is that, General, sir, if I may ask?"

"Because he can now live a little longer."

With that, von Berg walked up the steps into the Achillion, took an immediate right past the chapel, and walked back down the hallway to his study, where Franz sat with the Sonlar decoding machine, translating the cipher.

It was from Bern. The Barracuda reported that she had searched Andros's belongings, slept with him, and come to the conclusion that he was a genuine dupe. A full report was forthcoming, complete with photographs.

"So, Andros wants to do business," mused von Berg as he read the signal, "and wants one hundred thousand American dollars for it. Not quite the saintly icon Aphrodite paints of him, Franz."

"No, Herr Oberstgruppenführer."

Von Berg walked over to his wall safe behind the portrait of King Ludwig II and turned the dial several times to unlock the thick steel door. "Indeed, for a man who has pledged his love to one woman only, Herr Andros seems quite willing to accommodate the Barracuda's advances. Unless the Barracuda has once again over-estimated her charms."

Von Berg opened the door to reveal several stacks of papers along with his leather briefcase. He placed the signal inside his file marked ANDROS. He then pulled out a red folder labeled FLAMMEN-SCHWERT, looked at it for a moment thoughtfully, and put it back, shutting the safe and sliding the portrait over the door.

Franz asked, "So you think he's a spy?"

"Let's just say I'm wary of Greeks bearing gifts," von Berg replied. "This Red Cross ruse is obviously an excuse for something else, and not just to see Aphrodite. Greek channels in the Middle East probably tipped him off that she was helping to distribute food supplies in Athens. Why else would such a worthless individual make this sort of noble gesture?"

Franz shrugged.

Von Berg sat down behind his desk and drummed his fingers on the leather top. Hitler's weapons conference and von Berg's fortieth birthday were only a week away. Now that the fulfillment of his destiny finally was within his grasp, he suddenly felt vulnerable. Things were proceeding smoothly in the labs, but his timetable had been designed to tick away like a fine Swiss watch in the final days, and the unexpected arrival of Chris Andros was throwing off the second hand.

"Still," he mused, "this proposal deserves a response."

"Do you want him killed?"

"Oh, no. Not yet." Von Berg shook his head. "That would be terrible. Make him a martyr in Aphrodite's eyes, and he'd be immortal. No, Franz. She can never love me fully as long as she loves this distorted conception of Andros; he is more myth than man. We must destroy this image first, expose him for the fraud he truly is."

Franz furrowed his brow. "How do you mean?"

"Why, do business with him. Bring him to Athens, let Aphrodite see for herself what kind of coward he is. Then we can kill him, and it will be no loss to her."

Franz nodded. "Yes, I see. But at this delicate stage in your operations, do you think it's wise to allow yourself to be distracted?"

He pondered Franz's question for a moment. To unmask Aphrodite's idealized Andros as rabble was no distraction, he decided. She prized her freedom, so he would give her a choice, but he would make sure he was the better man for her to choose. To win her heart and kill Hitler at the same time would be the fulfillment of all his dreams. He could capture sanity itself and secure his future.

"Inform Bern that they are to permit Herr Andros safe passage to Greece," he told Franz. "They have forty-eight hours to make the necessary arrangements and issue the official papers. And tell Buzzini that Aphrodite will fly out this afternoon for Athens. You and I will be leaving tomorrow."

"Anything else?" Franz asked.

Von Berg stood up and walked across the floor to the glass case containing the Maranatha text. He leaned over and looked at the papyrus, pondering the significance of recent events and what seemed to him a fantastic convergence of the cosmos.

"Yes," he replied. "Inform the house staff that while we're gone, a certain Dr. Xaptz will be arriving at the Achillion as my guest. He does not know why. He is to be allowed access only to the upper floors of the palace and the Maranatha text in my study. Once he is here he cannot speak to anybody outside the house staff, in person or by phone. Until Aphrodite and I return together from Athens one week from today, Dr. Xaptz is not to leave here alive."

"*Zu Befehl,*" Franz replied automatically. "And then?"

Von Berg smiled. "Then it's off to Obersalzberg to make history."

45

There was music on the terrace of the Kursaal that evening when Andros and Elise came out from the little casino's gaming room. Here the gardens commanded a superb view of the Alps with the city of Bern in the foreground.

"I can only thank the Maker that the *boule* table has a five-franc limit," Andros said, looking up at the stars. "Between that and your little shopping sprees, Elise, you've drained my family fortune during our time together."

He looked at her in the dim light of a nearby lantern. Tonight she was wearing a stylish caramel-colored suit with a white silk blouse. The jacket was padded at the shoulders and nipped tight at the waist. Her snug-fitting skirt hugged her hips. All paid for by Andros; he would pass the cost along to the OSS.

She laughed and playfully stroked the sleeve of his white dinner jacket. "But the night is young, darling, and there is so much more we can see and do."

He thought they had done it all. He was tired of this ruse. He was tired of looking at her perfect features and scheming blue eyes. He decided to take advantage of the music and light atmosphere of the Kursaal gardens to bring up his visit to the German Legation. "Speaking of sightseeing," he began, "I saw your friend the other morning while you were shopping."

"I know, darling." Her voice was sad now.

"You do?"

"Why else would he call me this afternoon and tell me to give you this?" She produced an envelope from her fashionable purse. "Oh, do open it, Chris. I'm anxious to see how much time we have to spend together."

He opened it to see a train ticket for a one-way trip down the

Simplon railway to Brindisi, an Italian port on the Adriatic. From there, said the accompanying instructions, a boat would ferry him over to Greece. In the meantime, he was to maintain his room at the Bellevue Palace Hotel, where he would return after his conference with Germany's chief of Swiss industrial transportation, a certain Baron von Berg. Andros kept his best straight face as he looked up at Elise.

"What is it, darling?" she asked, trying to sound innocent.

He put on a brave show. "I'm afraid the money supply is low. It seems the man I need to see is in Athens."

"But, darling, are you sure?"

He looked at the ticket. It was stamped with that day's date: May 27, 1943. The train would leave at six. His watch told him it was already five. They weren't giving him much time. He folded the envelope and slipped it in his suit. "I'm afraid so."

"Oh, do be careful, Chris. I fear for you."

"I fear for myself should I stay with you, Elise. You're quite expensive." He gazed at the pretty face next to him, at this vain woman of undeniable charm.

She kissed him, and it felt almost genuine. "Oh, Chris, darling. You won't forget me?"

"How could I ever forget you, Elise?"

But he was looking at the Alps, thinking of what lay beyond. Twilight had melted the snowcapped peaks into a monolithic mound, an ominous black curtain through which he was about to pass. The other side promised another face, not quite as clear as the one next to him, but dearest to his heart.

46

The town of Brig slid away as the train Andros was on pulled out of the last station in Switzerland.

Several more châteaus and a castle moved by, and Andros caught a final glimpse of the Weisshorn and Mischabel mountain groups before the track curved toward the Simplon Tunnel, the longest in the world. Halfway through the twelve-mile corridor, under seven thousand feet of alpine mountain, they would cross the frontier between neutral Switzerland and Axis territory, and there would be no turning back.

He felt a sense of exhilaration, the same exhilaration he experienced after his first parachute jump at West Point. To be sure, the Germans in Bern had given him no guarantee of their cooperation, and the risks ahead were even greater. But he had cleared the first hurdle. Tomorrow evening he would make his connection with a ship in Brindisi. He was on his way home.

A few minutes later, there was a sharp rap on the door of his compartment. It was the Swiss porter, and with him was an Italian customs official. They addressed him in English. "Passport, *signore*."

Andros felt for the papers in his suit pocket and pulled out his special German diplomatic courier visa.

The Italian examined the passport and eyed him with a mixture of curiosity and fear. "Your destination, *signore*?"

"Brindisi. I have a trunk with me, too. Do you need to see that?"

"Trunks will be examined when we pull into Domodossola. We are just examining passports and hand luggage now." The Italian returned his papers. *"Grazie, signore."*

The door shut, and Andros settled back comfortably in his compartment. They were fast approaching the mouth of the tunnel, and soon he was swallowed by the darkness.

47

The outer harbor of Brindisi hummed as the dockers loaded the last stores onto the *Independence,* a Greek freighter from Andros Shipping that was part of the convoy about to depart Italy for Greece.

On the bridge was Captain Paniotis Tsatsos, a big, hairy bull of a man in a sailor's top and black baggy pants. He had a handlebar mustache, and his dark, swarthy face was crowned by silvery hair under a Greek captain's cap. He was barking orders between the steady stream of curses with which his Greek crew was well accustomed. Now that Andros ships, like all Greek ships, were banned by the British from sailing the Mediterranean, Captain Tsatsos was reduced to short runs between Italy and Greece. That meant spending less time with his first love—the sea—and more time holed up in ports dealing with German and Italian authorities. It made him more ornery than ever.

Tsatsos was now arguing with the commander of the Italian gun crew, Lieutenant Lamas, a thin fellow in uniform with a thin nose and thin mustache. They were leaning over the chart table, going over the route to Piraeus, when there was a shout from the deck.

Tsatsos looked up from his charts. Coming up the quay was a man in civilian clothes flanked by two Italian officers—the convoy commander and the port officer.

"What is it now?" he complained to Lamas. "The holds are full, and the deck is already a hazard with all the extra stores."

"Easy, old man," said the Italian. "I'll go see what they want."

Lamas went down the ladder, and Tsatsos watched him greet the party on the deck. They were too far away for Tsatsos to hear anything, but there was something about the civilian that seemed familiar to the old sea captain. He turned to his first mate, the clean-cut Karapis. "Give me your field glasses."

Tsatsos took the glasses and fixed the sights on the civilian. He could hardly believe his eyes. "Look!" he cried. "It is Christos Andros."

"The son of General Andros?" Karapis said. "Impossible. He's in America, been there for years."

"Heh?" Tsatsos pulled down the glasses and gave his first mate a sharp look. "I was sailing ships when you were bathed in a tub by your mother. You don't tell me it's impossible. Look for yourself." He was about to hand Karapis the field glasses when Lieutenant Lamas returned to the bridge.

"You have a passenger," the Italian announced. "A diplomat, it seems. The naval escorts can't take him because he's a civilian. Regulations. He says he would like to lie down and get some rest."

Tsatsos exchanged glances with Karapis. "My cabin is his, Lieutenant."

The Italian disappeared, and the old captain looked at his first mate and said, "Diplomat, my eye, Karapis. I taught that boy how to play his first *rembetika* song on the *bouzouki*. You think I can't recognize him? It is Christos Andros, I tell you."

48

Andros woke up when one of the ship's mates came in with coffee on a brass tray.

"South American," the sailor said, setting the tray down on the captain's desk. He offered Andros a cup. "Compliments of the captain."

Andros sat up on his bunk and took a sip. The cabin was quite spacious, with wood-paneled walls and a blackened porthole behind the desk.

"You've slept for hours," the sailor observed. "Captain Tsatsos sent me. He invites you to the bridge."

Old Tsatsos, here? Andros thought. The news was as much a shock for him as seeing the *Independence* flying the Italian flag. So much of a shock that Andros realized he wasn't as prepared as he had thought he was to see these faces from the past. Even now motion sickness, or something worse, was setting in. Perhaps it was the faint scent of hashish Andros detected in the room. Old Tsatsos was a smoker, one who refused to permit trifles like the law to stand in the way of his simple pleasures.

"All right," Andros replied, taking a gulp of coffee. "Let's go."

A baby-blue dawn was coming up over the sea when Andros went up on deck. They had just passed through the Corinth Canal, which was situated at the narrow bridge of land that connected the Peloponnese to the rest of Greece. Behind them was the Ionian Sea and before them the Aegean.

He found the captain on the bridge, standing behind the helmsman, barking orders as the ship's engines shifted below them. Tsatsos looked as crusty as ever.

"And how is our special guest the diplomat?" the captain asked playfully, fixing a knowing smile on Andros.

"Some motion sickness."

"You never liked the sea,"Tsatsos said cautiously.

"You never sailed still waters. . . ."

Tsatsos burst into a smile and embraced him. "*Yassou,* Christos!"

"You old sea dog!" Andros lifted his cup of coffee. "I see the war hasn't deprived you of the finer things. Where did you get this?"

"Why, that comes courtesy of Yanis Darprou of the *Minos.*"

"The *Minos*?" asked Andros. "But that ship is under Swiss registry. Where on earth did you link up?"

"Last month in Trieste,"Tsatsos explained. "The *Minos* had just come back from Brazil with a shipment of groundnuts and coffee beans for the Swiss. Whenever we're in the same port with another Andros ship, no matter what flag it flies, we trade."

"Under the noses of the Axis?"

The old rogue grinned. "All things are possible once you acquire a working knowledge of the black markets, young Christos. Bribery and other practices we regard as dishonorable are the everyday norm for these Axis officials. Indeed, not only can the disciples of the New Order be bought for a price, but they even pay us to keep our mouths shut, doubling our profits."

"Pay you?" Andros asked. "Whatever for?"

"Those groundnuts bound for Switzerland? The crates were transferred to the *Independence* while we were docked in Trieste. We brought them with us into Piraeus. The sentries patrolling the docks, the customs agents, they all turned a blind eye. So did we, for a price."

Andros said, "Sounds like a lot of trouble to smuggle groundnuts."

"Ah, but those crates did not have just groundnuts," said Tsatsos. "I checked for myself, I did. This wasn't the first time I carried mislabeled crates from Trieste into Greece."

Andros was fascinated by what old Tsatsos was telling him. "And what did you find?"

"Metallic uranium deposits,"Tsatsos said. "For what, I have no idea. It's bad enough knowing we have explosives on board half the time without worrying what else we might be carrying. I can only hold my breath and pray we don't blow up. At least with your father, there was a reason for such madness."

"There was?" asked Andros, uncertain of what Tsatsos was saying.

"The arms from Germany we slipped to Franco, to fight the Communists," Tsatsos explained. "Your grandfather Basil, he would have none of it, but your father, he knew better."

"Always," Andros replied dryly.

"It is his example that has given us the hope to go on." Tsatsos took off his hat in solemn remembrance. "Why, it was two years ago this Saturday that he died on Crete during the German invasion." He paused and then looked at Andros. "But enough of these sad songs. Even now Athens is alive with rumors of an Allied invasion. Your uncle Mitchell says the Germans confirm their fear with troop movements and defense buildups along the coastal areas."

"Is that so?" asked Andros. "Uncle Mitchell . . . he's at the house in Kifissia?"

"Moved in with the rest of the family as soon as your father died, before the Germans could requisition it without bloodshed."

"I see."

Tsatsos stopped, his face serious. "But tell me, what is the reason for this dangerous journey? Why now?"

Andros paused, remembering his childhood trips to the docks with the old captain and the mournful *rembetika* songs Tsatsos taught him to play on the *bouzouki* before his upper-crust grandfather took away the stringed instrument and forbade him to play the blues music of the Greek lower classes. But things were different now. *He* was supposed to be different. However much he wanted to be himself with his old friend, he couldn't. So he said, "I'm afraid it's not mine to say, Captain. Not now. Perhaps not ever. You must accept this."

Tsatsos wasn't pleased. Andros could see it in the old captain's eyes. But Tsatsos was one who knew better than to ask questions. He simply pointed and said, "Look, we've come!"

Andros followed the old man's thick finger as it stretched out over the blue waters of the Saronic Gulf. There, behind the veil of morning mist, was the harbor of Piraeus, and beyond it, Athens.

49

The sun was rising over Algiers when the young aide showed an exhausted but excited Captain Erin Whyte to the terrace of the Moorish villa at Dar el Ouad, headquarters of the supreme allied commander of the North African theater.

She found Churchill seated outside in one of the wickerwork chairs, hunched over a map of Greece spread across two trestle tables. He was wearing a light suit and dark tie. The aide disappeared through the French doors, leaving her alone before the great man.

"General Eisenhower is out riding and won't be back for another hour," Churchill said without looking up from the map. "You have news for me?"

"Yes, sir," Erin replied. "Colonel Huntington at Maison Blanche asked me to pass this along to you." She handed him a signal. "It's from Bern. Dulles says Andros was last seen at the railway station, boarding a train bound for Italy."

"Italy?" Churchill read the signal and nodded with visible excitement. "That must mean they'll ferry him over to Greece."

"They already have, sir." Erin passed a second signal along to Churchill. "SOE Cairo got word from Touchstone in Athens. Andros is arriving in Piraeus this morning aboard his own ship, the *Independence*."

"Really, his own ship?" Churchill read the signal with an expression that Erin thought bordered on admiration. "Von Berg certainly has an original touch," he commented. He looked up at her and said, "Touchstone also says the Baron arrived by plane in Athens yesterday, and Miss Vasilis the day before."

"Yes, sir."

"But we have no idea where they came from?"

"None, sir."

Churchill frowned. "Sit down, Captain." He gestured to a wickerwork chair and opened a file. "I confess I'm having second thoughts about dropping you into the Parnon Mountains to link up with the Greek *andartes.*"

Churchill's second thoughts didn't surprise her. She'd been through this with every male officer who briefed her before a mission, and she resented it. It was only a matter of time before the subject of Lyon would come up. "I've already gone over the flight route with MacDonald at the air base, sir," Erin replied. "He sees no problems. To him, I'm just another supply drop."

"Yes," said Churchill, "but to me you're still a woman, and a rather young woman at that." He glanced at the file. "Why, you're barely older than Andros."

"Old enough to have survived two separate missions to France, sir."

"So I see," said Churchill. "It says here you were caught by the Gestapo in Lyon and were raped before you made a miraculous escape, killing"—here he did a double take—"*eight* SS guards in the process. Unarmed, no less."

Lyon was the nightmare of her life; the mere mention of it brought on horrific chills. It was all she could do to suppress her emotions and not break down before the prime minister. She crossed her legs and said in a determined voice, "An unpleasant experience, sir. But I'm over it."

"Are you?" Churchill closed the file and eyed her. "According to this, you've quit your psychotherapy and have had problems taking orders from senior officers such as Colonel Prestwick. That's why you're a training instructor and not an agent in the field. Nobody can trust you."

The pang of disappointment she felt at that moment was dimmed only by her repulsion at Churchill for bringing her this news. Here she was, she thought, only hours away from parachuting behind enemy lines, beginning to wonder who the enemy really was. Churchill might as well have said she was to blame for Lyon. Or that it was her fault that both her male psychoanalysts had tried to join her on the couch. Churchill was beginning to sound like all the rest, ready to use her now and blame her later. Men, she cursed, they're all alike. That being the case, she'd rather face her fears than talk about them—or worse, run from them.

"Therapy has worked wonders for me, sir," she answered dryly. "I'm ready to go back in the field."

"You realize that you'll be fighting an uphill battle to win the respect of the Greek partisans, not to mention eluding SS storm troopers?"

"Of course I do, sir."

"Well, Captain, here are the new operation orders from the GHQ Middle East that you are to personally deliver to the National Bands of Greece."

Churchill gave her the top-secret enciphered directive with these ends spelled out:

1. *In event of invasion of the mainland of Greece:* to harass enemy lines of communication and generally to support invasion plans.
2. *If Axis troops attempt a general withdrawal from Greece or become disaffected:* to attack, harass, and pursue them.
3. *Should neither of the above occur:* to be ready at a later date and, at the right moment, to promote general, organized, and coordinated revolt.

Erin frowned and passed the order back to Churchill, who lit the corner of the paper with the burning end of his Havana and dropped it into the Arabic ashtray.

"Something the matter, Captain?"

"I think it's unconscionable to raise false hopes and mislead the Greeks into believing the U.S. Marines are on the way when that simply isn't so. We're invading Sicily."

Churchill nodded as if he had anticipated her objection. "If the Greek *andartes* don't believe the Allied invasion is coming, Captain, then neither will the Germans."

"But we're encouraging the Greeks to prematurely attack the German occupational forces in the false hope that we'll be there to support them in large numbers. We're sacrificing human lives for a lie, sir."

"There are other forces at work here, Captain, forces that even Prestwick and the Americans aren't aware of." Churchill looked down at the map of Greece. "As things stand, the Greek Resistance is in a state of virtual civil war between the right-wing National Democratic Army of Greece—EDES—and the left-wing National Popular Liberation Army—ELAS. Unfortunately, EDES is no match for ELAS."

"I'm aware of the situation, sir," Erin assured him. "Our senior liaison to the National Bands, Colonel James Doughty, used to head the Greek desk at SOE Cairo. He's been sending regular reports in from the field on the wireless."

"Then you're aware that ELAS is the military arm of the National Liberation Front, the largest and most powerful organization in Greece today," Churchill went on. "Bills itself as a popular movement and has recruited thousands of good Greeks. But Doughty and our other liaison officers in Greece believe it's controlled by the KKE."

That was the Communist Party of Greece, established by the Soviet Comintern, Stalin's international organization that exported communism abroad. Erin said, "I didn't know that."

"Neither do many Greeks," said Churchill. "But today the National Popular Liberation Army almost completely dominates free Greece and exists in practically every town and village. Indeed, ELAS lays claim to being the regular army of 'Free Greece.' Full-scale elections are being planned after the Germans leave. I need not stress to you how harmful it would be to Greek interests if the Communists gained power after the war."

Not to mention British interests, Erin thought. "In other words, that's why you set up the National Bands as an umbrella organization to coordinate the Resistance. You want to strengthen the republican-backed National Democratic Army in order to check

ELAS and prevent a Communist monopoly of power when Greece is finally liberated."

"I want to ensure that Greece doesn't slide into Stalin's sphere of influence," Churchill explained, "or else we'll be worse off when this war is over than when it began. The last thing we need is for Russia to have a stronghold in the Mediterranean. She'd dominate southern Europe and have easy access to the Middle East. Change the balance of power forever. We have future wars to think of, Captain."

"But we already have a senior liaison officer to the National Bands," she said. "Why send me?"

"Because I believe Stalin has planted a double agent within the ranks of the National Bands," Churchill told her. "A triple agent, in fact. Somebody who is passing along vital information from the GHQ Middle East to the Germans in Greece, information that betrays the location of our supply drops to non-Communist resistance forces and thus compromises their security to the Gestapo. Apparently, the Communists have discovered it's cheaper to get the occupying Axis troops to do their dirty work for them. Meanwhile, they make overtures of peace toward us."

So this was the real reason behind Churchill's Greek adventure. Erin could see it all now. "You think Colonel Doughty could be a Soviet spy?"

Churchill shook his head. "Who this triple agent is, we don't know—only that he goes by the code name of the Minotaur."

"And you want me to find out who this Minotaur is."

"That's right," said Churchill. "And Chris Andros is the key."

"Andros?" Erin started. "Then you believe he might actually steal the Maranatha text?"

"I have my hopes, Captain," said Churchill. "But it really doesn't matter. As much of a coward as we might have made him appear to the Germans, Chris Andros is still the son of General Nicholas Andros. His arrival in Athens will be perceived as a political event of the first order as far as the Greek Resistance is concerned. You can be sure that republicans and Communists alike won't take too kindly to the homecoming of a royalist."

"But he's not a royalist, sir," Erin corrected. "He told me himself that he hopes Greece would form a republic based on the American model."

"He's not a royalist—yet," said Churchill. "But he will be once he sees that the return of the monarchy is the only platform from which democratic reforms can take root in Greece. In any case, the prevailing perception of Andros is that he's a chip off his old royalist father's block. That may smoke out the Minotaur if he takes action. At the very least, if by some good fortune Andros actually comes out of Athens alive, I don't want him to reach the National Bands base only to have his throat cut."

Erin understood, and she realized something else. "So the submarine pickup with Prestwick is for me alone."

"And the Maranatha text, Captain," added Churchill. "Andros will stay behind to head the National Bands. By the time the Allies come around to liberating Greece, Andros will have earned the favor of the Greek people, thanks to his leadership within the Resistance. Also, as head of Andros Shipping, he will have the instant respect of the international business community and help restore the kingdom of Greece to its rightful place among the economies of Western Europe."

"You mean democracies, sir, don't you?"

"That's right, democracies," said Churchill. "So you see, I haven't written Andros off just yet. I have plans for him. Big plans. Plans to give Greece a future and a hope. I made a promise to General Andros and the Greek people. Keeping it is the least we can do for the cradle of Western civilization. Wouldn't you agree, Theseus?"

"Theseus?" Erin repeated.

"That's your code name," said Churchill. "That's how you'll identify yourself to all our agents in Greece."

Erin sat back in her seat. "Isn't that a rather provocative code name under the circumstances, sir?" she asked incredulously. "I mean, wasn't Theseus the name of the Athenian prince of Greek mythology who entered the labyrinth and slew the Minotaur?"

"Ah, then you know how the story is supposed to end, Captain," said Churchill, tossing the stub of his Havana into the ornamental ashtray. "For your sake and Andros's, see that there are no surprise endings. Remember, the Minotaur will be expecting you."

50

Prestwick moved out onto his terrace at the Hotel Saint George that morning and took in the spectacular view of the city below. Dazzling white terraces cascaded down the pine-covered hills to the ocean. The palm trees that lined the seafront boulevards swayed in the Mediterranean breeze.

"The French call the city *Alger la Blanche*—Algiers the White."

Prestwick turned from the terrace to see Erin standing in the living room. He hadn't heard her come in. But he certainly didn't mind. She looked ravishing in her uniform this morning, her earthy brown eyes as warm as ever and her ethereal blond hair catching some of the sunlight. "So I see," he told her as he stepped back inside. "Quite lovely."

She seemed to pick up his hint, because the corners of her mouth tightened, and she was formal with him. "The Saint George used to be the personal headquarters of the supreme commander before he moved to that Moorish villa," she told him. "I trust you approve of your accommodations, Colonel."

"Who wouldn't? But I must confess that I was looking forward to a tour of our OSS headquarters at Maison Blanche, not to mention our special training school Club des Pines. I've heard much about our demolitions program with that new C-3 explosive the French call plastique. But I've been here ten days, and still I've seen nothing." He took a step toward her.

She didn't back away, but she sounded evasive. "General Eisenhower felt it best that you keep a low profile during your stay here."

Prestwick took that to mean that he wasn't welcome here, that he and his bungled Operation Maranatha were an embarrassment that Eisenhower wanted to sweep under some Oriental rug. That didn't surprise him. Traditional military types rarely appreciated the subtle, more sophisticated work of the OSS. "A low profile, you say?" he asked. "So you've just returned from the supreme commander?"

Erin nodded. "Even as we speak, Andros is arriving in Athens."

It was the first piece of good news he had heard in a long time. A very long time. He stroked his chin and nodded. "That's fantastic!"

"That's not all," said Erin. "Your presence is requested aboard His Majesty's submarine the *Cherub* tomorrow. If all goes as planned, I'll rendezvous with you off the coast of Greece in a few days."

"Even more fantastic!" Then he saw the champagne bottle in the silver bucket on the table by the wall. "This calls for a celebration, Captain." Prestwick rubbed his hands together and walked over to the table where the champagne waited. He removed the bottle from the bucket of melted ice and eased out the cork from the bottle.

"I don't think so," said Erin. "I need to rest before my parachute drop into Greece tomorrow night."

"Yes, yes, you do that," said Prestwick, pouring slowly into two glasses. "In the meantime, however, I propose a toast."

Erin eyed him. "Is a toast all you're proposing, Jason?"

Prestwick smiled and handed her a glass. "Think about what we could do before your flight tomorrow, Erin. We could sip cold champagne, share a hot bath, and dance on the rooftop all night long."

"Or," she replied, staring down into her champagne, "we could simply save the celebrating until after Andros has accomplished his mission."

"To Chris Andros, then," he toasted. "May he retrieve the Maranatha text and find the meaning of the universe." He raised his glass to his lips and was on the verge of tasting the sweetness of success when she stopped him with her next remark.

"The meaning of the universe?" she asked, a frown on her face. "Is that what you really expect to find?"

He lowered his glass. "No, of course not. I was being facetious. There is no meaning. What's the matter with you?"

"You can believe what you want about the Maranatha text," she told him firmly, glaring at him. "But the mysteries of life can't be reduced to numbers. And even if you could see the future, without love, you're nothing."

"Did you say 'love'?" He looked at her and wanted to tell her she looked lovely when she was angry. "What are you driving at?"

"It was your fascination with futile speculations that got us into this mess," she said, setting her glass on the table. "But it will be Andros and his love for Aphrodite that will get us out."

"Is that so?" He flashed a conspiratorial grin. "According to what Dulles says in Bern, it was Andros's performance in bed with a Nazi spy that's gotten him this far."

The sting of disappointment was plain on Erin Whyte's face, and Prestwick took perverse delight in it.

"Did you train him for that, Captain?" he taunted her, pressing himself against her supple body. "Do you want to train me?"

"I taught him a lot of things," Erin replied calmly, "the last of which I'll show you first."

A tremendous explosion of pain erupted between Prestwick's legs. His face pinched in a grimace before his jaw dropped in a low groan.

Then Erin removed her knee from his groin, smiled, and sipped her champagne.

51

As the *Independence* moved into the great harbor, Andros could feel himself trembling with excitement. Here was Athens, the ancient capital of Western civilization. Here was home. He beheld the whitewashed city in wonder. The last time he'd felt such a sensation was on his first visit to America, when the ocean liner entered New York Harbor and he saw the Statue of Liberty.

Rising above the city was the Acropolis, and on top of it the pillars of the Parthenon stood proudly against the clear blue sky. The symbol of democracy, though desecrated by the Nazi flag flying overhead, still inspired hope for freedom. The sacred sight aroused in Andros the same pride and devotion he felt for the American flag. If Western civilization had a moral compass, his grandfather used to say, this was its true north.

Andros felt a hand on his shoulder. It was Tsatsos, who said, "Did you think the Parthenon would be gone when you came back?"

"To tell you the truth, I wasn't sure."

The old captain laughed. "And I tell you, it will still be standing long after these barbarians are gone."

The *Independence* dropped anchor, and the foul stench of defeat and occupation settled in. The Luftwaffe had bombed Piraeus more extensively than Andros had heard. As he surveyed the damage, he felt a surge of outrage.

"The German Stukas bombed the ports and ships, both war and merchant, as we were evacuating British troops to Crete," said Tsatsos. "Now it is the British RAF who raid the surrounding airfields and our ships."

The sober realization hit Andros that this was the last sight his father had had of the Greek mainland before he died. The memory of his father made him once again painfully aware that his own return to Greece wasn't at all what he'd been expecting. He was not in military uniform, disembarking from a troop transport. Rather, he was on his own family ship and dressed in civilian clothes. One man against the Third Reich.

And a powerful Reich it was. Patrolling the docks were SS guards toting Schmeissers. Rolls of barbed wire topped a concrete wall to shield the cargo ship as it sat at the water's edge.

Andros eyed the SS men as the gangway was lowered. "Baron von Berg's men?"

"They protect the transfer of his special shipments," Tsatsos said. "I see you are considered one of them."

As Tsatsos spoke, three black Mercedeses pulled up along the quay. Two men in black hats and overcoats stepped out of the first car.

"For me?" Andros asked.

"Gestapo," said Tsatsos, troubled. "They must be expecting you. Karapis, help our friend the diplomat with his luggage."

First Mate Karapis appeared with the trunk, which, like Andros, had survived the rigors of OSS training, a parachute drop into Switzerland, and the long journey to Athens.

Tsatsos glanced at the trunk and then fixed his dark, brooding eyes on Andros for a moment. "I don't know why you've chosen to come back, Christos," he said, his strong, rough hand gripping the scruff of Andros's neck. "But I must warn you to beware the kisses of an enemy, especially when you are among old friends."

"I take that to mean you harbor little love in your heart for collaborators?"

Tsatsos smiled broadly enough to reveal a few missing teeth. It was a menacing smile that required no explanation.

"Don't worry, old friend," said Andros as they parted. "Things aren't always as they seem."

He started down the gangway, Karapis and the trunk close behind. As soon as they reached the quay, the Gestapo agents relieved Karapis of the trunk and escorted Andros to the middle Mercedes. The driver got out and opened the rear door for him, and Andros heard a voice address him in coarse, ugly English.

"Welcome to Athens, Herr Andros. Please, climb in."

52

Andros got in and found himself sitting next to a young man not much older than he was. The man's smooth, pale features and almost white hair contrasted sharply with his dark suit. For a moment Andros thought his narrow eyes seemed to change color in the darkness of the cab, shifting from blue to gray to brown and then back to blue.

"Allow me to introduce myself, Herr Andros." His tone was oily. "My name is Werner. Jürgen Werner. I am an emissary of Baron Ludwig von Berg, your host. I am your escort to your family estate in Kifissia."

Werner extended his cold, clammy hand, and when Andros clasped it, a shiver raced up his arm. If this Werner was the kind of henchman von Berg surrounded himself with, Andros wondered what the Baron himself was like.

Then the door shut next to him, and the Mercedes started moving. "I wasn't expecting such a grand reception," Andros said.

"For your own protection, I assure you," Werner replied. "The Communists, they are everywhere, especially on the docks."

Andros glanced back at the shrinking port and could see Tsatsos and Karapis standing at the rail of the *Independence,* watching the motorcade leave the Piraeus district. Andros felt like he was six years old, returning from another day in Piraeus with his grandfather to the family's estate in Kifissia and having to endure the city sights in between. Once again he was catching a glimpse of how the majority lived, from the privileged comfort of a mobile observatory.

Athens had changed little since he last saw it six years before, except that it seemed grimier and even more disorganized under the occupation. The walls were littered with RAF slogans, old war posters, and various anti-Nazi graffiti. The Greek war cry, *"Aera,"* was chalked up everywhere in red and green. It meant "wind," as in "sweep them away like the wind."

The spirit of resistance was alive, Andros could see, though the flesh was weak. The back alleys revealed passing glimpses of barefoot children in rags picking through garbage heaps for scraps of food. If they could stay alive just a little longer, Andros thought, just until the liberation . . .

"I must say, Herr Werner," Andros observed, "your troops have given new meaning to the 'ruins of Athens.'"

"The German army did not come to Greece as an enemy but as a friend," Werner insisted, "to oust the British parasites who had been invited here by the criminal government of the Fourth of August. What you see is the destruction that plagued all of Greece during the British occupation."

"The British occupation"? thought Andros. Werner did have a way with words.

They were approaching Constitution Square. There was the old, aristocratic Hotel Grande Bretagne, host to so many of his childhood dances with Aphrodite. Now it was the headquarters for the German authorities. To their right was the Parliament building, useless since 1936, when Metaxas dissolved Parliament after the king had given him free rein. Andros remembered the furor surrounding the military crackdown. At least those were Greek troops in the city then. Now there were Axis sentries posted against the building's yellow walls and Axis tanks parked on its ramparts.

"I need not remind you, Herr Andros," Werner continued, "that the Germans helped Greece in her war of independence more than the British. What is now the Parliament was the original palace of Greece's first king, Otto, brother of King Ludwig of Bavaria."

What Werner failed to mention, thought Andros with a smile, was that the Greeks of Otto's day had kicked the seventeen-year-old monarch out.

Werner sighed. "If only King Otto's architects from Munich had proceeded with their plans for wide, straight thoroughfares, this could have been a great modern city. But the Greeks of his day complained they would bake on those boulevards without shade, and the shopkeepers would lose business on their little streets. As it is, the city is nothing but a labyrinth of twisting alleys and slums."

"Must make it difficult for you to track anybody down," Andros mused. "And so much easier to hide."

Werner had opened his mouth to reply when shouts came from the university. Andros looked out the window to his left and saw a motorized Axis column, four abreast, charging down University Street. He turned to Werner, who looked ahead stiffly.

"Unfortunately, Herr Andros, Communist-inspired elements remain unfriendly to the New Order and have yet to embrace the great ideals of national socialism. They disguise themselves as student demonstrators and insist on inciting riots and disturbing the public. The Italian *carabinieri* often must disperse them with bullets."

"Good riddance," said Andros, deciding now was the time to play the snob. "But don't such actions put a damper on the social life here?"

"Not at all," Werner replied, visibly pleased with the turn in his guest's attitude. "Baron von Berg sees to that."

"Baron von Berg," repeated Andros. "Yes, you must tell me more about him. All they told me in Bern was that he is some sort of liaison to Swiss industry for Germany."

"Not just a liaison but a great German industrialist. And a friend of the Greek people, a true philhellene."

"Is that so?"

"Oh, yes. His family has enjoyed a long friendship with the Greek people. I know his grandfather funded quite a few archaeological excavations on Crete. These days the Baron sponsors music festivals at the Euripides Theater and a number of charity events."

"How generous of him."

"The proceeds, you may be interested to know, go to Red Cross efforts to help villages terrorized by the Communists in the mountains."

"I can't wait to meet the gentleman."

"Indeed. Tonight he's throwing a little party and requests the honor of your presence." Werner handed Andros a formal invitation signed by Baron Ludwig von Berg.

"I recognize this address." Andros showed his anger when he looked up at the smiling Werner. "This is the Vasilis estate."

"Why, yes, the Vasilis family ran into financial troubles with the war. The Baron, recognizing the architectural value of their estate, is leasing it from them temporarily and overseeing its restoration. The family still lives there."

"How kind of him," said Andros, pocketing the invitation. "I'd be delighted to come."

53

They rounded a glade and entered the northern suburb of Kifissia. It was a gloriously sunny day. The rim of mountains that surrounded Athens often trapped the heat in the city, but here where Andros grew up, it was relatively cool. Here there were still flowers, green clover beds, and birds that sang in blissful ignorance of any human war. Pansies and lantana were coming out on the walls, and he recognized the familiar fragrance of orange blossoms.

Then he saw it—the family villa nested on its hill. The sight sent his heart racing, and for a moment he was in school again, coming home for the holidays. He could picture his father the general in the courtyard, holding the hand of his little cousin Helen, waiting with the house staff to welcome him with hugs and kisses. For all his misgivings about his father's politics and the question of the king, he longed for those days.

As the drive climbed through the shaded groves and the black Mercedes entered the open gates of the estate, Andros knew full well that it wasn't Nasos the family driver behind the wheel but a Nazi. The courtyard was lifeless when they braked to a halt.

Andros couldn't remember climbing out of the car; his eyes were fixed on the front door of the villa. When he turned around, all that was left of the Mercedes was a cloud of dust and his trunk standing on end in the middle of the courtyard.

He heard a creak and turned to see a curtain fall in the window. The front door opened, and a small figure flew out across the courtyard.

"Christos! Christos!" cried eleven-year-old Helen as she wrapped herself around his neck.

Andros lifted her up in his arms. Her blue-and-white sailor

dress fluttered in the breeze, and her braided black hair with a white bow swung around and gently slapped his face. "Helen, what a young lady you've become. Why, the last time I saw you, you were only five."

"She's still in love with her older cousin," said a familiar voice. "But I told her she can't marry you."

Mitchell Rassious emerged from the shadows of the doorway and crossed the sunlit courtyard to embrace him. He seemed heavier than Andros remembered and had less hair. But he looked good in his gray suit, open shirt collar, and dark tan. His silvering mustache and eyebrows gave him an air of distinction he had lacked when they were black.

Andros put Helen down. "Uncle Mitchell!"

"Christos!" Uncle Mitchell pulled his face forward with both hands. "Can it really be you? But how?"

"All in good time, Uncle."

Uncle Mitchell nodded and turned toward the open doorway. "Look who's here, Nasos," he called. "It is Christos!"

Nasos, the family servant and chauffeur, appeared in the doorway and, after making sure the Germans were gone, stepped outside. When he saw Andros, he cried, "*Yassou*, Christos!"

"Nasos!" Andros shook the strong hands of the former soldier who had served as his father's driver. He seemed smaller than Andros remembered but still had a full head of curly black hair and a youthful gleam in his eyes.

Uncle Mitchell said, "Look at him, Nasos. The spitting image of his father."

This time it was a compliment, Andros knew, and he smiled under their approving gazes.

Nasos felt his biceps. "And strong," he pointed out. "There is iron in those arms, I can feel it."

Andros remembered the similar remarks about his physique that Donovan had made at the Farm. It was another reminder that who he wanted to be and what he had to be here were two different people.

"Ouch," said Andros, rubbing his muscle where Nasos had gripped it. "I'm afraid I'm not as strong as you are, Nasos."

"Then we must feed you," declared Uncle Mitchell, putting his arm around him. "Nasos will unpack your trunk while your aunt Maria fixes us something to eat. Now, come inside and tell us what this is all about."

54

The family gathered in the living room, where Andros, with little Helen at his feet, did his best to explain his Red Cross mission and recount the latest news from the family in Boston. He hadn't been in Boston for some time, so that was difficult, but those in the room, with tears in their eyes, assumed his emotions were like their own.

Aunt Maria brought in a large tray with little cups of Turkish coffee. "This is yours, Christos," she said, pointing to the one set apart. "It is sweet, as you like it."

Bits of news and gossip were exchanged. So-and-so was betrothed, and so-and-so had died. Andros leaned back in his chair and looked about the tastefully appointed room. Everything, including his grandmother in her favorite easy chair, was as he remembered, only older: the massive walnut table, the elegantly upholstered sofas, the console with the gilt-framed mirror, and the elaborately carved grandfather clock from Vienna.

Uncle Mitchell, puffing away on his ornate pipe, observed that it was a miracle their furniture hadn't been commandeered by the Germans. Aunt Maria, pouring more coffee for Andros, offered him some of her homemade sweet-chestnut pie and apologized again for having nothing better to offer him.

"Food is scarce," Uncle Mitchell explained. "First the Germans keep cutting the daily bread rations. Then they take control of the fishing industry so that all fish caught here are packed to be sent to Germany. Our agriculture, our trade, our merchant marine—all destroyed. All that's left is famine and inflation. Were it not for the Red Cross supplies, even more would have died. So much for the so-called New Order."

Andros asked, "What about the family's ships?"

"The Germans and Italians bought what was left of the fleet at about sixty percent of its value. The exchange rate was absurd! The Germans called for fifty drachmas to the mark, the Italians sixteen drachmas to a lira. In the end, they paid us in special marks and drachmas that have no value outside Greece. We stay on and manage the operations."

Andros nodded. "And the Greek government here?"

"One puppet government after another. You know the Cabinet approved abolishing the royal regime? We are no longer the kingdom of Greece but the Greek state." He puffed harder on his pipe, his face turning red with anger. "Not only that, but we are no longer even Greeks! The Germans say we are not true Hellenes but corrupted by some Slavic blood. They say the real Greeks are the Dorians, who had German blood!"

Andros had heard it before, in countless discussions with his uncle and father before he left for America and whenever he returned on vacation. As usual, the women listened patiently, biting their tongues. He didn't want to remind his uncle, as much a Hellenist as Hitler was an Aryan, that there was some Turkish blood in the strain of many of his Greek compatriots as well as Slavic. Or that the tragic Great Idea to build a new Byzantium in 1923, though smaller in scale, was no less ambitious than Hitler's plan to revive the Holy Roman Empire.

"If only your father were here, he'd show them," Uncle Mitchell said. "We'd all show them, like we did the Turks and the Italians."

Andros was aware that his uncle was looking toward the other side of the room. In spite of himself, Andros finally allowed his eyes to drift until they rested on the one thing they had avoided since he entered the house: the portrait of his father hanging over the fireplace, with his military sword hanging below it.

Then his grandmother, having heard enough of her son-in-law and satisfied she had fulfilled her duties of being silent, said, "It is a wonderful thing you have done to bring more Red Cross food to our people, Christos, but why do this crazy thing now?"

"I wanted to see you before you died, *Yiayia*," he said to his grandmother. "But I see that won't be for a while."

"She'll outlive us all, I tell you," declared Uncle Mitchell, raising his hand. "And our children."

His grandmother eyed Andros carefully. "I know what you came back for. But that Vasilis girl is no good for you."

"I can't very well marry Helen here, *Yiayia*. That would be scandalous."

"Yes, marry me!" Helen said. "Please, marry me!"

His grandmother, ignoring the child, made the sign of the cross. "Lord, save us! After what she's done to us and the Mandrakis family."

Andros looked at his uncle. "Andrew Mandrakis?"

"Tell him, Mitchell," his grandmother ordered his uncle. "Speak some sense to this foolish boy."

Uncle Mitchell turned to Andros and said, "Andrew Mandrakis is dead. His own hand, they say. Remorse for having killed John Stampanos in a duel."

"John, too?" Andros said in disbelief. Two of his best friends from childhood. "What were they fighting over?"

"Aphrodite Vasilis. After they came back from the Albanian front, both boys pursued her. She, of course, pledged her love to you."

"But why a duel?"

"It was for honor. Her honor. Their honor. Because there is nothing better to do for young unemployed officers in Athens these days. They wanted her married to a Greek rather than live"—he took a breath and paused as if wondering whether to continue—"than live with that German Baron von Berg. After he killed John, Andrew killed himself when Aphrodite still refused him."

Andros rubbed his eyebrows in order to hide his distress, but his voice shook when he asked, "When did this happen?"

"It's been several months," Uncle Mitchell said. "This damn war has squeezed the life out of all of us. Things are different in Athens since you left."

"So it seems," said Andros, pulling out the invitation Werner had given him. "The man who brought me here invited me to a party this Baron von Berg fellow is throwing. I noticed it is at the Vasilis estate."

"The swine!" Uncle Mitchell grabbed the invitation out of Andros's hand and began tearing it up.

"What are you doing?" Andros cried, trying to stop him.

"You're not going to set foot in that den of collaborators."

Andros picked up the scraps of paper from the floor. "Now, now, Uncle, let's not be hasty in judging our neighbors."

"Mother of God!" Uncle Mitchell turned to the rest of the family. "Did you hear this boy, this son of Nicholas?" He glared at Andros. "No Andros shall associate with turncoats who betray their own countrymen." His nostrils flared, and he gnashed his teeth, revealing a flash of gold. "Unless the stories are true—that you have struck a deal with the Germans?"

So, Andros thought, the SOE rumor mill already was in motion. "Uncle Mitchell, please—"

His uncle threw his hands up to heaven. "That this traitor should live under our roof!"

Uncle Mitchell stormed out of the room, taking a crying Helen with him. Aunt Maria quietly withdrew after them, leaving Andros alone with his grandmother.

The old woman, who had seen more wars and more death than Andros cared to imagine, bit her wrinkled lip and shook her head. "You never should have come back, child," she said. "Aphrodite is beautiful, but she has made her choice."

Andros looked at the torn-up invitation. "No, Grandmother. That's where you're wrong. She never had a choice. Until now."

55

Upstairs in her bedroom at her family's estate that afternoon, Aphrodite Vasilis was busy unpacking her belongings and answering the relentless questions of her mother and father. Was she all right? Had the Baron harmed her? Where had she been for the last several weeks?

"Now, you know I can't answer that, Mama and Papa," she told them, self-consciously folding the nightgown Ludwig had given her.

Her short, balding father waddled back and forth across the floor in his tuxedo, nervously anticipating the party he had the privilege of hosting against his will. His fleshy face looked flushed from liquor, and his bow tie was crooked. "Well, thank God you're alive."

"Yes," chimed her mother from the other side of the room, making the sign of the cross. "We can't enjoy even an hour of sleep whenever you're gone. Not one hour's peace until we can see you with our eyes and know that you are fine."

Her mother was sitting in front of the vanity, admiring herself in the mirror. Outwardly, she looked as cool and elegant as ever, but her gaudy green dress was a bit much. So was her denial of what was happening to the family. The occupation had turned them into pathetic figures, and Aphrodite felt more sorrow for her parents than anger. The latter emotion she reserved exclusively for the Nazis.

"I'm not fine," Aphrodite replied, placing the nightgown in the top drawer of her dresser. "Nothing is fine as long as Kostas is in prison and Christos is in America."

She noticed that the picture of Chris she kept on her dresser was missing. "Mama, where's my picture of Christos?"

"I put it away in the bottom drawer," her mother said.

Aphrodite turned sharply to face her mother. "Why?"

Her mother held up her hands in a pleading gesture. "It makes the Baron jealous."

Aphrodite knew it was her mother who had always been jealous of Chris and her daughter's happiness. "Good," she said. "He should know that just because he holds my body doesn't mean he holds my heart."

"Aphrodite!" cried her mother, biting the knuckle of her clenched fist. "You mustn't say such things."

"But it's true, Mama." Aphrodite pulled open the bottom drawer and found the picture in the back, lying facedown. She took it out, wiped it clean, and placed it on top of her dresser, where it belonged. "We all know the arrangements of this estate," she went on. "You get to live here as long as I sleep with Ludwig. If I stop, then you two are out on the streets, where I don't think you'd find much sympathy from the 'peasants,' as you call them."

"See here," said her father. "Don't talk to your mother that way. She loves you, and so do I. We don't want to do anything rash. Yes, if we all keep calm, this whole thing will blow over."

"Blow over, Papa?" she repeated. "In case you haven't noticed, the old days are gone for good: Metaxas is dead, King George isn't coming back, and this country is going to hell. When is this all going to blow over?"

"After the war," he said resolutely. "You'll see."

She plopped down on the bed. "After the war, I'll be an old maid," she lamented, "despised by everybody."

"You'll be a beautiful, rich young woman, the envy of Athens, and the best catch," said her mother, admiring herself in the mirror one last time. She turned from the vanity and came over to the bed with a gold brush and began brushing Aphrodite's hair. "Love? What is that? You think I loved your father here? It comes in time. Hold your head still."

"Ludwig isn't even Greek, Mama. We're collaborators, traitors—"

"We are not traitors," her father insisted. "We are simply waiting for this godforsaken war to end. What other options do we have?

Sit and do nothing while the Germans commandeer everything we've worked for? Risk our lives to escape the country on some ramshackle caïque piloted by a Communist pirate who would probably slash our throats, steal our money, and throw us overboard for shark bait? Fight the enemy and die like so many other simple, misguided peasants who want to be heroes? No, I say we stay right where we are, where it's safe. We mustn't do anything drastic."

The truth, she feared, was that her father, ever the shrewd businessman and speculator, was simply hedging his bets. He didn't know there was a difference between finance and morality.

"Yes," her mother agreed. "Family loyalty is more important than anything, Aphrodite, more important than laws or love or even the church. Don't put your faith in some young fool who's never going to come back."

56

That evening the Vasilis estate was awash with light. Andros could hear the sound of music and laughter when Nasos stopped the car at the gate.

A German sentry emerged from the guardhouse, built since Andros last saw the estate. In awful Greek, the sentry demanded to see their papers before signaling to another sentry to lift the swing bar.

As they drove through the gate and up the long drive, a nervous Nasos asked, "You're sure you want to do this?"

For years Andros had dreamed of this night, of seeing Aphrodite, and already his mind cast forward to the moment they would see each other and he would know if she still loved him. "Wouldn't miss it for the world, old friend."

He realized that Aphrodite had been the most influential person in his childhood, next to his father. Perhaps that was because Aphrodite had never compared him to his father; she lavished him with unconditional love and affection. She had changed his life and the way he viewed himself because she didn't expect him to change or want him to. That was inconceivable to Andros, who felt that love was given to those who earned it. Yes, he thought joyfully, Aphrodite simply loved him for who he was. Her parents, meanwhile, had loved him for what he was—heir to the Andros Shipping dynasty. Every time Andros shook her father's hand, he could sense Vasilis mentally calculating his family's future good fortune and adding up the interest. Aphrodite's mother, an arrogant woman who shared Aphrodite's beauty but none of her warmth, had expressed her approval with a cool tolerance of the relationship.

Nasos pulled up to the entrance, where two SS footmen in spanking attire welcomed them. A white glove opened the door for

Andros, and another directed Nasos to park farther down the drive with the other cars. Andros, dressed in black tie and tuxedo, bade Nasos farewell and went up the steps.

Standing at the top of the steps, greeting their arriving guests, were Aphrodite's parents, the official hosts of the party. Vasilis, a short, meaty man stuffed into a tight-fitting tuxedo, was enthusiastically pumping hands while his taller wife, in a long, gaudy, bejeweled gown, welcomed them with an artificial, ingratiating smile. Upon seeing Andros, however, their jaws dropped and the blood drained from their faces, as if they had seen a ghost.

Finally, Vasilis found his tongue. "Christos? What are you doing here?"

"I'm a guest of the Baron's."

Vasilis and his wife exchanged nervous glances, and Andros thought they might physically bar him from entering the house. "Is Aphrodite here?" he asked.

They didn't answer but simply stared at him in denial, as if they hoped he would go away. Clearly, Vasilis now considered him a bad investment come due.

Andros, seeing that he wouldn't get very far with these two, said, "I'll have a look around," and left them standing there while he went inside.

In the main hall was a well-stocked bar, toward which Andros gravitated as he took in the surreal spectacle of German and Greek officers, politicians, and other dignitaries strolling about with lavishly dressed girls on their arms. The air seemed unusually carefree, he thought, considering the mixed attendance of victors and vanquished.

At the other end of the bar, he saw Werner, the Gestapo man who had greeted him at the docks that morning. He's been watching me, Andros realized, ever since I walked through the door. Werner smiled and waved like an old friend and walked over. "Hello!" he said, handing Andros a glass of champagne. "See any familiar faces?"

Andros took a sip from his glass and looked around, indeed recognizing some of the more prominent families in Athens.

Werner said, "Over there is Prime Minister Rallis, talking with

Dr. Hermann Neubacher, the Reich's chargé d'affaires in Athens. And in the corner arguing with General Wilhelm Speidel, commander of southern Greece, is General Vecchiarelli, the commander of the Italian Eleventh Army headquartered here. Most of the guests are outside in the garden. Let me show you."

As they crossed the ballroom and passed the great marble staircase, Andros noted that the hallway that led to the library was roped off and guarded by an orderly in a white dinner jacket.

They walked outside and stood at the top of the marble steps overlooking the garden. A full orchestra filled the air with music, and lavish spreads of food crowded the island buffet tables. Footmen in white dinner jackets carried trays of cocktails to the tables under the colored lights.

"Doesn't this violate the blackout order?" Andros asked.

Werner laughed. "Once we cut a party short because of a false air-raid warning, but the all-clear sounded soon enough. Besides, nobody's bombing Athens these days, certainly not the civilian population centers such as Kifissia. For the most part, Baron von Berg is willing to break the rules as long as he is fully apprised of any situations that might disrupt the enjoyment of his guests."

Andros followed Werner's gaze to the rooftop and noticed the silhouettes of snipers against the stars. "I see," said Andros. "And the servants in the white dinner jackets?"

"Waffen SS," Werner explained. "In addition to sporting the proper attire, each carries a Luger in a hidden shoulder holster. So you see, Herr Andros, you need not worry for your safety."

"I'm impressed."

Werner seemed pleased. "Oh, I see Baron von Berg now. The beautiful Vasilis girl sitting next to him, isn't she somebody you used to know?"

That was when Andros saw her—Aphrodite, seated with Baron von Berg and several other couples at a table at the other end of the garden.

Seeing her made his heart miss a beat. She looked more beautiful than he had imagined possible. Her long jet-black hair was braided and exquisitely piled on top of her head, and she was wearing something Greek girls never wore: a white bare-back summer evening gown, filled to ravishing splendor with her well-proportioned body. The girl he had proposed to in New York had become . . . a woman.

"Yes, that's her," he said at last. "You say the man next to her is Baron von Berg?"

"That's right."

Andros took in the Baron's full military dress uniform, the Knight's Cross at his throat, with oak leaves and swords for second and third awards. His heart sank. This man didn't look like a Nazi monster but, rather, the picture of distinction, an officer and a gentleman, everything his father had been and he himself had hoped to become. A man whom Aphrodite could even love.

"Come, Herr Andros," said Werner. "Allow me to introduce you."

Andros followed Werner to the table. The lighthearted conversation under way came to an abrupt end upon their appearance. All eyes were on Andros, but his were focused on Aphrodite. She looked at him curiously, not comprehending his presence at first. Then her big amber eyes widened in alarm and darted to von Berg, who rose to his feet as Werner made the introductions.

"Baron von Berg," Werner announced. "This is Herr Chris Andros."

"Ah, Herr Andros," von Berg said in his clear Athenian Greek. "We finally meet." They shook hands, each sizing up the other.

In Andros's mind, von Berg came out on top. He was a tall, broad-shouldered man of about forty with boyish good looks. Much too tall to have been a U-boat commander, Andros thought. His gold hair swept back from his broad forehead. His clean-shaven cheeks tapered down to a determined chin. On the surface, he looked like a distinguished Englishman: cultured, civilized, with a stiff upper lip. Furthermore, his piercing, aristocratic blue eyes made Andros uneasy; he felt as though the Baron could see right through this whole charade and was merely amusing himself at his expense.

"I believe you and Miss Vasilis are old friends, Herr Andros."

Andros smiled as he took Aphrodite's soft, warm hand and kissed it. "A pleasure to see you again, Aphrodite." He longed for some emotional response from her, but all he saw was terror in her face as she looked at von Berg.

The Baron was delighted. "So you are the son of General Andros," he said after allowing an uncomfortable minute to pass. "A great leader, your father was. I understand there's a memorial service for him tomorrow at the cathedral."

"You'll be there, Baron von Berg?"

"In better times, I would, Herr Andros. But these days my presence at the memorial of a fallen war hero may not be appreciated by some of your countrymen."

Andros glanced at Aphrodite, who was less than two feet from him but seemed so far away, and told von Berg, "You seem to get along with everybody here."

A cold glaze crossed the Baron's eyes, betraying the smile on his face. Before he could reply, a butler appeared at his side with the news that Berlin was calling on his private line.

"Excuse me, but duty calls," von Berg apologized. "I'll be back in a moment. In the meantime, I believe you two have much to catch up on." He patted Aphrodite on the arm and walked off.

The orchestra struck up a waltz. Andros turned to Aphrodite. Her eyes were big, round, and wet like a doe's. He held out his hand and smiled. "Shall we dance?"

57

He cut a dashing figure, and for a moment the sight of Chris Andros in the flesh had left Aphrodite breathless. The same dark, wavy hair. The same handsome face. The same mischievous grin that had won her over when she was a teenager and now made her fear for their lives.

"I've missed you, Aphrodite," he told her as they turned to the music. "It's been too long."

His voice was so calm, so matter-of-fact, as if nothing had changed in the years between his marriage proposal to her at the World's Fair and tonight.

"Four years this summer," she told him in a cool tone, hoping Chris could comprehend the hell she had been through.

His hazel eyes seemed to be searching for something in hers, something familiar, some sign of the girl he once knew. That girl, she feared, no longer existed, and thus neither did the luster that so captivated him in his youth.

"I'm sorry for the delay," he apologized. "I would have gotten here sooner, but a funny thing happened on my way to Athens. I think we call it the war. Better late than never, don't you think?"

She didn't answer him. She was overwhelmed with shame that he had seen her with Ludwig. Everything she had hoped to hide from him, as futile as that hope might have been, had been exposed.

"That's a lovely dress you're wearing," Chris went on. "I thought the next time I'd see you in white would be at the altar. Are those pearls a gift from the Baron, too?"

Her shame dissolved into rage. He had left her in the cold through no fault of his own, she realized. But he was also the kind of man who could never accept anything but angelic purity from her. Now that *that* was plainly lost, she feared he would consider her unacceptable. Once a goddess, now a slut. She would rather have him hate her than be disappointed in her—or worse, get himself killed by the Baron.

"You were a fool to come back, Christos."

"Call me a fool for love, but I've come back for you, just like I promised. Now we will be wed before God and married by the archbishop. I'll make an honest woman out of you yet."

His eyes seemed to be full of genuine love. But it was too much to believe he had come back to Greece on her account. "I know you, Christos. You're not here just for me."

He sighed in exasperation. "All right, then, I'm here to do business with your boyfriend, Ludwig."

Her heart sank in disappointment. "What sort of business?"

"You'll find out soon enough, but it would help tremendously if you could tell me where he keeps important documents. I'm looking for an ancient text, in particular. Have you seen anything?"

"So that's why you're here." She was angry at him because she was scared for him, scared at what the Baron might do to him, like he did to Karl or any man who came near her. She had to get rid of him, get him out of Athens. "I haven't seen any text. I see none of his papers. He keeps them locked away."

"But, of course, your father's safe is in the library. The Baron's study now, I presume."

Dear God, Chris, she thought, please stop. "Don't, Christos."

"Still hidden in the bookcase?"

She felt faint, and her knees seemed to buckle, but Chris held her up.

"Any spare keys?" he asked, relentlessly moving forward with his questions.

"He changed the lock," she found herself saying. "It's a combination. Only he knows. The locksmith who installed it . . . he died. Ludwig trusts nobody. Please, Christos, leave now while you can. Already you're in danger."

"Am I?" he asked in an almost mocking tone. "What about you?"

"I tell you, he doesn't want to involve me."

"How kind of him. You seem involved enough to me already. Are you sleeping with him tonight?"

The question, coming from Chris's lips, shocked and enraged her. "How dare you!" She slapped him in the face, tears streaking down her own. "How dare you throw this shame at me after you went to America and left me to this!"

Suddenly, she realized the music had stopped and she was in the middle of a sea of staring faces. She looked up at Chris and saw his surprise even as Ludwig emerged on the terrace to complete the picture of humiliation. Unable to stand there any longer, she fled the gardens and ran inside the house.

58

Fifteen minutes later, Aphrodite's mother watched Andros's car leave the drive from the window of her daughter's bedroom upstairs. She let the curtain fall and turned to her daughter, who was sobbing on the bed.

"What am I going to do?" cried Aphrodite.

"You stay with the Baron and forget Christos," her mother said firmly. "Shall we all die because this young fool returns to Greece?"

"But I love him," Aphrodite insisted.

"And your family? Shall we lose all we own? Our home? Our business? Everything your father has worked for? All for love? You're too young to understand, Aphrodite."

Her father came in and closed the door. "I heard them say goodbye in the hall while a footman fetched the car," he said. "Von Berg invited him over here for lunch tomorrow during siesta, to discuss business. I can only wonder what sort of business that would be." He began to pace the floor, thinking out loud. "You, young lady, will not be here when young Andros calls on the Baron. In fact, you're not to lay eyes on him while he's in Athens."

"What?"

Her mother said, "Don't throw your life away for some young fool! If he were smart, he would have waited until after the war to return."

"Oh, young Andros is no fool," said her father. "Mark my words, he's struck a deal with the Germans. I've heard as much, and now I believe it. Why else is he here? There's a real collaborator for you, Aphrodite. Don't let him trick you."

Her mother fixed herself in front of Aphrodite's vanity. "Come, we must see our guests and show ourselves. You can stay up here, child. And stay away from that boy tomorrow at the memorial service."

They turned off the light and left her to cry herself to sleep. But she could not sleep, distraught with all that had happened. Why did Chris have to return now, of all times? What was this document he was looking for? What would happen to them all? Her heart, ever since childhood, had belonged to Chris. But it belonged to her family, too, whatever their faults. That meant appeasing Ludwig. To help Chris would be to betray Ludwig and jeopardize her family. To betray Chris, however, would be to betray her heart. Who would deliver her from this inhuman suffering?

She began to pray to God but stopped herself when she realized her prayers had already been answered. Indeed, the lover she so desperately wanted to rescue her had arrived. But like the proverbial demon who returns to his place with seven more, so her original condition seemed mild compared to her present agony.

Before, she had lived in two separate worlds. One was the dream of her future with Chris, the other her existence with Ludwig. Those two worlds had collided, shattering the illusion that she could somehow survive in both. There was only one world now, and she trembled at the thought of what kind of world it would turn out to be.

59

Many of the same Athenians who had attended Baron von Berg's party the night before now packed the cathedral for the Saturday-morning memorial service. It marked the anniversary of General Nicholas Andros's death, two years since he had fallen defending Crete from the invading Germans. To pay their respects to the war hero was to prove their patriotism.

Chris Andros watched the spectacle in smoldering silence while altar boys swung their censers to the chants of the towering figure of Archbishop Damaskinos. A few pews ahead, seated with her parents, was an uncomfortable-looking Aphrodite, dressed in fashionable black.

Andros had never felt lower in his life. Last night's nightmare with Aphrodite had been bad enough. But to wake up to his father's memorial service and the harsh light of his own failures seemed unusually cruel. It was worse than death.

Since he knew no man could escape death, death never scared Andros. How a man died, on the other hand, was paramount, the ultimate epitaph on one's life. To die like his father, in battle, defending country, family, and friends, was the ultimate honor. It was just as good to live a long life like his grandfather, raise a large family, and die surrounded by people with whom one had left a positive legacy. Neither fate looked likely for him.

Life seemed so unfair in regard to his measure as a man, Andros thought. He would never be as revered as General Nicholas Andros, and yet he would never escape the sins of his father either. Furthermore, he had hoped to return to Greece a conquering hero, having proved his valor with the U.S. Army. But here he was, in the middle of the war, having proved nothing to anybody. Not to his uncle Mitchell, not to Aphrodite, and not to the Allies or himself. He had failed.

After last night's disaster, Andros felt more helpless than ever in his bid to save Aphrodite. Indeed, she seemed to have been managing for herself as well as one could expect before he showed up with an accusing finger. For him to inform her that she was no longer a pure, untainted virgin seemed cruel to him now, and he was sorry he had ever held that expectation over her head. He was also sorry he'd ever let an issue as frivolous as the role of a Danish king in Greece get between him and his father.

"Truly, all things are vanity, and life is but a shadow and a dream," boomed the archbishop. "For in vain doth everyone born of earth disquiet himself, as saith the Scripture. When we have acquired the world, then do we take up our dwelling in the grave, where kings and beggars are the same. Wherefore, O Christ our God, give rest to Thy servant departed this life, forasmuch as Thou lovest mankind."

Andros never understood the practice of praying for the dead. If man was appointed to die once and then the Judgment, then Andros failed to see how his prayers could alter the departed's eternal destiny if it had been determined. Moreover, how could this expression of love and remembrance after his father's death make up for what Chris had failed to express to him during his life?

He looked up at the domed ceiling, at Christ the Almighty gazing down from heaven. The Son of God seemed so distant up there in the celestial bodies, Andros thought, while here on earth, mortal men killed one another. Where was God now that the world was at war, now that lovers like him and Aphrodite stood so close to each other and yet so far apart, now that he was about to stare at the grave of a father whose side he had abandoned at the most crucial hour? Could God return what now seemed lost forever?

60

The First Cemetery was the Athenian version of Washington's Arlington National Cemetery. The approach was along Eternal Rest Street. Nasos drove up the slight grade through the main gate and stopped so that Andros could help his grandmother out. In his dark, conservative suit, Andros felt uncomfortably warm under the hot sun.

They made their way between the mausoleums and cypress trees toward the Andros family plot. To their right, the sculpture of the Sleeping Maiden, by the sculptor Halepas, graced the Afendakis family plot. To their left were other shrines, more famous for their art than for the souls whose memory they were intended to preserve.

Mourners had gathered around his father's simple grave, including his cousins and the Vasilis family. They kept a respectful distance while he and his grandmother made the sign of the cross and placed a bouquet of fresh flowers on the cold stone slab. Then little Helen came up and threw some wheat kernels on the tomb, a symbol of eternal life, and ran back to her father. Uncle Mitchell took her hand and glared at Andros, obviously displeased with him and his business in Athens.

As Andros grimly stood there before his father's grave, staring at death itself, Aphrodite's father approached and made the sign of the cross, whether out of respect for Nicholas Andros or his own fears, Andros couldn't tell.

"The same fate awaits us all," Vasilis said. "But as I once heard Metaxas say to a foreign dignitary, 'Death is but an episode for the Orthodox believer.'"

With those hugely consoling words, Vasilis rejoined his daughter and scowling wife, and they walked to their car. Before climbing in, Aphrodite glanced back toward Andros, and when he saw her sad eyes, he knew she still had feelings for him.

"Good God," remarked a voice from behind in perfect Oxford English. "Now we're quoting dead dictators like Holy Writ."

Andros turned to see a bearded Greek Orthodox priest standing next to him, staring down at the grave.

The priest said, "Now kiss my ring and look pious for all the mourners loafing about."

Andros bent over to kiss the priest's ring and saw the Union Jack insignia. When he straightened, he realized he was looking at Brigadier Andrew Eliot, the Athens SOE chief known as Touchstone. With a straight face, Andros asked, "Father, does the good archbishop know he's surrounded by false apostles?"

"His Most Holy Grace is quite on board, as you Americans say," replied SOE's master of disguise. "Let's take a stroll among the tombstones. Remember, I'm here to console you in your grief."

The two moved away from the mourners, who Andros hoped saw only a priest placing his hand on the shoulder of General Andros's grieving son, comforting him.

Eliot said, "I must congratulate you on your own exceptional performance, Chris. In under twenty-four hours, you've successfully established yourself as a thoroughly despicable individual. Athens is alive with talk that you've struck a deal with the Germans. You've been branded a collaborator."

"So it seems," Andros observed. It was a brutal fact of life he couldn't escape. As far as any Greek was concerned, he had become the kind of man he hated most. A turncoat. A traitor. A man who put his own selfish interests ahead of others. A Nazi. God, how he hated those bastards. The thought that he could be thrown in with that lot—especially Baron von Berg—brought bile to the back of his throat. "I'm everything I ever hated."

"Yes," said Eliot. "Even your uncle is a believer, and he's more than displeased with you. From what he's been telling his friends, you are an utter embarrassment to your family and to Greece."

Andros was beginning to worry that if the Germans didn't get him, some Greek patriot like Captain Tsatsos or his uncle Mitchell would. "You've heard this?"

"One hears many confessions in my occupation," Eliot replied with a smile. "You might want to read the latest edition of the resistance newspaper *Nea Eleftheron*. You're featured in the 'Portrait of a Traitor' column. Frankly, with such talk going around, I suspect you're the reason so many have come to pay their respects to your father. Tell me what happened last night. I understand you managed to infiltrate one of von Berg's parties."

"It was an invitation I couldn't refuse," Andros replied.

"You made contact with the girl?"

It was always "the girl" with these OSS and SOE types, thought Andros. Aphrodite had a name. Why didn't they use it? "*Aphrodite* says von Berg keeps important papers in the library safe," he snapped. "But she's too scared to even see me again."

"And von Berg?"

"Oh, von Berg and I are good friends," Andros went on in a stale tone. "He invited me to lunch this afternoon at the Vasilis estate."

"Perfect," said Eliot. "You can speak with Aphrodite while you're there, if you can get alone with her."

Andros turned and looked at Eliot. "I told you, she wants nothing to do with me."

"You must be bold, do something that will force her hand," Eliot said, putting his arm around Andros like a concerned man of the cloth, directing him back toward the mourners. "That's what the engagement ring is for. You will press her to marry you, to make her deal with you. In turn, that will force von Berg to deal with you."

"The Baron has already dealt with me most effectively," Andros said. "The question is, how do I deal with him this afternoon?"

"Very carefully," Eliot explained. "You'll tell him that the Andros ship *Turtle Dove* is already steaming toward Greece from Istanbul with a shipment of Red Cross food and medical supplies."

"It is?" asked Andros, alarmed at the pace with which events were now proceeding.

Eliot nodded. "That ship, which is under Swiss registry, is your

proof to von Berg that you can deliver on your promise to break
the British blockade. You'll ask him to reciprocate by allowing the
ship safe passage into Piraeus tomorrow morning. In the meantime,
you must convince Aphrodite to help you get into the Baron's safe
before that ship returns to Istanbul the next morning."

That was under forty-eight hours, Andros realized. "You're not
giving me much time."

"Nor, we hope, the Baron," Eliot replied. "We have to move
fast if we're going to pull this off, before the Nazis figure out what's
happening."

"What about you?" asked Andros. "Where will I find you?"

"After your meetings with von Berg and Aphrodite this afternoon, we'll rendezvous in the Royal Gardens near Constitution
Square. You'll be taking a stroll through the park at dusk, wearing
exactly what you have on now. You'll decide your shoes need to be
shined. A boy will offer to shine your shoes, and you will say, 'Like a
glass darkly,' and he will reply, 'But soon face-to-face.' He will hand
you further instructions."

"And in the meantime?"

"We'll listen in on your conversations with both von Berg and
the girl, courtesy of that ring box from Tiffany," said Eliot. "The
Germans have mobile direction finders roaming about, so we have
to be careful. You especially. One slip, and this could well be *your*
funeral next week. I see there's already a plot with your name on it."

61

Still dressed in his stiff three-piece suit from the memorial service, Andros arrived at the Vasilis estate at two and found Baron von Berg in the library, working through some papers. Von Berg was wearing a loose-fitting white sport shirt, slacks, and tennis shoes. The clothes gave the Baron an unhurried air of leisure, as if the only thing on his mind that afternoon, really, was getting in a few sets on the grass court in back before supper.

Von Berg looked up from his desk as Andros was ushered in by the orderly, and gestured him to a seat. He said nothing for a minute while he sorted through a pile of unopened mail.

The library was as Andros remembered it, with walls of books that had never been opened and a set of French doors leading outside to the gardens. If he remembered correctly, the Vasilis family safe was on the sixth shelf of the bookcase behind him. Aphrodite's father had had it brought over by ship from America. Vasilis alleged it was the same kind of safe favored by Chicago mobsters.

"Paperwork, Herr Andros. It will be the death of me yet." Von Berg pushed aside the papers and placed his silver letter opener on top of the stack to keep everything in place. "According to our legation in Bern, you offer an interesting business arrangement, to say the least. I have looked over the documents and navicerts you provided. They appear genuine."

"This surprises you?"

Von Berg smiled. "Not when I consider your financial situation," he said. "But I am surprised you're not more particular with your sympathies. I can't imagine your father would betray the Allies."

Andros could feel von Berg's eyes sweep over his suit and reappraise him. His glance seemed to fasten on the monogrammed gold cuff link Andros was fiddling with, the one with a large A embossed in the center.

"My father was a soldier, Baron von Berg," Andros explained with an air of condescension. "I am a businessman. So are you. Whatever you need, Andros ships can deliver into ports open to both Swiss and German shipping."

"So you claim, Herr Andros," said von Berg. "But what happens once these hypothetical consignments arrive in port?"

Andros said, "Once in port, such consignments, if properly handled, could mysteriously disappear from my Swiss ships and find themselves in the holds of German ships or on rail lines going into Germany."

"And the Swiss police and customs officers would look the other way?"

"The Swiss have appointed port commissioners whose job is to speed up the unloading of consignments and cut red tape," Andros explained. "When up to seven thousand tons are unloaded daily in Genoa alone, I think a few crates could be missed."

"For one hundred thousand American dollars."

"Not a penny less."

"I see." Von Berg leaned back in his seat. "And what if the Allies find out you are here talking to me about this? You realize by now dozens of British agents in Athens have reported your arrival."

Andros flashed a conspiratorial grin. "I'm counting on it," he said. "You see, I informed the American Legation in Bern that I was coming here. I told them it was on behalf of the Greek government in exile in Cairo to secure the safe passage of Red Cross relief supplies into Athens. Indeed, the ship is on its way and should be here by tomorrow morning. Whether or not you permit it through the counterblockade, the mere gesture on my part should speak for the altruistic intent of my visit. I do have an image to protect after this war ends, with both the Greeks and the Allies, not to mention Aphrodite."

Von Berg looked surprised. "So you intend to stay in Athens?"

"I wish I could. But I'll be on that Red Cross ship when it returns to Istanbul on Monday."

Von Berg smiled in admiration of Andros's depravity. "You seem to have thought of your way out, Herr Andros." He drummed his fingers on the leather desktop. "I'll inform the admiralty to instruct our submarines to let the ship pass; just have your office inform the port authority of its Sunday arrival so that proper distribution channels can be prepared."

"Thank you," said Andros. "There is one other thing, though. I'm afraid I didn't think Aphrodite would react so negatively to my arrival. You see, we were engaged to be married before the war."

Von Berg nodded. "That is my understanding."

"And that is still my desire." Andros pulled out the baby-blue Tiffany & Co. box with the hidden bug. He cracked it open to reveal the sparkling diamond.

"Lovely," murmured von Berg, leaning forward with interest. "So you plan on proposing to her again?"

"Strictly business, mind you," Andros said, snapping the box shut and pocketing it. "But all in Germany's best interests. After all, such a wedding could only complement your wonderful benefit concerts and parties here, proving yet again that life is good in the New Order."

"Such a wedding would also serve the interests of Chris Andros," von Berg observed with a wry smile. "Following the great Andros tradition, you would use marriage to consolidate the fortunes of two of Athens's wealthiest families, this time emerging from the war with a combined tobacco and transportation conglomerate that would be, I believe, the largest in Greece."

"Exactly," said Andros. "You must remember that, unlike the Germans or most Europeans, the Greeks and Americans have no established aristocracy, no titles that can be passed along at birth. Money, mind you, is the only measure of social status. And without money in America, I would be nothing. Here, however, I am something. Better a rich man in hell than a pauper in heaven, I say."

"I see, Herr Andros." Von Berg looked thoroughly disgusted

with him, his admiration for depravity obviously ending in matters concerning Aphrodite. Clearly, he considered her to be more than a war trophy. Andros was beginning to fear that she inspired as much devotion from the Baron as she did from himself.

"But first I'd like to ask you a favor regarding this Red Cross affair," Andros continued.

"Oh? And what is that?"

"After the *Turtle Dove* arrives tomorrow, I thought a dinner reception not unlike your party last night might be in order for the visiting Red Cross delegation. We could toast the goodwill of the German government."

Von Berg played along. "But of course."

"As a gesture of that goodwill, perhaps the German authorities in Greece would consider releasing some of the political prisoners they are holding hostage for impending reprisals. I have in mind the likes of Kostas Vasilis, among others."

Von Berg frowned. "Kostas Vasilis?"

"If I am to propose to Aphrodite, I need to know nobody is holding her back from making a free decision."

Andros had thrown down the gauntlet. Von Berg looked him in the eye. All pretense was shed. Business deals and the war itself seemed insignificant compared with Aphrodite. Knowing her free choice in the matter was clearly important to von Berg, whether or not he intended to let her go in the end.

"I see you are confident of your powers of persuasion with Aphrodite," von Berg told him. "But yes, all your requests will be met."

"Good." Andros rose to his feet. "In fact, I think I'll pay Aphrodite a visit on my way out."

"Oh, I'm terribly sorry," said von Berg, "but she's not here this afternoon."

"She's not?"

"No. She's at the Red Cross center, distributing food to the needy." Von Berg stood up and smiled. "Perhaps tomorrow evening at the reception?"

It would be too late then, Andros realized. "Yes, perhaps tomorrow evening," he said. "In the meantime, could I ask you one final favor?"

It took some visible effort, but von Berg managed to keep his smile. "Yes?"

"Since I won't be needing this until the reception," Andros said, pulling out the ring box, "would you mind keeping it in a safe place?"

"Not at all." Von Berg took the box. "I'll keep it locked and under Waffen SS guard. Is that safe enough?"

"Quite."

"Ah, that reminds me," said von Berg. "I have a gift for you."

To Andros's astonishment, the Baron walked over to the bookcase and removed several tomes from the sixth shelf to reveal the safe door. Von Berg didn't seem to mind revealing its location to him, rightly assuming that Vasilis couldn't keep his mobster safe a secret from his children's friends, what with his boasting.

Von Berg turned the combination with a few deft twists of the wrist and opened a single door, about six inches thick, to reveal a second, double door. He placed the ring box inside and began to search for something else.

"As you may know, Herr Andros, Hitler was impressed by the valor displayed by the Greek army in their brave fight against the Italians and, later, the Germans. So impressed that, after their defeat, he allowed the Greek officers to retain their swords and daggers. A gesture of tremendous respect on his part, considering his disdain for non-Teutons. It seems he regards men like your father as the descendants of Alexander the Great."

Von Berg turned around and presented to Andros a knife in a sheath.

Andros immediately recognized the embossed A insignia on the handle and realized it was his father's dagger.

"It was found on Crete after your father's body was returned to Athens and buried," von Berg explained. "A Greek partisan apparently lifted it when your father fell, and made good use of it against my countrymen. The initials and special seal on the handle told us who its rightful owner was."

Andros removed the dagger from its sheath and held it in his hand. It felt heavier than he had remembered, weighed down, perhaps, by his childhood recollections. He could still see his father showing the dagger to him and telling him how someday he, too, would have a dagger when he grew up and became an officer in the Hellenic Royal Army. He remembered falling asleep that night dreaming of future battles against the Turks and even facing Hadji Azrael, the devil himself. But life didn't turn out the way he or his father had expected. The devil wasn't Hadji Azrael. He was Baron Ludwig von Berg, a German aristocrat and a general in Hitler's dreaded SS. The self-styled "good sport" had wiped his father's blade clean of any blood but couldn't erase the swirl of suppressed emotions that overwhelmed Andros. He almost felt compelled to plunge the blade into von Berg's chest, a feeling that the Baron perhaps wished to encourage. But he remembered he was supposed to detest all forms of violence, so he kept his composure. He slid the dagger back into its sheath.

"And what am I supposed to do with this vile weapon?"

"Keep it as a symbol," von Berg said, escorting him to the door. "To remind you that there is still valor for those who lose."

He was referring to Aphrodite, Andros realized, and doing so with outrageous presumption. Seething inside, Andros forced a smile as he slipped the sheathed dagger into his breast pocket. He patted the bulge. "An excellent idea," he told the Baron. "Perhaps this would look nice on the fireplace mantel. His sword is there, you know. That's where these things belong, on wall displays, not in men's hands. I feel nervous simply having it on my person."

"So it seems." Von Berg frowned. "Perhaps I had you figured differently, Herr Andros."

"How is that?"

"I thought you were your father's son."

62

Aphrodite slipped away from the Red Cross food distribution center that afternoon, as instructed by the note Archbishop Damaskinos had passed to her. It took her half an hour to make her way from the Plaka district up the winding paths to Likavitos Hill, the highest point in Athens. At the summit was the white chapel of Agios Yioryios and a sweeping view of the city and the Saronic Gulf.

She stood there on the terrace, gazing out across the city, blinking in the setting sun. As children, she and Chris would meet here secretly, telling their parents they were going to Agios Yioryios to say their prayers. But times were different now. They were no longer children, and it was the Nazis they were eluding this time.

"You had no trouble getting here?" asked a voice.

She turned. It was Chris standing next to her, dressed in the same dark suit he'd worn that morning at the memorial service. He looked even better in the late-afternoon sun than the night before. It was their first time alone in four years.

"Eleni Lemnos covered for me at the distribution center," she said. "I put on one of the donated dresses as a disguise and slipped out the back. I have only a few minutes before I'm missed."

"One of von Berg's men is watching you?"

"Helmut long ago tired of watching me distribute food and comfort grieving widows," she replied. "The only things he watches in the afternoons are movies at the cinema down the block from the center. Still, there may be other eyes at the center that I'm not aware of."

There was an awkward silence. Finally, Chris said, "I'm glad you came."

"You're surprised?"

"I had my doubts," he said, rubbing his cheek. "That was some act last night. The slap across the face in particular—was it for real or just your flair for the dramatic? It *was* an act, wasn't it?"

"That depends on what you say next."

Chris paused to pick his words with care. "I know this insane war isn't your fault," he told her. "But seeing you with the Baron made me a little crazy. I'm sorry. I just want to know what happened."

He had said all she could reasonably expect him to say. "I'll tell you, Christos."

She told him how she'd met the Baron in the hospital, how the Gestapo had come for her brother, Kostas, and how the Baron had moved into her family's estate. The only thing she didn't tell him about was the Baron's retreat on Corfu. She remembered Ludwig's dire warnings of doom should she ever reveal its location. Although it was Berlin that Ludwig seemed to fear more than Washington, she wasn't about to put her family or Chris in any further danger over something as insignificant as the Baron's personal taste for peace and quiet.

When she was finished, all Chris could say was "I'm sorry it was you and not me who stayed behind."

She watched the sun melt over the blue gulf, turning the ruins of the Acropolis black against the Aegean sky. So symbolic of their relationship, she thought, for from this high ground, they once again enjoyed perspective not only of the city but of the tattered fragments of life.

"Why did you come back, Christos?"

"I told you last night," he said. "I came for you."

She recalled her father's talk about some sort of turncoat deal with the Germans to save Andros Shipping. "Is that what you told Ludwig this afternoon at my house?"

"Among other things," he said. "Actually, we discussed the release of your brother."

"My brother?"

He smiled at her. "Tomorrow an Andros ship with Red Cross supplies will arrive in Piraeus," he explained. "When it leaves on

Monday, your brother and several other political prisoners will be on board. Von Berg already has agreed to it."

"And you believe him?" she asked. "Where is the ship going?"

"Istanbul," Chris said. "Your brother will be sent on to Syria, Lebanon, and ultimately Egypt. There he'll undoubtedly volunteer to join the Greek army in exile. Maybe he'll salvage your family's tarnished image as collaborators before it's too late."

"And you, Christos? What will happen to you? What will happen to us?"

His smile vanished. "A lot depends on you. Von Berg is going to throw a reception for the Red Cross delegation tomorrow night. During the party, I'm going to break into your father's safe. Inside are papers vital to the defense of Greece."

"But I told you last night," she insisted, "only Ludwig knows the combination."

"Not if my friends are listening."

She didn't understand what he was saying and suddenly felt light-headed. "Too fast, Christos. Things are moving too fast. I can't keep up with you."

"That's okay, as long as von Berg can't, either," he replied. "The hallway to the library is too well lit and guarded. If I'm going to have any chance at all of getting in, it will have to be from the garden outside, through the French doors. I noticed last night that von Berg had a man posted on the patio."

"Yes," she said. "Hans and Peter share guard duties during parties."

"Hans and Peter?" he asked, raising an eyebrow. "I didn't know you were on such intimate terms with your captors."

"They're not as bad as you make them out to be," she found herself saying. "They didn't ask to be in the Baron's employment, and Hans happens to be a wonderful dancer."

"Is that so?" he said, looking somewhat annoyed. "When do they rotate shifts?"

"There are three shifts of guards. Hans usually relieves Peter at nine."

"When it's Hans's turn to relieve Peter, make sure you two are dancing together like everybody else," said Chris. "Meanwhile, I'll go upstairs to your room and change into the SS uniform you will have placed in the bottom drawer of your dresser."

"An SS uniform? How am I supposed to—"

"Your maids do the washing for von Berg's staff, don't they? Give me one that's waiting to be washed. I don't need anything immaculate. It will be dark enough when I climb down from your bedroom balcony to the garden. You know the drill—we practiced it often enough as teenagers."

"But Peter will still be on the patio outside the library, waiting for Hans to relieve him."

"Perhaps, if he hasn't gone to fetch him. Otherwise, I'll relieve him."

"Relieve him?" she asked nervously. "How?"

"Don't worry about me. Just keep Hans so happy that he forgets the time. I need at least five minutes to get in and out."

The audacity of Chris's proposal began to sink in, and it was all she could do to persuade him to stop the madness. "But Ludwig will know something is up."

"He'll be too busy with his Red Cross guests."

"It won't work."

"Von Berg won't notice anything is missing until morning," he reassured her. "By then you and I and our families will be long gone."

"Gone?"

"We're going to Cairo to get married." Chris put his hands on her shoulders, gently but firmly. "You still want to marry me, don't you?"

Aphrodite's heart skipped a beat at the thought that such a dream was still possible in this miserable life. "More than anything, Christos," she said, looking into his longing eyes. "But if something goes wrong . . . my brother. . . ."

"Your brother will be just fine," he said. "Von Berg won't back out of any international understanding he's reached. If something goes wrong, I'll be in trouble, not you or your family."

Despite the danger, a wave of relief swept over her. Chris really was on the Allies' side. He was not a collaborator after all. Perhaps the end to their suffering was at hand. "So the invasion comes soon, like they say?"

Chris shrugged. "Like I said, a lot depends on you."

She looked at him and felt like a little girl again. Her anger from the night before had vanished. Only fear remained, fear and a drop of doubt that she was as important to Chris as what was inside Ludwig's safe. "Christos, I'm scared."

"That makes two of us."

She felt his finger reach under her chin and lift her face toward his. She closed her eyes and let their lips touch. The world around them seemed to melt like the setting sun. He still loves me, she thought. Chris truly loves me and has come for me.

63

Dusk was already falling across the forty acres of park when Andros had Nasos deliver him to the Royal Gardens for his rendezvous with the SOE. Children were still at play in the shadows of the Parliament and Hotel Grande Bretagne while German soldiers strolled about in small groups.

He was buoyed by the joy of his reconciliation with Aphrodite. The masks had been dropped, their true feelings confessed. They were of one mind. She hadn't let him down. All he had to do was make sure he didn't let her down.

He passed an old Greek in a tattered army uniform, selling rotten chestnuts beneath a canopy of trees. The man was resting on a wooden leg, having lost his own in the war, though from the looks of the veteran, Andros suspected it was the Great War. He reached into his pocket and tossed the veteran a silver sovereign. Then he wandered down a path that opened into a flower circle. There by an ancient stone seat was a row of shoe shiners, mostly young boys and a few old men.

How anybody could make money shining shoes these days in Athens seemed impossible to Andros, until he noticed a couple of German soldiers walk up to the first boy in line. One of them put his jackboot on the small pedestal and pointed to it with a thick finger. The boy started shining as if his life depended on it.

"Shoe shine, shoe shine!" said the fourth boy down the row as Andros walked by. "Shoe shine, mister?"

The boy himself had no shoes, only a smiling face black with soot and two large animated eyes. Andros stopped to look. The street kid started to perform all sorts of acrobatics with his brushes, juggling them in the air with a spin and catching them behind his back.

"Where is your family?" Andros asked.

The boy shrugged as if to say he didn't have any.

"Where do you live?"

"Everywhere. Do you want a shine or not?"

Andros paused, wondering why the SOE would resort to using children instead of some of the older men down the line. With some hesitation, he proceeded to place his shoe on the stand. "Like a glass darkly."

The boy smiled. "But soon face-to-face."

The boy started scrubbing away, and Andros looked about the park and its ponds, green with thousands of exotic plants Queen Amalia had brought in from all parts of Greece and Italy in the 1840s.

When the boy finished, Andros paid him not in hyperinflated drachmas but with a silver sovereign. The boy responded by giving him change in drachmas. Pasted on one coin was a note instructing Sinon to follow the path to his right to a certain fountain.

Andros had started to leave when he heard an argument. He turned. The two soldiers had refused to pay the first boy for shining their boots, and now the boy was tagging along, demanding payment. The one German swung his heavy hand across the boy's face, sending him to the ground. The other soldier laughed, and they both walked on. But the shoe-shine boy was determined to get his drachmas. He got up and ran after the big German, wrapping himself around his leg. For several paces, he was dragged across the pavement before biting the German's leg.

"*Ach!*" cried the German, and hit him on the head. The boy, like a little dog, kept clinging.

To save the boy from dying from another blow to the head, Andros approached them. "See here," he said to the boy. "I'll pay you."

He handed the boy a silver sovereign, and the little boy, more dirty and bloodied than ever, grabbed it. Before he could run, the German gripped his wrist and squeezed until the boy screamed and opened his tiny fist. The coin dropped with a dull clink, and the other soldier picked it up.

"You rob little children now?" Andros asked, barely able to suppress his rage at the sight of the boy being beaten by these animals.

"Save yourself, man," said the big German in broken Greek.

Andros took off his hat as if to seek his pardon, but he secretly pulled the pin from above the rim. Without thinking, he rammed it into the German's neck like Erin Whyte had taught him, killing him instantly. The other soldier, shocked to see his companion fall to the pavement without a sound, reached for his gun, but Andros drew his father's dagger and shoved it into the soldier's stomach. The coin that the dying soldier clutched rolled onto the pavement, and the little boy grabbed it and ran.

Andros heard a whistle and saw another German soldier some way down the park avenue wave his hand. A whole group of Germans came into view and moved toward him. Andros started running. He ran past the fountain toward the street. A glance over his shoulder showed the Germans closing in on him.

He reached the street only to find his way blocked by a black Mercedes. Several members of the Security Police got out, pointing machine guns.

The commanding officer, a colonel, smiled at Andros with fiendish glee. "My, aren't we in a hurry tonight?" He nodded to one of his underlings, who proceeded to shove Andros into the backseat with the barrel of his gun.

Andros looked over his shoulder again and saw the pack of angry soldiers slow down as they approached the curb. The SP colonel flashed his papers to the sentry with the whistle and asked for a count of the wounded.

"Two of our own dead, Standartenführer," the sentry reported, trying to look into the Mercedes and glimpse the killer's face. But the SP man with the machine gun pushed Andros farther back, out of view. "That man there."

The SP colonel nodded. "We have him now."

"*Zu Befehl,* Standartenführer. We know the drill."

"Then get it over with," snarled the SP colonel. He got into the front of the Mercedes, next to the driver.

Andros looked out through the rear window as they started to pull away. The soldiers who had chased him were grabbing innocent passersby, women and children, and lining them up against a wall. He looked in front. "What are they doing?"

"Retribution," the SP colonel explained. "Your heroics have just cost your countrymen their lives."

"But women and children?"

"You killed two Germans. I wouldn't be surprised if they executed the first hundred Greeks who happen to walk by."

Andros heard the gunfire and screams as he looked back. "You bastards."

"Yes," said the SP colonel. "We bastards just saved your life."

They passed Hadrian's Arch, and the driver cut the lights before swinging a hard right down a side street toward the Plaka district.

"Where are we going?" asked Andros.

"Stissihorou Street," said the SP colonel. "Gestapo headquarters."

"But Stissihorou is the other way."

The SP colonel nodded and addressed the man with the machine gun in back. "Burger . . ."

Andros saw the butt of the gun and felt a tremendous crack against his skull. Then all went black.

64

That night in the Parnon Mountains, situated some two hundred miles south of Athens, fifteen Greek *andartes* and their British liaison officer left their secret base on horseback and headed toward the designated dropping zone. The *andartes,* drawn from the ranks of the rivaling right-wing EDES and left-wing ELAS, wore rags for uniforms and sheepskin caps with the initials EOE, which stood for National Bands of Greece. Their liaison officer to the Middle East GHQ, Colonel James Doughty, rode at the head of the line.

The crack signal that was broadcast by the BBC on the radio back at the National Bands base told them to expect three Royal Air Force planes to pass over at 0100 hours.

It was ten minutes past the hour already, and Stavros Mou-djouras of ELAS could still hear the thunder of German Junkers 88s in the distance, bombing the fires they had lit on dummy dropping grounds earlier.

"Go ahead, blast away, you Boche!" Doughty shouted at the night sky. "There's nothing there!"

The tough New Zealander always amused Stavros, but Stavros never forgot that Doughty served the interests of the British, not those of the Greek people. The same was true, Stavros was beginning to suspect, of the National Bands of Greece, which he had joined in the first place because he would rather fight Germans than Greeks.

The NZ initials on Doughty's cap, in particular, reminded Stavros of his enemy General Napoleon Zervas, the head of EDES. In his younger days as a senior army officer, Zervas had made his money playing cards and gambling. Whenever he found himself short of money, he would threaten a revolution in the army to shake the financial markets. After the exchanges took a dive, he would call off the revolution and split the proceeds of the rising market with the financier who worked with him. Such antics incensed Stavros, mostly because he never grasped the concepts of capitalism and distrusted a system that made blackmailers like Zervas rich—and honest, hardworking Greeks like his father poor.

The presence of EDES colonel Alexander Kalos, riding next to Doughty in his British-supplied battle dress uniform, boots, and pearl-handled pistols, did little to ease Stavros's fears. Kalos was a Zervas bootlicker with ambitions of his own, a Cretan and former cavalry officer who controlled the Peloponnese for EDES. He had secured his reputation with the Greek Resistance through his part in the destruction of the Gorgopatomos Railway six months earlier. The railway had been providing 80 percent of Rommel's supplies to North Africa, and its destruction was undoubtedly the highest achievement of the Resistance thus far. Kalos was only a captain in the Greek army back then, like me, thought Stavros, but Zervas had taken the unauthorized liberty of promoting him to full colonel before promoting himself to general. Now, in the eyes of the British in Cairo, Kalos was the highest-ranking Greek army officer in the integrated National Bands of Greece.

What supplies Cairo was dropping tonight was anybody's guess. But Stavros's younger brother, Michaelis, offered that whatever they might be, he had bad feelings about the rendezvous. This prophecy did not surprise any of the older *andartes,* least of all Stavros, who looked at his youngest brother and saw a slight, nervous, and sickly figure riding beside him.

"You have bad feelings about everything," Stavros said. "'I think we'll drown in that canal,' or 'We'll fall off this cliff if we try to climb it,' or 'The rocks will fall on us.'" Stavros adjusted the Sten submachine gun slung over his shoulder and grunted. "We have girls who are stronger partisans!"

"I'm here, aren't I?" Michaelis insisted.

As far as Stavros was concerned, that was the problem. His brother had abandoned the discipline of school life to join the free and wild atmosphere of the *andartes* in the mountains six months ago. Michaelis had become violently ill the day after the British had made a supply drop to partisans outside their family's village in northern Greece. It turned out he had eaten the new gelatin explosive known as plastique, thinking it was toffee. Stavros blamed the British and insisted they provide medical attention and keep him out of harm's way. With things heating up between EDES and ELAS, the family sent both of them to the National Bands in the Peloponnese.

Now Stavros never saw Michaelis do anything but work the soft putty of plastic explosives from recent supply drops into manageable ten-pound blocks. This was his eternal chore, not studying for school or playing with other boys or building the "better life" the Communist Party had promised, but making bombs. Over time the stuff had managed to work its way under Michaelis's nails and into his skin, and Stavros blamed that for his brother's headaches. Or maybe he blamed himself and the Party. Looking at his little brother, he wondered what he was fighting for. Deep doubt and a gnawing sense of guilt rose within him. He tried to suppress his misgivings with dialectic Marxism, but the superstitions and fears of his home village still had a powerful hold on his psyche.

By the time they arrived at the dropping zone, the rumbling of the Junkers had faded and a gray mist had settled upon the hillside. They waited in the scrub near the edge of the small clearing.

A few minutes later, Stavros could hear the distinct roar of a B-24 Liberator, closely followed by two more.

Doughty shouted, "Now!"

Two *andartes* scrambled into the clearing to light the signal fire.

When the planes passed overhead, they dropped their stores, each container popping off a small white parachute. The squadron leader tipped his wing in signature fashion before turning around and leading the others back to sea.

Michaelis pointed to the squadron leader and cried, "It's him! It's him! Did you see the wing, Stavros? Did you see?"

"I saw," Stavros answered without enthusiasm. The pilot was some daredevil named MacDonald, who advertised his exploits by planting notes inside the stores he dropped to the Resistance. Apparently, he wasn't getting much recognition back home.

As the containers fell gently to earth like snowflakes in the night, Colonel Doughty shouted with joy, "Manna from heaven!"

When the stores hit the ground one by one, the *andartes* rushed forward, eager to open them and find out what was inside. One of the canisters contained a complete radio outfit. Another had enough plastic explosives to blow up Mount Olympus.

Stavros secretly hoped that in addition to rifles, machine guns, ammunition, and explosives, he would find at least some chocolate and whiskey in his container. What he found instead was a strange uniform with the English initials SF on the shoulder and an American flag patch.

"That's for my friend," observed a strange voice from behind. "He's coming later."

Stavros turned. Stepping into the dim light of the clearing, dragging her white chute behind her, was a woman. A woman in a jumpsuit and boots with a sidearm strapped to her leg.

"Hello there," she said with a smile, extending her hand to the bewildered Greek. "I'm Theseus, Captain, Royal Marines."

65

The stars shined brightly over the treetops as Erin Whyte and the *andartes* ambled through the hills back toward the base. The landscape was bleaker than she had imagined, wild and undeveloped. Outside of an occasional forest of firs and pines, such as the one they were passing through, the rugged interior of Chris's homeland seemed remote and forbidding, one steep, sterile mountain range after another. For the Nazis, this must be hell, she thought, and for the Greeks a heaven-sent playground, because even in the darkness, the *andartes* seemed to know every cave and crag in the barren world.

"So this is Free Greece," she said to Doughty, who was riding next to her. "Rather desolate country."

"Stone Age," Doughty said. "Perfect for our purposes. There isn't a soul around for miles, only a few native Tzakonians our wide patrols run into every now and then, but they don't cause any problems."

Erin looked up toward the front of the line in the moonlight. She had counted fifteen *andartes* ahead of them in their rags and sheepskin caps. They had stashed half the stores in a nearby cave, which they kept as a secret munitions dump. The rest they strapped to their backs.

Leading the way back to base was the big one they called Stavros, wearing an old Greek army officer's tunic under the four bandoleers of ammunition that crisscrossed his massive chest. He was a fiery-looking man, Erin thought, big and swarthy, with a rough beard. As soon as he saw her back at the dropping zone, his dark eyes betrayed a hot temper with a spontaneous flash. He obviously wasn't pleased with her or the Middle East GHQ.

"What's the word on Stavros?" she asked Doughty in a whisper. "He looks like the revolutionary leader of some banana republic."

"We found him with his friends roaming the country, looking for trouble with the enemy," Doughty explained. "At night they sabotaged the railway lines, blowing up the trains that the Germans were using to bring in more reinforcements and supplies. Experienced in the use of heavy-infantry weapons. Regularly knocked out German trains by firing bazooka shells into locomotives with unerring accuracy and spraying the rest of the armored trains with equally murderous machine-gun fire."

"I see," said Erin. "And what does he do for fun?"

"Spends his off nights raiding Wehrmacht warehouses and ammunition dumps," Doughty replied. "Once he ran into a German convoy that included a panzer division and held it up for over thirty-six hours. In the process he managed to knock out several tanks and capture a German mountain artillery gun with ammunition."

"A regular one-man army," she remarked. "You've trained him well."

"Unfortunately, that privilege was Moscow's."

Erin remembered Churchill's suspicions about a Soviet mole and said, "He's a Communist, then?"

"A *kapetanios,* to be more precise," the New Zealander explained. "A guerrilla chieftain for ELAS who is more at home in the mountains, with his elite Black Bonnets, than at any Party plenary. In fact, some of the Party fanatics call him a *prodhotes.* It means traitor."

"A traitor?" Erin repeated. "Why is that?"

"He signed a Metaxas confession when he was in jail in 'thirty-nine."

"A confession?"

"A fascist form of inquisition devised by Metaxas's minister of security, Maniadakis, after the Fourth of August regime came to power," Doughty told her. "By renouncing their communism and signing a public 'declaration of repentance,' political prisoners could obtain their release. Copies of the declaration were sent to the authorities in the home villages of the 'penitents,' thus sowing seeds of distrust in the various Communist Party organizations and ensuring a life of misery for those released."

Erin looked at Stavros again. He didn't strike her as a man who would break under pressure, even under the refined police interrogation techniques of Maniadakis. "What induced him to sign?"

Doughty shrugged. "The rumors vary, but it seems that the Metaxas police were torturing his younger brother, Michaelis, and threatened to kill him unless Stavros renounced his communism."

Erin looked at Michaelis, riding behind his brother. The boy didn't look a day older than fourteen. His straight black hair, which needed to be cut, hung over his large, animated eyes. Whenever he looked back at her, which he often did because he was either curious or smitten, she noticed his shy smile. "Why, he's just a schoolboy."

"A little pyromaniac, that's what he is," corrected Doughty. "Quite adept with explosive and demolition accessories—fuses, timers, caps, and other items required to detonate everything from dynamite to half-pound blocks of TNT and plastique. Young enough to waltz into any taverna, leave the bomb behind, and walk out under the noses of the Nazis. After the explosion, there are never any witnesses left to identify him. He'll do anything to be like his brother."

At that moment Colonel Alexander Kalos, who had been at the rear of the line, rode up alongside her and Doughty. With the keen-eyed expression of a hunter, he said, "If I were Michaelis, I would do anything *not* to be like my brother."

"Theseus, meet Colonel Kalos," said Doughty. "He served a distinguished role under Napoleon Zervas in the destruction of the Gorgopatomos Railway viaduct last November."

"I'm impressed, Colonel."

"So you should be," said Kalos, taking her aback with his smug demeanor.

Erin watched him ride to the head of the line to relieve Stavros, who turned his horse around to go to the back of the line.

Doughty explained, "They switch off every so often so each can play the leader."

"Kalos is quite a cowboy," she observed, finding this bid for supremacy amusing. "Have you ever seen him use those pearl-handled Colts he's packing?"

"You noticed them, did you?" Doughty smiled. "Seems he saw a lot of American westerns before the war and fancies himself marshal in the mountains when it comes to Communists. When he's not on a horse, he swaggers around in riding breeches, boots, and spurs. But don't let his swagger fool you. He's a born leader of men. He's also the best shot I've ever seen."

"Really?" asked Erin. "Dare I ask how the cowboy from EDES and the *kapetanios* from ELAS get along?"

"They don't, as you can see," Doughty answered. "The brutalities of men like Stavros Moudjouras have given the Greek Resistance a rather bloodthirsty image. That's why we've checked him with a man like Kalos, equally quick with the trigger, just in case Stavros gets it in his head to try something to redeem his name in the eyes of the Communist Party."

"You think he would?" Erin asked, realizing that Stavros was no longer simply a suspected mole but a mole with a motive.

Doughty shrugged. "Overall, I think his personal ambitions are pure, even if his movement's are not. Fully devoted to his mission."

"Which is?" Erin persisted.

"Oh, the usual party line," Doughty replied. "The liberation of Greece, no less."

66

An hour later, they came over a ridge between two hills, and Erin could view the entire National Bands base spread out below: a cluster of shepherds' huts, tents, tarps, and a stable for horses. Dominating the scenery on the near side of the camp was a gorge carved out like the sliver of the moon, encircling half the camp. Over the gorge, the *andartes* had built a bridge, next to which was an amphitheater-style clearing.

On the surrounding hills, Erin could pick out the silhouettes of the other *andartes* Doughty had placed. They greeted the arriving convoy with sporadic gunfire. Stavros raised his Sten straight up and replied with a burst of his own, laughing the whole time.

Erin looked at Doughty. "What's that all about?"

"They're just blazing off for the hell of it," Doughty said. "An annoying waste of ammunition. I've come to my wits' end trying to explain to them that our factories in Britain and the States aren't working around the clock to manufacture ammunition so they can shoot it off whenever they feel like it. Or that planes get downed and ships sunk trying to get it to them. They consider themselves wild men of the mountains."

They began crossing the wooden bridge in single file. The planks groaned under the weight of each passing horse and rider, and Erin made the mistake of looking down into the mouth of the gorge as she passed.

"A good nine hundred feet to the bottom," Doughty said from behind. "The gorge widens as it goes out to sea, about twelve miles on the other side of the base."

As they came down into the camp, more *andartes* ran along beside them to take their horses and mules. All of them stared at her with such intense curiosity that Erin began to feel nervous;

she was aware of whispering and even some laughter. When she dismounted, Doughty led her toward the clearing. A fire burned in the center of the earthen floor, around which more *andartes* had clustered.

"Ah, food's awaiting," the New Zealander observed.

"At this hour?"

"The middle of the night is the middle of the day for us," Doughty explained. "Our diet usually consists of bread and beans. The bread comes from rough maize flour, and the beans we boil in water. An infernal standard fare and the source of my eternal state of diarrhea. But tonight, because of the supply drop, I believe they've prepared something special."

Erin could see that the *andartes* had spread a rug on the ground in front of the fire for her. "You're not worried about that fire attracting the enemy?"

"The Krauts are done for the night," Doughty assured her. "As long as we give the Junkers enough targets for their so-called precision bombing, they're satisfied and go home like clockwork. Now for a quiet meal."

As soon as they sat down, however, Erin was bombarded by questions from the curious Greeks. "What are the Allies doing in the Middle East?" they asked. "When is the invasion coming? Is Turkey coming into the war? Are you a real Royal Marine?"

Bewildered by the questions, she turned to Doughty for help.

"They demand to know everything," he told her in English. "They don't understand the meaning of the words 'privileged information' or 'security precautions.'"

Young Michaelis offered her a piece of the strange-looking meat he was turning over the fire. It resembled a long, thin sausage.

"*Kokkoretsi*," Doughty explained. "The cleansed intestine of a goat, stuffed with the choppings of the animal and some herbs and spices. A real treat."

Erin politely declined, but Doughty joined the others in helping himself.

At that moment Stavros walked up to the fire, his huge hand

holding a half-empty bottle of brandy. "Since our food isn't delicate enough for her to digest, perhaps the brave captain would prefer something to drink?" he asked, his voice dripping with sarcasm.

Erin was at a loss as to how to treat such a gesture. She realized it was foolish for her to expect suffering, proud home-bred Greeks like Stavros to hide their contempt for foreigners like her, a woman no less. But she knew she'd lose their respect if she didn't hold her ground. She glanced at Doughty, whose poker face told her she was on her own, and then looked the big Greek guerrilla in the eye.

"Pour me a glass, soldier."

The *andartes* around the fire produced a shot glass for her, and Stavros poured her some brandy.

"I propose a toast," announced Stavros. "To our British defenders for sending us so fine a military adviser as Theseus."

The *andartes* raised their assorted tin cups, mugs, and bottles in unison and cried, *"Kaly eleftheria!"*

"Kaly eleftheria," she replied, and swallowed her shot in one gulp. She knew the words meant good liberation or deliverance. But she didn't feel liberated and knew that the only way to be delivered from this insufferable situation was to play the game. So she held out her glass to Stavros for more.

67

It had taken several shots for Erin to shut up Stavros and prove her mettle. Now the brandy was having its way with her. With Doughty's help, she had found her *kaliva*, or shepherd's hut, then promptly collapsed onto her cot and fell asleep.

She dreamed she was back in the Gestapo cellars in Lyon. Cell number two. She was naked and cold and curled into a ball to keep warm. Her wrists and ankles were raw from the hand and leg chains that had held her for six days. She felt nauseated from the dank, suffocating stench of her own urine.

Looking down at her with his scornful smile was her interrogator, Standartenführer Hoffer. He was a young man, about her age, with a powerful build and an arrogant face. Next to him stood a sergeant holding a camera and flashbulb. They were cataloging her like some specimen for experimentation.

"For the record, please," Hoffer demanded. "State your name."

"Joan of Arc."

"I repeat," he said sharply, "state your name, age, and rank."

"Go to hell."

He struck her across the face, and she could feel the skin beneath her cheekbone split open.

"Let the record state that the subject, age twenty-seven, is a captain in the Strategic Operations Executive, British Secret Intelligence Service. She is known to the French Resistance as Erin. Isn't that so, Captain?"

She crouched there silently. The blood from the cut across her cheek was dribbling down her face. She rubbed her chin against her shoulder, smearing a streak across her collarbone.

"Isn't that so, Captain?"

When she looked up, he started urinating in her face. She tried to move away, but he kicked her in the stomach with the toe of his jackboot. The pain seared through her insides, and she collapsed in her corner, retching like a run-over dog, coughing up blood.

"As you know, Captain Erin, you are being charged with espionage and acts of sabotage against the Third Reich," Hoffer informed her. "Under the rules of the Geneva Convention, spies have no rights. Your existence is not even acknowledged by your own country. You will be hanged. You will be forgotten. But we will remember you for our own records. Sergeant."

The sergeant readied his camera. Hoffer reached over and pulled her head up by her hair until she screamed. He turned her battered face toward the camera, and an explosion of light burst from the flashbulb. She blinked, and Hoffer let go of her hair. Her head fell to the floor.

"Sergeant, leave us," said Hoffer. "Tell the others to join us in a few minutes."

She heard the sergeant leave the cell and lock the door. She and Hoffer were alone. Perhaps she still had a chance to come out of this alive.

Hoffer said, "Tell me the other names in your network, and perhaps we can reach accommodations."

She thought of the LaRoches, who had been hiding her and little Michelle. "I'm the network," she said, and spat a ball of blood in Hoffer's face.

He wiped the blood off his cheek, looked at his red fingertips, and cursed. "You little bitch."

"Guess you'll have to kill me, Frederick."

Upon hearing his first name, uttered with such haunting familiarity, Hoffer suddenly went cold.

"That's right," she said. "I know you. You're the son of Mark Hoffer, the Lutheran pastor."

His eyes narrowed into slits, his pupils shifting to the right and the left, as if he were afraid they could be overheard. Then he grabbed her throat and started shaking her. "Is that what those British bastards told you?" he demanded. "It's a lie!"

"Nobody told me, Frederick."

After a few moments the pupils rested on her, and his eyes grew wide with recognition. "Oh my God," he muttered in horror, taking his hands off her. "You're Francis Whyte's daughter!"

"I wasn't sure you'd recognize me without my Sunday-school dress," she said. "Then again, it was over ten years ago when your village church helped my father build his little school for Chinese peasants. We were just sixteen."

Hoffer looked terrified, his eyes rolling like those of a fox caught in a snare. He started pacing the cell, clutching his head between his hands. "This isn't happening!"

"Oh, yes it is," she said. "Just look at me."

He wouldn't. He couldn't.

She watched him with contempt, wondering how the handsome young man she had once admired from a distance could have become such a cowardly monster. A surprising number of former Protestants from independent churches—Lutherans, Presbyterians, Evangelicals—had joined the SS. That was because in the early '30s, Hitler still carried a Bible with him during public speaking engagements and appealed to their love of country and hatred of the urban radicals, the Jews, the Communists. Most of all, unlike Catholics, these young Protestants professed no allegiance to the pope or any other spiritual or political leader outside Germany. By the time they had suspected Hitler's secret agenda was to destroy Jews first and then the Church, these SS men had been brainwashed into professing faith not in the person of Jesus Christ but in an impersonal deity or destiny.

"How can you live with yourself?" she asked him.

He turned and glared at her, hatred filling his eyes. "We're just two good soldiers who happen to be on opposite sides of the war, Captain."

"What's the good soldier going to do now?" she asked. "Hit me again? Spit on me? Beat me? Crucify me, Centurion?"

He pointed an unsteady finger at her. "We both know you're no innocent victim," he said. "You knew what you were in for when you signed up for this war."

"So what's *your* excuse?"

Hoffer opened his mouth to say something, but footsteps could be heard rumbling down the passageway. He stiffened with iron resolve and told her, "We all have our jobs to do."

The cell door swung open. Six young SS men entered the cell. What stone they had crawled out from under, Erin could only guess. Their faces looked flushed from drink, and none of them seemed to be in his right senses. Their eyes flickered with hatred, their mouths twisted in perverse smiles.

"She won't talk, gentlemen," said Hoffer, assuming an impersonal air. "Perhaps you can persuade her."

Erin had heard how the Gestapo broke female agents down: multiple rape. But until now she had refused to believe it. I won't break down, she resolved, I won't.

Even Hoffer couldn't stomach what was about to happen. "I'll return in thirty minutes," he told the others. Careful to avoid looking at her, he walked out and closed the cell door.

She heard the key turn with a sickening click. There was a great cry, and the six guards rushed to her. She felt their hands crawling all over her, squeezing her, hurting her.

"Let's take her for a ride!"

"I bet she hasn't had a ride in years."

"Take a number, men," shouted the first one, a chunky, red-faced youth. "I get her first! The rest of you get what's left." He clutched her breast with his greasy, stubby fingers. She squirmed out of his grasp. "Where do you think you're going?" He unbuckled his belt and slid it off. Coiling it like a whip, he shouted, "Come back here!"

She felt the cold buckle bite her back as he flogged her. She let out a cry and slithered toward a corner of her cell, trying to get away.

He whipped her in a frenzied fury. "I'll beat you to death!"

"Stop it!" warned one. "You'll kill her."

She had reached the corner when she felt the cold hands grab her feet and drag her back. The first guard seized her shoulders and propped her up against the stone wall.

"I'm going to kill you," he said, slamming the back of her head against the stone. "When I'm finished, my friends are going to rape your corpse!"

She felt him hard against her, trying to get in. She screamed in pain.

"What's this?" he shouted, trying to part her thighs, but her ankles strained at the ends of the chains. "Unlock her leg chains! Hurry up!"

She felt the chains loosen and slip off. Then came two quick kicks to spread her legs. Before she could respond, she felt a searing pain as he thrust himself into her. She gasped in agony and stared into his crazed eyes. His sweaty face dripped, and his tongue flicked across his wet lips. He crushed his mouth onto hers.

"Save some for us!" cried the others.

"There's plenty to go around," the first one yelled. "Isn't there, bitch?"

The laughter in the cell was deafening, and the crude brute on top of her thrust deeper, harder, as if he could drill through her to the wall.

"My turn! My turn!" shouted another, aroused simply by watching her.

"She's all yours." The first one pushed himself away from her. "Take your turn, she'll take you all for a ride."

There was an outbreak of laughter, and she felt a dozen hands converge on her at once. She made a feeble attempt to ward them off, but they all collapsed on her, pinning her to the floor.

It was feeding time at the zoo.

Two of them pinned her legs down; a third sat on her face. The others took turns entering her, howling in laughter, shouting some crude song.

"Who are your friends, bitch?" they chanted. "Give us their names."

"No!" she screamed.

The leader grabbed her throat and started choking her while the others struck her face. "Give us their names, bitch!"

The blows to her head began to take their toll. Her mind began playing tricks on her. She thought she could see her father standing in the corner by the cell door. His face was sad, and tears were in his eyes. His hands were at his side as he stood there, watching.

"Father!" she cried out. "What are they doing? Oh, God, help me!"

Her father held his hands open, and she could see the holes in his wrists. "They know not what they do," he seemed to be telling her, then dissolved away.

"Don't leave me here!" she cried. "Don't go!"

But the image was gone, and she was barely conscious, numb from the pain, suffering one blow after another.

"Give us a name, bitch!" demanded their leader.

She started choking, gasping for breath.

"Give us a goddamn name!"

She couldn't hold out any longer. She couldn't stand the pain.

"LaRoche," she wheezed. "The LaRoche family hid me."

"Joseph LaRoche? That miserable little theater producer?"

She nodded.

"Excellent." With a deep laugh, he let go of her neck.

Her body fell limp on the floor of the cell. She looked up to see him wipe his hand across his smiling mouth.

Oh my God, she thought, they broke me. "What are you going to do to him?" she asked desperately.

"Nothing." He laughed. "It's what we'll do to that little girl of his that will make him talk."

Not little Michelle, she thought. What have I done? Dear God, don't let them get their hands on her! She had resolved not to break down. But those bastards had beaten her into submission, and God had abandoned her.

"It's about time we made Michelle a woman," said the leader. "This one's all used up and good for nothing. Aren't you, bitch?" He kicked her in the side.

She heard a crack and then another—two ribs gone. "God help me," she cried out, "I'll kill you all if you bastards touch that little girl!"

There was an explosion of laughter. "That's going to be a little difficult, considering where you're going." They all started kicking her, chanting, "Beat the bitch! Beat the bitch! Beat the bitch!"

Each blow unleashed a fury inside her until something finally snapped. She was furious at God for letting this happen to her and terrified to think that Michelle was next. She had to save her, because nobody else would. She had to survive if only to see these bastards dead and save poor Michelle.

"Good-bye, bitch!"

She was on her last gasp when she managed to free a leg and kick one of the guards in the groin. He moaned in pain and collapsed to the floor.

"You need to learn some manners!" said the leader, and brought down his belt with a swinging blow.

But she blocked it with her cuffed hands, grabbed it, and pulled him down on her knee. He groaned in pain. She brought the cuffs crashing down on his skull so hard that everybody could hear the sickening crack. She pushed him off her until he rolled across the floor, a halo of blood forming around his head. She picked herself up and got on her feet.

There was a stunned silence as the four standing guards stared at the corpse.

"You killed him!" someone said.

Another said, "She's hard as nails!"

"I'll break her in two!" One of them came forward, swinging wildly at her.

She ducked, turned, and drove her knee into his testicles. The blow brought his head forward and down, and she followed by delivering a chin jab full force, using the weight of her body to drive the heel of her hand up into his chin, spreading her fingers so as to reach his eyes. She dug them deep into the sockets, and he cried out in pain. Then she pulled his skull forward and drove it into her knee again, knocking him unconscious and dropping him to the floor.

The remaining three guards closed in on her.

She felt a terrific pain as one of them seized her by the hair from behind and pulled her head back. In one rapid and continuous motion, she grabbed his wrist and arm with a firm grip and swiveled into him, twisting his arm.

"Hey, what are you doing?"

She stepped backward as far as possible with her right foot, jerked his hand from her head, and twisted it down and back between her legs. This sent him headfirst toward the ground.

"Stop her! She's breaking my arm!"

One of the two remaining guards moved in to help. Keeping a firm grip on her captive's wrist and arm, she followed up with a smashing kick to his face, sending him into his friend's arms with enough force to make them both stumble backward and crash both heads against the wall. They dropped to the floor, unconscious.

The last guard came forward, fury in his bloodshot eyes. She stepped out of his reach, wrapped her chains around his neck, and pulled as hard as she could. For a wild moment he spun in circles, practically carrying her on his back as he tried to pry the chain loose, choking desperately. He slammed her against the wall, but she wouldn't let go. Finally, he dropped to the floor.

Breathing hard, feeling dizzy, she looked around at the bodies strewn across the cell. She threw up. Doubled over, she could see blood dripping down the insides of her thighs, and the horrible pain between her legs made her fall to her knees.

There was no time for pain, she told herself. In a few minutes Frederick would be back.

She dragged herself over to the guard who had unlocked her leg chains and found the key. With a little work, she managed to unlock the wrist chains. As she rubbed her sore wrists, she heard a soft groan. She looked over to see a semiconscious guard starting to stir.

Oh, God, she thought, it wasn't over. Not as long as they knew about the LaRoche family. She would have to make sure they were all dead. If only she hadn't broken . . .

She found a half-empty bottle of beer on the floor, smashed it, and picked the most useful shard of glass. Crawling on all fours, she approached the semiconscious guard and slit his throat. The moaning stopped instantly.

She proceeded to move from one unconscious guard to another, slitting their throats, even the one whose skull she had crushed and the one she had strangled. She couldn't afford to have one of them wake up on this side of death. She didn't want to think about what they would find on the other side.

When she was finished, she found a guard who looked about her size. She stripped off his uniform and put it on. She slipped her swollen feet into the oversize jackboots, snatched a cap, and stood up, leaning against the wall to keep her balance. She rolled her hair up into a ball and put the cap on.

She waited by the door, drawing deep breaths, waiting for Frederick to return. He would open the door and see the bodies strewn across the floor. That moment of confusion would be her chance. She would kill him. She would snap the neck of Frederick Hoffer, a preacher's kid like her, and she would feel no remorse. Then she would kill the sentry at the back door and stumble into the misty night.

A few minutes later, she heard the echo of Hoffer's steps coming down the hallway. The key hit the lock, and she held her breath. The door opened, and a hulking figure entered the cell and turned toward her. But it wasn't Hoffer.

It was Stavros.

She woke up, gasping for breath, wet strands of hair plastered across her face. She sat up in terror.

It was early morning, still dark, and she realized she was in her hut at the National Bands camp in the middle of nowhere, drawing deep breaths. It was only a dream—this time.

But it had happened for real once before. That meant it could happen again.

68

When Andros opened his eyes the next morning, he found himself lying on a green divan in what he discerned by the architecture to be an old Turkish house in the Plaka district. The living room bay protruded over a lonely street like the poop of an ancient galleon, affording the man who had knocked him out an unobstructed view on three sides of the neighborhood.

He remembered the night before in the Royal Gardens: the meeting with the shoeshine boy, the fight with the German soldiers, his capture by the Gestapo, and the rounding up and shooting of innocent Greeks. Their haunting cries echoed across his conscience. He could also feel a throbbing pain where the butt of a Schmeisser had crashed against his skull.

"Bastards," Andros said, touching the cold, wet cloth wrapped around his head.

The man turned from the window. "Like I said last night, we bastards just saved your life," he said in English. "Good thing our uniforms put the fear of God into them. They didn't see your face."

Andros sat up. The dawn's early light revealed a land of saddle rooftops covered with crumbling brown tiles, clotheslines that crisscrossed over twisted alleys, and the whitewashed facades of houses with yellow oak doors and green-shuttered windows. He looked at the man. "British?"

"SOE. The name's Jeffrey. Burger to the Germans. Have some tea. The others will be in shortly."

"I see." Andros felt his head and looked resentfully at Burger, or rather Jeffrey, who now poured some tea from the tray on the table. "You make a rather realistic Nazi."

"Thank you. And you were rather dumb. Your little escapade in the Royal Gardens made the morning papers."

Andros picked up the copy of *Eleftheron Vima* on the table. The front page carried an official notice by the German garrison commander whom Andros had seen at von Berg's party.

> During the night of May 29–30, two German sentries were slain in the National Gardens by unknown terrorists. A strict inquiry is being instigated and the perpetrators will be punished with death.
>
> The German military authorities have endeavored to act in every respect favorably to the Greek people. On the basis of the facts and ascertainments set forth above, the conduct of the city at large toward the German armed forces has again become less friendly. Furthermore, the press and public opinion among all classes are still sympathetic to resistance workers and British agents who are in hiding.
>
> Cooperation will be sought to locate and punish the instigators. In the event the orders of the German armed forces are not obeyed, the severest sanctions will be regretfully imposed.
>
> Athens, 30 May 1943.

Andros was still reading when a voice said, "Next time don't try to help orphans and widows. Do your job, and nobody else will get hurt."

Andros looked up to see Brigadier Andrew Eliot walk in from the kitchen, again dressed as a priest on this quiet Sunday morning. With him were the other former Gestapo agents, now dressed as peasants. They sat down around the coffee table.

"And how are you feeling this morning?" asked Eliot.

Andros heaved a heavy, heart-aching sigh. "Considerably better than those poor souls in the Royal Gardens last night."

"An unfortunate consequence of your bloodlust against the Germans. I gather you derived some pleasure from your first enemy kill of the war?"

"None," he replied as he absently rolled up his left sleeve.

"What's wrong?"

Andros looked down at the floor and around the coffee table. "I lost a cuff link."

"You'll survive," said Eliot. "Lose anything else?"

"Nasos," said Andros, suddenly remembering his driver. "He was waiting for me."

"We had a man dressed like you get into the car just before the mess started," Eliot said. "Nasos drove him to Kifissia and heard the full story on you along the way. Later this morning he'll take our man to Piraeus, where you'll already be inside the Andros Shipping offices. You'll walk out as yourself, and our man will walk out as a dockworker. Tonight Nasos will be integral to your escape from Baron von Berg's Red Cross gala."

"So you know about it?"

"Know about it? You made us break out in hives with that reckless move of yours to hand von Berg the ring box."

"So you were listening."

"All the way to the bank—or, more precisely, von Berg's safe," Eliot replied. "He opened it again a few hours later."

"And?"

"We were all ears. Here's the combination."

Eliot handed Andros a slip of paper with four double-digit numbers. Andros memorized it and handed it back.

"What's the word with the girl? Will she help?" Eliot asked.

Andros said, "I think so."

"Good God, man, you can't think. You must know."

"I know she'll see to it that the outside door to von Berg's office is open. I also know she'll delay one of his guards from getting to his post, long enough for me to slip in and out. What I don't know is if we can pull it off undetected."

"Which is why you'll need this." Eliot handed Andros what looked like a gold cigarette lighter but opened to reveal a camera lens. "Just in case the Maranatha text isn't there but something else is. All you do is point and click. We don't want von Berg to discover anything missing if we can help it."

"Just tell me how Aphrodite and I are going to get out of here alive."

"After the reception, Nasos will appear to drive you straight home," Eliot explained. "But along the way, you'll switch cars, and we'll take you to Piraeus. There, the same ship that brought you from Italy, the *Independence,* is scheduled to make a supply run to the Luftwaffe air base on the island of Kythira at eleven P.M. About halfway there, it will make an unscheduled stop off the east coast of the Peloponnese, near Monemvasia. During that time you'll cast off in a lifeboat. A reception committee of *andartes* will be waiting onshore to escort you back to the National Bands base."

"Captain Tsatsos knows about this?"

"Both Captain Tsatsos and your uncle Mitchell know only that an agent code-named Sinon will be leaving Athens for the National Bands base. Neither has the foggiest idea who Sinon is, so you'll have to identify yourself to them later this morning."

"That should prove amusing." Andros smiled at the thought and then grew serious. "Will Captain Whyte be waiting for me at the base?"

Eliot nodded. "Landed last night. You'll hand her everything you've got and wait for your submarine pickup tomorrow night."

"What about Aphrodite and our families?"

"We'll stow them away aboard the Red Cross ship, the *Turtle Dove,* before it returns to Istanbul tomorrow."

Andros shook his head. "It's too risky for them to wait until I'm gone before they escape."

"It's too risky for us if they disappear before you."

"Prestwick said they were coming with me."

"I don't know what your American superiors told you, Andros. But here in Greece, the British are in charge, and I'm not going to let anything jeopardize your escape."

Andros leaned back and crossed his arms. "I'm not leaving without her."

Eliot looked at his watch and sipped his tea. "It is now almost six A.M., and the *Turtle Dove* is due to arrive in Piraeus in a few hours. If you're not at quayside to oversee the distribution of Red Cross consignments, if von Berg has even the slightest suspicion that it was you who killed those two sentries last night, then we're all in trouble. You, your beloved, and her brother included. Andros, you've tried it your way. I bailed you out. Now it's my turn. You'll do as you're told."

69

A ndros arrived in Piraeus dressed as a docker and made his way past the other stevedores into the shipyard offices of Andros Shipping, overlooking the harbor. Uncle Mitchell and Captain Tsatsos were hunched over a chart table when he walked in.

"Reviewing the route for this evening's run to Kythira, Uncle?"

Uncle Mitchell looked up from his chart and beheld his prodigal nephew. "Why are you wearing those rags?"

"Why, to help you out," Andros replied cavalierly. "The *Turtle Dove* should be arriving shortly, and I want to do my part in distributing the Red Cross relief supplies."

"As if you've done even one day of honest work with your hands." Uncle Mitchell glared at him. "You never came home last night. You didn't even bother to show up at church this morning. I suppose you couldn't break away from your duties at the Vasilis estate. All of Athens knows you are a collaborator. I am ashamed of you for your father."

Andros assumed the seat behind his uncle's desk and fanned himself with a ship's manifest. "Oh, Uncle. I'm no collaborator. I'm simply a realist."

"I should strangle you right now, to keep such filthy words from pouring out of your mouth."

"I thought you were going to congratulate me, Uncle. Tonight I plan to propose to Aphrodite."

"You will still marry that slut?"

"Bite your tongue, or I'll cut it out for you."

"Strong words for such a puppy. And where will you get married? You think the archbishop will marry you two?"

"Probably not, unless he wishes to come to Cairo."

His uncle looked at him. "Cairo?"

Andros nodded. "The king will be there, along with other dignitaries who have nothing better to do these days. I hope you'll join us."

"Have you ever heard such nonsense, Tsatsos?" Uncle Mitchell asked the old skipper, who had been silent the whole time. "This boy's gone mad!"

Andros put down the manifest and grew serious. "Secret storage has been prepared for you on the *Turtle Dove*, Uncle. Get Yiaya, Aunt Maria, and Helen, and be ready to spend the night on board. You'll leave in the morning. I'll leave tonight with Tsatsos on the *Independence* for the run to the National Bands base."

His uncle and Tsatsos exchanged nervous glances. "What are you talking about?"

"Don't tell me you've forgotten the myth of the Trojan horse?"

His uncle stared in wonder. "You? You are—"

"Sinon, Uncle."

His uncle crossed himself in wonder and looked up to heaven with a great smile. He kissed Andros on the cheek and started crying. "Mother of God, you *are* your father's son!"

70

Baron von Berg was looking through the report that had just arrived from Istanbul when Werner entered his office and took a seat opposite the desk. "Well?" von Berg asked without lifting his eyes.

"The *Turtle Dove* just docked in Piraeus," Werner reported. "Altenburg, Neubacher, and the home administration are greeting the Red Cross delegation while the consignments are being loaded onto trucks and other ships for distribution. Herr Andros is there directing the effort."

"And?"

"Your suspicions are confirmed. It was Andros who allegedly was captured by our own security police in the Royal Gardens last night. The soldiers who chased him picked this up off the sidewalk." He held up a gold cuff link with a large A embossed in the center.

Von Berg took the cuff link and looked at it. Herr Andros, he could see, was a man of considerably more depth than he had given him credit for. "What does our Gestapo chief say?"

"Wisliceny doesn't have a clue."

"And now Andros pops up in Piraeus like nothing's happened."

"What do you want me to do now?"

"Nothing yet. According to your observations, Andros also met with Aphrodite yesterday atop Likavitos Hill. What did Helmut have to say about his negligence?"

"He was quite speechless, Herr Oberstgruppenführer."

"And now?"

"Quite lifeless."

Von Berg sighed and looked out the French doors to the gardens, where orderlies were setting up tables and lights for the Red Cross reception that evening. He was furious that Aphrodite could still love this man. "What do you suppose they talked about, Werner?"

"Who can say, Herr Oberstgruppenführer?"

"We might try Aphrodite. Bring her to me."

Werner went out. Von Berg walked over to his safe and removed some photos and looked at them. A few minutes later, Aphrodite came in. Werner ushered her to a chair.

"Please make this quick, Ludwig," said Aphrodite. "There's so much to do before the reception and so little time."

"Yes," von Berg responded coolly, "of that I have no doubt." He walked over to the French doors and turned around. "You saw Herr Andros yesterday."

She seemed too shocked to deny it and said nothing.

"What did he say to you, my love?"

"He wishes to marry me, Ludwig."

"Still? How faithful of him. What did you say?"

"I . . . I didn't know what to say."

Von Berg paused, photos in hand. "I was hoping I wouldn't have to show you these. But I thought you should be informed of your former fiancé's behavior before you make a wrong decision."

He spread the photos before her. They showed Chris with a blonde at dinner in Switzerland, on the streets, in bed.

"It seems your fiancé is not as faithful as he pretends, Aphrodite. I can only wonder what his true motives are for coming back to Athens. Perhaps you could tell me what he's told you. I couldn't bear to see you get hurt."

She looked up at him with angry, confused eyes. She seemed painfully aware, as he was, that the time to choose sides had come.

71

The reception for the Red Cross delegation was in full swing when Andros arrived at the Vasilis estate at half past eight. He looked for Aphrodite as he strolled about the gardens filled with diplomats and dignitaries, but he could not find her. The host of the party, however, was at his elbow instantly.

"Ah, there you are, Herr Andros," said Baron von Berg, once again sporting his decorated naval dress uniform and aristocratic air. "For a moment I doubted your arrival."

"Why, I wouldn't miss this for the world, Baron von Berg. Things in Piraeus kept me busy all afternoon."

Von Berg nodded. "Where is the rest of the Andros family?" he asked, looking about. "They are noticeably absent."

"Yes, well, my uncle doesn't approve of all this, you know. His archaic political views cloud any civilized perspective of the modern world."

"And business sense, perhaps?" Von Berg smiled.

"Yes, and business sense." Andros laughed. "Speaking of which, I'd like to conclude the deal we outlined in your office yesterday and propose to Aphrodite tonight. I suppose I should have the ring. Then I can find a private place to pop the question. That's if I can find her. Have you seen her?"

"Oh, she's up and about somewhere. Be careful which place you choose. You no doubt heard what happened in the Royal Gardens last night?"

"Who hasn't? I was there myself when the commotion started, but I quickly jumped back into my car and ordered my chauffeur to drive us away. Dreadful, that such thugs should be running about Athens. Why, that could have been me they killed. Any leads?"

Von Berg looked at him keenly. "None, unfortunately."

"Communists, you know, all of them. They—"

Andros stopped as Aphrodite appeared at the top of the steps overlooking the garden. Her hair was down tonight, falling gracefully behind her bare bronze shoulders and outshining her elegant black dress. The orchestra struck up a waltz, and Andros excused himself from von Berg. "You'll pardon me, Baron, but I'd like this waltz."

"But of course," said von Berg with an understanding smile. "I'll get your ring."

Despite her impeccable glossy exterior, Aphrodite seemed nervous as Andros took her hand and they danced beneath the sparkling lights in the twilight. He caught von Berg watching them before the Baron went up the steps inside the house.

"You have the uniform?" Andros asked her.

"Upstairs, in the lower right-hand drawer of my dresser."

"Good. And you'll take care of Hans?"

She nodded. "I've already promised him a dance and have been delaying him as long as I can. He's waiting by the buffet table."

They turned in a circle, and Andros glimpsed the reproachful Hans, immaculately dressed, impatiently looking at his watch.

"Excellent," Andros said. "It's eight-forty-eight, so I should be making my way to your bedroom and be back a little after nine. In and out in just a few minutes."

"Christos," said Aphrodite, "I don't think I can go through with this."

"Of course you can," he told her firmly. "Now is not the time for second thoughts."

"Ludwig knows something's up. Maybe not about the safe. But he suspects you want to take me away from him."

"You think he's a genius because he figured that out?"

"Please, Christos. Don't do anything foolish."

"What do you want me to do, Aphrodite? Run away?"

"Yes," she said. "Forget whatever is inside Ludwig's safe. Go home tomorrow morning on the *Turtle Dove*. You've brought food to Greece. You've freed my brother. Isn't that enough?"

"No, it's not." He was aware that time was slipping away. By now he should have been on his way to the Baron's study. "I came here on a mission, and I'm going to fulfill it."

"I'll get into the safe," she told him, squeezing his hand with unmistakable determination. "Tell your British friends that I'll give them what they want after you and Kostas are safely away."

"And leave you behind?" He groaned inside. "Why the hell do you think I came back to Athens? To see the sights?"

She looked confused, as if she couldn't believe him. "Just tell me one thing, Christos. Did you love her, or was that business, too?"

He looked into her curious amber eyes and felt his heart miss a beat. He prayed to God she wasn't talking about Elise.

"The woman in Bern," she said. "Ludwig showed me pictures of you two."

"She was a spy, Aphrodite, one of von Berg's, to test me and my love for you. I hate myself for what I did. But I had to do it."

"That makes two of us."

Before he could ask Aphrodite what she meant, Andros saw von Berg standing at the top of the steps. He felt a tap on his shoulder and turned.

"May I?" asked Hans.

"Of course."

Andros handed off Aphrodite, who looked back at him helplessly as Hans led her toward the center of the dancing. Andros walked up the steps to join von Berg. Together they watched Aphrodite and Hans waltz gracefully under the stars.

"Quite a charmer, that Hans," Andros told the Baron, trying to sound a bit flustered.

"Isn't he? I'll have to talk with him about his manners. To think that he would cut in on one of my honored guests."

"Oh, it's my own fault. I won't have a chance down there with

Aphrodite. I'll have a word with her later, if I can find the right time and place. Would you happen to have the ring?"

"Certainly." Von Berg handed Andros the blue box.

"Thank you," said Andros. "In the meantime, I think I'll try some of that fresh fish inside." With that, he excused himself and went into the house.

72

The clock in the hallway by the bar said it was two minutes to nine. Andros walked to an island of food, looked it over for a few seconds, and then went past a sentry up the stairs to Aphrodite's bedroom, the second door to the right down the corridor. But when he walked in, he found her mother sitting on the bed.

"You!" she said. "What are you doing here?"

Andros looked at his watch. It was nine o'clock on the dot. There was no time to have it out with the woman, so he started to take off his tuxedo.

"What on earth are you doing?" she said.

"Why, I'm about to propose to your daughter."

Her hands came to her face in horror, and she left the room cursing. Andros locked the door behind her and immediately went to the dresser.

The SS dress uniform was tucked away underneath some silk nighties. He quickly slipped into the pants, buttoned up the tunic, and fastened the belt with the German eagle on the buckle. He had to admit it felt good to be in uniform again, even if it was the wrong side's. He picked up the cap and put it on his head at a slight angle, just the way Hans had it on in the garden.

"Perfect," he told himself.

It was then that he noticed his picture on the dresser, taken in the States four years ago. How often had Aphrodite looked at it, he thought, the way he had looked at hers at West Point? How did von Berg feel about it, knowing it was up here? Not now, he told himself, and shook off any emotion he was feeling in order to concentrate on the task at hand.

Andros slipped the camera Eliot had given him into the uniform's pocket, along with Aphrodite's lighter. Then he parted the curtains and walked out onto the balcony.

It was dark outside, music drifting from the gardens around the corner. He firmly gripped Mrs. Vasilis's precious mango tree, for years his ladder to Aphrodite's bedroom, and softly descended to the gardens.

As Andros turned the corner, he could see the black cutout of a sentry on the patio outside the library. It was Peter, smoking a cigarette, pacing impatiently and glancing back and forth between his watch and the gardens, obviously itching to go. Andros was about to step forward when, from behind him, came two dull thuds—mangoes falling to the ground from the shaken tree.

Peter spun around. "Hans, is that you?"

Andros nodded and tapped his watch.

"You're late," Peter scolded, and without waiting for a response, he darted off toward the gardens.

Andros watched him leave and took a quick look around. Satisfied that nobody was near, he walked up, pushed his hand against the French door, and felt the catch give way.

73

The library was dark as Andros made his way to the bookshelves, careful to avoid running into von Berg's desk. Fortunately, there was enough glow from the gardens to throw some light on the floor through the windows. Andros moved cautiously but quickly. It would be only a minute or two before Peter saw the real Hans dancing with Aphrodite.

He pushed aside the volumes of Greek dramas and German philosophy and found the metal door to the safe. Following the numbers Touchstone had given him, he turned the dial to the right, to the left, back to the right, and one final turn to the left. He turned the handle. Nothing happened.

He tried it again, and again the handle wouldn't turn. Then he heard voices in the hallway. Through the slit of light beneath the door, he could see shadows moving on the other side. He held his breath, and after a moment, they passed.

Once more he gave the dial four swift turns. There was a wonderful click, and the handle turned smoothly. He pulled the heavy door, and it opened.

He flicked on his lighter, quickly scanned the contents of the safe, and pulled out three folders. The first was marked FLAMMEN-SCHWERT, the second LUDWIG VON BERG, and the third HUSKY. He realized he would have to skim them and choose what seemed important enough to photograph.

He opened the FLAMMENSCHWERT folder. In it, he found aerial photos of coastal fortifications, along with maps of minefields and artillery defenses. Also listed were various supply runs of Andros ships under Swiss registry, with their manifests, including metallic uranium from Brazil in crates marked for groundnuts. But he found nothing resembling an ancient text, only a report that was written in neither Greek nor even German but Danish.

The report's title, from what Andros could make out, spoke of "the passage of charged particles through matter." Scribbled on the cover was a note that said, "This manuscript must not fall into Nazi hands." Signed Niels Bohr. The Nobel Prize–winning physicist? thought Andros, looking closer. On top of Bohr's note was another note, typed on official Nazi stationery by an SS Oberführer Werner Best, suggesting that "Bohr's project be brought under our direction." Further military orders addressed the question of "atomistics" and mentioned "the off-site laboratory Achillion."

Andros looked again at the aerial photographs. On the back of one of the photos was writing that said it had been taken by an American B-17, and the word "Achillion." Perhaps this was the pilot MacDonald had told him about, the one shot down over Greece.

A photograph of a photograph would never do, Andros realized. So he left the pictures but took one of the negatives in the folder, as this would be less likely to be missed by von Berg. He slipped the negative into his pocket and moved on to the second folder, the one marked LUDWIG VON BERG.

74

The SD report on von Berg was quite thick. On the black cover was a square of white paper with the title spelled out in jet-black letters: LUDWIG VON BERG, SS NO. 96669. Too long to read here, Andros thought, but he had to open the report and at least skim the first page. He did and was hooked.

Baron Ludwig von Berg was born in 1904, the son of a certain Maximilian von Berg, an undistinguished professor of music at the University of Munich. What did distinguish Maximilian was that he had been orphaned at birth when his mother, a recently widowed Baroness Teresa von Berg, died during complications in his delivery.

Or so Maximilian—and later his son, Ludwig—believed.

Maximilian never knew the fantastic truth that he was none other than the illegitimate child of King Ludwig II of Bavaria and Empress Elizabeth of Austria. Neither would his son, were it not for a series of extraordinary circumstances.

It was no secret that Ludwig II adored and idealized his cousin Elizabeth. The two had grown up together on Lake Starnberg, Elizabeth in a beautiful home at Possenhofen and Ludwig across the waters in Berg Castle. Whenever the empress returned from Austria on holiday to her family at Possenhofen the lonely Ludwig was there, reveling in her company.

The summer of 1871 found the cousins especially intimate. Both were disenchanted with the aristocratic life and had secluded themselves from society. For the

33-year-old Empress Elizabeth, that meant escaping the intrigues of the Austrian court. For the 25-year-old King Ludwig II, that meant retreating from the politics of a new, united Germany. William, king of Prussia, was now hailed as emperor, and for the first time, King Ludwig feared for the future of his beloved Bavaria. He was particularly troubled that by refusing to marry and have children, he had failed to secure the succession of the Wittelsbach family line. Elizabeth understood, and one night in a fit of passion, the two cousins cast aside their platonic pretensions.

Max was born the next spring, while Elizabeth continued her seclusion in Merano with her sisters. By now she had been absent from Austria for almost two years, and the clamor of court gossip had reached such malicious levels that she was forced to return in May. But not before she left young "Max von Berg" in the charge of a childhood friend in Munich, a spiritualist named Countess Irene Paumgarten. The countess saw to Max von Berg's care and education. As a baron, he enjoyed enough social advantage to escape poverty but remained far enough away from a life in the court that had so disappointed his parents.

For the next 14 years, Elizabeth would often visit the countess on the pretext of spiritual guidance, but in reality to check up on young Max, who was being trained for a life of music in the grand tradition of Wagner, the one person King Ludwig II claimed understood him besides Elizabeth. Nobody else, however, could understand the enigma that was the Bavarian monarch. For it was during this time that Ludwig II retreated into a netherworld of fantasy, chasing grandiose dreams and building his fabled castles of Neuschwanstein, Herrenchiemsee, and Linderhof.

The "mad monarch," as he was widely known by that time, was finally declared insane and removed from government at the age of 40. In 1886 he drowned in Lake Starnberg under mysterious circumstances, and to this day there is debate as to whether he committed suicide or was assassinated. Because Ludwig left no known successor and because nobody knew about the illegitimate Max or whether he would be accepted with his dubious pedigree, Prince Luitpold became regent of Bavaria within the United Germany.

After Ludwig's death, a grief-stricken Elizabeth retreated to the Greek island of Corfu. She cited health reasons, but it was really to escape her pretentious and altogether miserable existence in the Hapsburg court once and for all. She lived to see Max enjoy a brilliant career as a composer of music and a fortunate marriage to Johanna Guber, the daughter of a prosperous German industrialist. Only Max's occasional acts of eccentricity, which charmed society but alarmed his family with their increasing frequency, gave her cause for concern. Elizabeth's last thrill in life was to attend Max's first Wagnerian production, staged by the Berlin court opera to critical acclaim, on September 10, 1898. At the age of 60, she was assassinated by the Italian anarchist Luzzeni on Lake Geneva in Switzerland. Max was 26.

It was several years later, on June 2, 1903, that Max von Berg's wife, Johanna, gave birth to their first and only child, a son whom they ironically chose to name Ludwig. When the child was christened in their local Catholic church in Munich, neither Max nor Johanna nor the priest nor any of the family friends attending had any idea that this was Ludwig III.

From the beginning, Ludwig von Berg's childhood was marred by tragedy. First there was his father's descent into madness—a shocking and disturbing development to family and friends who knew nothing of Max's heritage. Then came the outbreak of the Great War. To 11-year-old

Ludwig, both seemed to occur simultaneously and with equal devastation. Even as he saw his father deteriorate into a state of insanity, he witnessed the power of the British blockade choking the life out of his country. By the time he was 15, his father had died in an insane asylum, and Kaiser Wilhelm II's Reich had collapsed.

At this point Ludwig von Berg himself started to show signs of mental imbalance, hearing loud voices and having hallucinations. The thought that the madness all around him could also be inside him so terrified Ludwig that he hurled himself into those athletics in which he could excel as an individual: fencing, hunting, horseback riding, swimming, sailing, and marksmanship. To assert himself, to dominate and conquer, was to somehow keep ahead of the encroaching darkness that could swallow his soul at any moment. Whenever he did this—pursued technical perfection in any endeavor for its own sake—the voices stopped. As a result, he could never be still but constantly had to keep moving forward, terrified the voices would return.

In school he excelled in chemistry, physics, and mathematics, as well as classical and modern languages, but he found philosophy, morality, and his mother's Catholicism to be rather worthless on the whole. They did little to answer his honest questions concerning a meaningless universe and offered little comfort for his isolation. Only Hegel, Nietzsche, and Heidegger aroused any sort of interest; the result was an odd synthesis of existential thought that reached its nadir when Ludwig concluded that learning was futile and knowledge vanity. He dropped out of the university in 1922 and, at the age of 19, joined the navy for what he hoped would be a life of adventure.

He rose quickly through the ranks of the officer corps. After a brief tour of duty aboard the admiral's flagship, the cruiser *Berlin*, he was attached to naval intelligence. He was posted to the top-secret signals interception and code-breaking unit at Kiel. There he used his superior technical and language skills to crack enemy ciphers in defiance of the Versailles Treaty. He also qualified for the navy pentathlon team and taught fencing at the military sports school at Wünsdorf.

But to Ludwig von Berg, these were all mere games. The excitement of naval intelligence faded sooner than he expected, and worse, the voices returned. In need of an immediate remedy, he had his grandfather Guber pull strings with Admiral Raeder at fleet headquarters to secure him command of his own submarine.

Ever since the Great War, Ludwig von Berg had been spellbound by the submarine's ability to submerge and become invisible to the enemy. Such stealth offered not only protection but the offensive advantage of surprise. He could go anywhere in the world, even those parts of the sea dominated by the enemy, and launch an underwater torpedo attack without warning. This power, this independence, gave him a sense of control over his destiny.

But destiny caught up with Ludwig von Berg one day in 1936. That was when the 33-year-old baron received an urgent call from Wilhelm Canaris, his former first officer from the *Berlin*. Canaris, now an admiral, wanted to "talk about things."

It had been several years since the two had met, and much had happened in Germany in the meantime. Three years earlier the Reichstag had passed an enabling act that did away with parliamentary government and granted absolute power to Adolf Hitler. Since then the Nazi Party had dismissed the Bavarian state government in Munich, consolidated power throughout the rest of Germany, and crushed all opposition.

Ludwig von Berg spent most of his time at sea, so these were events he read about in the newspapers and did not concern him. But Admiral Canaris, who was head of the Abwehr—the German military secret service—looked troubled when he arrived at the Guber estate in Munich where Ludwig resided.

There was a transcript from recorded surveillance:

"These Nazis, they are bent on ruining Germany," he told von Berg in the parlor. "Now they want me to give them the noose to hang us all. You must help me."

Von Berg had heard similar grumbling among the officer corps. "How does this concern me?"

"You undoubtedly are aware of the SS?"

"Smart black uniforms, twin lightning flashes of silver on the collars. How could I miss them? Schutzstaffel—Hitler's so-called protection squad. Headed by that old schoolmaster and chicken farmer, Himmler."

"Well, in addition to protecting the Führer and the Nazi Party, the SS now concerns itself with protecting the security of the entire Reich. The Reich Security Main Office—or RSHA, as they now call themselves—is usurping every function of the state and armed forces. They even have their own secret intelligence service—the Security Service, or SD. Its chief is Himmler's deputy, Reinhard Heydrich."

"Heydrich?" said von Berg. "I know that name from somewhere. Wasn't there a midshipman on the *Berlin* by that name?"

"There was indeed."

"I saw him at the German officers' fencing tournament at Dresden once," von Berg recalled. "After he lost a match in the preliminary rounds, he smashed his saber to the floor and threw such a fit that the umpires had to restrain him." Von Berg looked at Canaris. "I heard he was expelled from the navy altogether. Surely this can't be the same man."

Canaris nodded. "Criminals, I tell you, from the top to the bottom. Now the military and political secret services are expected to 'collaborate.' I'm working with Heydrich to draw the lines of jurisdiction between his SD and my Abwehr."

"So again I ask you, Admiral, how does this concern me?"

"To achieve a common platform, Heydrich is modeling his organization along Abwehr lines. The SD is looking for someone to head its industrial espionage section. Your background with the B-Dienst code-breaking unit at Kiel and your family's connections with foreign industry make you ideal. I want you to join the SD and be Heydrich's industrial intelligence chief."

"And spy for you?"

"For Germany."

Von Berg raised an eyebrow and looked at Canaris. "Isn't that what Heydrich is going to say to me when he asks me to start spying on you and your traitors on the General Staff? That would place me in a most impossible position."

"The SD is rounding up anybody they consider a threat to the Reich—Communists, Jews, certain aristocrats." Canaris emphasized this last class as he looked at Baron von Berg. "Heydrich has secret dossiers on hundreds of thousands more locked in his personal safe, information that can be used against anyone. Let your conscience be your guide, von Berg."

"And if I have no conscience?"

"Then listen to reason. Heydrich's got a file on you, too."

Von Berg laughed. "On what, my politics? It must be a rather flimsy file. I have no politics, you know that. As for my family, my grandfather is the quintessential conservative German industrialist. He squandered I don't know how much helping that Bormann fellow finance the restoration of the old Barlow Palace down on the Brunnenstrasse for their party headquarters."

"All I know is what I heard," said Canaris. "That two years ago, after the bloody purge of the brownshirts by the SS, Heydrich seized all SA documents, including records of their interrogations at Stadelheim Prison here in Munich."

"Politics, politics, Admiral. I fail to see how this could possibly involve me."

"It seems that one of those interrogations extracted a rather extraordinary confession from a member of the Bavarian political police before the SA executed him. It concerned your father and the cause of his madness."

This instantly aroused von Berg's interest. "You are sure of this?"

"Of the file's existence, yes. What's inside, no."

Von Berg was silent. The thought that there could be an answer to the enigma that had been his father and a reason for his own signs of madness was something he had written off long ago. But now . . .

"If what you are saying is true," he said a moment later, "then why would Heydrich trust me to work for him?"

"Precisely because he has a file on you. He understands that self-interest will secure your loyalty, because without the protection of the SS, your future is doubtful. His ranks are full of former enemies who serve him well. Heinrich Mueller, the head of the Gestapo, was himself once a member of the Bavarian political police."

"I'm no Nazi, Admiral. I'm not much of anything when it comes to articles of faith."

"Your ideology—or lack of one—is second to your usefulness. The SD needs your skills. Germany needs your loyalty."

And von Berg needed the secret that was locked inside Heydrich's safe.

Less than one month later, SS colonel Ludwig von Berg
reported to SD headquarters on the Prinz Albrechtstrasse
and Wilhelmstrasse in Berlin. There he joined two
hundred so-called specialists from every imaginable
field—economics, physics, linguistics, arts, religion.
Among them he also found arsonists, forgers, kidnappers,
and murderers. All wore the black SS uniform with a red
armband bearing a black swastika on a white background.
Together they managed what had become a worldwide
criminal organization with three thousand full-time
agents and fifty thousand part-time agents.

Von Berg's industrial espionage section belonged to
Department III of the RSHA and tracked the world's vital
industries in munitions, fuels, rockets, and nuclear fission.
For Baron von Berg, this was a simple task. After his
grandfather's death, he had inherited more than a dozen
seats on the boards of such major German industrial
giants as Krupp, Zeiss, and I. G. Farben, not to mention the
family's equally prominent Guber Industries.

To the outside world, Baron von Berg was a former
naval officer and German industrialist who conducted
business abroad. Where possible, von Berg would
establish shell corporations in neutral countries such as
Switzerland as fronts to purchase vital technology from
foreign countries. He would also use legitimate German
enterprises abroad to enter into an intricate economic
web with American, British, and European corporations.
As a result, he was able to break the Versailles Treaty by
obtaining various parts for submarine, missile, and other
research from a number of different companies around
the world. These components would then be assembled in
Germany.

Inside the Third Reich, however, Standartenführer
von Berg of the SS remained under the watchful eye
of his superior, Heydrich, who, at meetings with RSHA

department heads, often referred to him as "our shady
Baron from military intelligence." To Heydrich, Baron
von Berg would always personify the old Germany, the
conservative establishment, and the naval officer corps
that had rejected him and that his twisted mind sought to
destroy.

Too many minutes later, utterly astounded, Andros reached the
final page of the summary section of the report:

> Because Ludwig II left no known successor, Prince Luitpold
> assumed the office of regent of Bavaria within the united
> Germany from 1886 until he died in 1912. The next year
> his son assumed the kingship and declared himself
> Ludwig III, only to be dethroned in 1918 with the brief
> establishment of the Soviet republic that preceded the
> doomed Weimar Republic and the rise of the Third Reich.
> By this time Ludwig II's son and true heir by birthright,
> Maximilian von Berg, had died in an insane asylum. The
> line of succession now falls to Ludwig von Berg.
>
> As far as the world is concerned, only two of us are
> aware of Ludwig von Berg's true identity. All members
> of the Bavarian political police aware of this rumor have
> been eliminated; Gestapo chief Heinrich Mueller knows
> nothing. As for others who might be aware of Maximilian's
> legacy, it is doubtful that—if they are still alive—they
> would come forward to confirm the rumor, much less
> stake their lives on it.
>
> Nevertheless, the legend of Ludwig II's son still
> fires a fierce monarchist movement in Bavaria, and the
> Wittelsbach family has worn the emperor's crown three
> times before. Should the secret of Maximilian von Berg's
> true identity be known, such sentiment could be strong
> enough to put Ludwig von Berg, the true Ludwig III, on
> the throne—if not by certain Germans, then by the Allies.

> Thus, in the final analysis, U-boat commander Ludwig
> von Berg of the Imperial Navy can only be considered an
> enemy of the Reich. Recommend special treatment. Heil
> Hitler!

Andros knew that "special treatment" was the SS euphemism for murder. The report was signed by the SS staff officer who had prepared it and was initialed by Heydrich. Heydrich, in turn, had the man executed the following day and added his own handwritten addendum to the bottom of the page:

> Now I am the only one who is aware of Ludwig von Berg's
> true identity. Genetics dictate that the Baron should be
> completely mad by the time he is 40. That would be June 2,
> 1943. In the meantime, he can still be of use to the Reich.
> He shall be brought under my direct supervision, where I
> can personally observe the signs of his progressive mental
> decline and perhaps encourage them. If, at the age of 40,
> he is still psychologically sound, I shall see to it that he
> receives very special treatment indeed.

75

Andros closed the report and looked outside to the gardens, recalling that Heydrich never made it to Berlin. Czech assassins had ambushed the Protector's green Mercedes as it made a hairpin turn outside Prague. The exploding grenade had fatally wounded Heydrich. It took him over a week to die at Bulovka Hospital.

All great stuff for the OSS, but no Maranatha text.

He put down the Von Berg file and picked up the Husky file. At last he'd found what he was looking for—copies of an ancient Greek text, juxtaposed with mathematical formulas.

The accompanying report, curiously, was written in . . . English.

English? Andros took a closer look and suddenly found himself staring at the Allied plans for invasion of Sicily. The plans said the Americans would be landing in the Gulf of Gela and from there would advance up the west coast of the island. The British were to land near the southwest tip of the island and move quickly to take Syracuse. The plans even detailed the movements of General Patton's Seventh Army—to which he and Hayfield had been assigned at West Point.

Sicily! According to the report, Greece was only a cover.

Von Berg's handwritten notes in the margins said that the Americans would never make it beyond the beaches. Hermann Goering's panzer division would move down toward Gela from its positions around Caltagirone and would be waiting to greet them.

Andros thought of Hayfield and knew he couldn't allow this scenario to happen.

He also thought of something else: Prestwick and Donovan lied to me.

His heart started to race as everything sank in. His own life, not to mention Aphrodite's, seemed less certain with each passing second.

Andros set the folders on von Berg's desk and pulled out his camera. He had to move fast, he realized, and switched on the desk lamp only to find Werner seated behind the desk, pointing a Česká at him.

76

The mournful strains of *rembetika* music faded into the night as Captain Tsatsos stepped outside the quayside taverna and lit his hand-rolled cigar. It was getting late, and darkness had fallen across the port of Piraeus. He drew a deep breath and looked past the row of shipyard warehouses to the docks. Anchored at the pier was the *Independence*, waiting to make her run to the Luftwaffe air base on the island of Kythira.

Tsatsos looked at his watch. Ten after nine. Curfew was at ten. Andros wasn't expected to arrive until shortly thereafter, when the entire harbor would be blacked out in the event of Allied night bombing.

Tsatsos strolled along the quay to the *Independence*, whistling softly in the dim light. The crew were dallying about with the cranes and the last remaining drums of fuel, trying to look as busy as they could. But Tsatsos could sense their restlessness on his way up the gangway. When he finally reached the bridge, his first mate looked worn and hunted.

"We've been stalling for as long as we can," Karapis reported anxiously. "Lieutenant Schneider from the port authority is demanding to know what the holdup is."

"Lieutenant Schneider." Tsatsos spat on the deck. "My favorite port officer."

Karapis said, "I told him you were drinking at the taverna, that you weren't aware our departure time had been moved up."

"And our cargo?"

"Even with the delays, the last stores are ready to be loaded," Karapis replied, "all except one."

Tsatsos nodded. "Andros."

"Do you think he'll make it?"

Tsatsos shrugged. "Lights out soon," he observed grimly. "If Christos comes, we want to be sure we're still in port."

Karapis, clearly losing patience, replied, "But the crew has stalled too long already."

Tsatsos turned his gaze a few piers away to the ghostly *Turtle Dove*, emptied of her stores and crew until her departure in the morning, or so it seemed. "What about our other friends?"

"Mitchell Rassious, his wife, daughter, and mother-in-law are all safely stowed aboard the *Turtle Dove*," Karapis reported. "We got them aboard before the last consignments were unloaded this evening and the SS guard detail moved in. It's we who will be in trouble if we don't cast off."

Tsatsos could see that his exasperated first mate could wait no longer. "Come, then, Karapis, let us talk to our friend the port officer."

They didn't have to travel far, because at that moment an annoyed Lieutenant Schneider walked onto the bridge. He was an oily, sniveling, and pretentious landlubber who had developed an abrupt passion for the sea the previous fall when he discovered that his battalion would be moving on from Athens to the cold Russian front. How he finagled his new post was a source of endless speculation among the Greek dockers.

"So that's what smells so foul in here," said the German, frowning at the cigar in Tsatsos's mouth. "You're smoking hashish."

Tsatsos shrugged. "Arrest me, Lieutenant. Then who will pilot your stolen wares?"

Schneider was still new to this miserable job and apparently had decided that insubordinate old dogs like Tsatsos weren't worth the trouble. "You're going to Kythira tonight," the port officer said with an authoritative voice. "But I see you have no gun crew or escort flotilla."

"Yes, it seems friends are in short supply for these little night runs to the Kythira air base." Tsatsos took a puff on his cigar and smiled. "Perhaps it has something to do with the highly explosive barrels of fuel we have on board." He tapped his cigar and with delight watched the German's eyes anxiously follow the flickering ashes to the floor. "Why do you ask? Would you like to join us?"

"No, not at all." Schneider sniffed. "In fact, the port authority has cleared you for departure. For over an hour now. You're to leave at once."

Tsatsos glanced at Karapis. "But of course. Just as soon as we load our last stores *and* fix that troublesome leak in the boiler room. You will check on it, Karapis?"

It took a few seconds for the first mate to understand. "Yes, sir, of course, sir. I'll go down right now," said Karapis, and left the bridge.

Tsatsos looked at Schneider. "Perhaps you would like to wait here with me while we test the leak. Our method is foolproof, you know."

"Is that so?"

"Yes," Tsatsos replied. "We fire up the engines, and if we don't blow up, we know the leak has been fixed."

"Thank you," said Schneider, "but other duties demand my attention."

Tsatsos noticed that Schneider was looking over his shoulder. He turned and looked out the window. At the end of the harbor, two *Kübelwagen* carrying a dozen SS guards emerged onto the docks. They drove past the quayside warehouses, tavernas, and *kafeneons*, rounding the harbor on their way toward the pier. There, they set up a checkpoint. Tsatsos looked at Schneider. "What's going on?"

"Extra security precautions for the blackout," Schneider explained. "Our orders are that nobody leaves here until tomorrow morning. Nobody except you. Now, off with you. What if the RAF bombed us and we couldn't get our planes off the ground for lack of fuel?"

"Why, that would be tragic."

"Yes, it would, Captain Tsatsos, for all of us."

Tsatsos nodded sympathetically. "Indeed, your vacation would be over, and you'd have to report to the Russian front."

Schneider left the bridge without another word, leaving Tsatsos alone to enjoy a commanding view of the harbor. He looked across the black blanket of water to the city. The moon hovered over the Acropolis, the Parthenon casting an ominous glow.

In a few minutes, Karapis returned to the bridge with the helmsman and engineer behind him, their faces awash with fear. Tsatsos knew he could stall no longer and heaved a deep sigh.

"Fire up the engines," he told them. "Tell the crew to prepare to cast off."

77

"I must say, you make a rather dashing Nazi, Herr Andros." Werner waved his Česká casually inside the library at the Vasilis estate. "Please sit down."

Andros, numbed for a moment, slowly moved his hand to his side.

Werner snapped up his arm with the Česká, a bulbous silencer screwed onto the end of the barrel. "I wouldn't, Herr Andros. This still makes a little cough, and I would prefer not to attract the Baron's attention just yet."

Andros sat down while Werner sifted through the open files, careful to keep his gun trained on him.

"What was it you were looking for? Coastal defenses for Greece, perhaps? Or an ancient Greek text? Ah, I see the Baron is conducting atomic experiments without the Führer's knowledge. Jewish physics. I thought we were through with all that when the Norwegian Resistance sabotaged the Norsk Hydro heavy-water plant and then Allied bombing finally destroyed it. Hmm, the Reichsführer will be very interested to know that work proceeds on the *Flammenschwert.*"

"Himmler doesn't know?"

Werner smiled. "Take your pictures, Herr Andros. Go on, quickly."

Andros hesitated, puzzled by this instruction, but he proceeded to shoot the film.

Werner said, "Now leave the camera on the desk and return the folders to the safe and shut the door."

Andros did as he was told and turned around.

"Yes, I think it would be better for my own life if it appeared I caught you and killed you before I had any chance to see the contents of the safe," said Werner. "But first you must explain to me how you got the combination. I've been trying for months."

"The ring box," said Andros, carefully dipping his hand into his pocket under Werner's watchful eye. "It has a listening device. I could hear the tumblers."

Andros held out his hand, and Werner moved closer, interested. But when Andros opened his fist, nothing was there. Andros quickly swung his leg up and kicked the Česká out of Werner's hand. He grabbed the letter opener on the desk and lunged at Werner, driving the blade up through his stomach and into his heart.

Werner's eyes flashed surprise, and with a wince, he dropped to the floor.

78

It was easy for Hans to forget the time as he danced with the lovely Fraülein Vasilis. But the sight of Peter walking into the gardens made him panic, especially as he was heading toward the Baron, who was talking with some Greek and Swedish representatives from the Red Cross.

"You must excuse me, Fraülein," he said, and gallantly kissed her hand.

"Oh, please, not yet," Aphrodite protested.

But he insisted, looking over her shoulder at the Baron. "Duty calls."

The music began to fade as he left the gardens and rounded the house to the library. Hans had managed to avoid a debacle with the Baron by not being seen at the same time as Peter, although he wondered why Peter would simply leave his post.

Still, Hans was rather happy with himself and slowed down as he approached the patio outside the library. After all, he had danced with two Italian countesses, three Wehrmacht communications officers, and finally but not least, that last waltz with the Baron's mistress, Fraülein Vasilis. All in all, a wonderful evening; those damn dance classes in Hamburg while he was at university really did pay off.

Then he noticed what seemed to be movement in the library. He slowed down and pulled out his Luger as he approached the French doors. One was ajar. With a kick, he burst inside and saw a sentry in the dark. "Who's there?"

"Hans, look on the floor."

Hans swung his flashlight to the floor and could see Werner lying on his back in the halo of light. "What happened?"

There was no answer, so he swung the light to the sentry's face. Instead, he saw Andros with a Česká pointed at him.

"You!"

Hans opened his mouth, but there was a cough, and the last thing he saw was a flash of light and then total darkness.

79

Andros realized he had little time to act, so he quickly repositioned the bodies, placing the Česká in Werner's hand and the letter opener in Hans's hand. He kicked Hans's Luger off to the side.

This way, Andros hoped, it would look like Werner had come in snooping and was caught by Hans. But Werner pointed his Česká at Hans and made him drop his Luger and shot him, perhaps. But not before the good SS guard could grab something sharp from the desk and kill Werner. It would have to do.

Now he heard von Berg's voice outside the door, then the rattle of the key in the lock. The doorknob began to turn. Andros snatched the camera and hurried through the French doors, closing them behind him the instant the door opened and von Berg's dark figure filled the square of light.

80

Von Berg looked at the bodies of Werner and Hans on the floor of the library. Franz, who had run in behind him, whipped out his Luger from beneath his white dinner jacket and proceeded to check out the rest of the room, making his way to the French doors and poking around outside on the deserted patio. He was about to blow his whistle to alert the others when von Berg cut him off.

"Close the doors, Franz."

Franz did as he was told, and von Berg immediately walked over to the safe. He opened it and made a swift but thorough check of its contents. Apparently, nothing had been touched. The lock wasn't damaged, and nobody knew the combination. Still . . .

"Franz, come with me."

Franz followed von Berg out of the library, down the corridor, and toward the party out back. There, from the top of the steps overlooking the garden, von Berg could see Aphrodite dancing with Chris Andros.

81

Aphrodite could barely contain her hysteria. Chris had returned only seconds before Ludwig appeared with Franz at the top of the steps. Now Ludwig was motioning for Peter to come over.

"Did you find what you were looking for?" she asked Chris as they danced.

He looked over her shoulder at Ludwig and Franz. "Not exactly. But I got enough."

She could smell sulfur from his hand. He had fired a gun. He had killed somebody in her family's home. Dear God in heaven. "What happened?" she asked him. "Something went wrong, didn't it?"

"Von Berg came in just as I was leaving," Chris explained. "I managed to slip around the corner and climb back up the balcony to your room."

"What about Hans?"

"What's done is done," he replied. "I stuffed the uniform into the same drawer I took it from. You'll have to take it with you when you leave tonight."

She decided now was the time to tell him. "I'm not coming."

He looked at her incredulously. "What do you mean, you're not coming?"

"You got what you wanted," she said coolly. "Now leave me alone."

"You're what I want," he pleaded with her. "That girl in Bern—she was nothing."

His voice was rising with his passion, and she glanced around to make sure nobody had overheard him. He was losing his head and becoming unreasonable. She would have to do the thinking for both of them.

"I know that," she said. "But the Baron isn't about to let me out of his sight for one second. If I stay here at the party, at least you might still have a chance of getting out of Athens alive."

Chris put his two firm hands on her shoulders and pulled her close to his desperate face. "You're coming with me to Piraeus," he said, shaking her. "You hear me? We've got less than an hour to get there, and I'm not leaving you behind!"

But she was staring at a red stain on his white tuxedo shirt. "Your shirt, Christos," she gasped. "There's blood!"

His eyes dropped to his shirt and came up horrified. "Aphrodite," he gulped, "you've got to help me!"

She glanced around helplessly and then saw Ludwig, Franz, and Peter starting toward them. "Oh, God, Christos, I don't know what to do!"

"Come with me to Cairo!"

But she would have none of it and grabbed a glass of red wine from a floating tray and flung it at him. The wine splattered across the front of his tuxedo, and she smashed the glass on the ground, bringing the dancing and music to an abrupt halt.

"I hate you, Christos!" she screamed. "I could never marry you!"

Andros, his white shirt drenched in red, watched in horror as she turned around and ran up the steps of the garden into the house.

"Aphrodite!" he called.

But it was too late. She was gone by the time von Berg came up to him.

The Baron glanced back at the house and then looked him over curiously. "I can see you've had a little too much wine tonight, Herr Andros."

Andros nodded grimly as he borrowed a white linen napkin from a passing orderly and patted the stain. "She's right, you know," he said. "I never should have come back."

Aware of his guests, von Berg suggested, "Perhaps you should leave, Herr Andros. We can discuss business first thing tomorrow morning before you depart on the *Turtle Dove*."

Andros nodded reluctantly. "As you like, Baron."

As Andros walked away, von Berg turned to Peter and said, "Follow him. Don't let him out of your sight."

82

Nasos was waiting by the car and opened the rear door for Andros. Once behind the wheel, he started the engine and looked in the rearview mirror. Andros nodded numbly and they began to move slowly down the drive to the gate, where the sentry raised the bar and let them through.

"Everything go as planned?" Nasos asked.

Nothing had gone as planned; Andros was still sorting out what had just happened. But he could see his driver's anxious eyes in the mirror and knew he had to provide some reassurance if they were to complete the last leg of this escapade.

"Not quite, Nasos, but we'll see."

The lights of the Vasilis estate faded behind the stately cypress trees as they moved on into the darkness. Kifissia was silent this time of night. A few minutes later, Nasos looked up into the rearview mirror and said, "We are being followed."

Andros turned and could see two headlights in the distance. "You know the plan."

Nasos nodded. "Yes, next bend in the road, you jump out and I drive on home. Later, I slip out through the back on foot."

"You sure you won't join us in Cairo?"

"I will join Colonel Psarros's men in the hills," Nasos replied. "I still have some *thrasos* left in me."

Andros sensed both sadness and strength in the voice of his father's faithful driver. He put his hand on the old man's shoulder. "Take care, my friend."

They came around the bend, and Nasos slowed momentarily while Andros opened the door and jumped out. He barely made it into the shrubs and ducked before the lights of the oncoming car passed over his head and moved on.

He sat there waiting. A moment later, he could hear the low hum of a car and saw the two flashes of light as the Gestapo car that had picked him up the night before in the Royal Gardens came around the corner and braked to a halt.

Lieutenant Jeffrey was behind the wheel. The rear door opened, and Eliot poked his head out. "Come on, inside now. We'll barely make it to Piraeus in time as it is."

As they moved off, Eliot looked at Andros and saw the wine-soaked shirt. "Good God, Andros, you're bleeding."

"Relax, it's not mine."

"Did you find the text?"

"Found where it is, among other things."

"That will have to do," Eliot said, handing over several envelopes. "Here are the orders you are to pass out when you reach the EOE base. And here are your false identity papers for the ship, just in case there's a last-minute dock inspection, and some stevedore's clothing. Change now."

"I want to wait for Aphrodite," Andros said, unbuttoning his dress shirt. He knew she'd said she wasn't coming. But there was always a chance she'd change her mind. "She might be right behind us with her family."

Eliot glared at him. "I told you not to muck things up, Andros. What if, in attempting to escape, she tips off von Berg? Where will that put us when we arrive in Piraeus?"

Andros thought of Werner and Hans on the floor of von Berg's study, of the film negative that von Berg was sure to miss, and finally, of the determined look in Aphrodite's eyes when she told him she wasn't coming.

"You needn't worry," Andros replied. "I don't think things could get any more mucked up than they already are."

83

It was after blackout when the Mercedes arrived in Piraeus and drove down to the docks. Straight ahead was the *Turtle Dove*, guarded by a dozen SS, who blocked the quay with their two *Kübelwagen*.

Andros was alarmed and asked, "Where's my family?"

"Safely stowed aboard," Eliot reassured him. "No need to worry. I'll handle this."

Jeffrey stopped the car, and a young SS captain walked up with his pistol. When the German saw the green piping of Eliot's uniform, he stepped back in fear and clicked his heels. "Standartenführer. An unexpected privilege. How may I help you?"

"Keep your eyes open," Eliot replied in perfect German. "There is devilry afoot tonight, and we expect something to go down before dawn. Nobody but nobody is to enter that ship without your inspection."

"*Zu Befehl*, Standartenführer." The SS captain motioned one of the *Kübelwagen* to back away and allow the Mercedes through.

"Carry on," said Eliot, and they proceeded down the quay toward the dock where the *Independence* was moored.

Jeffrey stopped the car, and Andros got out, joining the other stevedores in carrying the last consignments aboard the ship. The ship's engines rumbled as Andros quickly made his way to the bridge.

Tsatsos was ecstatic. "You made it!"

"How much longer can we wait?" Andros asked, hoping against hope that somehow Aphrodite would arrive shortly.

"We can't wait any longer," said Karapis, the first mate. "The port authority has cleared us. It's now or never. If they decide to inspect, they'll discover you."

Andros looked at the nervous faces of the crew and realized that too many other lives were at stake besides Aphrodite's. Who was he to say that his beloved was more important than them or their loved ones? Or the men who would soon embark on the greatest invasion in human history?

"All right, then," Andros said angrily. "Let's go."

Tsatsos shouted the orders, and slowly, the *Independence* moved out to sea.

Andros reached into his stevedore's shirt and drew out the film negative he had stolen from von Berg's safe. When von Berg noticed it was missing, Aphrodite would bear the brunt of his wrath. Andros wished he could sneak back to the Vasilis estate and put it back in the Baron's safe.

But it was too late to turn back now.

Tsatsos got off the radio and turned to him, his face aglow from the compass, and exclaimed, "By God, Christos, we did it!"

But the words rang hollow in Andros's ears. Three days ago he had come to Athens in the hope that he could once and for all exorcise the demons of his past. All he had managed to do, however, was destroy any future happiness he and Aphrodite might have shared if the war ever came to an end.

He looked back helplessly at the shrinking harbor, worried sick about her. Any hope he had of saving her was vanishing before his eyes. A gnawing sense of hopelessness and despair began to haunt him, the same emptiness he'd felt two days before when he stood at his father's grave. Aphrodite seemed forever beyond his grasp.

Finally, he said, "I've failed, Tsatsos."

84

Baron von Berg stood on the front steps of the Vasilis estate, bidding farewell to the last of his guests. "Good night. . . . So good of you to come. . . . Good night. . . . Yes, thank you, the food will help so many of the city's starving children. . . . Good night."

Franz walked up from behind. "The *Independence* just left Piraeus."

"And the *Turtle Dove?*"

"Under guard since dusk. Nobody is getting aboard unless we know."

"Good. Where is Andros now?"

"According to Peter, he headed straight home."

"I'd be very much surprised if he remains there. What about Aphrodite?"

"Upstairs in her room. I have guards posted outside her door and below her balcony."

"I'll deal with her in the morning, before we fly to Corfu," von Berg concluded. "First I want a word with her parents."

85

The spray of salt water slapped Andros's face as he stood at the rail of the *Independence,* watching the black mass of mountains of the Peloponnese move against the starry sky. In the ship's wake lay the island of Hydra, sleeping on the Aegean.

Andros tried to light a cigarette but couldn't. To his dismay, he realized he was using the phony lighter containing the secret camera. He had left the lighter Aphrodite had given him in his tuxedo, which was in Eliot's car back in Athens. His folly was complete, he decided. Not only had he not come out of Athens with Aphrodite, but he had lost his only token of their relationship.

Thank God his family was safe on the *Turtle Dove.*

Andros removed the microfilm cartridge from the lighter and looked at it in the moonlight. In all probability, the information it contained was worthless. All it confirmed was what his OSS masters had known all along: that the Allies were invading Sicily, not Greece. Clearly, they had expected him to be captured and to spill their precious lie to the suspicious Baron von Berg. Only, he had escaped, and von Berg presumably was more suspicious than ever. To top it off, he had seen nothing resembling an ancient Greek text and was beginning to wonder if it even existed. He put the microfilm in his pocket and grasped the hollow shell in his hand. Cursing the name of Jason Prestwick, and himself for his naïveté, he hurled the good-for-nothing lighter into the sea and went up to the bridge.

Karapis stood by the helmsman while Tsatsos scanned the darkness with his night glasses. Andros moved to the chart table and examined their route, trying to push Aphrodite out of his mind.

"I still don't understand," Andros said a minute later. "According to the charts, there's nothing north of Monemvasia."

"Ah, nothing now," said Tsatsos, handing him his night glasses. "But soon you'll see."

Andros took the night glasses and looked out at the wall of mountains to the starboard side. Still a monolithic mass, he thought, until he saw a flicker of light, and then the wall seemed to part like angels' wings, revealing something like a valley of stars between two dark peaks.

"The Villehardouin Gorge," Tsatsos explained. "It starts wide by the sea and narrows through the mountains for twelve miles, with only a stream at its bottom. The National Bands base is situated in a defensive position on the high ground between the gorge and the sea."

Andros continued to scan the shore until he saw a light. "I see something. The signal, I suspect."

He gave the glasses back to Tsatsos, who looked for himself. "That's it," said Tsatsos, lowering the glasses. "We'll signal back while you and Karapis get ready. Remember, once you're ashore, send Karapis back immediately. We must make up for lost time."

Andros nodded and went to the deck, where the crew lowered a lifeboat and its pilot, Karapis, into the water. Andros climbed over the side and descended a rope ladder one sagging rung at a time. Then he dropped into the bobbing boat, and they cast off.

As they peeled away, Andros could see Tsatsos standing by the rail on the deck of the *Independence,* waving good-bye. "You've made an old sailor proud, Christos!" he called out as he was swallowed by the darkness.

Andros waved back dutifully and said, "Farewell, old friend."

The sea was rough as they approached the cliffs along the coast, but soon they rounded a promontory, and Karapis eased the small boat into the inlet of a bay.

"An ancient Minoan harbor abandoned for centuries," Karapis informed Andros. "Guillaume de Villehardouin used it in the twelfth century as a secret supply dock during his three-year siege of Monemvasia. The two piers were built later by the Venetians. One of them is a good six feet underwater, so we have to watch it going in to keep from ripping the hull."

Andros could see the other pier, an old, crumbling stone peninsula jutting into the water, and on it a row of dim, ragged figures holding torches.

86

Erin Whyte stood at the end of the pier and watched anxiously while the boat carrying Chris came in from the sea like a phantom raft crossing back over from beyond the river Styx. What had happened in Athens, she wondered, that he should return alive yet alone?

Standing next to her was Stavros, sporting three bandoliers full of ammunition, one around his waist and one over each of his shoulders. She watched him briefly finger the beautifully engraved handles of the knives that protruded from various parts of his ample waist before he readied his Sten gun.

"Easy, big fella," she told him. "He's on our side, remember?"

"Humph," grunted the Greek.

She ignored him and watched the caïque approach. She was looking forward to finally seeing a friendly, familiar face in Greece.

When the caïque bumped up against the pier and Chris stepped onto the stone in his docker clothing, Erin immediately was struck by the disappointment on his face. She walked up to him, waiting to let him speak, fighting the urge to throw her arms around him and welcome him to "Free Greece."

"Well, Captain, here's what I have," he told her, handing over a microfilm cartridge and a film negative. "And that's all I have."

He did not greet her or show any emotion, and his lifeless eyes disturbed her deeply. Suddenly, she didn't want the film or even the Maranatha text itself; she only wanted Chris to be like he was before this mission. Like she was before Lyon. But that was impossible, she realized, and she could sense he knew it, too.

"You keep them for now," she told him, passing them back. "We don't have the facilities to develop them here, so we'll wait until we link up with Colonel Prestwick on the submarine." She dared not mention Churchill's change in plans.

"Prestwick," Chris muttered as he put away the negative and the microfilm cartridge. "I'm looking forward to our reunion."

It was then that Doughty, wearing his New Zealand battle dress uniform with parachute wings on his chest for the occasion, greeted Chris in Greek on behalf of the National Bands of Greece.

"Chris Andros, I presume," said the red-whiskered New Zealander, shaking Chris's hand. "So good to see the great general's son. Welcome to Free Greece."

At the name of Andros, whispering broke out among the ranks of the *andartes*. Stavros, it seemed to Erin, seemed particularly thunderstruck. The big Greek passed a torch in front of Chris's face and studied him closely. "You are the son of that monarcho-fascist General Nicholas Andros?"

"Yes," Chris shot back, glancing at her and Doughty. "I'm the son of that monarcho-fascist."

Stavros said nothing, but Erin could see from his suspicious expression that his Marxist mind was at work. Perhaps he could guess that the British wanted to install Andros as the leader of a united Greek Resistance, all under the banner of the National Bands of Greece. It was news she would have to break to Andros the next morning.

"An ugly bunch, aren't they?" she told Chris lightly, and to the rest gave a shout. "Let's move!"

They launched Karapis and his boat back to the *Independence* and produced a sorry-looking mule for Chris to ride to the base.

"I forgot," said Chris, reaching into his pocket and producing three sealed envelopes. "Touchstone wanted me to give you these orders."

Erin looked at the envelopes. The first was for her, the second for Stavros, and the third for Kalos. She slipped them into her tunic and nodded. "I'll pass these out tomorrow. In the meantime, I suggest we get moving."

As the column of *andartes* climbed the rocky trail, Erin noticed Stavros looking back over the long line of horses to glimpse her and Andros, side by side, bringing up the rear. Stavros then looked ahead resolutely and proceeded to lead the column of *andartes* in song: *"Better one day of freedom than forty years of slavery. . . ."*

87

Aphrodite slept in such fits throughout the night that when she awoke the next morning, she was surprised by the serenity that had descended upon her family's estate.

She got out of bed, slipped into her dressing gown, and walked to the balcony. The sun was up, the birds were chirping. It was so pleasant that the previous night seemed to fade like a dream, as did the past several days. Then she saw the stain of blood on the stone balustrade.

She thought of Chris and prayed that he was all right. She could still hear him begging her to come with him and could see the hurt in his eyes when she refused. But he never would have escaped if he had tried to bring her.

Suddenly, she remembered the German SS uniform and walked over to her dresser and pulled open the bottom drawer. She found it stuffed behind her nightgowns. It was soaked with blood. As she looked at it, she heard a knock on the door.

"Aphrodite?" It was Franz speaking.

She froze, the uniform still in her hands. "What is it?"

"The Baron wishes to have a word with you in his study."

She quickly stuffed the uniform in the drawer and pushed it shut before calling back. "I need a few minutes to freshen up."

"He wishes to see you now, Fraülein." His voice was harsh.

She stepped away from the dresser and moved toward her bed. She heard the key rattle in the lock. A chill ran up her spine as the door opened.

"This way, Fraülein."

Franz led her down the corridor and stood on the landing while he watched her descend the stairs. He's going to search my room, she realized. Oh, God, please don't let him find the uniform, she prayed frantically. When she reached the bottom of the stairs, she looked back up toward the landing, but Franz was gone.

She proceeded toward the library, picturing in advance the sight of Hans—or whoever was responsible for the blood on Chris's shirt—on the floor. But when she walked into the room, there were no bodies, there was no blood on the carpet. Only Ludwig seated behind his desk, dressed in the black uniform of an SS general. The French doors were open, she noticed, and a fresh breeze came in from the gardens.

"Aphrodite, please sit down." His tone was icy. He gestured to the chair in front of his desk.

She sat down, realizing that the last time she had seen him in black was that fateful night when he "saved" her family from the Gestapo. "Something wrong, Ludwig?"

"Very. It seems Herr Andros and his entire family have disappeared. Not only that, but so has a film negative from my safe."

Aphrodite followed his eyes to the safe and feigned surprise at its wide-open door. "Oh?"

"You wouldn't know anything about that, would you?"

Aphrodite tried to suppress the panic rising up inside her. "No, Ludwig."

"That's too bad, love," he replied, his steel-blue eyes piercing right through her. "Because we may have a problem with your brother's send-off this morning."

"Please, Ludwig, don't tell me Kostas won't be freed."

"Oh, your brother will go," Ludwig replied. "I promised the Red Cross that Kostas Vasilis would be freed, and so he shall. A deal is a deal. Unfortunately, neither his family nor I will be able to see him off."

"What do you mean?" she demanded.

"I mean I will do what I can to intercede on your father's behalf, but I'm afraid the evidence is quite incriminating," Ludwig said, pointing to the open safe. "After all, he more than anybody else would know how to break into his own safe."

Aphrodite knew he was not above using an implicit threat to her father's safety to make her talk. But she refused to believe he would follow through on it.

"I don't believe it," she said simply. "And neither do you, Ludwig. My father is a shrewd businessman and has been more than accommodating to you. Since only you know the combination, he wouldn't know how to open the safe in the first place, much less attempt it."

"That has crossed my mind, and I must admit I am puzzled by this affair," Ludwig answered. "I would like to believe there's been a terrible mistake here and that your father will be vindicated. Your mother did her best to defend him. She tried to be diplomatic about it, told us something about Andros being in your bedroom last night, exposing himself to her."

Franz walked in, carrying the bloodstained uniform she had hidden in her dresser.

"Ah, I see now." Ludwig's eyes flashed hurt and finally anger, as if the myth she was in his eyes had evaporated.

She sensed that something had snapped inside him. Any affection he ever had for her was broken, and she felt defenseless. "Ludwig, please, I can—"

"You told Andros about Corfu, didn't you?" His stern blue eyes were looking right through her.

"No, I didn't," she replied truthfully.

He seemed genuinely puzzled. "Where did Andros say he was going?" he demanded. "Come, now, it's too late for him. But not for you or your parents."

"Salonika," she lied. "He hopped a train to Salonika and jumped off halfway. He said the British had a caïque by the sea to take him to Turkey. But you're too late, Ludwig. He's long gone, and your secrets are with the Allies. He's a hero. He's beaten you."

As she spoke, the phone rang.

Ludwig looked at her and said, "We'll see about that," and picked it up. "Put him through." He paused. "Yes, I know who you are." He started writing out numbers on a pad of paper. "North of Monemvasia? Excellent. Of course. Double your usual reward."

He hung up, a sinister smile crossing his face as he looked at

Franz. "That was our friend the Minotaur. Seems that Herr Andros has made fools of us all. While our eyes were on the *Turtle Dove*, he slipped out last night on the *Independence*. Fortunately, he's still within our grasp if we strike before tonight."

"No, Ludwig!" she screamed. "Please—"

"You lied to me," he told her coldly, ignoring her pleas and handing Franz the orders he had written. "Relay the coordinates of this rebel camp to our Luftwaffe base on Karpathos. I want Stukas for this job. Meanwhile, have Colonel Ulrich and his paratroopers drop in north of the encampment for the mop-up."

Franz hesitated. "But Colonel Ulrich is dead, sir."

For a moment Ludwig looked confused. "Yes, of course," he said, regaining his senses. "I don't know where my head was. Tell the new one, Colonel Spreicher, to have his *Fallschirmjäger* on the next Junkers 52 transport available. And inform the airstrip to have my personal plane ready. We're flying out to Corfu: you, me, and Fräulein Vasilis here. We've wasted enough time in Athens. There are fewer than forty-eight hours before my birthday—I mean, before the Führer's weapons conference."

"*Zu Befehl,*" said Franz, and walked out, taking the bloodied uniform with him.

When Ludwig turned to her, his eyes had a deathly glaze. He looked at her triumphantly, and she turned cold inside. For a wild moment she sensed it was no longer Ludwig behind those eyes but someone else. Someone hideously evil. The Baron of the Black Order. Ludwig von Berg, she realized, was gone forever.

"Your friend is quite a clever man, love," he told her. "Clever and foolish. And to leave you behind," he added, "knowing you might suffer the same fate as your parents. That's not very nice, is it?"

Aphrodite realized she hadn't seen her mother or father since last night. A terrible fear gripped her, and her voice trembled. "Where are they?"

"In the garden, love." The Baron sat back and folded his hands.

Wordlessly, she stood up and walked through the French doors onto the patio and around the back into the garden.

As she entered the garden, she saw them hanging from separate mango trees, the bodies of her mother and father. They were under the watch of two SS guards with gray-green uniforms and Schmeisser machine pistols. At the foot of each tree was a sign in Greek that said SUCH IS THE FATE OF ENEMIES OF THE THIRD REICH.

Aphrodite screamed, breaking the silence of the morning and bringing the Baron out from his study.

"They're so sorry they couldn't say good-bye," he told her, calmly gripping her arm while giving the guards parting instructions: "We're leaving now. Permanently. See that our hosts here remain available to visitors for the rest of the day. Their presence is such an eloquent warning to others against future disobedience in the New Order."

88

It was midday siesta at the National Bands base when Erin Whyte walked into Chris's *kaliva* and found him fast asleep. He had taken off his seaman's shirt from the night before and looked handsome yet sad as he lay sprawled across the hard cot: an angel with broken wings. She decided not to disturb him and left the Special Forces uniform she had brought with her on top of the small, rough-hewn table. Then she went out in search of Colonel Kalos and Stavros Moudjouras.

She found them not in their shepherd's huts but a mile away, outside in a clearing they had converted into a firing range. Instead of German cutouts in front of sandbags, they had placed empty bottles of brandy on top of barrels at the target end. Stavros stood at the designated firing line with a special collection of weapons laid out on a crate while Colonel Kalos blew the tops off the bottles with an American Colt .45. Looking on were young Michaelis and a dozen EDES and ELAS *andartes*.

"Not bad," said Stavros, rendering his verdict on his rival's performance. "But a Colt's no good in Greece if you don't have bullets, and a forty-five-caliber can't chamber Axis ammunition." The ELAS *kapetanios* reached over and picked up the standard Wehrmacht pistol, the Walther P-38, tiny in his giant hand. "Now, this fires the nine-millimeter Parabellum round, which we can take off any dead German, and it can be fired single or double action."

Stavros fired the full eight rounds of the magazine at the bottles, the slide clicking forward after the last round was unloaded. The ELAS *andartes* on hand applauded, but he missed three bottles.

"I'd stick with your Sten if I were you," Kalos commented, to the howls of the EDES *andartes*. "Good for spraying bullets when you're outnumbered, at least, and it can chamber Axis ammunition as well."

Erin cleared her throat and broke up the gathering. "Now that we're all familiar with the weapons of the enemy, I suggest we move on to winning the war."

"Ah, Captain Whyte," said Kalos. "Perhaps you might try?"

Erin paused, feeling the enthusiastic glances of Michaelis and the others. There was nothing in the world she'd like better than to show up these macho Greek males, but this wasn't the place or the way to do it.

"Don't make the lady embarrass herself, Kalos," said Stavros, who had already reloaded the Walther and was gamely offering it to her.

It was a challenge she couldn't refuse without losing the respect of the others, she realized. And to lose their respect would mean losing her best defense against unsolicited physical advances or, worse, challenges to her authority. Reluctantly, she took the Walther and ran her hand over its smooth black steel barrel.

"You boys make it look so easy," she lamented as her arm swung up effortlessly. Without taking any apparent aim, she blew away the three remaining bottle tops. She laid down the gun and smiled at the slack-jawed Stavros. "But then, it is."

Young Michaelis's dark, animated eyes grew wide in wonder. The rest of the Greeks were silent. Now that she had succeeded in securing their attention, it was time to get down to business.

"Stavros, Kalos, you come with me on patrol," she said sharply, with an authority nobody questioned. "I have your new orders from the Middle East GHQ."

89

Stavros could only wonder what Cairo was going to ask of them this time. They found a small, private clearing a mile away and squatted in a circle. Michaelis, who had insisted on coming along, was watching their horses on the other side of some pine trees, playing with the portable transmitter in Captain Whyte's saddle sack.

"Here are your orders," Whyte said, passing specially marked envelopes to him and Kalos after opening one for herself. "They're in Greek but encoded in the C cipher," she added, "so it may take a minute for you to translate. Read them, memorize them, then destroy them."

"We're just going to blow another damn bridge," Stavros muttered, tearing open his envelope. He hated codes and ciphers, in part because he was a poor reader even without the extra burden. He often relied on Michaelis, who had at least some schooling. "I don't see the reason for . . ."

But even Michaelis would not understand this message, Stavros realized with a shock, because the code had come from Moscow. Stavros looked up at Captain Whyte and then glanced back at his note, which read:

> We have discussed the possibility of the day when you would fulfill the mission for which you were originally trained. That day has come. Now that Stalin has dissolved the Comintern, you and your comrades in the Central Committee in Greece will take your orders directly from me.
>
> With the liberation of Greece at hand, the British will attempt to install the king and his monarcho-fascist government. They will use Zervas and his EDES swine or the

front they call the National Bands of Greece as their means. You will not let that happen.

You will assume command of the EOE and will not give up your arms until Greece has popular rule as well as national liberation. Such a democracy leaves no room for any resistance movement other than the National Liberation Front. It alone is the legitimate representation of the Greek people and must be recognized as such.

Toward that end, immediately upon destroying this order, you are to kill the following three monarcho-fascists: the agent code-named Theseus; the son of General Andros; and the British liaison officer to the EOE.

Fulfill your orders and your transgressions will be forgiven. Fail and you will bear the punishment of all comrades who have renounced their faith.

THE MINOTAUR

The Minotaur is in Greece, thought Stavros, trembling at the return of the Soviet agent he hadn't heard from in so long. Too long, really. He glanced up to see Kalos walking back to the horses. Captain Whyte was smiling at him.

"Have it memorized?" she asked him. "Good. Now burn it."

Stavros struck a match and touched it to the order. He watched it burn into nothing as he slowly turned the implications over in his mind. He knew he needed to redeem himself before his comrades, but was murder the way to do it? He could understand killing the son of General Andros. But kill Theseus, a woman? Kill Colonel Doughty, their most respected military adviser, and probably destroy any chance of future arms supplies?

This is madness, he thought, and yet the terrifying realization gripped him that if the Minotaur could so manipulate events that a British officer could hand out her own death sentence, he could do anything.

Captain Whyte could see his confusion. "Is there something you don't understand?" she asked.

"Yes," Stavros replied, slowly raising his Sten gun and training it on her.

Captain Whyte took in the barrel of the ugly submachine gun and then looked into his eyes. Without even a trace of fear in her voice, she calmly stated, "So, I've finally met the Minotaur."

Stavros, aware that his own voice was trembling, said, "I'm not the Minotaur."

"You're not?" she asked.

Unable to bring himself to pull the trigger, Stavros lowered the barrel. "No," he said, and sighed. "I'm not."

"I'm disappointed," she replied.

"So am I," said Kalos, who stepped forward from the pine trees, pointing one of his pearl-handled Colts at Stavros and the other at Captain Whyte. "She is our enemy, comrade. She has to be stopped, just like Andros must be stopped."

"You?" said Stavros in disbelief, shocked to discover that the right hand of General Zervas was a Communist. "You are the Minotaur?"

"I answer to him, as do you," Kalos replied as he moved slowly and deliberately toward him and Captain Whyte. "My orders are to kill you if you should fail in your orders."

"But killing our British military advisers?" Stavros asked, glancing at Captain Whyte. "How can this possibly advance our cause?"

"She and the colonel were getting suspicious, about to send some damaging reports about me and the Minotaur to the foreign office in Cairo," Kalos explained, the barrel of his Colt now at the captain's back. "And I don't need to remind you, Stavros, that when the liberation comes and the Germans are gone, the British will try to reinstall the king and his monarcho-fascist government. We cannot let that happen."

Stavros said, "What do you propose?"

Kalos dug the barrel of his Colt into Erin Whyte's spine until she gasped in pain. "First, that the lovely captain here hand over the microfilm Andros brought from Athens."

"I don't have it," she said.

Kalos pushed harder with his pistol. "I don't believe you."

"Andros has it," she insisted, "back at the base." She managed to smile. "You'll just have to overcome half the EOE to get it."

"You'll just have to die so I can search you," Kalos said. "Stavros, kill her. Kill her and restore your honor before the Party. Only then will I consider you worthy to assume the command of the EOE, or what's left of it after we slaughter the EDES *andartes* in the camp."

"And then?" demanded Stavros. "Where does it end?"

"After I deliver the microfilm Andros obtained from the Germans to the Minotaur, I will return to Zervas, kill him, and assume command of EDES, calling you and our comrades in ELAS my sworn enemies."

Stavros saw everything, this plot the Minotaur was hatching. With Kalos as head of EDES, the National Liberation Front would effectively control its rival organization and consolidate power. "I cannot go along with this deceit."

"Then your end has come, *kapetanios*."

Kalos raised his Colt, but before he could pull the trigger, a voice shouted, "Stop it!" Michaelis emerged from behind the trees with a Thompson submachine gun shaking in his hands. "Put your gun down, Colonel."

Kalos smiled contemptuously and replied, "No, boy, *you* put your gun down, or the captain here gets a bullet in her back." He turned her toward Michaelis, making her a human shield.

Erin shouted, "Be careful, Michaelis!"

Stavros could see the confusion on his younger brother's face as he began to waver. "Don't do it, Michaelis."

"Too late," said Kalos, and his other Colt came around from behind Erin and exploded three times.

"Michaelis!" cried Stavros.

Before Michaelis could lift the heavy barrel of the Thompson to return the fire, the bullets had punched three holes across his chest, blowing him back several feet to the ground.

"No!" Stavros dropped his Sten gun and ran over to the limp, bullet-ridden body and held his brother's head in his arms. When he looked helplessly into the eyes that had once been so full of light and life, he saw only his own horrified face. He set his brother's head back down on a pillow of dust and turned angrily toward Kalos.

"I'm going to kill you!" he vowed when an explosion of machine-gun fire sent Kalos running into the woods for cover, leaving Stavros and Erin in the clearing as a column of gray-green uniforms and rimless helmets emerged from the trees.

Erin, thinking fast, picked up the Sten gun from the ground and unloaded a full clip at the SS paratroopers, killing several and pushing the rest back behind the trees. "What are you waiting for?" she shouted.

Stavros was staring at his brother's corpse, unable to leave. He felt her take his hand and drag him away. "We've got to get back to the base and warn Andros and the others!" she cried as a shower of bullets descended on them.

90

A ndros was still a bit blurry-eyed when he stepped out of his *kaliva* and made his way to the edge of the encampment wearing his Special Forces uniform. Doughty was sitting on a log, thoroughly enjoying a smoke from his pipe, now that he had real tobacco from the latest supply drop instead of cut-up leaves.

"There you go, a real American operative," the New Zealander observed.

Andros shrugged and sat down next to Doughty. "I'll be gone with tonight's submarine pickup, so I don't see the point."

Doughty smiled. "Had enough of us already, have you?"

"Some of you."

"Oh, don't mind Stavros. I suspect he considers the presence of Colonel Kalos and the arrival of General Andros's son a threat to his authority." Doughty puffed on his pipe. "You still have the roll of film?"

"Taped to my chest," Andros replied. "Along with that film negative. What I can't find is Captain Whyte."

"She's on a patrol with Stavros and Kalos." Doughty looked at his watch. "Hmm," he murmured. "They were supposed to be back by now." The New Zealander tilted his head as if his ears had picked something up. A frown crossed his face as he looked over Andros's shoulder.

Then Andros heard the high-pitched whine and swung around. A swarm of Stuka dive-bombers appeared over the trees like black vultures, sweeping down the hillside toward them. There must have been at least two dozen of them. The planes passed over in an instant, followed by a turbulent wind and a thunderclap that shook the trees.

"Dear God!" said Doughty, the pipe falling out of his gaping mouth as he and Andros jumped to their feet. "Let's get the hell out of here!"

He pushed Andros toward the wireless tent. The wireless operator Dimitrios was breaking down the set when they burst inside. "Bad news: our escape routes are cut," he said, furiously cramming the components into a suitcase. "One of our patrols reported a column of SS paratroopers closing in from the north before their transmission went dead."

Andros looked to Doughty, who was clearly doing his best to remain calm. "What about the pickup for Andros here?"

"I haven't been able to raise the submarine on the set, sir."

There was a tremendous crash outside as the Stukas let go of their first load of bombs. Then another, this one louder, rocking the ground beneath them.

"How did they find us?" Doughty muttered, then turned to Andros. "We've got to assume the pickup is on and get you out of here with the film."

Andros nodded but realized that if they were cut off from the sea and a German column was advancing from the north, their prospects for escape were limited, if not nonexistent.

"Over the gorge," Doughty said. "But we have to hurry, before they blow the bridge." He lifted the flap of the tent to reveal the chaos outside. Most of the *andartes* were running after their guns and horses as great orange balls of fire blossomed around them. The Stukas circled back for another run.

"See the woods on the far side of the clearing, Andros? On the other side are the amphitheater and the bridge. Think you can make it?"

Andros nodded and followed Doughty outside. They cut across the open encampment toward the trees. Andros was halfway across when he stumbled. The Stukas thundered in, lower than before, shattering the air and making the earth reverberate. Andros could feel the vibration in his bones as he looked up in time to see Doughty reach the edge of the woods.

"Come on, Andros! This way!"

The Stuka engines crescendoed into a shrill scream that lifted the hair on the back of Andros's neck as he got to his feet and scrambled toward the woods. He plunged into the pine trees just as the first Stuka let go of its second load of bombs. The explosion crashed across the encampment, the force hammering at Andros's back.

Andros looked toward the wireless tent, where he and Doughty had stood with the communications officer only a moment before. A hot orange ball of fire expanded rapidly, ripened, and burst into an ugly black pall of smoke. When it lifted, the tent had vanished. The next moment he was following Doughty through the woods.

The musty smell of cordite filled the air as they ran wildly through the trees, Stukas shrieking overhead. More bombs plowed into the *kalivas*, tents, toolsheds, latrines, and ammunition dumps, exploding bits of broken metal that cut down every *andarte* in their radius.

The gorge was coming up. Andros could make it out beyond the trees. Then there was an explosion of light. A fir tree, struck by a bomb, came crashing down nearly on top of them, blocking the path.

"This way," said Doughty with a poise and speed that awed Andros.

They emerged from the woods into the clearing that served as the camp's amphitheater, the gorge to their right and the bridge up ahead. Then a low-flying Stuka let go of its payload. A flash of light was followed by the thunderous clap of an explosion. Flames gushed up in its wake, and charred pieces of wood rained down around Andros.

The bridge was gone, just like that, and with it, thought Andros, any chance of escape.

When Andros looked back to Doughty, he wasn't there. Then, a moment later, he heard the voice calling him. "Andros . . . over here."

It was Doughty, his face splattered with blood, dragging himself over with his arms, leaving a trail of blood behind him. His chest was one red mass. "You've got to make it out of here with that film," he said, his speech garbled by the blood he was spitting up. "You've got to get to Sparta. There's a taverna in the square called Theo's. Ask for the Yankee Clipper . . . escape route to submarine . . . the barman knows . . . Tell . . ."

Then there was a flash of recognition. He opened his mouth to say something more but closed his eyes instead. His face plopped into the dirt.

Again the ground shook. Andros looked up to see a stampede of horses coming his way, *andartes* on their backs, three Stukas buzzing overhead, chasing them toward the abyss. Andros could barely move himself out of the way of the stampede, leaving Doughty's body to be trampled beneath a hundred hooves.

Andros watched as one horse after the other leaped into the air, hovering over the gorge for a few seconds before plummeting out of sight. Andros was aware of screams and shouts, but they were strangely muted as he watched what seemed like a silent slow-motion dream. He couldn't tell whether they were actually trying to make the impossible leap over the gorge or purposely killing themselves before the Germans got them. And yet a few of them almost made it, the front hooves of their horses barely scratching the other side, clawing madly before both horse and rider tumbled backward into the mouth of the insatiable abyss.

All Andros knew was that somehow he had to make it over.

It took another explosion to shake him to his senses. He snapped into action. Inching his way along the ground under the flying shrapnel, he made it to a fallen tree. There he found Doughty's field glasses and crept toward the edge of the gorge to take a look.

The bridge was gone, blown to bits. And still the horses and *andartes* shot into view, jumping into the inferno like lemmings.

Andros put down the field glasses. There was no way to cross the gorge, and it was nine hundred feet to the rocky bottom. But the *andartes* were right, there was no other way of escape.

He spun around, frantically searching the chaos for another way out. He spotted a mare without a rider. She was a big one, probably the biggest he'd seen at the camp.

With each explosion, the mare ran in an opposite direction until the sound of fire was so close that she simply stopped in her tracks in terror. Andros grabbed her loose reins and, after two failed tries, mounted her. Somehow he would get out of here, he resolved, somehow. There had to be a way.

Andros was alone in the middle of the clearing, the dumbstruck mare turning in circles in the wide-open area even as the explosions began to close in. A great flash of light flickered across the sky, and a tremendous explosion shook the ground. The mare bucked as Andros looked up to see a great shadow falling upon him. He covered his face and heard a thud. When he lowered his arms, another fir tree that had stood before him was gone, just like the tree that had almost crushed him and Doughty.

Then something sharp clipped him in the leg, and Andros fell forward. He would have slipped off his saddle had he not clung to the mare's mane. Pain shot up Andros's spine. Where he had been hit, he couldn't tell. All around him, the sounds and explosions were growing louder.

This was the end. The Baron had won. All was lost. He remembered the words of the archbishop at his father's memorial service: "Into your hands I commit my spirit . . ."

And then there was silence. Choking on dust, the taste of oil in his mouth, Andros wiped the grime from his teary eyes. The Stukas were gone, and he was alone in the clearing, the smoke rising around him in black columns and the stench of scorched metal, oil, and flesh in the air.

Straight ahead, the gorge was clouded in ugly vapors that seemed to bubble up from the depths and roll across the clearing like dark death clouds. When the black fog lifted, the gaping chasm became clear in the light. Andros blinked, his eyes blurred again by the smoke, his mind blurred by the impossible hurdle before him.

He had little choice. The mane of the mare seemed to prickle with electricity, and the hair on the back of his neck lifted at the sound of the hum. The Stukas were closing in again.

He grabbed the reins and tried to get the horse to move, but she wouldn't. He had lost all feeling in his legs, so he struck the mare's rump as hard as he could with his fist. Again nothing.

With one last effort, he pulled his father's dagger from its sheath and jabbed the horse's rump. She shot off toward the black gorge, which glowed mysteriously beneath the dark shadows of the dust clouds on the surface. Andros pressed his head down against the mare's mane as she picked up speed.

The horse and rider hurled themselves across the open gorge. Just when he expected them to plunge to the bottom, they seemed to float over the gorge. Andros heard the sharp clap of hooves beating against rocky soil. He glanced back to see the half-moon sliver of the gorge fall behind them like a reaper that had barely missed its prey.

Death behind him, darkness before him, the last thing Andros remembered was clinging to the horse as if she were life itself, hurtling into space.

PRESENT DAY

91

Sam Deker's body convulsed in the metal chair in the DARPA labs beneath the VA Hospital in Los Angeles. General Packard and Wanda Randolph looked on as a helpless Dr. Prestwick stopped the light-wave bombardment to Deker's brain and the photosynthetic algae drip to his artery.

"I don't understand," Dr. Prestwick said. "I'm not doing anything now."

Packard said, "The 34th Degree program, Doctor. Shut it down."

"It *is* down!" Dr. Prestwick said. "Deker is doing this all by himself."

Deker's body arched in pain and then slumped in the chair, his head rolling back, lifeless.

"Dear God," Randolph whispered. "You killed him."

Dr. Prestwick said, "No, his vitals are fine. Look at the monitors. This is something else."

"You mean a coma?" Randolph said, and started slapping Deker. "Wake up, Deker! Wake up! You gotta come back. Come back!"

Nothing seemed to work for the next two hours, and then they gave up trying.

"Now what, Doc?" Packard asked.

Dr. Prestwick said, "The monitors will automatically tell us when there is a change in Deker's condition. We post a couple of nurses and wait for him to eventually wake up."

"And if he doesn't?" Randolph asked. "You're not cutting up that poor boy's brain."

Dr. Prestwick looked at Packard, who looked at Deker. "If he's so lost inside that he goes six months, we'll reconvene to discuss next steps. But knowing Deker, he'll find a way. He always does."

1943

92

On the island of Corfu, Commandant Georgio Buzzini was in his office on the second floor of the Palace of St. Michael and St. George when his aide Sergeant Racini returned from the airstrip to report that General Ludwig von Berg had arrived and was safe at the Achillion.

"Too bad," said Buzzini, still smarting from his last run-in with von Berg. "Did he ask why I wasn't there to greet him personally?"

"No, sir," Racini replied. "He didn't seem to care."

"He didn't?" Buzzini frowned.

"He simply wanted to know if his friend the German professor had arrived. I told him he had, two days ago. I also gave him all his cables from Berlin on the spot." The sergeant from Palermo quickly added, "To save him another trip to the office here."

"You mean save us another visit from that bastard." Buzzini looked out the window over Corfu Town's *spiniada*. "Was his so-called nurse with him?"

"Yes, but she didn't look well at all. I think she's suffered some trauma. She said she was going to drown herself, and the Baron said she could be his guest."

"And why shouldn't she, Sergeant?" Buzzini turned from the window. "Her parents are dead, hanged by the SS in Athens!"

"Mother of God!" cried Racini.

"Yes," said Buzzini grimly. "If he could, the Baron would murder the Virgin Mary herself before she could bear the Christ Child." He held up the communiqué his radio operator had picked up while Racini was gone. "This is from General Vecchiarelli's headquarters in Athens," he said, waving the flimsy piece of paper wildly. "The Baron's nurse, it turns out, is none other than Aphrodite Vasilis of the tobacco family. It was her parents the Baron murdered."

"No!" said Racini.

"Yes, Sergeant," said Buzzini, relishing this rare display of superior knowledge. "Not only that, but it seems none other than the son of General Andros paid the good Baron a visit in Athens."

"The son of General Andros?" repeated Racini, his face flushed from these revelations.

Buzzini decided to drop his final bombshell. "Furthermore, radio traffic is heavy with news from the Peloponnese," he went on. "Even as we speak, a German air strike is under way against Greek partisans in the Parnon Mountains of the Peloponnese."

Racini looked flabbergasted, much to Buzzini's satisfaction. "But what does this mean, Commandant?"

Buzzini, enjoying himself, said, "Consider what we know so far, Sergeant." He held up a finger to make his first point. "The German First Panzer Division is on its way from France along with further reinforcements to bring a total of four German divisions alongside our own Italian Eleventh Army in Greece."

The sergeant from Palermo nodded.

Buzzini held up a second finger. "The Germans have relieved us of control of the minefields we've laid all along the west coast of Greece. Indeed, German R-boats now patrol the waters surrounding these islands and the coast."

Racini received the second volley of information with a simple "This is true."

Buzzini held up three fingers. "Then there is this air strike against increased partisan activity in the mountains."

Racini shrugged. "Again I must ask you, Commandant, what does this mean?"

Buzzini smiled triumphantly as he held up four fingers. "And now the Baron himself returns to the island in a fury and cloisters himself behind the gates of the Achillion. The only conclusion we can draw is that the Allies are about to invade Greece."

"But where in Greece?" pressed Racini.

"The German Naval War Staff said it last week in that cable to

General von Berg when they suggested that landing attempts will most likely be here on Corfu."

"Here?" cried Racini. "But when?"

"That, unfortunately, I cannot tell you," Buzzini admitted as he turned to the window once again and looked out across Garitsa Bay. "But I'll wager you one thing, Sergeant: the Baron knows. Oh, yes, he knows."

93

What was left of the National Bands of Greece base was being mopped up by the SS Death's Head unit of Standartenführer Spreicher, a man who delighted in this sort of thing, personally picking off any wounded men who were half dead. Medics, he reasoned, were unnecessary baggage in these sorts of operations. After all, he himself had lost half his face in Crete and managed to survive. If any of his own men were wounded, they were to fight to the death or be shot by their brothers in arms. It was simpler that way. All for one and one for all.

Spreicher worked his way through the debris and bodies, searching for Andros. He spotted a British battle dress uniform by the gorge and found the man sprawled facedown, still alive and groaning in pain.

Digging the toe of his jackboot under the man's body, Spreicher kicked him over. "Hey, Englishman," he said in crude, brutal English. "It's morning. Face your maker."

Death-glazed eyes looked up at him from the ravaged face. Out of the dirt-encrusted mouth came a spurt of blood that dribbled down the chin and matted in the red beard. Half torn from the soiled uniform was a New Zealand insignia.

"Where's the film negative?" he demanded. "Where's Andros?"

When he received no answer, he put his jackboot on the New Zealander's skull and began to apply pressure. His second in command, Oberführer Borgman, ran over with the S-phone. "Linder wants to know if there are any prisoners up here."

Spreicher looked down at Doughty. "Well?"

When there was no reply, he dug the heel of his boot deep into the skull until there was a crack and he crushed it. Then he turned to his second in command and said, "None up here, Oberführer. What does Linder say at the bottom of the gorge?"

"His party had nothing to report down there."

Spreicher moved to the edge of the gorge and looked down the nine-hundred-foot cliff walls. Linder and his men were busy looting what little they could find among the smashed bodies of the Greek *andartes* strewn among the rocks. Spreicher spat and wiped his nose. The stench of burned horse and human flesh was foul. He told Borgman, "Looks like you'll have to inform General von Berg that we have no prisoners or survivors, so far as we can tell. Nor any film."

Borgman looked terrified. "You want me to say we found nothing?"

"Tell him we're still searching." Spreicher frowned as he surveyed the destruction and devastation. Damn, he thought, I missed all the fun on this one. Furthermore, he hadn't obtained the microfilm, and he knew all too well from his predecessor, Ulrich, what happened to those who failed von Berg.

He heard a shout from across the gorge and saw Miller waving his hands. "Go see what he wants," he told Borgman.

While Borgman left, Spreicher looked down at the New Zealander's head on the ground and watched the blood seep out of the cracked skull.

Borgman returned with good news. "Miller and his men found tracks on the other side of the gorge, sir," he reported. "They're not ours, and they're fresh. Someone must have made it over the bridge before she blew, perhaps someone from that patrol we ran into during our advance."

"General von Berg's orders are clear," Spreicher said with a gleam in his eye. "We must hunt this man down. We'll turn over every village between here and Sparta if we have to. Andros cannot get away. Let's move."

"*Zu Befehl!*" replied Borgman.

Yes, thought Spreicher, surveying the destruction, the fun was just beginning.

94

His mother was in a life jacket, her arms wrapped around him as they floated in a sea of fire, bodies everywhere, some swallowed up by the burning oil from the sinking ocean liner in the distance. As the crest of a wave lifted them up, his mother's tired arms loosened, and the wave parted them forever, her screams of "Christos! Christos!" fading in the darkness of night. For Chris, there were no words he could form, only a helpless cry as he turned in his bed, soaked with sweat, aware of another presence.

"Better to enter the kingdom of God with one leg than to have two and be thrown into hell."

Andros blinked his eyes open to see two eyes, alive with light and compassion, looking down at him. Then a sharp pain shot up his leg, and he shivered.

The voice said, "You have both of them, don't worry."

Andros felt for his leg, but another wave of darkness washed over him. He groaned in agony. A pair of soft, soothing lips kissed him gently on the mouth, and he reopened his eyes.

It was Erin, her face shining like that of an angel in the shaft of sunlight falling through a crack in the roof of what seemed to be a cave.

Andros groaned. "How long?"

"You were out for a couple of hours," she told him. "Good thing we found you and got that shrapnel out. Either infection would have set in, or the Nazis would have found you. Looks like that microfilm of yours is more significant than we thought."

Andros was fully awake now, his nausea gone. Only the pain in his leg remained. He looked down to see his thigh wrapped in bloodied strips of linen. His thigh and nothing more. His pants had been removed.

"I was changing the dressing when you woke up," she explained. "It's not like I haven't seen a man before."

Andros held up his hand to tell her that was enough, thank you. He propped himself up and had a look around, careful to avoid making eye contact with Erin. He was in a small cave, which he was sharing with three horses and a cache of weapons, several dozen Sten guns, ammunition, grenades, and what looked like four hundred pounds of plastic high explosive in quarter-pound bars wrapped in cellophane.

"You'll have to excuse the accommodations, but it was the best we could do under the circumstances," Erin said. "This is one of several storage facilities the EOE has in these parts."

Andros saw daylight at the entrance to the cave, which was screened by a forest of pine trees. "Where are we, exactly?"

"No-man's-land," Erin explained as she prepared the new dressing. "Somewhere between Free Greece and the German zone."

Andros remembered the destruction of the base, the carnage, Doughty. "Free Greece?" he repeated hoarsely. "Our camp was blown!"

"You managed to survive," Erin replied, carefully peeling the old wrap from his thigh.

The pain came back with a vengeance. "Oh, God," he gasped. "It kills."

"Not if you sit still." She started to apply the new wrap to his thigh.

Andros grimaced as soon as the dressing touched his skin. But his attention was diverted to the distant roar of a low-flying aircraft somewhere outside the cave.

"Reconnaissance plane," Erin explained. "Searching the hills and valleys for us. Probably in radio contact with ground forces. We're going to have to stay put and keep quiet until dusk."

"I'm not going anywhere," Andros replied, feeling another wave of pain coming on as Erin wrapped the new dressing.

"This might hurt a little," Erin said, applying more pressure.

Andros started to protest, but Erin once again fixed her mouth to his and muffled his cries while her firm hands held his body steady on the outside. He was surprised to find himself responding to her touch, and if Aphrodite weren't foremost in his thoughts, he might have been disappointed when the pain finally subsided and Erin let him go.

Andros gasped for breath. "What are you trying to do?" he asked. "Kiss me or kill me?"

"Kill you if you don't shut up," she whispered. "We can't be found out. We have to make sure that microfilm gets to the Allies."

Andros said, "And how are we going to do that?"

"We're going to make that submarine pickup tonight, while we still have a window of opportunity," said Erin with impressive determination. "That is, if you're up to it."

"And if I'm not?"

"Then it's only a matter of time before von Berg's goons get us," Erin said.

"I guess I'd rather live with the pain than let von Berg put me out of my misery."

"I'm glad you see it that way." Erin opened a crate of clothing and found a pair of baggy trousers. "Here, try these." She tossed them into the air, and he caught them with one hand.

"Turn around," he told her.

She shrugged and turned her back toward him. "I've seen everything you've got, Andros. Besides, you might need some help."

"You've helped me enough already, Captain."

Two painful minutes later, he had slipped the pants on. But when he tried to stand up on his wounded leg, an electric jolt shot up his body. He leaned against the rock for support. Erin was at his side instantly.

"Are you okay?" she asked, looking intensely concerned.

"I'll manage," he told her. "So where's the submarine pickup?"

"Off the coast of Kalamata."

From where Erin had placed them, that was all the way over in the neighboring province of Messenia, on the other side of the Taygetos range. He laughed in despair. "We'll never make it in time. Not on horseback."

"That's why we're going to Sparta," Erin replied. "There's an SOE safe house waiting for us there, along with false papers and motor transport. Then we'll drive like the devil up through the Taygetos Pass and down to Kalamata."

Sparta. You must get to Sparta. There's a taverna in the square called Theo's. Ask for the Yankee Clipper. The barman knows . . . Those were Doughty's last words. Andros said, "That safe house wouldn't be Theo's taverna, would it?"

"As a matter of fact, it would," Erin replied, a puzzled look crossing her face.

"Doughty told me before he died," Andros explained as he considered Erin's plan to go to Sparta. The ancient city and present-day capital of Laconia lay at the bottom of the fertile Evrotas Valley, the formidable Taygetos mountain range rising up behind it. "You realize, don't you, that to even get there we first have to cross the Evrotas plains in the open?"

"Fortunately, the sun sets early behind the Taygetos, so we should have the cover of darkness by the time we cross the plains."

"And then we somehow sneak in and out under the noses of the German garrison?" Andros shook his head. "There's no way."

"It's the only way," Erin insisted, "and the one they'd least expect."

As Erin was speaking, Andros heard the crunch of boots on pebbles outside. He shot her a worried glance. A black figure filled the circle of light in the mouth of the cave, holding a Sten gun. The hulking giant stepped forward into a shaft of sunlight, and Andros saw that it was the ELAS *kapetanios,* Stavros.

"It's okay, Chris," said Erin. "It was Stavros who found you in a creek and brought you here."

The picture of a stream in the country came to his mind and then faded. Andros nodded. The big Greek sat down on a crate of plastic explosives. "The noose grows tighter and tighter around our necks," he reported. "It's only a matter of time before we join my brother in the grave."

Andros looked at Stavros and then at Erin. "Michaelis is dead?"

"Kalos did it," said Stavros. "He murdered my brother."

"I suppose this means you'll wage a personal civil war with EDES?"

"Kalos is ELAS," corrected Stavros. "He is not what he seems." The big *kapetanios* began to weep for his lost brother.

Andros glanced at Erin, who confirmed the story with a sad nod. "It happened just before we were ambushed by SS paratroopers," she said.

Erin then told Andros about Churchill's hunch about a Soviet mole within the Greek Resistance; her mission to discover the identity of the Minotaur; and what had happened with Kalos before von Berg's Death's Head battalion attacked.

When Andros had heard it all, he shook his head. "That ought to shake up Zervas and the Middle East GHQ. But if Kalos isn't the Minotaur, who is?"

"Maybe our station in Sparta will know," she said.

"Sparta?" asked Stavros. "What's in Sparta besides Germans and collaborators?"

"A safe house, a wireless, British agents who can get us to Kalamata in time for our submarine pickup," said Erin. "You coming with us?"

"I told you," said Stavros, "Sparta is crawling with Germans and collaborators. One look at me and I'll be hanged."

"I'm afraid if you're seen at all, it will be the end of you," Erin replied. "I'm sure that Colonel Kalos, if he's still alive, has already reported your demise and wouldn't take too kindly to having you seen walking around. Of course, you could go north to your headquarters and try your luck with Saraphis, Siantos, Velouchiotis, and the rest of your ELAS comrades at Petrouli. That's if you can make it that far and if they don't hang you anyway. This way, at least there's hope. You might even be able to clear the name of ELAS by exposing Kalos."

Stavros considered his options. "You are quite convincing, Captain Whyte," he told her. "Okay, we go."

"The trick will be convincing those we run into in Sparta that we're peasants," said Erin, returning to the open crate of clothing.

"Our uniforms will attract more than a little attention once we cross the Evrotas River and enter town. So I suggest you slip into something more convincing while I wait outside."

Andros waited until she left before he joined Stavros in rummaging through the rags. Unfortunately, the only thing large enough for Stavros was a big black cassock.

"A priest?" said the *kapetanios*. "I won't do it."

"It will have to do," said Andros. "Anything less would give you away."

"Hurry up," called Erin, walking in. Her voice was flat, her face tense. "We have more company. Bring me some field glasses, Stavros, and let's take a look."

Stavros picked up a pair of field glasses and walked out with Erin. Andros, now fully alert, followed close behind, dragging himself across the rocky floor of the cave to the entrance. They hid in the shadows as the low hum of an airplane buzzed overhead.

Andros could see it over the treetops, a Nazi seaplane flying in low over the valley, the glint of bright sunlight bouncing off its wings.

"An old-fashioned Savoia-Marchetti," Erin observed through the field glasses.

Andros squinted and followed the plane out to sea. "For us?"

"More likely on his way to scour the sea for our submarine."

"A bad sign," said Stavros. "We better hide in the cave until dusk."

"I don't think so," Erin said, handing Stavros the field glasses. "Look down there."

Stavros had a look. "I see what you mean," he said, and passed the glasses along to Andros.

Andros raised the glasses and adjusted the focus. Beyond their screen of trees, German troops jumped into view. They were about three miles away, making their way in columns along the opposite side of the ravine. They had a number of mules in each column; these seemed to be carrying mortars and heavy machine guns as well as the usual camp equipment.

"Alpine Corps. Good mountaineers," he reported after spotting their green uniforms. "Where did *they* come from?"

"Sparta, probably," Stavros said. "There's an SS Death's Head battalion down there, too. We don't want to meet them." He glanced back at the cave. "Still, it would be a pity to allow such a generous cache of arms to fall into their hands. . . ."

They decided to take Sten submachine guns, because they could be broken down into parts small enough to conceal once they reached Sparta. They also packed some plastique. For good measure, Stavros plunged his giant hand into one box and grabbed several grenades like a bunch of grapes, and Andros took a Walther .38. Erin worked quickly and carefully to lay several charges and fix the Cordtex for simultaneous firing.

When the charges were laid and a time delay was set, the party of three quietly led the horses out of the cave and down the foothills. They heard the explosion an hour later as they emerged at the edge of the plains.

"Put that in your pipe and smoke it," Stavros huffed.

Andros and Erin exchanged surprised glances and looked at the *kapetanios*, who sheepishly explained, "Doughty used to say that, and it would always make my brother laugh. Now they're both laughing together, laughing at those of us who must remain in this godforsaken life . . ." But he couldn't finish.

In the distance they could see Sparta, a brightly lit island grid of twentieth-century civilization floating in a dark sea of ancient orchards and olive groves that rolled on under the evening skies. Assured that it was sufficiently dark to cross at a gallop, they mounted their horses and set off at a good pace.

95

Von Berg was sitting in his study, staring at the portrait of his grandfather King Ludwig II, when Spreicher phoned in from the police station in Sparta to report that Andros had survived the destruction of the secret Greek Resistance base and had eluded the Alpine Corps.

Von Berg, sitting on the edge of Kaiser Wilhelm II's leather chair, could barely contain his rage. "Idiots! I don't want him leaving the province!"

"He can't go back to Monemvasia," Spreicher said. "And we're overturning every town and village in Laconia, sir. There's no way out for him. The Parnon Mountains are behind him and the Taygetos Mountains before him. In between are the Evrotas Valley and our garrison here in Sparta."

Von Berg said, "What about the Gulf of Laconia? Andros must not reach the water!"

"The waters are mined, and we have motor torpedo boats patrolling the coast," Spreicher assured him. "It's only a matter of time. Between air reconnaissance and ground sweeping, I don't see how much longer he can last."

"It had better not be too much longer, Standartenführer, for your sake."

Von Berg slammed the phone down and went to the glass case containing the Maranatha text. He stood there, looking over the ancient parchment, hands behind his back. There was a knock at the door, and Franz escorted Dr. Xaptz into the study.

"Ah, Dr. Xaptz." Von Berg sat down behind his desk. "Has the Führer's personal consultant in spiritual matters completed his analysis of the Maranatha text?"

"Yes, Oberstgruppenführer." The professor looked disheveled and disoriented.

"Well?" the Baron asked. "Do you believe this text to be authentic?"

"In its antiquity, yes," Dr. Xaptz answered. "But its contents are another story. I'll have a complete report for you tomorrow."

"Tomorrow?" Von Berg frowned. "That's the eve of the Führer's weapons conference. Why so long?"

"You must understand, Oberstgruppenführer. I don't have the resources here that I have available in Berlin."

That's how much *you* know, Herr Professor, von Berg thought. "You mean you don't approve of your accommodations?"

"Beautiful as these grounds may be, Oberstgruppenführer, I have been here several days, and still I have yet to see more than my suite and the text here in your study. Even then it is under the eyes of your house staff. Indeed, I have been hindered in my efforts to enlist the aid of others outside the premises, either in person or by phone. As a result, I have been performing the tedious translations and alphanumerical calculations on my own."

"Then I won't keep you." Von Berg gestured to the door. "But I must have the report by tomorrow evening. We leave the next morning for Obersalzberg."

The professor seemed visibly relieved to hear him speak in the plural. "But of course, Oberstgruppenführer."

"We don't wish to disappoint the Führer, do we?" said Von Berg. "Franz, I'd like a word with you."

Franz waited until Dr. Xaptz was gone and clicked his heels. "At your orders, Oberstgruppenführer."

"Where is Aphrodite?"

Franz looked confused. "Why, she's swimming."

"Swimming? But it's almost time for supper. Who said she could go swimming?"

"You did, sir."

"I did?" Von Berg couldn't remember anything of the sort. "That's ridiculous. Go call her back in."

"Yes, Your Highness."

"What did you say?" Von Berg looked closely at Franz, who stood stiffly at attention.

"I said, yes, sir." Franz looked thoroughly confused. "Are you feeling well, Oberstgruppenführer?"

Von Berg knew he was hearing things now. He rubbed his temples, which were throbbing in pain. "I seem to have a slight headache."

"Is there anything I can get you, sir?"

"Yes," von Berg snapped. "You can get me Aphrodite. I'm going to get some fresh air."

Franz clicked his heels. "*Zu Befehl,* Oberstgruppenführer," he said, and left.

Von Berg looked up again at the face of his grandfather, King Ludwig II of Bavaria, and the terrible truth sank in.

The voices had returned.

He hadn't heard them since his childhood days, when his father, Maximilian, was going mad in the sanitarium and Kaiser Wilhelm's Reich was crumbling all around him. Now they were back, making their murmuring, disturbing presence clear. First, the increasing regularity and intensity of the headaches, which he had previously attributed to his gunshot wound. Then his lapses in memory, such as forgetting that he had killed his field underling Ulrich. Now these imaginary proclamations of his royalty from Franz.

Damn, he thought. He'd hoped he had licked them, these demons from the past, but he realized the discipline, focus, and intensity he had used to keep them at bay had slipped since he fell in love with Aphrodite.

"Yes, some fresh air," he told himself. "That's all I need. I've been away too long."

Von Berg stepped outside into the gardens. He wandered past the statues of the dying Achilles and Empress Elizabeth toward the terrace overlooking the Chalikiopoulos Lagoon.

He wondered how his melancholy grandmother had felt whenever she stood here, looking out from this same breathtaking vista. Did it feel like paradise to her, or prison? To him it felt like both, he realized. The Achillion was his retreat, not from the intrigues of the Hapsburg Court, but from Hitler's Third Reich. Unlike Elizabeth, he wasn't trapped by an impossible marriage or the knowledge of a forbidden affair and illegitimate child.

Yes, von Berg decided, my grandmother had nowhere to go. But I, I have a destiny to fulfill. And it will ultimately bring me glory or death.

He was terrified of death, because it cast him in the same lot as every other man. And he was not like any other man. He was the rightful king of Bavaria, the only man who could topple Hitler, end this insane war, and bring peace on earth. That a leader destined for such greatness could die before his time was inconceivable to him.

Nothing would jeopardize his ambitions now. Not Aphrodite, nor Andros, nor Himmler, nor the Führer. Nothing would stop him from fulfilling his destiny of becoming Germany's rightful king and the leader of a united Europe. Hitler's war had served its purpose: Europe was one. It was time for a new leader and a new world order.

Across the dark waters of the lagoon and under the pink skies, he could see the shimmering lights of Corfu Town. Somewhere down in those waters was Aphrodite, taking her evening swim.

It was her fault, he decided. She had made him weak, had made him actually care enough for her—a mere woman!—to waste his precious, limited time on Andros when Hitler's weapons conference was the day after tomorrow. On his birthday, no less. The day he turned forty. The day all his fears—or dreams—would be realized.

Perhaps it was his fault. Perhaps she could detect unconsciously his knowledge that Andros was still running about in the mountains. Once Andros was dead, truly dead, and she had come to terms with that, then she might love him.

Despite his bitterness and dejection, he could not find it within himself to kill her. Her parents, yes. Andros, yes. But Aphrodite? Never. All he could do was hope that she would have a change of heart and learn to love him. To have to rely on hope at all made him despair even more. He didn't believe in hope. He knew better. He knew that the best indicator of a person's future behavior was his past behavior. But knowledge be damned! The end of logic was madness, after all. Perhaps Aphrodite was independent enough to change her feelings for him. She had the will. She could find a way. If she wanted to. . . .

"*Vernunft wird Unsinn / Wohltat Plage,*'" he sang quietly, recalling the wistful sentiments of his favorite childhood poet, Goethe. "'Reason becomes nonsense / Boons afflictions.'"

Aphrodite, he reasoned, was his affliction.

96

Aphrodite was swimming in the Chalikiopoulos Lagoon while Peter watched her from shore. Beyond the SS bodyguard was the Achillion on its hill, the sun setting behind it.

Everything had changed, she realized, and yet nothing had changed.

Chris had come to Athens and left without her. Her parents, whom she had stayed behind to protect, were dead. Her brother, for whose freedom she had slept with the Baron, had been released. She was all that remained, abandoned to live the rest of her days on this island prison with the man who'd stolen her virginity and murdered her parents. Better off if she were dead than to live in this tropical purgatory, she thought. She had already decided to drown herself before the sun set.

There was only one thing left for her to do.

She looked across the rippling waters to the islet of Pondikonissi, with its whitewashed Church of the Pantokrator. The church looked strangely dark and forbidding this evening.

She glanced back at Peter, who was watching her with hateful eyes. He blamed her for Hans's death, she realized; he knew that it was only by a stroke of good fortune that he hadn't been the sentry Chris had killed in Athens. He wouldn't mind if she drowned herself. Indeed, it almost seemed as if the Baron and his staff expected her to take care of this final unpleasant task—getting rid of Aphrodite Vasilis. She wouldn't disappoint them.

"I'll be back before dark," she told Peter, and swam toward the church.

This time there were no shouts for her to come back, no concern about her welfare. There were also no robe and slippers for her at the foot of the steps. She found it chilly as she climbed to the top of the hill and entered the tiny church.

It was even colder and darker inside. No candles, no warmth, no life. The Orthodox priest who had told her to trust in the Lord with all her heart was gone. With rising fury, she wondered if Ludwig had carried out his threat against Father John. She couldn't even confess her misery and bitterness to God before she killed herself. She had never felt more alone in her life and began to cry in the dark.

"What's the matter, child?" asked a voice.

She turned to see a bearded face hovering behind the flicker of a candle. "Father, it's you," she said, and told him everything that had happened in Athens. About Chris, the Maranatha text, and the death of her parents.

"Truly, the Lord is merciful," said the priest. "He has spared his servant, and now he has spared you."

"Spared me?" she asked. "What about my parents? What about Chris? He's probably dead. What is there for me to live for?"

The priest looked at her with sad, knowing eyes, strange eyes that seemed to comprehend her pain all too well. Aphrodite looked away. Through the church's tiny stained-glass window, set in a rotting wooden frame, she could see it was dark outside. It was time for her baptism.

"I've got to go, Father."

"You most certainly do."

His response startled her and she looked at him curiously. "I do?"

"You must complete what your love began," he told her, and put his hand on her shoulder. "You must steal the Maranatha text from the Baron."

His voice resonated with a depth that stirred her soul, and when she looked up into his dark eyes, she could see her own face dimly. And then in the candlelight, she could see that this priest was not the one she used to confess to, but somebody else.

"Where is Father John?" she asked, voice trembling.

"Killed by the Baron, I'm told."

"Oh my God," she said. "It's my fault. I brought him to ruin just like everybody else I've loved."

"There's no need for you to bear the sins of the entire world, child," the priest said. "Our Savior has done that for us already. Rest assured, the Baron will receive his reward in due time."

"Who are you?"

"I, too, am a survivor, of a different sort. My brothers faced the same end as your family—at the hands of the Baron."

He ran his hand down the long gold chain draped around his neck and then held up his large, ornate cross in the candlelight. In its center was a glittering sapphire, though the cross's beauty was marred by a large indentation on one of its arms.

"My name is Philip."

97

The stars were out by the time Andros, Erin, and Stavros reached the Evrotas River and tied their horses to some fig trees in an orchard along the banks.

Andros looked across the river to Sparta's neat rows of neoclassical houses that rose up on the other side. Somewhere in town there was an SOE safe house and motor transport to take them to their submarine pickup. All they had to do was cross the river. He stared at the broad, icy waters and tried to picture himself swimming across in pain.

"I suppose we have no choice?" he said.

Stavros said, "You could take the Geraki Road that crosses over into town and try your luck at the German checkpoint."

Andros looked to Erin, but she was already half naked. He unbuckled his belt. The thought of her was too seductive to resist, however. Against his will, he tried to steal another glimpse of her. But as his gaze floated up, it met hers. She had been watching him, he realized, longing for him, and she didn't seem embarrassed that he knew it. But to embrace Erin now, if only emotionally, was to admit he had given up on Aphrodite. He wasn't ready to do that and doubted very much whether Erin would think him a better man if he did. So he stuffed his clothing into his satchel and resolutely waded into the water.

It was even colder than Andros had imagined, but the cold had the therapeutic side effect of numbing the pain in his leg. Soon he could no longer touch the bottom with his feet and panicked. At one moment he thought he heard his mother's cry in the night wind. But he fixed his eyes on his destination and kept working his limbs, afraid that if he stopped for even a moment, he'd sink to the bottom. The sight of Stavros ahead of him and the knowledge of Erin behind him spurred him on. Swallowing water and choking all the way, he eventually crawled up on the opposite bank of the river, exhausted. Ten minutes later, they were in dry clothes and hopped a low wall, safely on the outskirts of town.

They moved like phantoms past houses and down dark alleys toward the center of town. Stavros grumbled that his cassock was too short to hide his boots. A few dogs who smelled them barked, but by then they were already passing strollers in the streets. Unlike many Greek towns, this one had streets laid out at right angles—all the easier for an armored car to roll up from nowhere and keep the populace in order. Considering they had no papers, the sooner they were in a crowd, the better.

"The big tavernas are just off the *platia*, if I remember correctly," said Andros, leading the way.

They walked down Palaiologou Street, one of the two main boulevards lined with palm trees that swayed in the wind, turned onto Evrotou Avenue, and emerged in the *platia*, the large town square. The evening was alive with crowds of Greeks and Germans strolling about the square and filling up the tavernas.

Theo's was just across the *platia* from the town hall and the headquarters of the German garrison. It was an open-fronted building on the square with straw chairs arranged in front under the orange trees. Erin took a seat at one of the open-air tables outside while Andros and Stavros went inside.

The taverna was packed with German soldiers. Andros and Stavros moved confidently through the tables to the counter and asked for Theo. The bartender who stepped up was slight, dark, and visibly irked at being pulled aside on such a busy night. "What do you fellows want?" he asked.

Andros slipped a reichsmark note across the counter. "I'm looking for my friends and would like a cup of tea."

Theo took the note, saw the words "Yankee Clipper," and looked up with a start at Andros. Another look at Stavros seemed to send him into shock. "Heh, Nick," he called to one of his waiters, "two ouzos for these fellows." He disappeared into the back while a young waiter came with the ouzos.

Andros stole a glance at Stavros, who stiffened with fear beneath his cassock.

"Stavros, what is it?"

"Take a look behind us."

Andros looked over the big Greek's shoulder. On the wall above a table of German soldiers playing cards was a WANTED poster with Stavros's picture, a relic from the witch hunt for Communists under Metaxas. The reward for any information leading to his capture was three hundred thousand drachmas.

"You're more popular than I thought," Andros whispered. "Three hundred thousand drachmas. I'm impressed."

So was one of the Germans, it seemed, because Andros caught him eyeing Stavros over his glass of beer. Andros made sure that the next time the German looked their way, Stavros's back was turned.

"Face the counter and look straight back into the kitchen," Andros ordered. Stavros obeyed and asked for a second glass of ouzo. Andros looked over the tables to the *platia*. Erin was still outside, watching for trouble, when Theo came back.

"Why don't you two take a stroll around the square and come around the back in five minutes," Theo instructed them.

Andros replied, "I've got another with me who shouldn't linger outside."

"Tell both your friends to follow you in," said Theo, "but in ten minutes."

When Andros entered the back five minutes later, he was taken upstairs to a room overlooking the *platia*. Seated at a table was a man with a handlebar mustache, smoking a silver pipe, playing cards with another man who had a submachine gun lying across his knees.

"Gin," said the man, laying down his cards. He looked up at Andros. The face was different without a priestly beard or SS uniform, but the playful eyes were familiar. Andros recognized none other than Touchstone.

98

"So good to see you alive," said Brigadier Andrew Eliot, whose face, Andros concluded, was capable of assuming any shape. "Come, sit down. We've been looking all over for you."

"So have the Germans," Andros replied, taking a seat at the card table.

Eliot nodded to the man across the table with the submachine gun. "Meet Orestes, one of our communications officers. He's in charge of the station here in Sparta."

Andros looked at the nondescript fellow, who shared Eliot's ability to blend into any crowd. "Nice to meet you," said Andros, and he turned to Eliot. "What's the word from Athens? Did Aphrodite and my family get out?"

Eliot started shuffling the cards. "Your family left Piraeus safely this morning with Kostas Vasilis aboard the *Turtle Dove*. Right now they're en route to Istanbul."

So far, so good, thought Andros. "And Aphrodite?"

"She's in better shape than her parents. Von Berg had them executed in the family gardens early this morning."

Andros flinched at the news. "That goddamn Nazi bastard." He let his face drop to his hands. "They were his last bargaining chips with Aphrodite. I didn't think—"

"That the Baron would play his trump card so soon?" said Eliot, dealing him a hand. "Neither did we. Unfortunately, that means he's using brute force on the girl now. She was last seen boarding the Baron's plane before it lifted off from Athens. I think we can safely assume he's not planning on coming back."

"Where did they go?"

"We were hoping you could tell us. You have the film?"

Before Andros could answer, their host, Theo, came into the

room, his anxiety revealing itself through his strained smile. He was followed by Stavros and Erin. Erin took a seat at the table with Eliot. But the *kapetanios* moved to the window and nervously looked out over the *platia*. Theo left them and closed the door.

"Your big friend here needn't worry," Eliot told Andros. "The Germans have already broken in here once before. When they discovered what we were 'really up to'—gambling, or so they thought—it put their suspicions at ease. Since that night, I can't tell you how many times a Kraut has been in that chair you're sitting in for a good game of rummy. The proceeds of their considerable losses have kept Theo's bar well stocked."

Stavros stood by the window. "Tell him about Kalos, Andros."

"Colonel Kalos of EDES?" asked Eliot. "What about him?"

"He betrayed us, all of us," Andros said. "The National Bands, EDES, even ELAS." He explained what had happened.

Eliot swore under his breath. "Colonel Kalos a Communist? That will indeed shake them up in Cairo." He looked at Stavros. "If it's true."

Stavros turned from the window. "I swear to you, it is true."

Eliot raised an eyebrow. "Then aren't you on the same side?"

"I am of the mountains; Kalos is a disciple of Moscow's. Greece is for neither the British nor the Russians; Greece is for the Greeks."

"We can handle Kalos," said Eliot. "The hard part will be handling your escape. Orestes, get back to your place and raise Cairo on the set. Tell them the Yankee Clipper is ready to sail. Andros, you cut the cards."

Andros watched Orestes walk out the door with his submachine gun tucked under his coat. Then he cut the deck. "So what now?"

"The situation is, to say the least, fluid." Eliot dealt everybody a hand. "Submarine pickup tonight off the Gulf of Messenia. When you leave here, you'll be dressed as farm laborers, driving a produce truck on an olive and grain run to the port of Kalamata. A small fishing boat will be waiting to take you out to sea and link up with the submarine. Prestwick will be on board, anxious for your information. Now, pick up your hand."

Andros did as he was told. Inserted among the playing cards was an official identity card that gave him the name Troumboulas. "Where did you get this?"

"Courtesy of a certain gendarme," Eliot explained.

Stavros, suspicious as ever, asked, "Perhaps a local police chief I know personally?"

"Just because plenty of Greek police officials work under the Nazis and Italians doesn't mean all of them are collaborators, Stavros," Eliot said. "Quite a few are genuine patriots helping the Resistance. This one contacted us some months ago, saying he wanted to join the guerrillas in the mountains. We told him to stay at his post, that apart from carrying out his unpleasant duties as humanely as possible, he could also be of some service to us. I have more for the rest of you."

"I won't be needing one," said Stavros. "This is as far as I go. After we get out of here, I must get back to my village."

Eliot looked at the *kapetanios* with disdain, as if Stavros were a loose end that refused to be tied. "Fine," he said.

Andros asked, "So where is this truck, and who will be driving?"

Eliot led him to the open window overlooking the *platia*, throbbing with evening strollers and patrons of the tavernas. "See that fountain over there? In ten minutes you will go take a drink of water. A man will appear behind you, telling you to save some for the fish off Kalamata. He's your conductor. You'll follow him to a warehouse on the outskirts of town. That's where the truck is. You simply ask to see Stella. We don't have much time: curfew is in under an hour."

"What about us?" asked Stavros, glancing at Erin. "You expect us to wait up here with a hundred Germans downstairs?"

"Andros will park the lorry in the rear and load you in the back. The less you two are seen, the better. All of you will take the main road out of Sparta and drive through the Taygetos range to Kalamata."

"And simply float through the checkpoints?" Stavros asked.

"Inside the glove compartment of the lorry are papers signed by the local German garrison commander himself. They'll get you past the checkpoints here in Sparta, outside Kalamata, and onto the docks. Our man Niko will take you in his fishing caïque to the submarine. The caïque is moored to the second to last pier. Understood?"

"Understood," said Andros.

"Good, I'll go secure the arrangements. Andros, you follow me in five minutes."

When Eliot left the room, he closed the door and went downstairs to the phone in the kitchen. There, amid the background clatter of plates and glasses, he dialed a local number. "This is the Minotaur. Andros just turned up. I'm sending him your way. He'll do as I say, and so will you. Now listen . . ."

99

Andros was only too happy to step out onto the *platia* after spending too much time in a closed room with a nervous Stavros. He crossed the *platia* and approached the fountain as Eliot had instructed and stood behind two women. He bent down to take his drink. When he looked up, he saw a convoy of German trucks pull up in front of the town hall. They were the Alpine Corps they had spotted from the cave earlier, back from a fruitless excursion in the mountains.

A voice from behind him said, "Save some for the fish off Kalamata."

Andros turned. Before him was a small, dark man with a gray mustache. The man took some water and then, in passing, whispered that they must get going. "Follow me at intervals."

They crossed the *platia* and made their way past the cathedral, turning down a narrow alley. Although the streets were laid out at right angles, Andros quickly lost his sense of direction as he followed his conductor through the maze of alleys toward the edge of the town. The odyssey ended in a ghostly courtyard under a big moon. The warehouse in back could barely stand, its caved-in roof supported by rotting walls with broken windows.

The conductor creaked open the gate, and they walked around back. He knocked quickly four times and waited. A moment later, the garage door slid open.

The man who stood there in dirty overalls was wiping the grease from his hands with a blackened cloth. He wore a handkerchief knotted over his head in the manner of the Cretans, and his angry eyes looked Andros over from his soot-smeared face. "What do you want?"

The conductor answered, "We came to see Stella."

"She's inside, but I don't know if she wants to see you."

The conductor motioned for Andros to go inside while he stayed outside.

The warehouse was simply one large garage with two small rooms and a kitchen in back. In the middle of the garage sat the sorry-looking lorry, its condition hardly better than the garage's. It was filled in back with sacks of grain.

Andros walked around the truck and opened the hood. "Stella looks sturdy enough for the streets in town," he told the mechanic, "but how will she do in the mountain passes?"

The mechanic angrily retorted, "You don't like the arrangements?"

"All I want to know is how she'll do in the mountain passes."

"You'll never know." The mechanic's right arm came up holding a pearl-handled Colt revolver. "Spread your feet," he ordered. "Hands against the wall."

Andros did as he was told and could feel the rough hands run over his body. "If you're looking for a gun, I don't have one."

The mechanic spun him around and pushed the cold barrel of the Colt under his chin. "The film, fascist," he said, breathing heavily. "I want the film!"

"Too late," said Andros with a smile. "It's back at the camp."

"Liar!" The mechanic kicked him in the groin.

The blow sent Andros doubling over in agony. He slid against the wall to the floor, groaning in pain.

The mechanic reached down and tore open his shirt, saw the film cartridge and negative taped to his chest, and ripped them off. "You're in the hands of the National Liberation Front, traitor," he told Andros. "And it is in the hands of the National Liberation Front that you will die. Now, get up and walk toward the kitchen slowly." With the sharp point of his boot, he kicked Andros in his wounded leg. Andros roared in pain, his body writhing in agony.

"You call yourself the son of General Andros," scoffed the mechanic, looking down at him. "You're not much to look at." He screwed up his eyes. "I said get up!"

Andros tried to brace himself, but the blow from the boot came too fast, crashing into his back with such force that he was sure his back was broken. In spite of the jarring pain, he managed to stand. He stood staring at the revolver, trying to piece together what was happening.

The mechanic barked, "I said move."

Andros felt the hard barrel of the Colt press against his back, pushing him through the warehouse to the kitchen. There he saw Brigadier Eliot, sitting in a chair, sipping some tea, a Mauser on the counter beside him.

"Ah, you made it, Andros." Eliot nodded toward an empty chair. "Please sit down."

Bewildered, Andros sank down on the chair while the mechanic used one hand to keep the Colt revolver trained on him and the other to place the cartridge of microfilm and the negative on the counter for Eliot to see.

"Excellent work, Comrade Kalos," Eliot said. "Although I must say, from what I heard happening out there, I wasn't sure I was going to see Andros walk in here alive."

Andros glanced at the mechanic and realized he was looking at Colonel Alexander Kalos. He then looked at Eliot. Suddenly, he saw it all. "You're the Minotaur."

Eliot smiled with satisfaction. "Ever since that fateful autumn afternoon on the campus at Cambridge, when I had the unexpected pleasure of running into an elderly gentleman by the name of Orlov," he explained. "For me, an ungrateful son of a barrister and disillusioned veteran of the Great War, what he offered was the opportunity of a lifetime. Two years later, I joined the British Secret Service."

"As a spy for the enemy," said Andros.

"That, I suppose, depends on your point of view." Eliot smiled. "The way I see it, as the ranking SOE officer in Greece at this moment, I can persuade the Foreign Office in Cairo to support ELAS and the nascent democracy growing in Greece. Even if they don't, I can ensure that the National Liberation Front's army has the weapons it needs to boot Zervas out with the rest of the fascists."

Eliot put his cup of tea on the counter next to the Mauser and the cartridge of microfilm. "The irony is," he went on, "if Commander Lloyd had reached the monks in Meteora before von Berg, I already would have had the Maranatha text, and the OSS wouldn't have sent you in. None of this would have happened."

Andros wasn't sure what Eliot was talking about, but the British brigadier and Soviet spy had confirmed that a text did exist. At least Prestwick and Donovan hadn't lied to him about that. But Andros realized the text contained more than the Germans' enciphered defense plans for Greece. The Maranatha text, as Eliot called it, had to be a religious document, if it involved monks from Meteora.

"Since when is an atheist like Stalin so interested in a religious text?" asked Andros, stalling while he tried to think of a way out.

"From his seminary days in Tbilisi," Eliot said. "He has a thorough understanding of how men use religion to manipulate and oppress entire societies. He simply stripped it of its stained-glass facade. And for that, he's called a cruel dictator while those pious bastards in the Church of England have their rings kissed by the royal family and are called holy men of God. Isn't that the case with the Greek Orthodox Church?"

Andros said nothing.

"Nevertheless," said Eliot, "you've surpassed my expectations for an OSS man by actually managing to break into von Berg's safe in Kifissia."

Andros glanced at the counter on which Eliot had placed the film negative and microfilm cartridge. If the Maranatha text wasn't in von Berg's safe, where was it? The answer, he guessed, was on the film negative and not the microfilm exposures Werner made him shoot. Furthermore, wherever this Maranatha text was, there he would probably find Aphrodite.

Eliot could see his mind at work. "When we picked you up after the party and drove you to Piraeus, I was tempted to take the film from you then and there. But then I would be failing in my duties as a British agent and would tip my hand to my underlings in the car, whose loyalties to the Crown are quite unquestionable."

"And because you knew you had Kalos at the National Bands base." Andros looked at Kalos, who had pulled a bottle of brandy from the sideboard and was pouring himself a glass.

"And Stavros, before he buckled," said Eliot, who picked up his Mauser and pointed it at Andros. "As they were the ones going to make the actual raid to steal the text, I was confident it would eventually come back to me if they succeeded. They would steal it—all for Mr. Churchill, of course—and Stavros would kill Doughty and the other British officers."

"But why?" asked Andros, beginning to worry about Erin back at Theo's.

"Doughty was getting suspicious," Eliot explained. "According to Kalos here, he was about to telegraph some reports to the Foreign Office that, if interpreted with other goings-on in Greece, would implicate me."

Andros said, "So you gave the Nazis the location of the base."

"That's right," Eliot replied.

"Then von Berg's men blew up the base and we came here," Andros concluded. "So I suppose there never was an escape route for us tonight."

"Oh, but there is," said Eliot. "Can't risk it being said that I haven't been faithful in my capacities as chief of SOE Athens. I'd let you go right now if you didn't know Kalos's identity. Unfortunately, my role as the Minotaur calls for me to kill you."

"It won't work," Andros said. "Stavros told us about your plans to destroy Zervas and consolidate power."

"Stavros can talk all he wants to the Gestapo," said Eliot. "Kalos, the phone, please."

Kalos pulled a phone from beneath the sideboard and handed it to Eliot, who put his Mauser on the counter while Kalos covered Andros with his Colt.

"You don't mind if I make a local call, do you?" Eliot asked Andros as he dialed. A moment later, he cleared his throat and spoke in precise German. "You may be interested to know that none other than the Communist terrorist Stavros Moudjouras is at this moment hiding out in a room over Theo's taverna. If you move quickly, you may yet catch him." He hung up and looked at Andros. "I hate loose ends."

"I suppose you'd include me in that category?"

"Most definitely."

Andros realized that it was now or never. If he didn't get out of there this minute, Erin and Stavros would be caught by the Gestapo, and they'd all be dead.

"Can I at least have some brandy?" Andros asked. "Or a cigarette?"

"Kalos, give him a cigarette."

Kalos extended an open carton of black-market cigarettes while Eliot kept Andros covered with the Mauser. Andros withdrew a cigarette and allowed Kalos to give him a light. Kalos produced a familiar-looking gold lighter. "A gift from Brigadier Eliot," he said, and flicked it open. "You like it, heh?"

It was Aphrodite's lighter, the one Andros had left behind during his escape from Athens. Seeing it in the filthy hands of this criminal only furthered his resolve to get out of there somehow. He leaned forward to touch the end of his cigarette to the flame and then sat back and inhaled. He glanced out the window. It was pitch-black outside. Erin and Stavros were either worrying about what had happened to him or had no time to worry because the Germans had gotten to them.

"Well, Mr. Andros," said Eliot, raising the Mauser, "I'm afraid it's time to die."

"Can't I finish my cigarette?" Andros inhaled and held his breath as he looked into the Mauser's barrel.

A curious look crossed Eliot's face, and he lowered the Mauser. "Fine," he said. "Two more breaths."

Andros exhaled smoke and casually leaned over to tip the ashes of his cigarette.

Eliot smiled. "You have one breath left."

Andros nodded and quickly swung his arm to knock aside Kalos's revolver. He then kicked the chair out from under Eliot, who crashed to the floor. Eliot reached for his Mauser, but Andros stepped on the outstretched arm until the grip loosened around the pistol. He bent down to pick it up when Eliot grabbed his legs and pulled him to the floor. An unbearable shock of pain jolted Andros.

"Kalos!" called Eliot.

Andros looked up in time to see Kalos walk up holding an ax over his head. Raising his trembling arm, Andros fired a bullet into Kalos's chest. Kalos stumbled backward and was brought to the floor by the weight of the ax.

Eliot tightened his grip around Andros's legs, sending further ripples of pain up his spine.

Andros swung the butt of the Mauser against Eliot's skull and heard a sickening crack. He could feel the man's arms loosen from around his legs.

When Andros stood up, he saw that the Minotaur was dead. He also smelled something burning, and when he turned, he saw that his cigarette had started a fire by the baseboard. A curtain of flame shot up the wall and started licking the ceiling. It wouldn't be long before the entire tinderbox of a warehouse came crashing down on him.

He thought of Erin and Stavros at Theo's taverna. I have to get back to them before the Gestapo does, he thought. No time to waste.

Grabbing the microfilm cartridge and negative from the counter, he headed toward the garage. There was the lorry, pointed toward the closed garage door. He ran over and climbed into the cab behind the wheel. He turned the key in the ignition, and the engine roared to life. Then he shifted gears and stepped on the accelerator.

The lorry lurched forward and crashed through the door. Suddenly, he was in the courtyard and could see the moon through the windshield. He shifted to high gear and headed straight for Theo's taverna.

100

Stavros and Erin were upstairs in the parlor over Theo's when the door burst open and Theo entered. "SS paratroopers," he said breathlessly. "They're downstairs!"

Stavros moved to the window overlooking the town square and lifted the curtain. Several armored cars, troop carriers, and *Kübelwagen* appeared in the *platia,* and armed soldiers were converging on the taverna.

"The Baron's Death's Head battalion!" Stavros cried. "The ones I said we don't want to meet."

"Any ideas?" asked Erin, standing beside him.

Stavros dropped the curtain. "The alley," he said. "If we can cut through the kitchen."

They had started down the stairs when they heard the rumble of heavy boots coming up.

"This way," said Erin, ducking into another bedroom.

They closed the door as the jackboots moved past them toward the parlor they had just vacated. They stood before the open window facing the alley, garbage strewn out below in the darkness.

Erin said, "We'll have to jump."

"You can't be serious!" said Stavros.

But the pounding on the door followed by the heavy shout *"Raus! Schnell!"* outside in the hallway convinced him otherwise. The two crawled out the window and were hanging on to the sill by their fingers when the Germans crashed through the door.

Breathlessly, they hung outside in the darkness while the Germans overturned the room. Suddenly, Stavros was aware of voices below. He looked down and saw the helmets of SS men searching the piles of garbage in the pool of light from the kitchen. Had they simply looked up, they would have beheld the strange sight of a big priest and a young woman hanging in the air.

As it was, fed up with the stench and finding nothing outside, the Germans disappeared into the kitchen. But before Stavros could relax, he heard a rumble down below and the screech of brakes as a shadow moved in the dark.

"It's the lorry with Andros," whispered Erin. "Let go and we'll drop onto the sacks of grain in back."

"What? How do you know?"

"Let go, I tell you. The sacks of grain will break the fall."

Before Stavros could respond, the window above them slid open, and he looked up into the disfigured face of an SS officer who stared down at them like the devil with a crooked smile.

Before the German could make a sound, Stavros felt Erin slip her hand into his cassock, remove a dagger from his belt, and hurl it into the SS officer's chest with such speed that all Stavros saw was the flash of the blade and the German lurching forward. Erin reached up, grabbed the German's uniform, and disappeared as she pulled the dying German down with her into the darkness below.

Stavros clenched his teeth and released his grip. He landed with a thud among the sacks, just as Erin had said. He could see her removing his dagger from the dead German and hiding the corpse behind a sack of grain.

She wiped the blade clean against the rough sackcloth. "Better that his friends don't find him at all than find him dead," she said, handing Stavros's dagger back to him, handle first. Then she called to Andros in the cab, "We're in!"

The lorry lurched forward. Stavros looked behind at the dark alley and saw a German poke his head outside the taverna window, look about curiously, and then, seeing nothing, disappear.

"It's not over yet," Erin warned as they turned the corner.

101

The *platia* was ablaze with searchlights trained on the taverna as Andros rolled by in the lorry. The SS had sealed off the entire square and were searching every house and assembling all the men between sixteen and sixty in the street, holding the crowd in check with armored cars and automatic weapons.

Andros drove past the town hall and rounded a corner. At the checkpoint on the edge of town, several armored cars and SS men were waiting.

"I hope this pass works," Andros muttered to himself as he slowed down. He called back to Stavros and Erin in the rear, "Get down!" He braked to a halt while a young SS captain approached with his pistol. With him was a Greek policeman.

"Identification, please," the SS officer demanded.

Andros pulled out the identification card Eliot had given him back at Theo's and handed it to the German. "What's going on?"

"Communists."

"Oh, I see."

The SS officer eyed him closely. "What's your name?"

"Troumboulas."

The German turned to the Greek gendarme. "Check that name against our list of popular pseudonyms used by British agents."

The gendarme did as he was told and shook his head to indicate there was no match.

Still the German wasn't satisfied. He flashed his light in Andros's face. "Where are you going?"

"Kalamata," Andros answered. "Grains for shipment. I'm late, you know."

"It is not my concern if you spend too much time at the taverna, you lazy pig," said the German. "It will cost you two sacks." He turned to the gendarme, with whom Andros presumed he split the black-market proceeds. "Does that sound right?"

The gendarme nodded nervously. Meanwhile, three German guards walked around to the back of the lorry and poked their flashlights among the sacks. Andros watched them disappear in the rearview mirror and froze in his seat, expecting the worst. Instead he heard a voice say in German, "Carry on."

Andros started the engine. It was only when the lorry moved toward the gate that Andros looked again in his rearview mirror and realized there was nobody behind the truck. The German guards were gone. Only the SS captain and the Greek gendarme stood in the street, equally bewildered, until the German realized what had happened and pulled his gun. "Stop them!" he shouted to the guard-house, and had started firing when a burst of machine-gun fire from the back of the lorry cut him and his Greek friend to the ground.

Andros took his eyes off the rearview mirror in time to see the swing bar dropping in front of the windshield. He hit the accelerator and crashed through. Suddenly they were out of Sparta and in the open foothills.

102

His Majesty's submarine the *Cherub* slowly made its way beneath the surface of the Mediterranean en route to its rendezvous with the OSS agent code-named Sinon, off the southwestern coast of the Greek Peloponnese.

For Lieutenant Commander Eric Safire, its captain, things had been touch and go for several hours, ever since the submarine's radio operator had picked up word that a Luftwaffe air strike had decimated the National Bands base in Greece. But under a half hour ago, Orestes in Sparta had radioed that Sinon had survived and was on his way to the rendezvous as planned. Or rather, almost as planned. That was what worried Safire, but he had said nothing about it yet because he had learned not to question his orders.

A young man of medium height, the twenty-six-year-old captain wore his straight brown hair long enough to tuck behind his ears. He would have resembled a girl were it not for the three-day growth on his face. He had said good-bye to his razor blade back in port because at sea they had to conserve their fresh water, and shaving with salt water packed too much of a sting.

This mission was his third in a remarkable series of special operations. First came the North Africa landings, Operation Torch, when he was an officer aboard the submarine HM *Seraph* and they had slipped General Mark Clark ashore to secretly contact the French before the Allied invasion. Next came Operation Mincemeat, when they dropped the body of "Major Martin" off the coast of Huelva, Spain.

This time around, Safire was the master of his own mint-condition submarine, and his company was neither a distinguished general nor a pseudonymous corpse but an American OSS colonel named Jason Prestwick, who stood beside him in the control room, thrilled to be "in the field," as he called it.

The American had joined them in Algiers and had made himself an annoying if amusing nuisance to the young crew. The tall, awkward professor seemed harmless enough at first, bumping his head against the short doorways and threatening only his own well-being. Soon, however, he was putting the entire crew in danger. What with his endless fascination with new technology, he was always touching this button or turning that dial. For one wild minute the submarine was in danger of sinking after a curious Prestwick had removed the sea hatch from the floor and was surprised to find water bubbling up into the control room.

Safire turned to the old professor, noted the Band-Aid on his forehead, and asked, "Your Joe ever done this before?"

"*I've* never done this before, Commander, let alone Andros," Prestwick replied with a sour expression. "But if he comes out of Greece alive, he'll have information vital to the war. Information that Churchill and Roosevelt are anxiously awaiting."

"It's going to be tricky," Safire warned, showing Prestwick the charts. "The signal we picked up from Orestes said that the caïque carrying Andros is going to launch from Kalamata. That's in the Gulf of Messenia."

Prestwick followed Safire's finger as it traced the route on the chart. "So what?"

"Our orders in Alexandria were to rendezvous six miles off the Cape of Koroni. That's beyond this peninsula at the mouth of the gulf."

"I don't see the difference," said Prestwick. "Rather than take the land route all the way to Koroni, they're going to launch from Kalamata and cut across the gulf waters. What are you getting at?"

Safire pointed to a mass of X's on the chart, off the port of Kalamata. "See these markings? The Germans have mined the Gulf of Messenia. Andros will never get out of there in one piece."

"Good God!" said Prestwick. "Can't we stop them?"

Safire rubbed his stubbled chin. "A little late for that, I think. They've probably left already from Sparta, and it's too risky to surface right now. What I can't understand is why. It was SOE agents in Athens who provided Cairo with the location of the German minefields for our charts in the first place."

The American's hands trembled as he lifted the chart and looked for himself, his green eyes squinting from behind their glasses. "What can we do?"

Safire wanted to tell him they could turn back, that it would be foolhardy to jeopardize the *Cherub* and its crew by straying anywhere near that minefield in the futile search for an agent who would not be there when they surfaced. But Prestwick was the senior intelligence officer here, and Safire had learned early on in his naval career that when a superior asked for his opinion, it was better to offer options and not advice.

"We could try to surface at the designated rendezvous in the unlikely chance that your Joe is there," he answered. "Or we could call it a day and head back to base."

"Turn back?" Prestwick put down the chart and looked at him, his angry eyes turning into green slits behind the fogged-up glasses. "You turn back, Commander, and I'll have you brought up on charges of insubordination and see that you are stripped of your command."

The nasty tone in the American's voice tempted Safire toward violence, but he restrained himself. Striking a superior officer, however inferior a man he might be, would do little to boost his naval career or help the Allies.

"Of course, sir," said Safire, and turned to the helmsman. "Full ahead."

103

It was at least thirty miles to Kalamata through the rocky, snow-capped slopes of the Taygetos range, Andros calculated, pushing the engine hard as the lorry climbed the dramatic Langada Gorge. But with mountain road conditions being so intolerable, they'd be lucky to make it in an hour in this crate. Of course, crashing through the checkpoint on their way out of Sparta probably had put every German and Italian checkpoint ahead of them on alert.

Andros glanced over his shoulder toward the back and shouted, "I'm going to pull over!"

"What's wrong now?" asked Stavros.

"Nothing, we're changing drivers. You're up front. Any descriptions or pseudonyms that have been radioed ahead belong to me."

Andros pulled the lorry over to the side of the road. He left the engine running and walked back to the rear of the lorry while Stavros, now wearing the uniform of a German, climbed into the cab and shifted gears.

As they drove off, Andros crouched in the rear of the lorry among the sacks of grain with Erin, who was still stripping a uniform off one of the dead Germans.

"Whatever happened to silent killing?" he asked.

Erin shrugged sheepishly and rolled up her hair and put on the SS officer's cap with the Death's Head badge.

Andros counted four bodies in the back. "I saw only three soldiers at the checkpoint."

"Stavros and I picked up this one earlier." Erin pointed to the closest corpse.

Andros glanced at the naked body, twisted among the sacks. Separated from his companions, with no uniform or symbols of fascism on him, he looked like an ordinary young man, much like the cadets back at West Point. He had a powerful build with rippling muscles now stilled. Then the lorry hit a bump, and the head bounced, turning up to reveal a face that was badly burned on one side. Andros looked away.

"You came just in time back there," Erin said casually, checking a Schmeisser. "What happened at the warehouse?"

"I was tied up by your friend the Minotaur."

Erin stared at him. Her eyes, what Andros could see of them in the moonlight, seemed to grow larger. Finally, after a long silence, she said, "Eliot. It was Eliot."

"Along with his friend Colonel Kalos," Andros added.

"I should have known," she said, cursing herself. "I should have seen it. I never should have let you go alone to pick up the lorry." She gripped his shoulder and opened her mouth to say something, but she couldn't seem to find the words.

Andros gently lifted her hand from his shoulder and returned it to the Schmeisser. "It's okay," he told her. "You trained me well. They're dead and we're alive."

"Thanks to you," she said.

"It's about time I returned the favor. Now what?"

She looked strangely still in the moonlight in spite of the jerky bounces of the lorry. "You tell me, sir," she said in a manner that clearly signaled a shift in their relationship. "My orders were to defer to the judgment of my commanding officer in the field once he had proved himself."

Andros could see that she was referring to him. "And have I, Captain?"

"Yes, Colonel."

Andros was taken aback. "Colonel now, is it?"

"Churchill's orders."

"Since when does the British prime minister bestow promotions within the U.S. Army?"

"Hellenic Royal Army, sir," she corrected. "King George signed the papers."

Everything seemed to fall into place for Andros. "This submarine pickup was planned for you, wasn't it? I was supposed to stay back at the National Bands of Greece to legitimize it."

Erin nodded slowly.

At that point Andros was aware that the lorry was slowing down as they approached the Taygetos Pass at the top of the ridge of mountains.

"About half a mile ahead of us," Stavros called from the cab, "an Italian staff car blocking the pass, two soldiers holding hands up for us to stop."

Andros exchanged glances with Erin as the lorry braked to a halt.

"Identification, *signor,*" demanded a harsh voice in passable Greek.

Andros heard the shuffle of papers and Stavros's irritated voice. "I'm running behind schedule. Hurry."

"But of course," came the smart reply. "Now step out slowly or I'll blow your brains out."

The Italian must have been pointing a gun, because Andros heard the door open and Stavros get out.

"Rudolf, check this ape. Ah, a gun. Carrying a gun is worth the death penalty."

"Protection," Stavros explained. "From bandits like you."

There was a great smack, and Andros could almost feel the butt of the pistol strike Stavros's face. "Rudolf, check what they're carrying in the back."

Andros and Erin crouched low behind the sacks while a flashlight beam searched the back of the lorry. Apparently not satisfied, Rudolf climbed inside for a further look. As he bent over, Andros slipped his arm across the man's neck and pulled until he heard the awful snap.

Outside, Rudolf's superior was getting impatient. "Hurry up, Corporal. I haven't got all night."

When Andros finally came around from behind the lorry, he cut the figure of an Italian commando, rifle at the ready.

"Well, Corporal?"

"All clear," answered Andros, stepping forward into the light of the guardhouse.

The Italian's face fell, and he reached for his pistol, but Andros shot him in the arm. The Italian reached for his sleeve in agony. "Please, no more!"

"Next time you'll join your friend," Andros said, and called to Stavros and Erin, "Take care of the truck while I take care of this one."

The Italian looked terrified and begged for mercy.

"Just shut up and strip," Andros ordered. "Erin, pardon the stain on the sleeve."

Andros marched the naked Italian into the fir forest on the other side of the ridge. He forced the man to lie flat on the ground and struck him on the head like Erin had taught him at the Farm. Then he used a rope he'd found in the guardhouse to tie him up in knots that would make old Captain Tsatsos proud.

When Andros returned to the road, there was no sign of the lorry, only the Italian staff car. The engine was running, and Erin was behind the wheel. Stavros, dressed in an Italian uniform, sat sulking in back with the submachine guns.

"I hope she knows what she's doing," the *kapetanios* griped as Andros climbed into the passenger seat next to her.

Erin ignored the remark, hit the accelerator, and they were off. As soon as the lights of the checkpoint faded from the rearview mirror, she told Andros, "Check the glove compartment for papers."

Andros rummaged through the compartment and produced a visa. "Signed by the Italian garrison commander of Kalamata himself."

"Perfect," she replied.

They descended the other side of the Taygetos Mountains toward Kalamata along the Nedonas Gorge, clearing the next two checkpoints without a hitch.

104

The port of Kalamata was used by the Italians for shipping supplies between Italy and the Aegean Islands. But at this hour, the streets of the capital of the province of Messenia were deserted as the Italian staff car carrying Andros, Erin, and Stavros rolled through the center of town, passing the Italian garrison on its way toward the beachfront a long mile down.

They stopped behind a warehouse across from the marina. The smell of fish was strong, the mournful wail of a *bouzouki* from some distant taverna barely audible above the rhythmic creaking of boats in their slips.

"Nice and slow," said Andros as they proceeded. "Remember, we're patrolling the piers, just like the others on foot."

As Erin drove along the quayside, past the strung-up nets and occasional swinging lantern, Andros was aware of several dark vehicles coming up fast on their right. He looked into the side-view mirror, only to be blinded by the headlights of *Kübelwagen*.

"It's a trap!" said Stavros, opening fire, trying to knock out the lights.

Erin stepped on the pedal, but more lights appeared at the far end of the harbor. She roared down the quayside and swung a hard left into the second-to-last pier, the *Kübelwagen* and cars closing in.

She braked to a halt, and they all jumped out and started running. A hundred yards away was the end of the pier, lit by a lantern swinging on a rope. Behind them the *Kübelwagen* and Gestapo cars were blocked by the Italian staff car. The Germans got out and started shooting.

As they ran down the pier, Andros could hear an engine revving in the water. Soon he saw it—a fishing caïque bobbing at the end of the pier. The pier light had been knocked out. A figure popped out of the wheelhouse, aiming a rusted Thompson submachine gun at them as they climbed aboard.

"Your uniforms, I wasn't too sure," the skipper said, dropping the formalities when a spray of bullets from the quay showered splinters of wood. "Inside, now!"

They crammed into the wheelhouse, and the surprisingly powerful engine roared to life. The old fishing caïque peeled away from the pier at an unbelievably high speed.

"What do you have under there?" asked Stavros, pointing to the engine room.

"Tank engine," the skipper boasted. "This caïque belongs to the British, but I get to keep everything at the end of the war if I'm still afloat." He switched on the radio to a special frequency to pick up Axis traffic. "We're not out of this yet. They've alerted every patrol boat in the gulf. They will try to cut us off."

Several German and Italian motor torpedo boats were converging up ahead in the open sea. But they were too late. The engine shot a pitch higher, and the caïque cleared the boats trying to close them off, leaving them behind to be swallowed by the darkness.

The skipper said, "They won't follow us now."

"How can you be so sure?" asked Andros.

"The waters we are in, they are mined. That is why the patrol boats don't follow us." The skipper started laughing. "But I, Niko, know the way, I think. If they have not changed things too much."

105

They weaved their way through the minefield in the Gulf of Messenia, a fiendish grin crossing Niko's face as the boat headed toward the Cape of Koroni and the open sea. The tossing proved too much for Andros, and he retched over the side, convinced that if they didn't strike a mine, they were going to die one way or another with this daredevil.

As Andros leaned over the splintered railing, the raw feeling of gravel in his throat, it occurred to him that the Minotaur would take whatever precautions necessary to minimize even the most remote risk of losing the microfilm. If such was the case, Eliot would cover his bets by placing his own man on the getaway caïque. Andros straightened and turned to see Niko in the wheelhouse with Stavros.

Stavros must have been thinking the same thing, because he picked up the rusted Thompson on the deck and pointed it at Niko. "The British give you this, too?" he asked. "It doesn't even work."

The skipper shrugged. "It was too much of a chore to clean every day, and I got tired of it."

Stavros pointed to several flags visible beneath the pile of ropes in the back of the deck—German, Greek, Egyptian, Turkish. "And those?"

"Depends on which waters I travel."

"What else did the British do for you?"

"SOE also gave me this," Niko said, proudly holding up a luminous signal ball. "Works well in the water and will help us with the submarine pickup off Koroni."

As Niko held up the signal ball with one hand, he reached under the chart table with the other and released a spring catch. A flap fell down, and a Schmeisser machine pistol dropped from its secret compartment into his hand. He raised his arm and pointed it at Andros and Stavros. "The National Liberation Front orders you to hand over the film to me before I throw you out among the mines," he demanded. "I, Niko, am—"

His throat seemed to catch on this last phrase as a terrible grimace crossed his face. He doubled over to reveal a harpoon rising out of his shoulder like a flagpole and, behind it, Erin holding the gun.

"You, Niko, are too small a fish to kill," said Erin.

Stavros reached over and grabbed the wounded Niko by his sailor's shirt. "But you seem to have enough hot air to float." Stavros pulled the harpoon out of Niko's shoulder and, in a single fluid motion, hurled him into the sea. In seconds he drifted behind them and disappeared.

Andros moved quickly to man the wheel. "That was quick thinking, Erin."

"Not quick enough. Look."

He glanced over his shoulder. Lights appeared on the horizon.

"German motor torpedo boats," Erin explained. "Looks like they plan to fire at us from a distance. Now what?"

"Now we make for the Cape of Koroni and wait for the signal from the submarine," he told her, pushing the engine to a full-throttled roar. "And hope those torpedoes don't catch up with us."

Suddenly a torpedo struck a mine two hundred yards away, exploding into a giant fireball that lit up the night and exposed them to the Axis ships.

Andros steered a zigzag course and soon had the caïque zooming through the waters, bouncing off the waves. With each chop, he winced in pain and feared that his knees would break, or that they'd strike a mine and disintegrate.

"They're still back there!" shouted Erin. "What do you suggest?"

"We toss a grenade in their direction. The Germans will think we struck a mine and died."

"I'm ready," Stavros announced.

Andros turned and started. The *kapetanios* was holding a grenade in one hand and the pin in the other. "What are you waiting for?"

Stavros hurled the live grenade into the mine-infested waters as the caïque peeled away. Twenty seconds later, the grenade blew, detonating a mine. The explosion lit up the Gulf of Messenia, and by the time it dimmed, they were engulfed in darkness.

106

It was still the middle of the night when the caïque cleared the promontory of Koroni. To starboard Erin could see the coastal fortifications of Koroni's Crusader castle, high on a cliff overlooking a sandy bay. Beyond the peninsula were the offshore islands of Sapientza and Skhiza. They had reached the open sea. A few more miles and they would rendezvous with the submarine.

Inside the wheelhouse, Stavros and Erin were sharing the first watch while Andros nursed his wounded leg down in the hold. Stavros had the wheel. He also had an anxious expression.

"How do we know Eliot hasn't talked to the British already and lied about us?" Stavros asked as they passed the Cape of Koroni. "How do we know they won't kill us?"

"We don't," said Erin, wiping the salty spray off her face. "Do you want to go back to Kalamata?"

Stavros said, "What happens to us once we are aboard your submarine?"

"We tell them about Kalos and the Minotaur. You'll be vindicated."

"No," he replied. "I am a dead man already. Didn't you see back there in Sparta? The British betrayed me to the Germans. They, like my comrades, wish to see me gone. I can never remove the black stain on my name for signing the Metaxas confession. I have committed the unpardonable sin and have betrayed the cause. This is my punishment."

"Because you saved your brother's life?" asked Erin. "That hardly seems a crime to me."

"You don't understand, Captain Whyte," the *kapetanios* told her. "When a Communist falls into enemy hands, his imprisonment is nothing personal but part of the class struggle, a political blow to the Party. He must not waver, not under torture, failing health, nothing, or he betrays the Party."

There was pride in his voice, and Erin began to grasp the similarities between them. Her breakdown before the Gestapo in Lyon wasn't all that different from Stavros's public renunciation of Marxism. Perhaps she had allowed her apprehensions about him as a man and a Communist to get the best of her back at the National Bands base.

"You know, my father the missionary endured unbearable pain for the cause of Christ in the Far East," she said, her voice softening. "You two are very different men, but I'll wager that you're alike in one way: Becoming a Communist was probably the most unselfish, idealistic, and sacrificial decision of your life. And the day you betrayed your cause for the sake of your brother was equally unselfish, for you thought of him and not your reputation. Quite unlike Peter the Apostle when he denied Christ. But Jesus forgave him and restored him."

"The Party is not so kind," Stavros replied.

"Wasn't your brother's life more important than the cause?" asked Erin. "Aren't people like your brother the reason for the cause?"

"What do you mean?" Stavros gripped the wheel and watched their heading.

"That if the souls of men like your brother live eighty or so years and die, then the Party, the state, the cause, are indeed more important, since they can last for generations. But if the souls of men are immortal, then individuals are more important than the state, than kingdoms that rise and fall and whose names we no longer remember."

"Ah, now we are entering deep waters," Stavros replied. "Waters in which a simple man such as I cannot swim." He killed the engine and handed Erin the luminous signal ball. "Get ready. We're near the rendezvous."

She had opened her mouth to say something when the hatch cover popped open and Chris climbed up on deck beneath the night skies. He must have sensed they had entered smooth waters and seemed relieved to get out of the cramped, uncomfortable hold. "How are we doing?" he asked.

"Shhh," said Stavros, holding a finger to his lips. "Listen."

There was a heavy silence as the caïque rose and fell with each small swell, the only sound the lap of water against the wooden hull. Then came an unmistakably faint, dull clacking noise.

"I think I see it," said Andros, pointing. "The silhouette of the submarine."

Erin held up the signal ball, palm toward the sea. But she was looking at Stavros. "Are you sure you won't come with us?"

Stavros shook his head.

"Come on," said Chris. "You could join one of the Greek army units training in Egypt or Lebanon."

"The Hellenic Royal Army," Stavros corrected. "No, Andros. The war is here, in Greece. And this caïque should make a nice addition to the ELAS navy. It will be my peace offering to them."

Erin said, "And if they still consider you a traitor?"

Stavros shrugged. "That is their concern. But I will not betray my conscience. I will not give up my arms until we have popular rule as well as national liberation. We don't need King George or the Party. We Greeks must be master in our own house."

The *kapetanios*'s integrity made a deep impression on Erin, because she had seen it in her father. If Stavros had been a Party hack blindly following his misguided faith, she might have felt differently. But he *knew* there were corrupt leaders waiting for him back at Party headquarters, and still he insisted on going back to confront them, like a lamb to the slaughter.

"Good luck, then," Andros said, and shook the *kapetanios*'s hand. "I hope we don't meet again in battle, for both our sakes."

Erin watched Chris stuff the film negative and microfilm cartridge into a waterproof satchel, grab a life preserver, and wait for her by the wooden rail.

"Ladies first," he said, gesturing overboard.

But she couldn't leave Stavros alone.

Stavros could see her hesitation. "What are you waiting for?"

"You've got to come with us," she begged him. "If you don't, what will I tell them in Cairo?"

"What will you say?" repeated Stavros. He started to sing an old klephtic song from the days of the War of Independence against the Turks:

> *"If our comrades ask you any questions about me,*
> *Don't say I stopped a bullet, don't say I was unlucky,*
> *Just tell them I got married*
> *In the sad lands overseas . . .*
> *With a big flat stone for a mother-in-law,*
> *New pebble brothers, and the black earth for my bride."*

Erin realized there was nothing left to say, so she gave Stavros a big hug, turned around, and dove over the side of the caïque into the water, waiting for Chris to follow. He landed beside her with a splash, his arms locked around the life preserver.

Erin held up the signal ball. There on the horizon, visible now and then through the curtain of clouds in the moonlight, was the *Cherub*, like a great gray whale sitting atop a wave.

Stavros, meanwhile, had started the caïque's engine and was slowly motoring away.

Treading in the wake of the caïque, Erin watched the *kapetanios* dissolve into the night, a tragic figure whose future, she realized, was about as dim as Greece's at this point, no matter who won the war.

107

It was the middle of the night on the island of Corfu, and Aphrodite lay awake in her bed at the Achillion. A warm breeze off the sea blew through the open windows, and the curtains rose with a flutter and a ripple, casting wicked shadows across the moonlit floor. It seemed as if the long, twisted fingers of a giant claw were reaching across the covers of her bed to grab her, then retracting whenever the wind died.

She rolled over and looked at the grandfather clock in the corner of the room. It was just after three. She wanted to make sure the house staff was asleep before she went downstairs to the Baron's study. That was where he kept the Maranatha text, she had concluded, the same text Christos had asked her about in Athens and which the monk Philip had told her she must destroy.

She had no choice, for now she knew what it was Christos had been looking for in Athens and what it was she had failed to tell him. If the text wasn't in her father's safe in Athens, it had to be here at the Achillion. Why else had the Baron forbidden her from ever revealing the Achillion as his residence to anybody, even her parents, whose last days were filled with anxiety whenever she disappeared from Athens for weeks at a time? Why else was she forbidden to enter the study downstairs? What else could the Baron be hiding that was more valuable than all his other art treasures? It had to be the Maranatha text.

Yes, she told herself, earlier that afternoon she had been ready to die. But now, thanks to Philip, she wanted to live a little longer, if only to help the Allies. May God only forgive me, she thought, for my failure to tell Christos about the Achillion in Athens for fear of the Baron.

She sat up in bed and looked around the room. It was a creepy room, she decided, her eyes darting about. Just beyond the foot of the bed was the wardrobe where the Baron had hanged Karl the week before. Had it been only a week? Several times since then, she had woken up from her sleep, believing she heard a knocking sound coming from inside, as if Karl were still there and wanted to come out. She also had the feeling that she was being watched and at times found her eyes unconsciously drifting back to the eerie portrait of Elizabeth of Austria staring down at her from above the headboard.

She would have passed off these feelings as flights of imagination if not for the indifference with which the staff had treated her since she returned from her evening swim. The Baron was nowhere to be seen, and when she asked where he was, nobody would say. Franz, Peter, Helga—everybody was behaving differently. Then there was the new guest, that hideous little man they called Professor Xaptz. It was as if something sinister were afoot within the palace, a conspiracy in which they were all involved.

She slipped out of bed, put on her robe, and opened the bedroom door. The palace was quiet, but the landing outside was dark, and it was a long way down the stairs to the Baron's study.

Gathering her courage, she crossed the landing and softly descended the grand staircase. She had reached the sixth step when she stopped. What if the text wasn't there, either? What if it was in Berlin? She pushed the thought out of her mind and continued down the stairs.

She reached the foyer on the first floor and looked around. Then she started down the long corridor toward the study near the end of the hall. About twenty feet before she reached the door, she could see that it was open and a light was on. In her mind she rehearsed her speech if she was caught. She would say she was worried about Ludwig and had gone down to the study to see if he was there.

As she approached the open door, she remembered how she'd once seen Ludwig and several guests walk into the study, but only he walked out. Another time three guests walked out of the study whom she'd never seen walk in. But the only door to the study was the one before her. At least, it was the only one she was aware of.

Standing in the open doorway, she looked inside.

Nobody was in the study.

She crossed the floor toward Ludwig's desk and stood before the large painting of King Ludwig II of Bavaria on the wall. Something about the picture bothered her, something she couldn't put her finger on. It was the same eerie feeling she had lying in bed upstairs beneath the brooding eyes of Empress Elizabeth of Austria.

She slowly turned to survey the rest of the room, taking in the window overlooking the gardens, the heavy drapes, bookshelves that lined the walls, and . . . a glass case standing in the corner.

Moving toward the case, seemingly tugged by some invisible cord, she could see the ragged fragment of the papyrus beneath the glass. It had been mounted flat, pressed between two other sheets of glass. She stood there in silence, beholding the document that men had killed one another to possess.

She lowered her face to the glass to see if she could read the words scrawled across the papyrus. A few phrases were familiar to her, but classical Greek differed too much from modern Greek for her to comprehend the contents. Unfortunately, she would have to destroy the text without knowing exactly what it said.

Placing her hands on the glass lid of the case, she tried to lift it off. But it was sealed shut, and she could see no latch or hinge. The only way to remove the text would be to break the glass. The problem was how to do that without making too much noise and arousing attention.

She looked around and spotted a bronze bust of Achilles on a shelf, much like the statue outside in the gardens but smaller in scale. It was heavy enough that she had to use both hands to lift it from the shelf and carry it over to the glass case. Cradling the bust in one arm, she lifted the bottom of one of the heavy drapes from the nearby window and spread it across the top of the case. Slowly, she eased the bust onto the cloth cushion until it rested almost entirely on its own weight. As soon as she heard the first crackle of glass, she lifted the bust before it could plunge straight through and placed it back on its shelf. She returned to the glass case, pressed her hand down on the curtain draped over it, and punched down the shards of glass, cringing when they shattered against the glass-plated text and made some noise.

She pulled the curtain aside and dipped her hands into the case, carefully brushing aside the broken glass until she could get a grip on the text. Her fingers grasped the corner, and she lifted it up, the glass from the case sliding off. As she eased the plate out of the case, she became aware of a red streak dribbling down her arm. She then saw the cut on her forearm and suppressed a cry.

When she had freed the glass plate from the case, she slowly turned around. Standing there beside his desk, smiling at her, was the Baron.

"So that's what Herr Andros was looking for in Athens," he told her. "The Maranatha text!"

She went cold and almost dropped the text on the floor. She glanced at the doorway, wondering how he'd gotten in.

His eyes lit up as if he had finally fathomed some great mystery. "I never would have guessed," he said. "Your friend came to steal my secrets, but now I believe I know his."

Aphrodite thought about what the monk Philip had told her. She had to finish what Christos had started. She couldn't give up now. "One more step," she warned him, "and I'll smash this plate to the floor."

"Oh, I wouldn't do that if I were you," the Baron told her in a cool tone. "Not that it would make any real difference to me. After all, I've had the contents translated, photographed, and copied. But then I'd have to punish you, and the world would lose another work of art."

Aphrodite didn't know if the Baron was referring to her or the Maranatha text. "I'd rather die than live as part of your collection."

Before the Baron could answer her, an entire section of the bookcase opened up to reveal a secret passageway. Franz entered the room, stopping abruptly when he saw her.

"Don't mind her, Franz," said the Baron. "What is it?"

"This came in from Oberführer Borgman in the field just now."

Speechless, Aphrodite watched Franz hand the Baron a lengthy communiqué. When he finished skimming the report, he looked at her with his piercing eyes. "So, it's over," he said. "The caïque carrying Andros struck a mine and blew up in the Gulf of Messenia."

With those words, Aphrodite felt something drop to the floor and shatter. But when she looked down and saw the glass plate in her hands, she realized it was her heart that had broken. She fell to her knees, still clinging to the text, and started wailing.

"Murderers!" she cried. "Murderers!"

Von Berg sighed and gave the communiqué back to Franz. "And yet neither the film nor any wreckage has been found," he said above her cries. "Why is that?"

"What can I say, Herr Oberstgruppenführer?" Franz replied. "Two of our R-boat commanders saw the explosion with their own eyes. As for debris, we are searching by air, but as you can imagine, this is difficult at night. Our minesweepers with wooden hulls arrive in the morning. But it may take a good day or two."

"And what about Spreicher?"

"His body was found next to an abandoned lorry near the Taygetos Pass."

"That's too bad," the Baron said, and began to stare at Aphrodite. "How many Germans have died during Andros's little escapade through the Peloponnese?"

Aphrodite stopped crying, the streak of tears still running down her cheeks. She glanced at Franz, who appeared to be making some mental calculations. A terrible premonition began to form in the hollow of her stomach.

Finally, Franz said, "Altogether, if we include those killed at that ammunition dump in Laconia, thirty-seven Waffen SS."

"Thirty-seven of Germany's finest dead," repeated the Baron incredulously. "And how many Greeks?"

Franz said, "If we don't include the Greek *andartes* at the National Bands base, then one, sir. That Greek gendarme who was gunned down when Andros crashed the checkpoint outside Sparta."

"And he was working for us," quipped the Baron. "How many suspected accomplices were rounded up in Sparta?"

Franz said, "Fifteen—so far."

"That's less than half as many Germans who have died," the Baron observed. "That doesn't look very good, Franz, does it?"

"No, sir."

Aphrodite could feel her heart pounding.

"Then I suggest you do more than even the score in the revised report you'll forward to Berlin," the Baron ordered. "You can start by burning to the ground every single village those terrorists may have passed through and then round up two hundred locals in Sparta and Kalamata and have them shot. That would work out to about five Greeks to every one German. More than a fair rate of exchange, wouldn't you say?"

Aphrodite could take it no longer. "No, don't!" she cried. "Please don't kill any more people!"

The Baron smiled. "I'll double that number if you don't give me the text," he warned her. "Or I'll cut it in half, if you'll be reasonable."

Choking on her tears, she nodded.

"Good," he replied, and turned to Franz. "Make it only one hundred Greeks."

"Of course, Herr Oberstgruppenführer."

"Numbers, Standartenführer," said the Baron. "Berlin loves numbers. And at this point I don't want to draw any further attention by doing anything that suggests we're slacking off in Greece. Now, help me with Aphrodite here."

She said nothing as they helped her to her feet.

The Baron removed the glass-plated text from her hands. "There, now," he told her. "That wasn't so bad, was it?"

She watched him take the glass plate and put it in a wall safe behind the portrait of King Ludwig II. Then he and Franz led her toward the bookcase.

"Where are you taking me?" she demanded.

The Baron replied, "Why, to your new quarters in the lower levels."

When she resisted, they dragged her by the arms and practically hurled her into the dark passageway. But it wasn't a passageway. It was an elevator. Oh, God, she thought, what else can there be? Then the Baron and Franz stepped inside, the door closed, and the cage descended into the bowels of the earth.

108

A faint blue dawn was coming up over Algiers the next morning when Churchill finished reading Prestwick's signal. Churchill then reached for a match, lit his second Havana of the morning, and settled back in his wickerwork chair on the terrace of Eisenhower's Moorish villa.

The signal was marked: MOST SECRET AND PERSONAL. From the Commanding Officer, H.M. Submarine *Cherub*. Date: 31st May, 1943. To the Director of Naval Intelligence.

Churchill read it over a couple of times before he finally lowered his hand and looked up at Colonel Ellery Huntington, the OSS chief in Algiers who had personally delivered the message. "Are they sure?"

"Positive, sir," Huntington replied. "ALSOS confirms the authenticity of the technical papers Andros photographed and the atomic nature of General von Berg's research program."

Churchill nodded grimly. The ALSOS team was a select group of scientists who worked with the OSS in stealing information about experiments in nuclear physics by the Germans. Their code name came from the Greek word for "grove," after Major General Leslie R. Groves, director of the Manhattan Project, the American program to develop the atomic bomb.

General Eisenhower, who, for the last several minutes, had been pacing the terrace's tiled floor in his riding boots and breeches, let out a long whistle. "That boy Andros found more than either he or we bargained for," said the supreme Allied commander.

"I couldn't agree with you more," said Churchill, still dazed by the other signal from the *Cherub*, the encoded one from Captain Whyte that he would not be sharing with the Americans—for now. Her devastating revelation of Brigadier Andrew Eliot as the Minotaur would only jeopardize American confidence in future joint SOE-OSS ventures. In any case, Churchill resolved then and there that an SOE shake-up was in order, not only in Greece, but at the highest levels in SOE Cairo.

Eisenhower marched to the balustrade of the terrace, staring off to sea. "Good grief, Colonel," he said, addressing Huntington. "You're telling us that von Berg is building an atomic bomb below some palace on a Greek island?"

"So it appears, sir."

"And it appears that he's hidden this even from Berlin," Churchill added. "You are supreme commander, General. Any ideas?"

Eisenhower turned to Churchill. "You know damn well what we're going to do. This is a job for your boys in the RAF. Surgical strike, dawn tomorrow. We'll make it look like we're bombing Greece's coastal defenses, knocking out a key naval station, and softening up our target before the invasion. But I want this so-called *Flammenschwert* facility taken out, permanently."

Huntington cleared his throat. "It will take quite a pilot to pull it off, sir."

"You know as well as I do, Colonel, that there's only one pilot for this job."

"Jack MacDonald?"

"Tell him to have his squadron ready for takeoff at midnight."

"I'm on my way to Blida right now, sir." Huntington turned to leave through the French doors.

"Oh, and Colonel," said Churchill, stopping Huntington in his tracks. "Have Captain Safire set a course for Corfu. I want the *Cherub* to linger off the coast to survey the bomb damage."

109

The electric motor of the *Cherub* hummed as Andros made his way along the corridor toward the submarine's galley. Prestwick was sitting at the table under a dim light, enjoying a cup of tea, when he walked in.

"And how are we feeling, Chris? You slept for hours."

"Tried to," Andros replied, taking a seat opposite Prestwick. "And I thought surface vessels were hell. I'd hate to be trapped in this thing if we started filling up with water."

Prestwick nodded, but both men knew that seasickness wasn't the foremost concern in Andros's heart.

"She didn't believe me, Prestwick," Andros said after a long pause. "She couldn't comprehend that I'd actually come back for her. She thought I only wanted information to please some fool like you. Then again, I can't blame her. My performance, while less than exemplary, met your requirements for my cover."

"Yes," Prestwick answered without emotion. "An unfortunate development. Speaking of which, the film you brought us is extraordinary. My God, it's an intelligence coup. You're an American hero."

"A hero?" Andros nodded to acknowledge the alleged distinction, but did so in a way that showed he didn't really care. "Any reply from Algiers?"

Prestwick sipped his tea. "No response yet about that roll of microfilm. But your family arrived safely in Istanbul aboard the *Turtle Dove*, along with a rather angry Kostas Vasilis. Right now I suspect they're en route to Cairo, where they'll join the Greek government in exile."

"And Aphrodite?"

Prestwick shook his head. "Who knows? I'm afraid all we can

do at this point is wait until we reach Algiers, see what else they've learned."

Andros watched him sip tea. "Why the lies, Prestwick?"

Prestwick paused. "Whatever do you mean?"

"You never expected me to get this far, did you? You thought I'd be caught by the Germans and spill that precious lie you told me about the Allies preparing to invade Greece."

Prestwick took another sip. "You don't think we are?"

"I saw the Operation Husky plans in von Berg's safe. I know it's Sicily we're invading."

Prestwick almost dropped his cup. "I think you'd better elaborate."

"Relax, Prestwick. Werner acted as if he'd already seen the report and was interested only in the *Flammenschwert*. My guess is that German intelligence suspects the Husky report is a fraud and has discounted it altogether."

Prestwick seemed to regain some of his composure. "But you don't?"

"Not after the lies you told me back at the Farm. It all makes perfect sense now."

"We never lied to you outright, Chris. We simply led you to believe what you wanted to believe. As for expecting you to fail in your mission, that doesn't mean we wanted you to fail. We were simply taking into account the realities of the war."

"Really? And suppose von Berg had caught me after I discovered the Husky plans in his safe? He would have known I was being set up and deduced for himself what it was you were up to." Andros paused and then asked, "What exactly *are* you up to, Prestwick?"

Prestwick set down his cup of tea. "Now that you know the secret of the Maranatha text, I don't suppose it would hurt to let you in on the whole story."

"The secret of what?"

So Prestwick told him: about the bogus Maranatha microfilm implying an invasion of Greece and how the OSS allowed it to fall into Nazi hands; about the real Maranatha text and how Baron von

Berg had beaten them to it at the Monastery of the Taborian Light; and finally, why Andros was recruited to steal the text—not because of his formidable skills as a soldier but because of his relationship with Aphrodite.

When his OSS superior was finished, Andros shook his head in disgust. "Lies, lies, lies, Prestwick. Do you always use innocents to clean up your messes, or am I a special case?"

"Very special, Chris," said Prestwick. "We sent you in to keep our secret from von Berg, but in the process you've discovered his, the *Flammenschwert*. As for that aerial negative you retrieved from the safe, we fed it through the enlarger. We should have a nice print soon enough."

"I'd like to take a look."

"You could, but I don't see the point," Prestwick said crisply. "Captain Whyte looked it over already." He glanced at his watch and took up his cup of tea. "It's three in the afternoon. We still have several hours until we reach North Africa and face hours of debriefing. Until that time, I suggest you get some more sleep. I'm sure Captain Whyte won't mind you taking her bunk in the captain's private cabin now that she's up and about."

Andros hesitated. Prestwick put a hand on his shoulder. "Chris, there's nothing you can do for Aphrodite right now. Maybe when you wake up, we'll have some news."

Andros nodded and left.

110

Instead of retiring to the captain's quarters, Andros made his way to the signals room. It had been converted into a makeshift darkroom. Erin was hunched over the developing tanks when he stepped inside. Her eyes lit up at the sight of him.

"You're up," she remarked in surprise, straightening under the safe lights. She was wearing a white polo sweater over a pair of denim overalls that the all-male crew had given her.

"Prestwick said you have something for me to see."

She hesitated, a disappointed and curious expression crossing her face. She pointed and said, "In the tank."

Andros looked at the image slowly materializing in the bath of fixing solution. The black-and-white picture of a castle by the sea was like something from a dream or a Hollywood studio set. "Looks like some sort of castle," he observed.

"The Achillion," said Erin, pulling the picture out of the solution. "It's on the island of Corfu. Built in 1890 for Empress Elizabeth of Austria. Later became the summer home of Kaiser Wilhelm II. The Greek government confiscated it in 1914 and let the French turn it into a hospital a couple of years later. That's what it still is, according to our data. Located about seven miles south of Corfu Town, on the east coast of the island."

"What is its military significance?"

She clipped the photo to a clothesline to let it drip-dry. "Take a closer look," she challenged. "See anything else?"

Andros reached for a magnifying glass and went over the photo. "There must be something here," he insisted, "something important enough for the Jerries to shoot down one of our reconnaissance planes." So far he saw nothing out of the ordinary. Perhaps he was looking in the wrong place. Perhaps what was important wasn't at the palace at all but somewhere else. . . .

Then it jumped into view—a thin line beneath the water.

Andros lowered the magnifying glass and looked at Erin. "A submarine wake!"

"Seems the Baron has tunneled a secret submarine station into the rock beneath the palace," Erin explained. "Now, that's a nifty trick."

Andros traced the line from the water back to the cliffs beneath the Achillion. It looked like the submarine must have just gone inside the mountain beneath the palace—or come out and submerged. A chill ran up Andros's spine. "This must be where von Berg has Aphrodite."

"Among other things," said Erin. "We'll have a better look when we surface."

"When we surface?" Andros gripped her arm. "We're heading for Corfu?"

Her face darkened. "I thought you knew."

"To rescue Aphrodite?" he asked anxiously.

She lowered her eyes. "Not exactly."

"What do you mean?" Andros tightened his grip until she winced in pain.

"My arm, Chris!"

He knew she could break his lock on her and strike him if she wanted to. But the pain in her eyes told him that her feelings for him were too strong. "Tell me," he demanded.

She swallowed hard and said, "Churchill's ordered an air strike on the island tonight."

"What?" Andros released his grip and stood there in shock.

She rubbed her sore arm. "I'm sorry, Chris," she said with genuine sadness. "I thought you knew."

"Loose lips sink ships, Captain Whyte," said a voice from behind them. "Or submarines."

Andros turned to see Prestwick in the doorway. On either side of him was a junior officer, their pistols at the ready.

"You liar," said Andros. "Why didn't you tell me?"

"Because I knew you'd be unreasonable, as you are now."

"Aphrodite held up her end of the deal in Athens, Prestwick. And paid the price. We have to rescue her."

"How do you propose to do that? Walk through the front gates of the Achillion?"

Andros pointed to the aerial blowup. "Through the back door."

"Oh, you mean that submarine tunnel?" Prestwick raised an eyebrow. "Assuming you were able to infiltrate the underground fortress and elude detection by von Berg's formidable SS guards, how would you manage to get out before the bombers blow it to kingdom come? Swim?"

"If I have to."

"Then you would finally qualify for the Olympic pentathlon after all," sneered Prestwick, and he shook his head. "Unfortunately, I can't risk sending you in at this point. You know too much. Besides, if you're caught, the air strike will lose its element of surprise."

"You expect me to sit here and watch the Allies murder Aphrodite?"

"If it means saving the lives of millions, yes."

"No!" Andros pulled out his father's dagger.

Erin pleaded with him, "Don't, Chris. He's not worth it."

"Poking holes in me isn't going to save your beloved Aphrodite," Prestwick added matter-of-factly. "I'm afraid that if you insist on being difficult, we're going to have to confine you to the captain's quarters until tomorrow morning, when this is all over. Gentlemen."

The two officers raised their pistols.

Andros glanced at Erin, whose alarmed eyes begged him to go no further, then back to Prestwick and the officers. Finally, he sighed in defeat and slid the dagger behind his back.

"There," said Prestwick. "Now you're being reasonable. Excuse us, Captain."

Prestwick moved behind him and, together with the officers, escorted him down the fore-and-aft passageway back to the captain's quarters. They made him lie on the bunk and handcuffed him to the rail.

"You'll stay here until after the air strike," Prestwick said. "I'll be back in the morning."

He stepped out and closed the green curtain, leaving Andros alone in the compartment.

111

In the operations building at the Blida air base, Captain Jack Mac-Donald reported to the intelligence room, as ordered. There he found Colonel Ellery Huntington, the senior OSS officer in Algiers, waiting for him.

MacDonald smiled and said, "To what do I owe this pleasure, Colonel?"

"Where the hell have you been, MacDonald?" Huntington replied, dispensing with the pleasantries. "We've been looking for you all afternoon."

"I'm a creature of the night, Colonel," MacDonald explained cheerfully. "I didn't think you boys cared what I did during the day so long as I showed up to work."

Huntington grudgingly agreed. "Yes, well, the prime minister wanted me to congratulate you on your string of successful missions, Captain. He also wanted you to perform one more special job for him."

"Another SOE or OSS job, I suppose?" MacDonald muttered. "What's the matter? Do the Swiss need more chocolates dropped on their villages? Perhaps the Greeks need more brandy? I hear there's a shortage of tarts for our men in France. What is it about this time?"

"Oh, about two tons of TNT."

MacDonald's eyes widened as Huntington spread out the map of the Achillion on the table, pointing out the palace, the cove, and the bunkers halfway up the hill between them.

MacDonald couldn't hide his delight. "The real thing!" he exclaimed. "It's about bloody time."

"I must warn you," Huntington cautioned, "the OSS Air Operations Section has determined this mission is impossible, considering the terrain of the target area and the strength of the enemy air defenses if you're detected."

"Nonsense, sir," he boasted. "Nothing's impossible for Jack Mac-Donald. When do we go in?"

"You'll strike at dawn."

"Dawn?" MacDonald glanced at his watch. It was already 2300 hours. "In a bit of a hurry, are we, Colonel?"

"You could say that." Huntington used a pointer to trace the flight route. "For most of the journey, you'll be in the dark; but as you approach the island of Corfu, day will be breaking, and you should see the fortifications of the Italian garrison in Corfu Town."

MacDonald noted the reference points to look for in his approach and nodded.

"You'll have to come in under the Italian radar net to avoid detection, you realize," Huntington went on. "That means one pass to surprise them before you and your planes are vulnerable to anti-aircraft guns."

"One pass is all we'll need," MacDonald assured him. "Just make sure the British Air Ministry has canceled any RAF missions that might interfere with our air strike."

"Done," Huntington said, and glanced at his watch. "With an estimated flight time of five and a half hours, that means you should be up in the air just after midnight. I suggest you assemble your men now."

MacDonald looked at Huntington with a gleam in his eye. "That won't be a problem, Colonel. Not when I tell them we finally get to bomb the Krauts."

112

Von Berg was back behind the desk in his study on the eve of Hitler's secret weapons conference, looking over the final report on the Maranatha text that he would present to Hitler at Obersalzberg the next morning. When he finished, he leaned back and looked up to see the wretched face of Dr. Xaptz, anxious with anticipation.

Von Berg said, "So, Professor, you don't believe it was the apostle Paul who penned the Maranatha text?"

"It could have been, or one of his disciples taking his dictation." Dr. Xaptz shrugged. "It's difficult to say who the author really is."

"But you don't think it's Paul."

"No," said Dr. Xaptz. "I think someone was pretending to be the apostle, to dupe the early church in Thessaloniki. Perhaps to further discredit the new Christian faith that threatened Rome."

"What makes you so sure?" asked von Berg.

"As I said in the report, several things," the professor said. "First, the emphasis on one's good deeds rather than faith in Jesus Christ for one's eternal salvation is anathema to Paul's gospel. Indeed, in another letter to the Galatians, the apostle said that if he or anybody else should preach a different gospel, that person should be eternally condemned."

"'Eternally condemned'?" Von Berg smiled. "Sounds like something Himmler would say to instill more discipline within the ranks of his Black Order."

"Paul was one of the most ambitious of men," Dr. Xaptz explained. "As Nietzsche said, his superstition was equaled only by his cunning. He was a much tortured, much-to-be-pitied man, an exceedingly unpleasant person both to himself and to others."

"Much like yourself, Herr Professor," von Berg mumbled as he flipped through the text. "In addition to exhortations that contradict everything the apostle believed in, I see you note some linguistic inconsistencies. You also mention the glaring omission of his personal signature at the end of the text." Von Berg looked up at Dr. Xaptz. "What does that mean?"

"Paul often dictated his letters to a secretary, such as Silas or Timothy," Dr. Xaptz said. "At the end of the text, he would take over from his secretary and write in his own hand. That was the distinguishing mark of all his letters—his seal of authenticity, if you will. The Maranatha text, or at least the fragment in our possession, has no such distinction."

Frowning, von Berg flipped toward the back of the report. "This is your translation of the Maranatha text?"

"A rough translation that will need further refinements," Dr. Xaptz cautioned.

Von Berg looked over the German. "These are strong warnings of God's wrath," he commented. "I wonder if anybody listened."

Dr. Xaptz nodded. "It would help explain why so many Thessalonians, anticipating the return of Christ, quit their jobs and hid in caves, awaiting the end of the world. That, in turn, prompted Paul to write them his letter telling them to work with their hands and be productive members of society."

"Unlike yourself, of course, Dr. Xaptz." Von Berg pointed to the underlined portion of the translation. "And this is the date when the world will end?"

"According to the alphanumeric code I extracted from the text. I had to convert the date from the Jewish to our Gregorian calendar."

"Interesting." Von Berg drummed his fingers on the desk. "So soon and yet so far away."

"Yes, General von Berg. That was my impression."

Von Berg closed the report and placed it on the table. "It's pure fantasy, you realize. The text speaks of a nation of Israel, and your calculations presuppose its existence. Why, there hasn't been a Jewish state for two thousand years."

"I admit it's a difficult concept to fathom."

"Come, now, Dr. Xaptz, it's impossible. You know as well as Dr. Stein did that when this war is over, there won't be a Jew left on the planet, let alone a Jewish state. Not with maniacs like Himmler, Streicher, and you floating about."

Dr. Xaptz bit his tongue in fear.

"No matter," von Berg continued, pressing a buzzer beneath his desk. "At least your description of the differences between the text here and the one represented on the intercepted microfilm is precise and convincing. There can be no question that the microfilm is a plant by the Allies to dupe the Führer."

The bookcase began to part, revealing Franz in the secret doorway. Dr. Xatpz's jaw dropped, and von Berg smiled.

"Franz, now that this quack has served his purpose, please escort him to his new cell in the lower level."

The blood drained from the professor's face. "Cell? But why?"

"Because I don't like you, Dr. Xaptz, that's why," said von Berg. "Besides, if Paul didn't pen this text, then all the rumors about encoded doomsday dates or formulas for unlocking the Führer's precious Greek Fire are groundless."

"On the contrary," Dr. Xaptz insisted, with resourceful enthusiasm, "there is the distinct possibility that the author of this text was unconscious of what he was writing. You of all people should appreciate this, considering your family heritage."

Von Berg went cold. "My heritage, Dr. Xaptz?"

"Reichsführer Himmler told me that the godmother who raised your father was none other than the countess Paumgarten. She was a so-called writing medium of note. It was said she had the ability of writing automatically, that her hand was guided by spirits while she fell into a dreamlike somnambulistic state. When asked questions, she would write down the answers given by the 'spirits.'"

"Hardly anybody but old maids took her seriously," von Berg said, maintaining his poise.

"According to the Reichsführer, Empress Elizabeth of Austria did," Dr. Xaptz said. "I understand that she and the countess were in touch for years, that Elizabeth used her stays in Munich for 'sessions' and sent written inquiries to the countess whenever she encountered problems in her life."

Those sessions were only a cover for Elizabeth's visits with her son, my father, von Berg realized. He felt a cold shudder pass through him but was able to keep it hidden from the heinous little professor, who was using the ploy to bargain for his life.

"Indeed," Dr. Xaptz continued, "according to very confidential reports the Reichsführer has obtained, it seems Chancellor Otto von Bismarck himself was concerned that the countess was using the empress's spiritualistic interests to exert political influence over her."

"And isn't that what you and the Reichsführer have been attempting to do with Hitler in recent months?" asked von Berg.

Dr. Xaptz was relaxed now, apparently confident that von Berg had appreciated the allusions to Empress Elizabeth.

Von Berg pressed, "What are you getting at?"

"Merely that, like the countess Paumgarten, the author of the Maranatha text may not have been aware of what he was truly writing even if his attempt was to deceive the early Church. Perhaps fate chose him as a channel through which to reveal the secret of Greek Fire in codes unknown to us until now."

"All of which gives me an interesting idea, Herr Professor." Von Berg rose from his chair and removed the portrait of King Ludwig II to reveal the wall safe. He opened it and pulled out his briefcase, which contained all the documents he had hidden in the library safe at the Vasilis estate. "I believe you're right. There are codes in this infernal text. Furthermore, I believe we've found them." Von Berg produced the Niels Bohr report on atomistics.

Dr. Xaptz looked through the report. "These are formulas from the world of nuclear physics."

"Come, now, Professor," said von Berg. "You think God doesn't understand physics?"

Dr. Xaptz looked puzzled. "I don't understand."

"It's very simple, really," said von Berg. "You are to insert these atomic formulas into the report you handed me and make it appear as if they were deciphered from the Maranatha text."

113

The clap of boots in the passage outside the cell woke Aphrodite. She tried to get up but discovered her hands and feet were strapped to the bunk. She was aware of the Baron's voice, the rattle of chains, and the metal door scraping open against the stone. A dark figure stepped inside.

"Aphrodite, sweet little Aphrodite," said the chilling voice, coming ever closer. "The sentry outside says our little princess has turned into quite an animal. I like to tame wild things."

She could feel his breath on her face. She tried to lash out at him, straining at the ends of her straps like a dog on a leash. She felt his cold hand grip her throat, and she became very still.

"That's better, little princess."

The cool, calm tone of his voice incensed her. "You killed my parents."

"The fools killed themselves," he replied, relaxing his grip on her throat. "Your young lover Herr Andros let them, just as he left you to die."

"You might as well kill me, too, because now that Christos is gone, I have nothing to live for."

"Silly girl." He stroked her hair. "Everything passes, even these misguided romantic yearnings of yours. You'll see. Tomorrow you'll forget this unpleasant interlude and join me at my side."

That he could demand her love after all that had happened infuriated her. "Never," she hissed. "I'll never love you."

"Never is a long time, love." His finger slid down her neck, and he slipped his hand into her nightgown and cupped her breast. "A very long time."

She became very still, almost lifeless in the dark, but she could feel her heart pounding as the Baron's hand made its way between

"Impossible!" cried Dr. Xaptz. "How will I prove it?"

"You'll find a way," said von Berg. "From what you've shown me you can draw pretty much anything you want to out of the Maranatha text."

"Only a madman would believe atomic formulas could be found in a first-century text."

"Precisely," replied von Berg, "and the Führer is such a man. Now, you'll do it from your cell, or you'll die. Oh, Franz? When you're through with him, tell Kapitänleutnant Myers I'll be down in the Omega room soon."

her thighs and pushed them apart. Numb with horror, she could barely speak.

"You've lost, Ludwig," she said in a low voice. "That it should come to this."

"You'll come around," he assured her, and leaned over and crushed his mouth on hers.

114

It was almost two o'clock in the morning when the *Cherub* surfaced several miles off the island of Corfu. Andros knew it as soon as the submarine's electric motor stopped humming and the *clack-clack* of its twin diesel engines took over. He lay there in his bunk, staring at the curving bulkhead, aware of movement outside in the fore-and-aft passageway. He rattled his handcuffs against the bunk's rail to get some attention.

Finally, Prestwick poked his head in. "What is it?"

"Captain Safire. Where is he?"

"On the bridge. Why?"

"I need some air, fresh air, and space. And a smoke. I've been cooped up in this sardine can for eighteen hours."

Prestwick said nothing and disappeared. Andros gnashed his teeth in despair, but the old professor returned with a key. He also was pointing a U.S. Army–issue Colt .45 pistol at him, his aim unsteady.

"Considering your fear of water, I don't suppose there's any danger of you swimming away," Prestwick said crisply. "But any funny business, and I'll have to shoot your leg."

"So this is how America treats its heroes," Andros complained as the cuffs came off and he got to his feet. "Just be careful where you point that thing."

Prestwick waved the pistol at the curtain. "You first, Chris."

Andros took a step forward, nudged by the poke of the Colt at his back, and spun around into Prestwick, passed his arm over the hand holding the pistol, and locked it. Prestwick was looking into angry eyes, unable to shoot him or release his arm from the deadly grip. Andros struck Prestwick across the face with the back of his other hand. Prestwick cried out in pain and released his hold on the pistol, dropping it to the floor.

"You can thank Captain Whyte for teaching me that trick," Andros said softly, stuffing one of Safire's socks into Prestwick's mouth before he could call for help. "And you can thank me for not going all the way with her instructions."

Prestwick mumbled nonsense while Andros twisted his arm behind his back and drove him face-first into Captain Safire's bunk until he was on his stomach. Andros reached for Safire's clothesline, tied Prestwick's wrists together, and forced his arms well up behind his back. He then passed the cord around Prestwick's neck and back and his wrists, bent his legs backward, and tied them together.

"If you keep still, you won't be hurt," Andros told him. "But if you attempt to struggle, you'll probably strangle yourself."

Andros reached down and picked up the Colt from the floor. He slipped it behind his back, along with his father's dagger and a flare from one of Safire's storage containers. He then looked at the Tiffany & Co. ring box on the oak countertop and lit a cigarette before moving toward the passageway.

"You're crazy if you think I'd let Aphrodite pay for your stupidity, Prestwick. You better pray she's alive, because one way or another, I'm coming back from that island. If it's not with her, then it's for you."

115

The stars were still out when Andros came up the ladder onto the bridge. The cool spray of salt water slapped his face as he took in a deep breath and exhaled. Dead ahead was the island of Corfu, sleeping on the dark, brooding surface of the Ionian Sea.

Also on the bridge, with his back to Andros, was Captain Safire, scanning the shoreline with his night glasses while he smoked his pipe. "A gem she is tonight," he said to himself, "sparkling on a velvet cloth for only God and us to admire."

"From a safe distance, anyway," said Andros.

Safire lowered his glasses and turned, surprised to see him alone. "Where's Prestwick?"

"Resting. This is all a bit too much for him." Andros looked at his watch. "Ten after two, Captain. Dawn is only a few hours away, and I have to reach shore before daybreak." He raised the pistol slightly so Safire could see it. "I'll need a dinghy to get across. Do you suppose you could produce one for me?"

"And if I don't?" Safire dared.

"I'll light up the sky with one of the flares I found in your compartment. Enough to attract the attention of nearby night fighters and torpedo boats."

Safire spoke into his piping down to the control room. "I need a dinghy up here."

"That's it?" Andros asked. "No questions?"

Safire smiled reflectively. "When I was off the coast of Spain a few weeks ago, in another submarine, the captain had me and the other junior officers bring up a mysterious six-foot canister the rest of the crew believed contained optical instruments. We knew this was only a cover, that the canister contained a secret weather-reporting buoy. You can imagine our surprise when we opened it and found a frozen corpse, courtesy of our dirty-tricks specialists at SOE."

"Major Martin?" asked Andros, remembering what he had seen in von Berg's Husky file.

"The same," Safire replied. "As you can see, our men have learned not to ask too many questions. Your request is par for this war."

The hatch on the trim foredeck below the bridge opened, and two ratings emerged with an inflatable dinghy. Andros watched them work while Safire smoked his pipe.

"Who is this young lady who inspires you to kill yourself?" Safire asked.

Andros told him, "She was my fiancée before the war."

"And the Baron has her captive?"

Andros nodded. "Aphrodite Vasilis."

"Vasilis?" Safire removed his pipe from his mouth and stared at it. "As in Vasilis Tobacco?"

"The same," Andros replied. "Von Berg had her parents executed."

"Now, that *is* a pity."

Andros watched the ratings lower the dinghy into the water. "Not as much as sitting here and watching her die at the hands of those whom she risked everything to help."

Andros went over the side and descended the ladder to the circular hull. The dinghy was already in the water, held by the ratings. Andros dropped in.

"The water is a bit choppy," called Safire from the bridge. "You ever try this before?"

"There's a first time for everything, Captain. Thanks for the lift."

"Let it never be said that Captain Safire stood in the way of true love."

Safire ordered the ratings to release the lines and watched the tide pull the rubber dinghy away from the *Cherub* and in toward the island. Andros reached for the oars and started to row.

As the tiny dinghy drifted off into the darkness, Safire saluted from the conning tower. "I hope she's worth it, Andros," he said quietly, "for all our sakes."

116

Andros could see the shore clearly as he rowed quietly. The white surf crashed across the sandy beaches and against the jagged cliffs rising from the sea. Every now and then, when a wave lifted him high enough, he could glimpse the Achillion waiting for him high atop its hill.

According to the blowup he had seen in the *Cherub,* the secret tunnel was in the back of a cove at the base of the hill, so Andros used the forbidding palace as his marker all the way in. But the cliffs were coming up fast, blocking his view, and the waves started getting choppy, forcing him to adjust his weight to keep water from pouring in.

Soon he was caught in a foamy current that was sucking him in to the soaring rockface. He immediately began to row in the opposite direction, but it was too late. For a terrifying moment, it looked like he would be slammed against the sides of the cliffs. Then he saw a flash of blue light, and the cliffs opened up to reveal a hidden cove between two jagged peaks. There, in the back of the cove, was the tunnel.

The entrance to the tunnel was marked by two blue lights. All he needed to do was clear the narrow passage. But the dinghy missed the entrance and bounced off a rock, throwing Andros over the side into the water. Never a good swimmer, Andros struggled before the water pulled him under.

When he surfaced, gasping for breath, the dinghy was adrift in the middle of the cove, and he had managed somehow to reach the shallow, sandy fringe. His panic subsided.

He had dragged himself across the sand near the mouth of the tunnel when he heard a shout in German. A dazzling white searchlight from the hill stabbed the water behind him, and the dinghy was caught in a flurry of machine-gun fire.

Andros pressed his back against the rock and held his breath in the shadows beneath the beam of light. The entire cove was awash with light, and Andros was aware of the crunch of jackboots and the sound of voices growing louder on the hill above. The talk, from what Andros could gather, was whether to salvage the dinghy or let it sink.

"Didn't see anybody inside," said one of the German sentries. "Probably lost its moorings in Garitsa Bay and drifted down, that's all. No need to make a fuss over nothing."

"We should check it out just the same," said another sentry.

This exchange was followed by the click of heels and fading footsteps.

Andros quickly searched the ground for something that could float and found an oar from the dinghy. He was about to enter the tunnel when he saw a disturbance in the current. The shadowy silhouettes of two harpooners rushed out past him toward the dinghy. They were unaware of him plastered against the rocks.

The sentries in the tower must have called the divers, Andros thought, and he realized now was the time to act, before they returned.

He paused to make sure no more divers were coming and then slipped into the water. Holding the oar in front of him with outstretched arms, Andros kicked his legs just beneath the surface and propelled himself down the long tunnel, helped by a favorable current.

A few dark minutes later, he floated into a vast cavern. A horseshoe-shaped stone quay had been hewn out of the rock. Nestled in its half-moon bay was a German U-boat. Its legend was not a number, like U-505 or U-515, but a name: *Nausicaa.*

Andros treaded as best he could beneath the shadow of its gray hull, surveying the surroundings. A lone sentry paced the other end of the loading bay. A buzzer sounded, and the sentry stepped behind a wall of crates and out of view. Quickly but quietly, Andros climbed out of the water and hid behind the other side of the crates just as the sentry returned.

The German must have heard something, because he began to approach the water. Andros snatched a harpoon gun leaning against the cave wall and aimed it at the sentry. "Stop right where you are," he ordered.

The sentry stopped cold, and at that moment the loading-bay phone rang.

"You'll tell them nothing," Andros warned, hoping the German understood English. He repeated his words in Greek, adding, "I'll pin you to the wall if your voice so much as shakes. Now, drop your gun and pick up the phone."

The sentry did as he was told and walked over to the phone. He looked at Andros and picked up the receiver. "No," he said. "Nothing to report." He hung up.

Andros ordered him to sprawl on the floor, facedown. "There's a girl here somewhere, isn't there? A very lovely girl."

"Fräulein Vasilis?"

"That's right. You tell me where she is, and you can live."

"The cell block one level below us, but you'll never find her."

"Thanks." Andros smacked the back of the guard's head with the butt of the harpoon gun. Not enough to kill him, but enough to give him a generous headache when he woke up later.

Andros dragged the unconscious German behind the crates, tied him up, and stripped off his uniform. He had just buttoned the pants and was about to step into the nearest corridor when a voice said, "Stop right there."

Andros turned. From the top of the submarine's conning tower, the *Nausicaa*'s chief engineer had popped up out of the hatch and was pointing a gun at him. Before Andros could open his mouth, he heard the click of machine pistols and found himself surrounded by von Berg's SS guards. Andros then realized the engineer had called the guards from inside the U-boat.

The engineer told the guards, "Inform General von Berg we have a prisoner."

117

As SS guards escorted him through the labyrinth that crisscrossed beneath the palace, Andros was both awed and angered by the extent of von Berg's facility. They turned and went along one particularly dark, menacing tunnel that felt oddly familiar. Andros shivered in the cold, damp air. He was aware of voices drifting down from the other end.

Moving toward the voices, they passed through an archway and stepped onto some sort of balcony that overlooked a cavernous manufacturing facility. Stone steps led down to the floor, where a vast array of machinery, pumps, and piping hummed. Engineers in white lab coats swarmed like mice around the banks of instruments under the direction of von Berg.

"Logic never interfered with the Führer's decisions before, Myers," von Berg was telling a short man in Kriegsmarine uniform. "So a demonstration of the power of *Flammenschwert* may be in order. I want the device loaded onto the *Nausicaa* immediately."

"So soon?" replied Myers. "But the detonation devices have yet to be tested."

"Circumstance has necessitated a change in plans. Now that the Allies no doubt are aware of this facility, they will seek to destroy it. No matter; it has served its purposes. The important thing is to keep the *Flammenschwert* mobile, out of their reach. That's your job. As for this complex here, whatever we have accomplished we can duplicate in Germany, if necessary, and on a much larger scale."

"*Zu Befehl,* Herr Oberstgruppenführer."

Von Berg dismissed the *Nausicaa*'s commanding officer and was about to resume his work. Then somebody pointed toward the balcony, and the Baron looked up to see Andros. "Ah, Herr Andros!" he exclaimed. "You keep crashing my parties."

Andros felt the jab of a Schmeisser at his back and descended the narrow steps along the wall. When he reached the floor, von Berg regarded him with genuine admiration.

"Your timing, I must tell you, Herr Andros, is quite extraordinary. You are witnessing a great moment in the history of the Thousand-Year Reich."

"Am I?" Andros took in the vast network of pumps and pipes. "Centrifuges, von Berg?"

"One thousand exactly," von Berg replied. "For enriching uranium hexafluoride gas."

"And I thought you were processing groundnuts from Brazil." Andros hoped to catch von Berg off guard with the extent of the intelligence he—and presumably the Allies—already had gathered.

"I see you've learned much on your little field trip, Herr Andros," von Berg replied, unfazed. "Unfortunately, natural uranium contains less than one percent of the isotope U-235. That's why I built this conversion and centrifuge plant, to concentrate the U-235 isotope to about ninety percent for weapons-grade material."

"Weapons-grade?"

"Why, enough to drive an atomic explosion." The corners of von Berg's thin lips turned up into a smile. "Come, Herr Andros, allow me to complete your education. I wouldn't want you to die an ignorant animal, unaware of how close you came before failing miserably. That would never do."

They proceeded across the floor, passing technicians and engineers busy at the controls. Andros was aware of von Berg watching him, obviously reevaluating everything through his nemesis's eyes and not wholly displeased with the effect it had on him.

"The process is called magnetic isotope separation," von Berg explained. "The vacuum pumps and piping move the chemically processed uranium from one centrifuge to another. It is this cascade that separates the U-235 component and produces weapons-grade uranium."

"I see," said Andros. "Quite a production you've pulled together here."

"I'm sure someday we'll consider this arrangement quite crude," von Berg replied. "But for the present it suits our purposes. You no doubt are familiar with the *Flammenschwert* legend of Greek mythology. How man stole fire from the gods. That's what I've done. I've stolen fire from heaven. The key to unlocking the power of the universe: Germany's first atomic bomb. And now we are about to transfer it from this lab to my submarine."

Andros looked on as von Berg stepped behind some oscilloscopes while several assistants began pressing buttons on another instrument panel. A low humming began.

"Synchronizing the centrifuges has been my biggest challenge," von Berg said over the noise. "Thanks to precision parts from Switzerland, I've been able to keep the centrifuges aligned and minimize friction. But I'm boring you with these details. Franz?"

At the snap of von Berg's fingers, the trusted aide materialized before Andros's eyes.

"Herr Andros has seen enough, I think. Would you do the honors?"

Before Andros could react, he felt a crash on the back of his head and remembered nothing more.

PRESENT DAY

118

The light faded, and Sam Deker woke up strapped to a chair inside the DARPA labs beneath the VA Hospital in Los Angeles. Nobody was there.

He removed the fiber-optic shunt from his skull and jerked from the spark inside his eyes. It was as if he had pulled a plug from its socket. Then he carefully removed the IV drip that had been pumping photosynthetic algae into his veins.

He staggered to his feet. He felt weak and exhausted as he looked around the lab. He was all alone. The computer systems were up and running, but there were no people. Only surveillance cameras. Always surveillance cameras.

He sat down at a console and got to work to hack into the security feeds. He didn't care who saw him. But when he called up the surveillance of the lab he was sitting in, he could see only himself in the chair. He dialed it back a few minutes, then a few hours, then a few days, and finally, weeks. Always he was strapped in the chair, completely out.

Just how long had he been here? And where had everybody gone?

He was about to get up when he caught sight of a label on one of the surveillance feeds: *Advanced Sleep Labs*. He felt the hair on the back of his neck rise as he tapped into the feeds, found the sleep lab in Century City, and eventually found a feed named "Sam Deker."

He dialed in to his last night at the sleep lab, before he'd ever heard of the 34th Degree.

There he was, checking in the night before at nine P.M. Giselle the "sleep aide" had helped strap him into his heart and sleep apnea monitor to record biology, given him some sleeping pills to help, and tucked him in.

The surveillance footage showed him restless for a full four hours. Finally, shortly after one A.M. he fell asleep. The image looked like a still photograph as he fast-forwarded. He stopped at 1:45 when a stab of light shot into the room. He expected to see Giselle again, checking in on him.

What he saw instead were three figures gather around his bed like phantoms. The sight froze his veins. They set up an IV drip and plugged a glowing purple line to his head.

"Goddamn monsters," he muttered.

They had been experimenting on him from the start, planting ideas, driving him insane.

He smashed his fist on the console and stood up. He had seen enough.

He looked at the camera in the corner and marched to the doors outside, where he expected to find a couple of MPs.

Here, too, however, he found nobody. Only the long dark corridor he had come through. He started walking into the black.

THE 34TH DEGREE

119

A dazed and bewildered Sam Deker woke up to find himself tied up again. Only it wasn't the steel chair beneath the VA Hospital in Los Angeles. It was a deep leather chair in Baron Ludwig von Berg's study at the Achillion on Corfu. Franz slapped him into consciousness.

"Wake up, Andros," Franz said.

When Deker came to, he saw no sign of Marshall Packard, Wanda Randolph, or young Prestwick. Nor did he see any sign of Aphrodite. Only Ludwig von Berg behind a desk. A brass clock on the desk said it was five-thirty, but Deker had trouble focusing. He looked around the large, ornate study to get his bearings in this smashed-up world of present-day Los Angeles and 1943 Corfu.

"Aphrodite," he said. "What have you done with her?"

Von Berg narrowed his penetrating eyes. "Is she all you were searching for?"

"What else would I want?"

"I had in mind the Maranatha text."

Deker refused to confirm or deny von Berg's words, in case this was all a trick, so he kept a straight face and said nothing.

Von Berg smiled knowingly. "Truly, Herr Andros, I can only marvel at the audacity of the OSS," he said. "Planting a cipher in a phony Maranatha text and allowing it to fall into our hands in the form of a microfilm—it's beyond belief. The irony is that you succeeded in duping the Führer. I suppose the plan would have worked had I not found the real text and you hadn't prompted me to take a closer look."

Deker watched the Baron remove a large portrait of King Ludwig II of Bavaria from the wall to reveal a secret safe. Out of this safe he removed a leather briefcase, and from there drew out what looked like a text pressed between two plates of glass.

"Here it is, Herr Andros," said von Berg, walking up to him. "The text that has cost the lives of many good men throughout the centuries."

The papyrus was brown and fragmented, and the ancient Greek characters looked dark and foreboding, as if they were indeed hiding some eternal mystery. Deker could understand Hitler's and Prestwick's interest in unlocking the text's secrets. He wanted to reach out and touch the glass, but his hands were tied.

"So close, Herr Andros, yet so far." Von Berg pulled the text away from him. "And it was all for nothing, you see, because I already knew the Allies intend to invade Sicily and that Greece is only a cover."

Deker sank in his chair. Von Berg knew everything. There was nothing to hide now.

"The truly astonishing irony," von Berg continued, "is that this text is nothing but a forgery."

Deker looked up. "A forgery?"

"Foisted upon gullible believers by a false apostle in the first century. If he were alive today, I suspect he'd be working for Himmler or Donovan."

"A forgery," Deker repeated, watching von Berg carefully slip the glass containing the text into his leather briefcase.

Von Berg laughed. "Don't despair, Herr Andros! Your failure has been my inspiration. This text may yet serve a greater purpose than anyone ever intended. You see, I intend to convince the Führer that he has indeed tapped the source of Greek Fire and that the formulas encoded in the text are atomic in nature. Anything to make him a believer in the *Flammenschwert*."

"Atomic formulas hidden in a text written almost two thousand years ago?" Deker asked incredulously. "Hitler will never believe it."

"The Führer is crazy, and he will believe it," von Berg retorted. "After all, atomic theories were formulated in classical times. There was Leucippus of Miletus, Democritus of Abdera, and Epicurus of

Samos. The ancient philosophers and mathematicians simply lacked the means to translate their ideas into reality."

"Reality? Come, now, von Berg. This is fantasy!"

Von Berg shrugged as if to say it didn't matter. "Whether it was Paul or some other false apostle who penned the Maranatha text, whether the text was encoded consciously by the author or unconsciously by some unseen hand, whether it is divine or of the devil, will be of little consequence to the Führer. The point is, Herr Andros, the text exists. More important, this text is proof to the general staff that the Allied microfilm Canaris's Abwehr agents intercepted in Istanbul is a forgery and that the Allies intend a landing in Sicily."

Von Berg placed the briefcase containing the Maranatha text inside his wall safe, shut the door, and spun the combination. He then swung the portrait of King Ludwig II back into place. "So you see, Herr Andros, I know everything."

"Everything?" said Deker, challenging the Baron's hubris. "Then I suppose you knew all along that Werner was working for Himmler."

The corners of von Berg's mouth tightened as he forced a smile, and Deker could see a flicker of doubt in his icy blue eyes.

"Oh, yes," said Deker. "In fact, I wouldn't be surprised if Himmler has a cell with your name on it."

Von Berg shrugged. "Then I'll simply have to kill Himmler and Hitler when I see them later this morning," he said. "As the new chancellor, I can then put a stop to this war."

"Stop this war?" Deker laughed incredulously. "Even if you did take out Hitler and Himmler, why would the Allies or anybody believe you'd be any better, much less make peace with you?"

"Because I am the rightful king of Germany!" von Berg cried out, and began to pace back and forth beneath the portrait of King Ludwig II. "I am the son of Maximilian von Berg and the grandson of Elizabeth of Austria and Ludwig II of Bavaria. I am King Ludwig III!"

Deker blinked. "You're crazy, von Berg. You're even worse than Hitler."

Von Berg's face turned red with anger, his facial muscles trembling as all the passion he had bottled up inside erupted. *"Ein ewiges Rätsel will ich bleiben mir und anderen!"'* he screamed, shaking an angry fist at heaven. "If I wish to remain an eternal enigma to myself and to others, that is my divine right!"

The emotional outburst caught Deker by surprise, and he watched in morbid fascination as it took a full minute and several deep breaths before the Baron could fully wind down and regain control of himself.

"The Allies will recognize the authority of King Ludwig III," von Berg announced, referring to himself in the third person. "If they don't, the power of the *Flammenschwert* will force them to make peace with Germany. Peace or the destruction of their cities. Yes, the war will be over in a matter of days. It's a shame you won't be alive to see it, Herr Andros."

The bookcase opened, and Franz appeared in the passageway. He regarded the red-faced Baron with trepidation and cleared his throat. "The *Flammenschwert* device is being loaded on the *Nausicaa*, Herr Oberstgruppenführer."

Von Berg drew a deep breath. "And Aphrodite?"

"Already on board, in your quarters."

"Excellent." Von Berg turned to Deker. "The crew of the *Nausicaa* believes the *Flammenschwert* device contains a new form of rocket fuel. Of the five officers and fifty ratings on board, only Captain Myers, Franz, and I know the truth."

Von Berg checked his watch. "It's a quarter to six, Franz. Take Andros downstairs to his cell and inform Myers to prepare to depart in ten minutes."

Ten minutes, thought Deker. That meant the *Flammenschwert* could be gone before the Allies' strike. It would all be for nothing. And he would be left here to die.

Von Berg seemed to read his mind. "You thought I'd stay for the fireworks, Herr Andros? With you here, your Allied friends can't be far behind, but by the time they arrive, I'll be long gone. And you'll be dead."

A few minutes later, Deker was thrown into a dank cell beneath the Achillion. Franz slammed the heavy metal door and turned the key. Deker could see the German's smiling face looking through the bars of the square window cut into the door.

"I trust your accommodations are adequate, Herr Andros."

"A bit damp, I confess."

"Oh, did the Baron forget to tell you? These cell blocks are flooded from the loading bay above us every time the *Nausicaa* departs. According to my watch, that should be five minutes from now."

120

The island of Corfu loomed large on the horizon as the squadron of RAF bombers skimmed the surface of the Ionian Sea and flew in under the Italian radar net. Their view of the coastline was obscured by a low mist over the waters.

Seated at the left-seat controls of his Liberator was Squadron Leader Jack MacDonald, excitedly scanning his airspeed indicator, which read 110 mph. Next to him sat Wing Commander Rainey, looking ahead nervously, a crushed fifty-mission hat clamped to his head by a pair of oversize earphones.

"At least the experts at our briefing in Blida were honest," said the baby-faced copilot. "We have poor visibility and dangerous terrain. I can't see a thing. We've got to climb."

MacDonald grasped the yoke of the control stick with his left hand and gripped the throttle with his right, carefully jockeying the bomber toward the shadowy outline of coast and mountains.

"We've got to climb, sir!" Rainey repeated.

MacDonald shook his head. "Any higher than six hundred feet, and we'll trip their radar."

"Any lower than six thousand feet," warned Rainey, "and their antiaircraft guns will shoot us down."

But dawn was breaking, and so was the low mist. The sky cleared, and MacDonald could see their reference points. At three o'clock was Corfu Town's Old Fortress. At noon were the two islets in the mouth of the Chalikiopoulos Lagoon. And there at nine o'clock high, sitting pretty on its hill, was the Achillion.

"We're going in," MacDonald announced. "Radio the others. This is it. The mother lode."

Rainey flicked the button on his microphone and relayed the order to the rest of the crew and squadron. "One shot, boys, and one shot only," he reminded them. "We've got to hit those bunkers halfway up the hill. Follow our lead."

MacDonald smiled like a maniac as he goosed the throttle just enough to maintain altitude and banked tightly toward the Achillion. "This is for you, Carol and Sarah," he said softly.

Rainey looked at him in disbelief and wiped the sweat from his forehead. "The wrong touch of the controls, the tiniest deviation from course, could send us smashing into the sea or the side of that hill. This is a fool's run!"

"And the fools are dead ahead," said MacDonald, looking straight at the palace coming up fast into their windshield. "Bombs away!"

121

It was just after six in the morning, and Commandant Buzzini, having been rudely awakened by General von Berg's call ordering him to have his plane ready at the airstrip, was sipping his usual espresso in his office when he heard the high-pitched engines of airplanes in the sky outside. He moved to the window and saw a wave of American B-24s thundering in from the sea, RAF insignias on their wings.

"Mother of God!" he cried, dropping the cup. "The Allied invasion. It has begun!"

He was reaching for his phone when Sergeant Racini came running in from the adjacent office. "Commandant, what is happening?"

"Can't you see for yourself, Sergeant? We're under attack!"

Racini went to the window, eyes wide when he turned. "What are your orders, Commandant?"

"Scramble whatever fighters we have before we lose our airstrip, and mobilize our ground and naval forces to prepare for an Allied amphibious assault," Buzzini replied, waving his hands wildly. "Put me through to Rome and Berlin immediately. We must warn them that the Allies are invading!"

122

Von Berg was in his study, gathering his papers, when the first payload hit the hillside, rocking the palace and sending the portrait of King Ludwig II crashing to the floor. Then Franz burst in and cried, "The Allies, sir! They're attacking!"

Von Berg ran to the window in alarm. The gigantic belly of a B-24 bomber streaked by as it came up the hillside, barely clearing the palace. A second explosion followed, shattering the window and sending von Berg diving for cover.

"Herr Oberstgruppenführer!" Franz ran over to help von Berg up from the floor. "Are you all right?"

Von Berg brushed the splinters of glass from his uniform and noticed blood on his silk handkerchief. "Just a few scratches, Franz."

"But how did they find us?"

"Andros, of course."

"What do we do now?"

Von Berg turned to the blown-out window. The curtains were twisting in the breeze coming through the gaping hole. He could hear the island's air raid sirens blaring and the rumble of his anti-aircraft batteries shooting fire into the skies outside.

"We're obviously not flying out of here," von Berg said. "Our only way out is aboard the *Nausicaa*. Let's get down to the loading bay before we find ourselves surrounded by enemy paratroopers."

They opened the bookcase and hurried into the secret elevator and began their harrowing descent into the quaking mountain. At the bottom of the shaft, the doors parted to reveal the *Nausicaa* in her cave, the throbbing diesel engines screaming to leave.

The submarine's crew was lined up on deck, loading the *Flammenschwert* device with the help of a hydraulic hoist. Myers was on the bridge, anxious to leave as he watched the atomic bomb sink below deck through the forward torpedo-loading hatch. Then he saw von Berg. "General."

"How are we doing, Kapitänleutnant?" Von Berg climbed up the conning tower and stood next to him.

"Once the bomb is chained and secured, we can move out," Myers replied. "About two more minutes."

Von Berg turned to Franz. "I'm going below to check on Aphrodite. You stay here. I want you to man the guns, because once we emerge from the tunnel, we're easy prey for aircraft until we dive. And stop anybody who wants to ride with us out of here. We can't afford the excess weight."

Franz nodded quickly and stepped behind the 37mm gun on the after-extension of the small deck behind the conning tower. Then he trained it on the loading dock as von Berg climbed down the *Nausicaa*'s hatch.

123

Aphrodite was inside the *Nausicaa*'s oak-paneled captain's quarters, strapped to Myers's bunk. She was aware of the tremendous explosions outside but could do nothing to free herself. Staring at the bulkhead, she felt as though she were lying in a coffin and somebody was shutting the door on her. Then the cabin's green curtain was torn aside, and in stepped the Baron.

"Troubles, Ludwig?" she mocked.

"I hope I won't have to gag you as well, my sweet." He seemed remarkably calm as he took a cup and saucer from the cupboard and helped himself to some of the captain's coffee. "It won't be long, Aphrodite. Soon this whole nightmare of a war will be over, and we can get on with our lives." His cup and saucer clattered with the shock of the next explosion.

"It's the end of you, Ludwig," Aphrodite insisted. "Christos has seen to it."

"Andros has seen nothing yet." Von Berg set the cup and saucer in the sink and spoke into the captain's intercom. "Myers. How are we doing?"

"*Flammenschwert* is loaded aboard, sir," came the response. "We're ready when you are."

Von Berg nodded. "Flood the cells. We're moving out."

124

Deker was in his cell when the walls started to shake and the sentries outside the door shouted. The shaking was followed by the unmistakable explosion of antiaircraft fire from above. Not waiting to be buried alive, the sentries escaped down the corridor, leaving Deker on his own as blocks of stone started to fall from the ceiling.

He took cover in a dark corner of the cell, crouching into a small ball and throwing his arms over his head for protection. At least the Allies had made good use of the intelligence he had provided them, he thought. Not that it mattered if von Berg managed to escape with Aphrodite and the atomic bomb.

From the next cell came the screams of another prisoner. "You cannot leave me!" the man cried in German. "I am Dr. Xaptz, personal counselor to the Führer! Don't leave me here to die!"

Deker heard a key rattling inside the lock of his own cell door. He lowered his arms and looked up. The iron gate scraped open, and in stepped an old man wearing a sentry's uniform. Quietly, he closed the door and turned around, two ramlike eyes shining out of a wizened face. To Deker, it felt like the devil himself had come from hell to fetch him, and he shrank back into the shadows.

"I know you," Deker said in a trembling voice. "I've seen your face somewhere before."

"Come," said the old man in Greek. "We must hurry. The Baron is escaping in his submarine. I saw him on my way in."

It occurred to Deker where he had seen that face—in a mirror at the Monastery of the Taborian Light in Meteora. He was very confused. That couldn't be.

Deker exclaimed, "You're Hadji Azrael!"

"My name is Philip."

Deker then remembered the destruction of the Monastery of the Taborian Light. "You died in the fire."

"Strange. That's what Aphrodite told me about you, Christos."

"Aphrodite?" Deker cried out. "We've got—" He broke off at the sound of an ominous rumble down the tunnel. Through the window slot in the door, he saw the sentries who had disappeared now running toward the cell, chased by a wall of water. "Get back!" he shouted.

Deker and Philip shrank back from the door and huddled in the corner of the cell, waiting for the torrent to burst through and flood the cell. But the thick door blocked the water, as did one of the captors, who slammed into the metal barrier and whose face plugged the window slot. Deker looked up at the German's eyes, turning round in terror. The entire door seemed ready to give way from the buildup behind it, and water started spurting around the edges, but the visible bulge in the center of the door flattened, and the blue face in the window slipped out of sight as the water receded.

Deker looked at Philip, who was making the sign of the cross. He then stood up and walked to the cell door. The force of the water had cracked the door's frame. After a few pushes, they were able to force the door open.

The entire network of tunnels beneath the submarine bay was flooded, they discovered, and all who were inside had drowned, including the prisoner in the neighboring cell. Deker found a couple of German corpses floating about and helped himself to a Schmeisser.

"I have to find Aphrodite," he told Philip as they waded through the sea water toward some stone steps and made their way up to the bay level.

Philip said, "She's on the *Nausicaa* with the Maranatha text."

"No," said Deker. "The text is upstairs in von Berg's study—unless you saw him take it aboard the submarine."

Philip shook his head. "I don't believe he took anything with him."

At the top of the steps, they reached a dry corridor outside the submarine bay, still below the surface of the hillside but undamaged by the flooding in the lower levels.

"You go after Aphrodite," said Philip. "I'll go after the text."

They were silent a moment, only dimly aware of shouts and gunfire in the distance. Deker looked into the old monk's eyes. He hardly knew this man and yet had so many questions he would have liked to ask him. Philip seemed to grasp a greater world than Deker knew. But the Baron was getting away, and both he and Philip understood that there was no time now.

"Good-bye," Deker said as they separated.

"God help you!" cried Philip, and he disappeared down the dark corridor.

Deker turned around, pulled out his Schmeisser, and started toward the submarine bay. Sirens blared, and soldiers ran past him in the opposite direction. He encountered no resistance, as everybody was preoccupied with their own survival. But when he entered the submarine bay, he was greeted by machine-gun fire from the aft deck of the *Nausicaa*, and he dove for cover behind some crates.

When the gunfire ceased, Deker peered over the crates and gazed out over the cavernous submarine bay. Large chunks of rock were falling from the ceiling. With all the smoke and confusion, Deker couldn't see the submarine and feared she was gone. Then a curtain of smoke parted, and he could see the unreal image of the *Nausicaa* slipping away. Behind her giant gun on the aft deck was Franz, who spotted him behind the crates. Franz swung the gun toward him and unleashed a burst of fire.

Deker ducked as the bullets drilled a neat row of holes into the rock over his head. The *Nausicaa*'s antiaircraft guns were designed to lock at a parallel angle, no doubt to prevent the gunners from tearing up their own deck. But in these circumstances, they frustrated Franz's attempt to point the barrels low enough to kill him.

Deker emerged from behind the crates and ran beneath the line of fire until he reached the end of the stone pier. Only ten feet of water separated him from the *Nausicaa*. But to him, it could have been ten miles. He froze in fear.

Franz reached for his Luger to pick him off. Deker saw him and quickly lifted the barrel of his Schmeisser, fell to one knee, and fired, knocking Franz off the aft deck of the escaping submarine. Deker took a deep breath and dove into the water, crawling wildly toward the *Nausicaa* before it could get away.

He climbed up onto the *Nausicaa*'s aft deck and lay sprawled on his back, gasping for air. They were slowly making their way through floating debris out of the cave. Behind them lay fiery destruction, before them a gaping hole and the open sea.

125

The *Nausicaa* was emerging from the collapsing tunnel and into broad daylight when Myers noticed Franz wasn't firing the guns anymore. He turned to discover that Franz was nowhere in sight, only the dark, drenched figure of Andros pointing a Schmeisser at him.

Andros said, "You have new orders, Kapitänleutnant. You are to proceed on your present course and present speed, but you won't take her down until I say so."

"But we are vulnerable to aircraft," Myers protested.

Andros raised the Schmeisser to Myers's head. "Right now you are vulnerable to many things. Where's von Berg?"

"My quarters."

"With Aphrodite?"

"Yes."

"How many are in the conning tower below us?"

"A helmsman and torpedo officer."

"And in the control room on the level below?"

"Four technicians," Myers replied. "The diving officer, a helmsman, and two planesmen."

"So six crew members stand between me and von Berg," said Andros, calculating the captain's quarters to be the first compartment forward from the control room. "And the *Flammenschwert* device. Where is it?"

Myers didn't respond.

Andros slid back the bolt of his Schmeisser, letting the loud click speak for itself. "I didn't hear you."

"It's in the forward torpedo room," Myers replied. "You'll never make it that far. There are thirty-five crew members below and only one fore-and-aft passageway."

"Let me worry about that. Now call your communications officer in the radio room."

Myers was about to speak into the intercom when Andros buried the barrel of the Schmeisser in the back of his neck.

"Not into the public-address system," Andros warned. "This is a private conversation. I know one of these pipes here connects you directly to the radio room, so choose the right one."

Myers nodded and spoke into his piping to the radio room. "Funkgefreiter Voigt."

"At your orders, Kapitänleutnant."

Myers looked up for further instructions.

"Tell Voigt to tune to the following frequency." Andros gave him the frequency, and Myers repeated it to the dumbfounded telegraphist.

There was a lengthy pause on the other end. "But that's an Allied frequency, sir!"

"That's an order," Myers barked.

Andros told Myers, "And when he's through sending the following message, you'll order everybody to abandon ship."

126

The *Cherub* was a few miles off the coast of Corfu as Erin Whyte watched the hillside and cove beneath the Achillion explode with columns of fire. She realized nobody could possibly survive that kind of destruction.

"It doesn't look good," she said softly as she peered through the periscope inside the conning tower.

"Let me see," demanded a liberated Prestwick, who was standing next to her. His wrists were still raw from being tied up, so he grasped the handles of the scope gingerly as he pressed his spectacles to the glass. "Good show!" he exclaimed. "Those bombers hit the bull's-eye."

"No thanks to you," remarked Erin, incensed at Prestwick's utter disregard for Andros. "It was Chris who led us here."

Prestwick kept his eyes glued to the periscope. "Thank you, Andros, wherever you are," he said with a shudder. "Your father would have been proud of you. My God, would you look at that."

Erin stepped aside as Captain Safire took a look for himself and removed his cap. "Aye, there's nobody coming out of *that* alive."

The radio operator climbed up the ladder from the control room and handed Safire a signal. "We just picked up a call from Sinon, sir."

"That's Andros!" Erin cried. "He's alive!"

Safire read the signal. "Sinon says *Flammenschwert* has his fire and has run off with *Nausicaa*."

"My God!" said Prestwick. "That means von Berg has escaped on his submarine and has an atomic bomb on board."

Safire nodded. "I'll see if we can break her back by air." He spoke into the piping to the control room, paused to listen, and turned to

Prestwick with a grim expression. "Our flyboys are long gone, high-tailing it back to North Africa. Looks like the Luftwaffe is giving them a good chase."

"Then it's up to us," said Erin. "How soon until we catch von Berg, Captain?"

"If his U-boat stays surfaced, she can do nineteen knots on her diesels," Safire explained. "Best we can do submerged is seven knots on our electric motor, eight if we push her."

"Then surface, for God's sake!" said Prestwick.

Safire put his eyes to the scope and shook his head. "Not in the daylight, sir, not with enemy warships on the surface and fighters in the skies."

The prospect of von Berg getting away alarmed Erin. If the Baron managed to disappear beneath the Mediterranean, they'd never find him. "If von Berg did submerge," she asked Safire, "how long could he stay underwater before surfacing?"

"Eight months," Safire replied, still looking through the periscope. "And he'd have enough fuel for almost seventeen thousand miles."

Prestwick gasped. "That means von Berg could conceivably cross the Atlantic for New York City, park his submarine somewhere in the Hudson, and blow the city off the face of the planet. Captain, we can't take a chance and let him submerge."

"Sir?" asked Safire.

"That submarine must not reach open waters," said Prestwick. "We must sink her at whatever the cost."

"Sink her?" cried Erin. "But what about Chris?"

"Whatever the cost, Captain Whyte," Prestwick repeated.

"You bastard."

Safire raised his hand to silence them. "I see her now, pulling away from the island."

"Then what are we waiting for?" demanded Prestwick, loosening his tie.

Erin turned to Safire. "Don't do it," she said. "We can stop the *Nausicaa* without sinking her."

"We can't afford to lose the element of surprise," said Prestwick. "You'll sink her or I'll have you stripped of your command."

Safire looked at Erin helplessly and shook his head at Prestwick. He spoke into the intercom to address the crew. "Action stations. Torpedo crews, prepare for attack."

127

Von Berg was with Aphrodite in his compartment when he sensed the *Nausicaa*'s engines had stopped. Suddenly, the Klaxon sounded, and Myers's voice came over the public-address system.

"All hands, abandon ship. All hands, abandon ship."

Von Berg frowned and went to his intercom. "Myers, what's happened? What's going on?"

The voice of Chris Andros came through loud and clear. "It's over, von Berg."

Von Berg stood in shock. Andros alive? he thought. But how? No human could have survived the cell blocks. But the fact was, either Andros was alive, or the voices of madness finally had defeated him.

Aphrodite, who had also heard Andros's voice, was unable to conceal her joy and pride. "You see, Ludwig, I told you," she said with newfound defiance. "He's come back for me *and* you. What are you going to do now?"

He glared at her. "I'll be back shortly," he said, and stepped out of the compartment.

The Klaxon was blaring and emergency lights flashing as he crossed the fore-and-aft passageway to the radio room. The radio technician, Voigt, was gone. Von Berg grabbed the microphone and adjusted the frequency selector. He started the distress call procedures. Then he turned to the radio room's phonograph and put the needle on a record. The music of Wagner's "Death March" flooded all the compartments.

Back in the captain's quarters, the sound of that macabre music crept up Aphrodite's flesh as she struggled in her bunk. "What are you doing?" she demanded when von Berg returned.

There was a wild look in his eyes, and he whipped out a Luger and put it to her head. She was sure she was about to die. Instead, he untied her and pulled her out into the fore-and-aft passageway, the Luger's cold barrel at her temple.

"Don't worry, Aphrodite," he told her as he pushed her through the galley and toward the forward torpedo room. "I won't let him hurt you. I won't let *anybody* hurt you."

He dragged her into the officers' quarters, the compartment just before the forward torpedo room. She squirmed within his arms, but like steel cords, they tightened around her. She tried to scream, but von Berg clapped his hand over her mouth.

"Come and get me now, Andros," he said softly. "I'm waiting."

128

Topside on the *Nausicaa*'s bridge, Deker and his captive Myers watched as the crew emerged from their escape hatches and cast off in dinghies. There was no sign of von Berg or Aphrodite.

Myers said, "You're wasting your time, Andros. Von Berg won't come up here. You'll have to go after him."

Deker pressed the Schmeisser harder against Myers's back. "You go join the others now, while you still have a chance. Remember, I can shoot you all from up here at any time I choose."

Reluctantly, Myers descended the ladder outside the conning tower to the deck and joined the last dinghy before it cast off.

Deker watched the tide take care of the rest, pulling the dinghies toward shore. Satisfied that they were far enough away, he climbed down the hatch and dropped into the control room.

Blue lights flashed eerily, and music filled the empty compartment. Deker scanned the unmanned banks of instruments to his port and starboard sides. Behind him clacked the abandoned engine room. He glanced about to make sure everything was clear and stepped into the fore-and-aft passageway.

When he reached the captain's quarters, he tore open the green curtain. The oak-paneled compartment was empty, but the Baron made his eerie presence felt through the crackling intercom.

"Welcome aboard, Herr Andros," said von Berg's voice. "Are you looking for someone in particular?"

Deker stepped outside into the cramped fore-and-aft passageway, Schmeisser at the ready. He briskly made his way along the corridor toward the galley. A creeping claustrophobia came over him as the bulkhead seemed to close in. Straight ahead was the hatch leading to the forward torpedo room.

At the end of the passageway, Aphrodite appeared.

"Aphrodite!" he called.

"No, Christos!"

Deker started toward her when he saw the barrel of a Luger at her head; then von Berg stepped into view.

"Stay right where you are, Herr Andros." Von Berg put the semiautomatic next to Aphrodite's ear. "Now, drop that Schmeisser or she gets it in the head."

Deker hesitated, and von Berg yanked Aphrodite's long black hair until she cried out in pain.

"Now or never, Herr Andros."

Deker lowered the Schmeisser and stepped forward.

"I said drop it!" von Berg called.

Deker stood still and dropped the submachine gun. It fell to the metal floor with a dull clank that echoed through the fore-and-aft passageway.

"Step into the shaft of light where I can see you."

Deker stepped beneath the galley's overhead hatch, glimpsing the circle of daylight overhead.

"Very good," said von Berg, coming toward him.

They were only a few feet apart, and Deker could see the manic look in von Berg's eyes, like that of an animal trapped in a snare, willing to bite off its own leg to get free. He kept a tight hold on Aphrodite, who struggled against him.

Deker said, "Let her go, von Berg."

"As soon as you're good and dead, Herr Andros."

Von Berg aimed the Luger at him and pulled the trigger. Deker moved to the side, but it was too late. Aphrodite screamed as the bullet plowed into his shoulder and spun him to the floor. Dazed, he clutched his bloody arm and looked up to see von Berg move forward to finish him off. "For you, the war is over, Herr Andros."

Von Berg raised his Luger when Aphrodite lunged toward them, screaming, "No, Ludwig!"

Von Berg half turned toward her as Deker fingered Andros's father's dagger and hurled it into his side. Von Berg cried out in pain, dropped the Luger, and rolled off into the shadows.

Aphrodite ran to Deker as he struggled to stand in the shaft of light. "Christos," she said.

"Later," he replied, and gently pushed her in front of him. "Come now, up the ladder and out the hatch. We don't have much time."

He helped her mount the ladder. When he saw her legs disappear through the hatch, he began to pull himself up after her with his right arm, his left dangling uselessly. He had entered the dark tunnel of the bulkhead when he felt a tug at his legs. He looked down to see the bloody hands and angry face of von Berg pulling him back.

"Christos, hurry!" Aphrodite called from above.

Deker looked up to see her face in a circle of blue sky. She reached down to help him up through the hatch while he tried to shake von Berg.

Their fingers touched briefly. But then a violent explosion rocked the submarine. Deker's hand slipped, and he fell back down.

"Christos!" Aphrodite screamed as the great metal hulk rolled, throwing her off into the sea, and all at once Deker felt himself sinking with the *Nausicaa* into the deep.

129

"Direct hit!" shouted Prestwick from behind the *Cherub*'s periscope. "She's sinking like lead."

Erin, who was standing behind Prestwick and Safire in the conning tower, pried Prestwick loose from the scope and had a look. The forward bow of the *Nausicaa* was pointing straight up to the sky. It would be only a matter of minutes before the submarine sank beneath the surface. She felt sick with worry for Andros. "Wait a minute," she said. "I see something floating in the water."

"Quick, let me see." Safire took the scope, paused as he looked, and snapped his head back. "Surface immediately!" he ordered the crew. "We've got a survivor."

The *Cherub*'s crew began to empty the ballasts, and slowly the submarine began to rise. Ten minutes later, they brought her on board, Aphrodite Vasilis, chilled to the bone and crying.

The crew stood at attention while Aphrodite climbed down the conning tower into the control room. Erin could tell that one look at her was enough to convince Safire and every rating aboard that mankind owed Andros a debt of gratitude for rescuing such a heavenly creature.

"Christos," she sobbed. "He's on that submarine."

"Good God!" said Prestwick. "You mean he's alive?"

Aphrodite, wet and trembling, was nodding when the signal officer came into the control room with a message for Safire.

"According to the radio traffic, sir, there's a flotilla of ships coming out from Mandraki Harbor."

Safire nodded grimly. "Helmsman," he ordered, "prepare to dive."

"But Christos!" shouted Aphrodite. "You can't let him die!" She turned to Erin. "You can't let him die!"

Erin could see the pain in Aphrodite's twisted face. It was a pain they shared. "Let's get you dry," she told her. "Colonel Prestwick here will take you to the captain's quarters, where you can rest up."

"What about Christos?" Aphrodite asked desperately.

"I'll do everything I can," Erin promised, even though she realized there was very little she could do.

The dazed girl could only nod as Prestwick helped her up and escorted her out of the control room.

When they were gone, Erin turned to Safire. "May I take another look through the scope?"

"You can look. But I'm afraid it won't do you much good."

Erin climbed up into the conning tower and put her eyes to the periscope in time to see the bow of the *Nausicaa* slip below the surface of the water. What had become of the Baron, she didn't know. But of Andros there could be no doubt: He was dead. And with him was an atomic bomb. They were on their way to the bottom of the Ionian Sea.

When she descended into the control room, Prestwick, Safire, and the crew were waiting for her.

"Well?" Prestwick asked, pausing for her to tell them what they already knew.

She swallowed hard, and without a word, she walked out of the control room and down the passageway to the captain's quarters.

Aphrodite was sitting on the bunk, shivering in her navy blanket, sobbing uncontrollably. Then Erin saw the empty blue box from Tiffany & Co. on the desk and looked at the diamond ring Aphrodite had slipped on her finger.

"Oh, Christos," Aphrodite cried. "You did love me."

130

The torpedo from the *Cherub* had ripped a hole through the *Nausicaa's* electric motor room, flooding the rear compartments and turning the submarine on end.

Deker and von Berg managed to climb into the forward torpedo room and shut the hatch, sealing themselves off from the rest of the ship but not the water, which already swirled around their knees.

Deker could feel the blood pumping out of his shoulder. He applied more pressure with his other hand as he leaned against the vertical floor. That was when he saw the *Flammenschwert* device for the first time. The atomic bomb stood upright before his eyes and was in danger of slipping off its chains.

Von Berg was laughing. "We share the same tomb," he said, a twisted smile crossing his agonized face. "The German and the Greek, the Nazi and the American, we all die."

Deker didn't reply. The water was up to his waist, and the *Nausicaa's* cracked hull was beginning to collapse like a tin can under the tremendous pressure. He searched for a way of escape.

"It's no use," von Berg said. "We're trapped. This is your grave, and you share it with me. There's no escape."

Deker considered the four circular hatches above his head, the doors to the torpedo tubes. "How do I launch the torpedo tubes?"

"I must say, you're full of ideas, Herr Andros," von Berg replied, then started coughing up blood. "Unfortunately, the tubes are fired on the captain's order from controls in the conning tower."

"I suppose these manual controls are completely useless?"

"A precaution against electrical failure, that's all."

"So if I push this button . . ."

"I wouldn't, Herr Andros."

Deker pressed the button. It released a charge of compressed air that ejected the torpedo out of the tube and into the water.

Deker said, "And you said it wouldn't work, von Berg."

The submarine pitched violently, and Deker was thrown against the bulkhead by the shifting water.

"I told you," said von Berg. "Without a diving officer in the control room, there's no way to compensate for the weight change."

Deker reached up and twisted the black handle until the torpedo hatch dropped open. More water poured in on their heads from the flooded tube. Then it stopped, and Deker hoisted himself inside.

"Crawl into your little tomb, Andros," von Berg called out after him. "Another minute won't save you from death. I'll still be waiting for you on the other side."

As he climbed into the tube, Deker could hear von Berg's hideous, rasping laugh. It was all he could do to keep from slipping down the sides of the slick tube back into the compartment of water below him. He glanced down at von Berg's bloody face before he pulled up the hatch, locking himself in a vacuum of darkness.

There was only silence in the tube, silence from the water, but it was black, and he had a little air left as he felt the whole sub sinking. He would get a proper burial at sea, at least, just like his forefathers.

The water rose slowly to his eyes, forcing him to lift his chin above the surface to breathe. Not a sound from the torpedo room below. Von Berg must be dead by now, but that thought did him little good. It would be only seconds before the salt water would swirl down his own throat and his body would sink like a lead weight.

And now he was choking on the water, coughing it up only to swallow more. He could feel the water filling up his lungs, could feel himself losing air and consciousness. As he sank to the bottom of the torpedo tube and the darkness overcame him, the last image of life that flickered in his mind was that of Aphrodite's sad face watching him die.

And then he felt a blast of compressed air beneath his feet and he was shooting up through a dark tunnel, as if in a dream. At the end of it was a light, a wonderful light, and for a brief, flickering moment, he saw his mother's face, and then everything faded to black.

131

He broke the surface of the Ionian Sea seconds later, gasping for air. The last thing he remembered was the *Nausicaa* touching bottom and exploding. But as he bobbed with the waves, he could feel his head attached to his body. He was in one piece, he realized. He was alive.

The explosion must have released the charge of compressed air that ejected him out of the tube and into the water. The only other possible explanation was that the Baron himself had pressed the launch button. But there was nothing across the smooth surface of the sea to suggest that Baron von Berg or the *Nausicaa* had ever been there.

Deker floated helplessly in ghostly silence, trying to get his bearings, then remembered he couldn't swim.

As the crest of a wave lifted him up, he thought he heard his mother scream, "Christos! Christos!" like she did in the darkness of that terrible night at sea long ago.

He turned and cringed at what looked like the ghost of the resurrected *Nausicaa* bearing down on him. But the legend on its superstructure said *Cherub*. And standing on the bridge were Prestwick, Safire, and Erin, and next to them Aphrodite.

132

A t the Achillion on Corfu, Commandant Buzzini was sitting be-hind what had been Baron von Berg's desk, surveying the bomb damage to the study while his men searched the rest of the abandoned palace. The shattered portrait of King Ludwig II on the floor beside him attracted his attention, and he leaned over to take a closer look. For an eerie moment the Italian sensed that it was Baron von Berg himself staring out through those shards of glass, smiling at him from the Great Beyond.

"Commandant."

"What?" Buzzini jumped up in his seat only to see Sergeant Racini standing in front of the desk.

"Sorry, Commandant, sir."

Buzzini regained his composure and frowned. "What is it, Sergeant?"

"The Germans are sending more divisions to Greece!" Racini handed the signal from Rome to his subdued superior. "Comman-dant, did you hear me?" Then Racini saw the blown-out safe in the wall and the Husky report lying on the desk in front of Buzzini.

"It seems I have accidentally opened the Baron's safe," Buzzini explained.

"You opened SS reports?" Racini crossed himself. "They will cut our throats for this!"

Buzzini pushed the Husky report across the desk to Racini. "Read it, Sergeant."

Racini picked up the report addressed TO THE LEADER AND CHANCELLOR OF THE STATE and marked MOST SECRET. As he read it, his eyes grew wide. "Mother of God!" he cried when he finished. "It is Italy the Allies invade!"

"The Baron himself confirms this," said Buzzini.

Racini passed back the report. "My sisters are in Palermo."

"And they'll probably shower the Americans with kisses when they come. Sergeant, we must think fast what to do."

Then Buzzini thought of something else. What would happen to him and his men should the Allies attack Italy? How would the Germans react? Will we Italians be treated like allies, he wondered, or enemies? The Italian commandant knew what to do.

"For our sakes and our families, Sergeant," said Buzzini, "we must pray the Allies land with the element of surprise."

Racini nodded, speechless, as Buzzini struck a match and torched the report, dropping the whole mess into a wastebasket.

"I never saw this," said Buzzini. "Did you?"

"Oh, no, never, Commandant."

"As for this ancient text the report speaks of . . ." Buzzini looked around the room and saw the broken glass case in the corner. "Look over there, Sergeant."

Racini walked over to the case and shrugged. "There is nothing here, Commandant."

Buzzini rubbed his whiskers. "The Baron must have taken it," he said decisively, "because it's not in the safe."

"Now what, Commandant?"

"Now we take care of the last remaining piece of evidence." Buzzini rose to his feet. "Tomorrow morning the Achillion is to reopen as a hospital. See that it looks like one. As far as we're concerned, it was never anything else."

"Yes, Commandant."

"And, Sergeant"—Buzzini looked up at his young aide with flashing, angry eyes—"do you swear to God to keep this a secret?"

The sergeant from Palermo crossed himself with trembling fingers and said, "To the grave, sir."

133

At Hitler's holiday house in Obersalzberg, the Führer and his generals had just viewed footage of Wernher von Braun's A-4 rockets when a grim-faced Himmler walked in on the weapons conference.

"Reichsführer," Hitler observed. "You don't look happy."

"I regret that I must be the bearer of bad tidings to my Führer." Himmler presented the signal from Berlin that said SS general Ludwig von Berg had been killed during an Allied air strike on Corfu. Himmler concealed his delight behind a mournful facade.

Hitler's fury was evident as he crumpled the paper in his hand. "And what has become of Dr. Xaptz?"

"Killed as well by the enemy."

"And the research von Berg was eager to show us today?"

"Lost, I'm afraid."

Hitler sighed and looked at the A-4 rockets on the screen. "No matter," he told the generals in the room. "We now possess the decisive weapons of the war. Production will begin immediately. Soon hails of fire will rain upon London."

Everybody in the room murmured their agreement except Admiral Canaris, who was lost in sobering reflection at the news of von Berg's death.

"As for this air strike on Corfu," Hitler went on, "it can only affirm that my intuition was right and von Berg's intelligence wrong about the Allies' intentions in Greece. General Jodl?"

The chief of staff of the Armed Forces High Command sat up in his chair. "Yes, my Führer?"

"The 194th Jäger and the First Gebirgs Divisions are to

join the German First Panzer Division in Greece immediately."

"Two more divisions?" asked Jodl. "That makes five additional divisions you've deployed to Greece in recent weeks."

"Yes, Jodl, I know that," said Hitler, glaring. "How often must I repeat myself around here?"

134

It was the stormy, moonless night of July 9, 1943, when American and British forces landed on Sicily, catching the Germans and Italians by surprise. Within seventy-two hours, more than five hundred thousand troops touched shore. It would be a matter of weeks before Italy surrendered to the Allies and declared war on her former ally Germany.

As a result, fierce fighting broke out among the German and Italian garrisons on the Greek islands in September. The German commandant of Cefalonia declared open season on Italians when he told his troops: "Hunters! The next twenty-four hours are yours." Four thousand Italians were shot that day. On Corfu, the fighting was especially heated, and the Italians and Germans clashed with such fury that a violent fire broke out and swept the island.

As for Corfu's former Italian commandant, Buzzini, he was no longer stationed on the island, having shrewdly managed to get himself and Sergeant Racini demoted by means of appearing incompetent. He was waiting on the beaches of Sicily the night the Allies landed, smug in the confidence that he knew something the Führer didn't.

Thus, when U.S. Army second lieutenant Billy Hayfield's landing craft touched shore, the dumbfounded Texan was greeted by one of the most unusual sights of World War II as Buzzini and other so-called defenders of Sicily helped his unit unload.

PRESENT DAY

135

Deker awoke from his nightmare, gasping for air. He sat up in his bed and let his eyes adjust in the columned room. Shafts of morning light streamed through the drapes and marble columns onto a vast mosaic floor. He stood up on the cold tiles and walked over to a table piled with ancient scrolls.

He pulled one out and unrolled it. He recognized the letters as Greek and was stunned to realize that he understood it. It was a copy of Aristotle's *Poetics*. There were others. Books about the arts, history. There was one about Rome's campaign in Germania, another one about the ancient battle of Jericho. The pile of scrolls collapsed from his touch to reveal a dirty, secret scroll hidden behind them all. This one, too, was in Greek: *The Revelation of Jesus Christ*, by John the Apostle.

He stepped outside into the adjoining courtyard, where a ravishing brunette emerged dripping from a bathing pool. Behind her was a gigantic, half-finished sculpture of herself. She wrapped a clingy gown around her supple, golden body. Then she turned to face him with her two round breasts.

"Aphrodite," he said.

"This year's model," she said, and kissed him on the lips. "But I'll always be your Helena."

He saw the tarp and tools next to the statue of Aphrodite, the goddess of love. "Did I do that, Helena?" he asked her.

"You with a hammer and chisel?" Helena laughed. "That would be a Greek tragedy. You're dangerous enough with your pen and your comedies. You don't like Colonius's work?"

"I do," he said, gazing at the woman before him and the statue of the goddess modeled after her. "Magnificent."

She smiled. "What are you going to do when I'm fifty cubits tall and you can only gaze at my naked stone body in the temple with all the other mortal men? Will you remember you once had me in the flesh, Athanasius?"

Athanasius. His head was a jumble of images and memories. That name was not one of them.

"I'm a Greek playwright," he told her, as if he had just remembered.

"The greatest," she purred as she kissed him.

"I'm from Athens, like my father. But my mother was from Judea."

Helena frowned. "I thought you were going to stop saying that. No good can come of it in Rome. Have you been drinking *kykeon* and smoking blue lotus leaves again? Or reading those old books? I am tired of your dreams about the fall of ancient cities like Jericho, or your nightmares of Greece conquered by Germania, or your visions of a future Rome beyond the Great Sea. Put away your psychedelics, Athanasius. Enough. You have me as your muse."

He stood still and said nothing, only listened to the breeze and smelled the scent of citrus from a nearby bowl of fruit. It was all very quiet, until the birds rose into the sky. Then came the unmistakable roar of the crowds, carried on the wind.

"What's that?" he asked Helena.

She shrugged and said, "That, I suppose, is the last of Flavius Clemens."

He staggered back inside the villa and roamed its chambers until he finally emerged on a terrace and took in the spectacular view of the city. Dazzling white terraces and marble columns cascaded down the cypress-covered hills to the winding river below. The roar of the crowds came up even louder, and he gasped at the sight of the great Colosseum.

He stared at his hands. They were his hands. He looked at the city. It was his adopted city. He was Athanasius. This was Rome.

The games, he realized, had only just begun.

ACKNOWLEDGMENTS

It was Simon Lipskar who first saw the promise of *The 34th Degree* long before anybody else, and for that I will always be grateful. Thanks, too, to my editor, Emily Bestler, for being the first to pull the trigger on that promise. None of this would have been possible, of course, without the help of Judith Curr at Atria, Louise Burke at Pocket Books, and Sarah Branham and the rest of the team at Simon & Schuster.